THE KILLING CAVE

Lady Fan Mysteries
Book Eleven

Elizabeth Bailey

SAPERE
BOOKS

THE KILLING CAVE

Published by Sapere Books.

24 Trafalgar Road, Ilkley, LS29 8HH

saperebooks.com

ISBN: 978-0-85495-573-2

CHAPTER ONE

August, 1799

"Papa! Papa!"

An urgent note in her son's treble voice alerted Lady Ottilia Fanshawe. She turned from contemplating the efforts of her nearly three-year-old daughters Diana and Elinor, who were somewhat inexpertly piling shingle onto their makeshift castle under the watchful eyes of the nursemaids.

"Papa!"

Luke was sprinting across Aldborough's rock-strewn shingle beach, heading towards the spot where Francis had been helping their adopted daughter Pretty hunt for fossils in the boulders. Her husband straightened up, his gaze trained on the little boy. He cupped a hand to his mouth.

"Take care, Luke! Not so fast!"

The child, not much to Ottilia's surprise, paid no heed. Now a miniature version of his father, in manly attire from his short blue jacket and buff breeches down to his little boots, Luke sped nimbly, shouting all the while.

"In the cave, Papa! Come and see!"

Instinct made Ottilia rise from the convenient rock she was using as a seat, a half-formed fear in her breast that her precious son would take a rattling fall, and at the back of her ever-curious mind, the inevitable question raised by Luke's words.

"I found it in the cave!"

Francis was moving now, his finger raised. "Wretch of a boy! Didn't I tell you not to go exploring in the caves without me?"

Luke slowed as the two of them began to close in. "I know, but I couldn't help it, Papa. 'Sides, it don't matter now."

"Oh, you think so? Well, let me tell you why it matters —☐

Luke cut him off. "There's a man in there, Papa. He's all dead."

Ottilia's heart gave a jolt. She started towards them as she saw her spouse freeze.

"What did you say?"

"I found a dead man." Luke grasped at Francis's coat. "You've got to come, Papa."

Ottilia's heart sank as an all too familiar look came over her husband's face. She could have predicted his immediate response.

"Are you sure he's dead?"

"'Course I'm sure. I saw Catkin dead, ain't I?"

Here Pretty put her oar in. "Numbskull! Catkin was a pony. And you should say 'haven't', not 'ain't', Luke. Speak proper English!"

"Pretty, this isn't the moment for a grammar lesson." Francis was beginning to sound exasperated.

He may as well not have wasted his breath, Ottilia thought, amused as Luke retorted with some heat. "He's just like Catkin, so that's all you know, jingle-brain! He's got a hole in his head."

Arriving in time to catch this last, Ottilia wasted no words on protest, turning to Francis. "We had best investigate, had we not?"

Her spouse groaned. "The prospect does not fill me with any great enthusiasm."

Ottilia held down the bubble of excitement. Not that she had hankered for adventure these past three years, what with the deleterious effect on her health in birthing her twin daughters

6

and the exigencies involved in the necessarily augmented household in caring for four children. She was a deal better, thankfully, and this spell away from home had come as a welcome respite. Luke's discovery of a corpse, if it proved true, might be counted a bonus. But she could not say so to Francis.

"Well, as yet we have no notion precisely what Luke has found."

Her son piped up at this. "I told you already, Mama. It's a dead man."

Ottilia gave him her attention. "Yes, and he looks like Catkin, you said."

"Yes, 'cos Papa had to shoot him when he broke his leg, remember? Catkin had a hole in his head too."

Ottilia could not suppress a sigh. "A shooting is a serious matter, my dear, when it comes to a man. Can you show us where he is?"

"That's what I've been saying. Papa has to come." Upon which, he turned to Francis and grasped his hand. "I'll show you, Papa."

Francis held back. "One moment." His brows were drawn together as he looked at Ottilia. "I'd better go and see first, Tillie."

"If you imagine I have any intention of being excluded, Fan, you must have windmills in your head."

A reluctant grin was drawn from her spouse. "I'm a master of forlorn hopes where you are concerned." He lifted his and Luke's joined hands. "Lead on, then, my brave soldier!" Luke started off in the direction towards the caves. "Easy now. Don't rush Mama."

"She can follow with Pretty."

Francis halted, turning his head to where their eldest was standing off to one side, seeming far too innocent for her known character. No doubt she had stayed silent on purpose. "You stay with the others, Pretty."

A pout appeared. "I want to come too. If Luke is allowed—

"Luke is only going to show us, and then he'll be sent straight out again. He wasn't supposed to go into the caves in the first place." Francis delivered this with an admonitory glance towards the culprit, who looked anything but abashed.

"Go, Fan, and I will follow," Ottilia said sotto voce. Then she put an arm about Pretty's shoulders and turned her away from the cliffs. "It won't be a pleasant sight, my dear. Go and help Di and Nell with their castle."

"Must I, Auntilla?"

"If you will be so kind. They won't have much longer to build it, for I fear Luke's find means we must all return to the house."

"Oh, why?"

"Because there will be formalities. This man's death must be reported to the proper authorities."

Her sober mien was having an effect. At nine, Pretty was beginning to show intermittent signs of early maturity. In her features too, as they were forming into a whole that matched her name. Ottilia had difficulty in recalling her real mother's face, which she had seen only in death. But she did remember being struck by the woman's blonde beauty, and it seemed Pretty was like to rival her in looks.

"Will you have to find the person who shot him?"

Little though she knew of Ottilia's crime-solving exploits, much to her relief, Pretty at least understood the significance of her 'Lady Fan' personality. Servants talked and Pretty, as her former nurse Hepsie reported, had vague memories pertaining to the tragic deaths of her parents.

Ottilia spoke with truth. "I dare say I may, my love. If the authorities allow."

This produced the unexpected glow of Pretty's bright smile. "You will in any event. It's your forty, that's what I heard."

"You mean *forte*. I wonder just where you heard that, young madam?"

When Ottilia entered the cave, Francis was just visible in the shadows, bent over what was presumably the corpse. It was hidden from her sight by a boulder, but the stench was palpable. Days must have passed since the death.

She turned to Luke, who was hovering at the opening. "Go down to the others, my love. You have done your part."

Her young son hopped from one foot to the other, his excitement all too reminiscent of Ottilia's nephews at a similar age. "But I want to see."

"You have already seen and that is enough. Go quickly, before Papa remembers he forbade you to come into the caves at all."

Luke was clearly crestfallen, but he went, albeit with lagging steps and regretful looks cast over his shoulder.

Once satisfied he was well on his way, Ottilia lifted her sprigged muslin petticoats and picked her way over rough stone, glad of the short, warm spencer as the chill of the cave struck. She had to move well into the interior to reach the spot where the man lay, folded up against the rough wall.

There was not much light, but enough penetrated from the entrance and from some source above to show the depth and height of the cavern. In the dimmer reaches there appeared to be a couple of low openings that likely led to inner recesses or tunnels. It crossed Ottilia's mind that this would make the perfect hideout for smugglers. She was assailed by a fleeting relief that her intrepid little son had been prevented by his find to be tempted to explore further.

Francis rose as she came up, his handkerchief held over his nose. "Whoever did this chose well. It's dim enough and far enough in to be missed."

"That rock conceals him too." Ottilia wrinkled her nose. "Although not for much longer, I suspect. I wonder if it was the smell that attracted Luke?"

"Impossible boy! He takes after his mother."

Ottilia trilled with laughter. "Fiend of a husband, how dare you?"

"Well, do you ever do as I tell you?"

She ignored the challenge, fixing her attention on the body at her feet. The trunk and head lay at an angle away from the wall, the legs folded awkwardly. "Might he have been kneeling, do you think?"

Francis had moved back to give her room. "I concede that it looks like it at first glance, but I'd expect his legs to be more parallel if he had fallen from a kneeling position."

Ottilia cast a glance down the body and back again. "I believe you are right. How very odd."

"Luke was right about the hole in his head."

A blackened aperture was clearly visible in the forehead, but Ottilia's attention was caught by two more peculiar circumstances. The man's hands had apparently fallen behind his back, but when she leaned over, a closer inspection revealed thin twine encircling each wrist with a trailing line between. His head was bare, but a swathe of cloth seemed to be laid across his eyes.

"This is interesting, Fan." Ottilia squatted down and reached for an edge, intending to tug it down, but it snagged under the head. Tied behind? If so, it had loosened, for when she pulled at it, the cloth came free. A loose knot?

"What's that, Tillie?"

"I believe it was a blindfold."

"Are you serious?" Francis dropped down beside her and took the cloth from her hand, flicking it out. "This is a country fellow's neckerchief." Ottilia watched him hold it up to what little light there was as he made an inspection. "It doesn't seem to be bloodied."

"It ought to be, do you not think?"

"Not necessarily. The mess is more likely at the back of his head. Inside, his skull is probably shattered."

"His hands are tied too. Not very efficiently. Do not you tie the hands tightly together in these cases?"

Her spouse was looking over the back of the corpse to verify her words, but at this he turned his head, regarding her with a frowning brow. "Which cases?"

"Firing squads."

"You are not suggesting…?" Francis emitted a curse. "For pity's sake! As if plain murder was not enough."

"I wonder…" Ottilia mused, the question forming in her mind. "If that notion proves out, it was a rather rough and ready way to execute a man."

Lord Francis Fanshawe regarded his wife's calm features with a rise of dismay. As if the inclement weather encountered in Suffolk over this alleged summer was not enough to ruin the family's sojourn by the sea. Not to mention his mother's peremptory demand to be included, despite her great age.

I will not give in to the advancing years, Sybilla had written, immediately contradicting herself with, *Besides, if you mean to take*

11

a lodging by the beach, that is precisely where Pellew advises me to go. Sea air will benefit my ageing bones.

The cavalcade had therefore been obliged to journey first to Polbrook in order to collect the dowager marchioness, who travelled in her own carriage, accompanied by both her companion and the maid who had replaced Venner, a sour creature now retired, much to the relief of his mother's household. To cap it all, she had insisted upon her French grandson tagging along as escort.

"One cannot be without a gentleman's assistance. Bastien may take care of my needs, thus relieving you, my dear son. You have enough females on your hands as it is."

Undeniable, but Francis had been moved to protest in the privacy of his and Tillie's bedchamber at Polbrook, whereto the whole party had repaired to await his mother's pleasure.

"Anyone would suppose she had not cursed those French offspring of my brother Randal's from here to eternity. I thought Mama could not abide them."

Ottilia had, as ever, been quick to soothe. "Don't fret, Fan. At least Bastien may endure the brunt of Sybilla's complaints instead of you, my poor darling. I do think Bastien has grown into a fine young man. Handsome too, with those fair locks. He favours his mother, I believe."

Francis had been disinclined to acknowledge the wretched fellow's looks, but he was obliged to admit, as the rain continued to make the journey to Aldborough arduous beyond bearing, that the presence of a strong and well set-up young man of a polite and cheerful disposition did much to relieve the strain upon his temper. Bastien shouldered any task assigned to him in a willing and efficient manner that could not but make Francis warm to him. Not even the miserable state of the weather that made the children bored and fractious appeared to have the power to dismay his brother's illegitimate son.

Every break in the black clouds and raging winds was seized with alacrity, as it had been today. It was too cold for swimming, but at least the children were out in the fresh air and able to explore freely. To some purpose, given the result of Luke's investigations.

Francis let out a heartfelt sigh and dumped the cloth he was holding onto the corpse. "This is the end of all things, Tillie. I despair, I really do."

His wife had risen when he did, and now she laid a hand on his chest. Even in the dim light, he perceived her warm smile. "You don't feel it offers a distraction?"

He threw a gaze heavenwards. "You always say that. It's well for you, but it's hardly going to distract the children."

"Is it not? I will wager Luke and Pretty are discussing the matter at length already."

He covered her hand with his own. "Witch wife you are. Very well, let us see what we can find out about this vile killing."

He released her hand as he spoke and Ottilia stepped back. "Guns are more in your line than mine, Fan. I will let you lead."

He looked at the body, measuring it with his eyes. "If we take it he was kneeling, his head must have been about here." He stretched out a hand and touched the wall. "Now, let us see."

Scouring the uneven cave wall around the selected spot, he could not see any indentation that might have resulted from a bullet passing completely through the top of the man's head. He brushed the wall with his palm.

"What are you looking for?"

"I've failed to find any marks possibly made by a bullet. If one did hit, there ought to be loosened particles."

"Could you also try it as if he were standing?"

Francis complied, repeating his motions higher up.

"Anything there, Fan?"

"Nothing. Which means the weapon was fired at a little distance." He was already moving round to where he might examine the head more closely. "What we need is a ball, and I am beginning to think it's still inside." He squatted by the head and leaned over, feeling through the hair. "No exit wound. He was definitely not shot at point-blank range." His finger encountered a protuberance. "Aha!"

"You have found something?"

"I can't see properly in this dismal light. Wait!" He pulled back and dug into one of the capacious pockets of his frock coat, feeling for his pocket knife. With a gesture of triumph, he brought the folding knife forth and flourished it.

"You look just like a magician, my dearest dear."

He threw her a grin. "An essential tool for a father on the hunt for fossils."

Bending to his task, he pulled the head around a little so that more light fell upon the back and once more felt for the bump. "I may make even more of a mess of this fellow's head."

"In the interests of a murder hunt, Fan. Science allows it, moreover."

Francis, intent upon cutting away the man's hair as close to the skull as was possible, the better to get at the suspect bump, made no answer. A hank of hair came away, and he set it aside.

"Ah, I can see it more clearly now."

Methodically, he gouged around the edges of the protuberance. Skin, fuzzy with the remaining hair, came away. Under it was embedded a semi-spherical lump, encrusted with a brownish dried goo that might have been blood or brains. Or both. A slight flattening showed the point of impact.

Francis drew back. "I'll leave the removal to the medical man. If I have gauged it right, this is a musket ball. The killer must have been standing off at some distance."

"How far off?"

Francis measured paces, crossing the wide cave, and halted, turning back to look at the body. "It's odd, Tillie. You'd think he couldn't have been farther than here with that boulder in the way." He took a couple of long steps back towards the body. "Close range for a musket and the ball hasn't gone through. Logically, I would put it at a good twenty yards or more, but it doesn't fit this notion you have of execution."

His wife made no answer, her eyes no longer upon his position, but looking down into the further reaches of the cave. Francis knew that look.

"What are you thinking?"

She blinked and turned to meet his gaze. "Could he have been much further off?"

"The one who fired the shot? How, in this confined space? At a greater distance, I'd call him a remarkably good shot." Ottilia nodded, but in an absent way. He pursued his own thought. "We've not yet thought who might have pulled the trigger."

She surprised him. "Smugglers?"

"That came pat. Is that what you were mulling over?" A thought occurred. "Revenge for a betrayal perhaps?"

"Or punishment." Ottilia's glance fell upon the body again and she swept her arm in an arc across the trunk. "These are not rough clothes, though."

Francis looked again the corpse. As far as one could tell with the lack of light, the man was clad in boots, buckskins and a cloth coat that looked to be well cut. A waistcoat and neck-cloth completed his attire.

"Agreed. Not that it alters your notion. If the stories one hears in the Cross Keys are anything to go by, it is not mere country folk who are involved in free trading. According to reports, half the inhabitants are in with a string of smugglers. Or they used to be. These riding officers come in for a good deal of criticism, but they are doing a better job these days, according to the *Ipswich Journal*."

During their stay in Aldborough, Francis had formed the habit of spending an hour or so in Woulmer's coffee house to peruse the papers and catch up on the progress of hostilities on the continent. The latest news, from Egypt where the British fleet was supporting the Ottomans against the French, recorded a depressing defeat by the upstart Corsican, Napoleon Bonaparte. If the London journals had not yet come in, the local newspaper supplied entertaining snippets such as a balloon having gone up, constables searching for disorderly women or livestock running amok, which at least had the merit of relieving the tedium.

It struck him anew that boredom was unlikely to be his lot as of this moment. "I had best report this at the custom house as well as alerting the local justice."

Ottilia's mischievous twinkle appeared. "Let us hope he is amenable to having his jurisdiction overtaken."

Francis had to laugh. "You wretch, Tillie. Very well. Resurrect the blighted Lady Fan if you must."

CHAPTER TWO

Sergeant Beith of Aldborough Custom House exhibited dismay tinged with a hint of resignation. He was a fellow much of his own age, Francis guessed, with signs of an incipient paunch under his red waistcoat and tightly buttoned blue jacket. Likely the extra flesh was caused by too much imbibing of ale rather than food, since veins were beginning to show red in his plump cheeks. He sucked them in on a hiss. "That'll be one of the gangs hereabouts, that will."

"Smugglers, you mean?"

"Aye, but they ain't gone so far as murderin' afore."

Francis's patience was wearing thin. It had begun to rain again while the party was making its way back to the lodging house. They had been obliged to hurry, the nurses carrying the twins, Pretty and Luke running ahead, while Francis sheltered his wife with the umbrella never far out of reach in this unpredictable weather. He saw Ottilia into the singularly misnamed Fisher Cottage, which was the last large house in the row along Crag Lane which, like the two main thoroughfares behind it, ran parallel to the shore. By the time he had set forth to begin upon his reports of the death, the drizzle was easing, but as he had been obliged to cross Crabbe Street and tramp almost the length of the High Street, he was damp, cold and deucedly uncomfortable.

"Well, what do you propose to do, man? Will you go and look?"

The sergeant scratched his chin. "Rightly speaking, it ought to be the lieutenant."

Having been resident in Aldborough for several godforsaken weeks, Francis was already acquainted with Chief Officer Lieutenant Radway, from whom he had learned much about local smuggling. "And is he here?"

"He's not, sir. He's gone off with Mr Yelford."

"The riding officer?"

"Aye. One of our informants heard as there's a cache been found in a barn."

"Very well, then the matter falls to you as deputy, does it not?"

Beith looked dubious. "Rightly speaking, if it is murder, sir, it falls to Justice Overy."

Francis controlled a pithy retort with difficulty. "Naturally, and he is next on my list. But someone must take charge of this body in the meantime."

The sergeant did not appear to relish the prospect, once again sucking in his cheeks. "Mebbe so…" Then he brightened. "Taplow! He's our boatman. I'll set him to it, sir. Will you show him where?"

Francis cursed. "I'll show you as the presiding officer. If you choose to leave this Taplow to watch the corpse, that is your business."

The sergeant sighed. "Suppose that's fair." He reached for a large ledger situated to one side of the desk and pulled it towards him. "First I've to log your visit and report, sir." He picked up a pen from a wooden standish and dipped it into the inkpot. "What was the name again, sir?"

"Lord Francis Fanshawe."

Beith was looking at the page, half covered with entries in a neat hand, to which he had opened the ledger, but at this he glanced up, eyes widening. Had the wretched fellow not heard him when Francis had introduced himself at the first?

"Begging your pardon, me lord, I hadn't realised. Lord Francis what was that?"

"Fanshawe." He spelled his name for good measure, irritation rising. At this rate, he would be at the business all day. He interrupted the sergeant's laborious scribing. "Must you do this now? Can you not fill in your report when you return? You'll have a deal more to write, I imagine."

Beith straightened, poking the end of his pen under his short brown wig in a reflective fashion. "It's a matter of protocol, me lord. I've got to enter the complaint along with your name."

"I would hardly call it a complaint." Though he might well complain of his son's unfortunate discovery, since it must inevitably involve his darling wife in yet another nuisance of a murder enquiry. The presence in the area of both customs personnel and Riding Officer Yelford, not to mention a division of the Norfolk Militia he knew to be stationed on the heights to the west of the town, gave rise to a faint hope that Ottilia's services might well be dispensed with. Would she relinquish the matter into authority's hands? He almost snorted aloud. When had she ever been content to let one of these puzzles escape her close attention?

To his relief, since his thoughts threatened to raise his ire, Sergeant Beith completed registering his initial entry into his ledger and set down his pen on the standish.

"Ready now, me lord. I'll summon Taplow as we go out."

Leaving the small building ahead of his host, Francis negotiated the steep stone steps outside the front door while Beith conscientiously locked it. The boatman was found lounging against a bollard, laughing with a young woman Francis recognised as one of several maids hired along with the lodging house. As she was carrying a basket, she had no doubt been on an errand. Francis refrained from commenting on her dally since she flitted off upon the sergeant calling for Taplow to accompany him.

The drizzle had given way to a weak sun, making the return walk to the cave less unpleasant than it might have been. Beith, the shingle crunching under his shoes, which he wore with gaiters in lieu of boots, whiled away the minutes with questions pertaining to the find — to which Francis had no answer, since he neither knew the identity of the dead man, nor his occupation, if any.

"How long has he been there, me lord?"

"I have no notion, except to say that he smells. You had best ask that question of a medical man."

"Smells?"

Was it apprehension in the tone? "There is always a putrid aroma around a corpse."

"Seen many, have you, me lord?"

"Too many." To avoid further explanation, he added, "I was in the army at one time."

"Ah, were you, me lord? Then I dare say you wasn't shocked."

The implication being that the sergeant would be? He certainly grew a deal more sober in his manner once he was obliged to examine the corpse. Indeed, Francis could swear his face lost a trifle of colour. His tone was both awed and fearful.

"He's been shot."

"That would be a fair inference."

The note of sarcasm passed the fellow by. The boatman, who had uttered a low-voiced "Gawd!" upon sight of the dead man, here took a hand. "Looks to me as if someone didn't mean fer him to be found, Mr Beith."

"Because of that, you mean?" Francis nodded towards the rock. "The culprit must have known the body would be discovered sooner or later. He, or they, might otherwise have dragged it further into the cave." He gestured. "Those openings may well lead to recesses or tunnels leading away from here."

Both boatman and sergeant looked impressed. The latter, still appearing a little shocked, managed a nod. "True enough, me lord." A hopeful note entered his voice. "Anything else you noticed?"

Francis had no intention of disclosing the notion of a possible execution. A supposition likely to imbue the investigation with an element of high drama that would no doubt attract gossiping attention was a matter only for the ears of the Justice of the Peace. The way news travelled in country parishes was all too familiar. From these two mouths to the world was but a step. He bypassed the question.

"I will leave you to make what arrangements you see fit, Sergeant." He paused. "Do either of you know this man?"

The boatman shook his head and the sergeant looked a little more closely at the dead man's face. He peered for a moment or two and then pursed his lips, straightening up again.

"Looks familiar, me lord, as one I might have seen about the town, but I can't say as I recognise him."

Since the face was carrying the marks of death, this was hardly surprising. "Let us hope someone can identify him. I'll be off now to report to Justice Overy. He will know what steps to take."

Francis turned on the words, ignoring a half-heard request to wait, and left the cave with haste.

Sybilla, upon hearing of her little grandson's discovery, fell at once — and predictably, to Ottilia's sighing resignation — into a mood of peevish complaint.

"If that does not set the seal on a singularly ill-considered expedition! Why in the world did I not expect it? You cannot go anywhere, Ottilia, without encountering a murdered corpse. I believe you are cursed. Or my son is so. Not that he may escape blame. Why he could not have consulted a weatherman before choosing to bring his entire family to a coast too well known for thunderous storms is beyond me!"

Ottilia cut in before her mother-in-law could become entrenched in this familiar theme. "Let us not dwell upon that matter, Sybilla. I was going to initiate a discussion on abandoning our plan to remain for several more weeks as we intended, but that is now ineligible."

Sybilla's companion, Henrietta Skelmersdale, here intervened before the dowager could enter a retort. "Oh, I cannot think Lady Polbrook would agree to leave, would you, ma'am?" She turned with dancing eyes to Ottilia. "She is in a fair way to winning a fortune at whist, you must know."

"Be quiet, Henrietta!"

Henrietta ignored this terse command. "She is twitchy this morning because she could not get a game. Poor Miss Ospringe is not well and did not appear."

Sybilla gave vent to one of her snorts. "A valetudinarian, for my part, suffering from *malade imaginaire*. She is younger than I, yet she succumbs to the slightest ailment. I've no patience."

Ottilia could not resist. "That is well documented at least."

A crack of laughter escaped Sybilla, but she smothered it, covering her mouth with one hand. "Don't be impertinent!"

Ottilia smiled. "You do not pull the wool over my eyes, ma'am. You will not demean yourself by asking me, but I don't doubt you are eager to hear the details."

Sybilla's lips twitched, but she maintained her peremptory manner. "And I don't doubt you are eager to spill them."

Ottilia detected a lessening of the querulous note and was relieved. The dowager was plainly feeling the frustration attendant upon the exigencies of an ageing body. She could no longer walk with the same briskness and her strength was apt to fail. Odd aches attacked her without warning and she was more prone to infectious ailments. But Sybilla, true to form, refused to admit to any such frailty, treating with scorn all suggestions made to ease her path and finding relief in displays of ill temper. Ottilia took immediate advantage of her improved mood.

"Well, I think you must be interested in the most telling aspect of the business."

"Which is?"

"It looks as if — or perhaps it is meant to look — as if the man was executed."

Sybilla's black eyes grew wide for an instant and Henrietta gave a gasp.

"Executed? Not merely slain?"

"His hands were tied and he was blindfolded, though both somewhat loosely. He was shot in the head. Francis found a musket ball embedded in the back of his skull."

Henrietta, who was seated in a chair near one of the wide windows, sank back, putting a hand to her cheek. "That is horrific, Lady Fan."

Sybilla, less shocked it seemed than intrigued, leaned forward in her chair by the fire — necessary even in summer in this present climate. "You say he was tied and blindfolded loosely. What does that mean?"

"The twine was tied at the wrists, but they were not tightly held together. The blindfold knot was loose, for it readily came undone. I would like to think these odd facts might be spotted by anyone else who examines the body, but —□

"But they won't, you think?" asked Henrietta.

"I fear they won't."

"Because most of us are not as observant as you are, Lady Fan."

Ottilia had to laugh at the admiring note, but the dowager wafted a hand. "No need to flatter her, girl. Ottilia is quite aware of her own merits."

"Oh, stop. I do have a knack of noticing, perhaps, but that is all."

"It is not all and you know it, Ottilia. False modesty is unbecoming."

Ottilia was obliged to suppress a rise of annoyance. Must Sybilla embarrass her? The dowager knew how much she disliked discussions of the kind. She hastened to turn the subject, rising from the long sofa, a flowery affair with its chintz-covered seat and cushions, into which she had sunk upon arriving in the parlour where the two other ladies were already seated. Situated on the first floor, it was the main apartment where the family gathered. There was a dining room to the back which served for all meals, and a big room just below the attics appropriated for the children's nursery, but the rest of the lodging house had been given over to bedchambers. The Fanshawes had hired the whole place, bar the ground floor — which was occupied by the owners, Mr and Mrs

Forncett and given over to domestic use — and still the accommodation was inadequate.

Henrietta had chosen to share with Pretty rather than take up a truckle bed with her employer, and Bastien was obliged to be content with the smallest chamber at the back. Ottilia and Francis occupied the second of the main chambers, leaving the front room that mirrored the parlour for the dowager. Apart from the nurses, who slept with their charges in the rooms assigned to the twins and Luke, which were situated next to the nursery above, most of the servants were housed in the attics. The house was reasonably well furnished, the parlour being set with the sofa, several chairs, a writing bureau and a card table. The curtains and wallpapers were not of fashionable style and the furniture was heavy, but all in all, Ottilia was satisfied that it served its intended purpose.

She moved to the fireplace, bending to make a show of warming her hands. "I am glad you caused a fire to be lit, Sybilla. It was warm out earlier, but the drizzle makes it cold."

This proved an unfortunate reminder. "It is positively freezing out. I wonder you have not all taken colds."

Ottilia bypassed the comment with haste, turning as she straightened, setting her back to the fire. "Where is Bastien, by the by? Did he not accompany you this morning?"

Henrietta took this. "He went off to the stables once he had assisted Lady Polbrook into The Rooms. You know his habit. If he is not out riding, he is hobnobbing in Woulmer's with his cronies and that fellow Frenchman he dotes on."

To Ottilia's secret amusement, Sybilla was quick to defend her excessively handsome grandson, notwithstanding his illegitimacy and the gold curling locks inherited from his despised mother. "He does not *dote*, Henrietta. Don't be absurd. It is natural the boy should seek out the company of one of his countrymen. Besides, he has made several friends here. I do not begrudge him such acquaintances. Bastien has been lonely, poor boy."

Ottilia's instincts clicked in. "Now there's a thought. Have you met these cronies of his, Henrietta? I've only seen them at a distance once or twice."

The young men accompanied Bastien to the occasional gatherings in The Rooms, such as they were in Aldborough, the town being but sparsely inhabited by gentry. The term described a sizeable house in the High Street, opened originally as a tearoom by an enterprising inhabitant, and subsequently expanded into two apartments on the ground floor, one for refreshments, the other for cardplayers and any who cared to make use of the books on the shelves to one side that passed for a circulating library. Above these, a larger chamber served for assemblies and the occasional theatrical performance by a visiting troupe.

Since Ottilia rarely attended, being invariably fatigued and having little desire to sit through indifferent musical performances or tread a measure to the sound of a scratchy fiddle, no occasion had yet arisen to present Bastien's friends to her. Only now did she feel the lack. Had not the corpse had the appearance of a gentleman?

"I have met them, yes." Henrietta wrinkled her nose. "I cannot say I took to them. A rowdy set of rascals. Bastien seems to be fond of this Grégoire. They converse in French together most of the time."

"He told me he likes to practise." Thus Sybilla. "Quite right too. He must not lose command of his mother tongue."

"He will scarcely do so, ma'am, when he and his sister speak only French together."

Ottilia cut in fast, before the dowager could argue the point further. "Yes, and with their parents too. I remember Randal usually converses in French with Violette and the children. But setting that aside, I must ask Fan if he has spoken to these young men."

Before she could say more, Ottilia found herself under the scrutiny of Sybilla's shrewd gaze. "Why did you bring them up at all? What have you in your head?"

"I might have guessed you would latch onto that, Sybilla. The dead man's clothes were not those of a common fellow. It occurs to me to wonder if one of Bastien's cronies may be found to be missing."

CHAPTER THREE

Bastien Guizot Fanshawe had fortuitously met his Uncle Francis at the coach yard adjacent to the smithy, where his horse was stabled along with the rest of the family's cattle and several coaches. Good that the coachmen and grooms were housed close by, there being no room for them at the lodging. He had no faith in his grandmother's groom, but Lord Francis's fellow had quickly earned his esteem. Ryde knew his business and might be entrusted with the care of Tonnerre, his prized stallion.

The horse proved skittish and he was engaged in soothing him when Francis walked into the stables.

"Ah, there you are, Bastien. If you are about to ride, come with me."

He had grown to like his uncle in these few weeks and smiled. "Willingly, *mon oncle*. Where do you go?"

"To see a Justice of the Peace. I've to report a murder."

"A murder?"

"Luke found the body." His uncle turned to the groom, who was hovering after releasing Tonnerre into Bastien's charge. "Saddle me a horse, Ryde."

"Right you are, m'lord. Shall I saddle up too?"

"No need. Monsieur Guizot will keep me company."

Bastien heard the words with a rise of pleasure. Alone among his relatives, Lord Francis used his true name, which he much preferred. He never introduced himself as Fanshawe, although he did not object when his father did so. *Maman*, of course, insisted upon him using his adoptive family name. It was not his policy to make waves and it served no purpose to rebel.

He watched as the groom expertly threw a saddle over one of the horses and Bastien ran a critical eye over the beast. A carriage horse, it was deep in the chest with strong legs, built for endurance rather than speed.

"I wish you luck with that mount, *mon oncle*. For my part, I would not ride him."

Francis laughed. "Nor I, my boy, had I the choice."

"His lordship has a tidy couple back at Flitteris Manor, sir, but we couldn't bring them as well."

"True enough, Ryde." Bastien came under that endearing tease in his uncle's quirking lip. "Moreover, unlike some, I've no wish to be in the saddle all day on a long journey."

Bastien grinned. "I do not sit in a coach if I may ride."

His uncle's eyebrow quirked as well now. "Especially if you are obliged to do so in company with my esteemed mama."

Bastien could not contain his laughter, but he spoke in a tone of contrition. "But I am most fond of *Grand-mère*. Her tongue is full of wit."

"I am glad you think so," said his uncle, mounting up. "Is that Tonnerre of yours raring to go?"

"I have not ridden him in a couple of days, and he protests much." He patted the horse's neck and set one foot in the stirrup. "He will not throw me, sir. He likes to tease me a little, that's all." He threw himself into the saddle and settled his feet in the stirrups. "Let us go, *mon oncle*."

He walked his mount out into the High Street and found Francis had followed suit. For a short time, they rode in a companionable silence, turning into Crabbe Street and riding its length to pick up the main road inland that led to Hazlewood, where Justice Overy resided. Presently, curiosity overcame Bastien.

"Tell me about this murder, if it please you, sir. Does it mean my aunt must again be Lady Fan?" The tale, when told, caused him both fascination and dismay. "But who would kill a man in such a fashion?"

"That is the pertinent question." His uncle spoke on a wry note. "Our first supposition was that smugglers are involved."

"That is possible. It is said that no one here pays duty for his liquor."

"So I hear too."

"I also heard it said by Woulmer that the tea merchant, Washbrook, has a secret cellar with tunnels. There he holds goods and barrels on behalf of smugglers."

Francis laughed. "I should doubt of that rumour having any truth. Lieutenant Radway claims to have searched Washbrook's premises several times, and found nothing."

Bastien let this pass, his mind returning to the murder. "Even if it is a smuggler, I ask myself why they make an execution."

"They might, if a man betrayed them. Although I admit Sergeant Beith has never heard of such a thing in this area. Moreover, if it isn't smugglers, the manner of the killing becomes even more puzzling."

"That is seen." A new thought occurred. "You say he seemed a gentleman, this dead man?"

"So your aunt believes, going by his clothing. Why, have you some idea in your head?"

"You do not know the man?"

"I do not. At least, I did not recognise him. The customs sergeant seemed to think he was familiar. A corpse's face undergoes changes and he'd been dead for several days."

"You think that is why one does not recognise him?"

"Precisely. Why did you ask?"

Bastien pondered. It was a long shot, but perhaps worth mentioning. "When you spoke of a gentleman…"

"Go on."

"It is perhaps nothing, but there is one who has not been seen for a while."

"Who?" Lord Francis's tone had sharpened. "It's important, Bastien."

"It is the brother of Miss Green. I have not questioned it, but he goes away sometimes, for a day or more."

"You mean one of those fellows you are often seen with?"

"That is correct. I engage with them because of Grégoire. He is their friend."

He received a sidelong look from his uncle. Shrewd? Or merely questioning? "You don't consider them friends, I take it?"

Bastien could not suppress a grimace. "If not for Grégoire, for whom I cherish a liking, perhaps such men would not attract me. Mundell and Rampton in particular — both strike me as insincere. He, Rampton — what is the word? — yes, he is arrogant. The other likes to make a joke, but his jokes show contempt. You know the type?"

His uncle's mouth curled. "Only too well. What of the fellow who is missing?"

Bastien gave a shrug. "Carlton Green is a good fellow, I think. It is hard to tell. He is friendly but quiet, not loud like the others."

"Hm. This may prove useful. I'd be glad if you will repeat this to my wife."

"I am happy to do so. Also, I have heard from Grégoire that Miss Green has become anxious."

Lord Francis sent him another frowning look. "Since when?"

"Yesterday she told Grégoire that her brother usually is only absent for perhaps two days. Now it is already four."

"That's why you mentioned it. I wonder, might you recognise Green, if the dead man is he?"

"Assuredly."

"Then we'll alert the justice. Once the corpse is brought in, we'll get you to take a look."

Bastien did not relish the prospect, but he saw his duty clearly. "Better me than Miss Green, no?"

"That's exactly what I'm thinking. There's no sense in distressing the girl unless the man proves to be her brother. In which case, we should leave it to my wife to break the news."

This was logical enough, but Bastien felt compelled to enter a caveat. "Yet my aunt does not know Cecily Green, I think. Would it not be better for Grégoire to perform this duty?"

He was treated to another of those sidelong looks. "Women are better at this sort of thing than the mere male. Does this Grégoire of yours have an understanding with Miss Green?"

"I do not think it has proceeded thus far, but Grégoire is infatuated."

"Miss Green likewise?"

An unwelcome fillip at his breast attacked Bastien. "I cannot say." He hoped not, in truth. Conscience intervened. There was a look in her eyes with his countryman which he had certainly not received. "Perhaps a little."

"Well, let us first find out if there is a need for anyone to break such news. I fear it will be some hours before we are able to ascertain the man's identity in any event. There are formalities to be observed before the body can be brought back to Aldborough."

An idea surfaced. "Can I not ride out to the place?"

"To see it in situ? I don't see why not. But Justice Overy must first be informed. It is his business to take charge of the affair."

As they rode on, Bastien was left to the reflection that if the corpse proved to be Carlton Green, the notion of an execution would be even more questionable. Who would want to kill him as a matter of justice? And more importantly, why?

The Justice of the Peace introduced himself as Tobias Overy, making several bows in the doing, seemingly uncomfortable in the presence of rank. He was dressed in country clothing of a brown frock coat over buff breeches, and in defiance of current fashion he adhered to his wig, a short brown affair with rolled curls at the back. He would not sit and Ottilia felt obliged to remain standing herself, using the mantel for support. Her strength was much greater these days, but increased exertion was apt still to tire her unduly. She did her best to put the magistrate at ease.

"I am glad to have this opportunity to meet you, Mr Overy. Thank you for taking the time to visit me."

The justice bowed yet again. "Your ladyship is most gracious. I should not have troubled you except that his lordship was kind enough to suggest you may have information to shed light upon this matter. A terrible business. I do not remember when I have been more shocked."

He looked more distressed to Ottilia's eye. She spoke in a soothing tone. "I dare say you do not have many such incidents with which to deal, sir."

At this, Tobias Overy pulled himself up, his globular eyes protruding the more. "Oh indeed, my lady, we have had our fair share of criminal activity. We dwell in a sorry area for smuggling, I fear." The dismay reappeared. "But not murder. In general, these fellows content themselves with punishments of a less drastic nature."

Ottilia picked up on the word at once. "You think this was a punishment then?"

His thick brows drew together. "His lordship spoke of certain factors that point to an execution." He gave a little shiver. "That is not the business of a citizen. Such acts must be left to the rule of law. Otherwise, where are we, my lady? Anarchy. Chaos. It does not bear thinking of."

Up to this point, Ottilia had been operating on routine, her mind not wholly on the matter at hand. The justice had arrived at an inopportune moment while she was engaged in quelling a near riot. Hepsie, the titular head of the nursery, but in practice guardian of the welfare of both Pretty and Luke, had sent to her for aid as her charges were in danger of coming to blows.

She had arrived in the nursery to find the pair engaged in hot argument, shrieking over each other while the twins, evidently excited by the cacophony, added their voices to the fray. Ottilia came in under the hubbub with her usual calm.

"What in the world is all this?"

She then stood still until the various parties noticed her presence and stammered into silence, her son and adoptive daughter both staring at her, guilt written large upon their faces. Diana and Elinor, breaking into smiles, ran to Ottilia, catching at her skirts.

"Mamma! Mamma!"

"Luke is naughty," offered Di, upturned face alive with mischief. Her dark curls rioted about her pretty little face, her brown eyes a-sparkle.

"You shush, Di!" Thus Nell, on a scolding note. She was like her sister, but not identical, with hair of a lighter hue and eyes similar to Ottilia's grey.

"Hush, both of you!" Ottilia dropped to her haunches and took a hand of each, holding them together. "Do not you start quarrelling as well, my babes." She paid no attention to the immediate protests, passing the hands to the now hovering nurses — "Take them, if you please!" — and stepping up to confront the warring pair.

Luke instantly pointed an accusing finger. "She started it!"

"I did not! You began by bragging of finding the body."

"I wasn't bragging. I only —□

Ottilia cut them short. "That is enough. I don't wish to hear excuses. I have just this to say: if you again make it necessary for Hepsie to request assistance, be aware that it might be Papa who comes."

This was enough to make the children look at each other in lively consternation. Francis was notoriously more ruthless in dealing with recalcitrants. Ottilia knew well it was adoration of their father that made his scolds harder to bear.

Luke was first to recover. "Beg pardon, Mama. I won't fight with Pretty again."

Ottilia hid a smile. "A vain promise, my darling. But if you do, pray keep it within bounds."

A huge sigh came from Pretty. "It's my blame. I'm the eldest. I shouldn't let myself be provoked."

Ottilia patted her shoulder. "We are all provoked sometimes, my love. I must request, however, that you won't talk of Luke's find in the hearing of the twins."

Here Hepsie intervened. "That's exactly what I told them, my lady, but would they listen?"

Ottilia smiled at her. "They won't do it again. If you take my advice, Hepsie, you will send them at once to their separate rooms when they become unruly."

"Oh, no!"

"I won't go!"

The protests were uttered sotto voce, but as Ottilia was about to respond, a knock at the door produced the footman, Tyler.

He bowed. "I am sorry to interrupt you, my lady, but a magistrate has arrived, sent by his lordship."

Obliged to hurry from the room, her mind only half on the happenings of the morning, Ottilia was preoccupied as she joined the visitor in the parlour. It was, to her relief, now empty of its former occupants, the dowager having retired to take a rest and Henrietta seizing the chance to walk out in search of some necessities she wanted to purchase.

Ottilia, noting the effect of the unprecedented murder upon the unfortunate Justice Overy, found her attention fully back on the event. She was obliged to hide a rise of amusement at the dire results he anticipated, but she could not help feeling sorry for the man. He was clearly out of his depth.

"Well, let us hope you may find this particular piece of anarchy to be nowhere near as disastrous as you anticipate."

Mr Overy fetched a sigh. "I hope so indeed, my lady." His gaze became questioning. "His lordship gave me to understand that your ladyship has some experience in these affairs."

Ottilia had to smile at the note of disbelief. "I dare say you find that odd, sir, but it happens to be true. Too much experience, in fact." She was glad Sybilla had left the room, in her mind hearing the snort that would no doubt have greeted this remark.

"I should not presume to suggest his lordship spoke an untruth."

Ottilia bypassed this. "Speaking of my husband, where is he, by the by?"

"Ah. He has ridden back to the scene, my lady. The gentleman who accompanied him has gone with him. It may be that this moosoor knows the man who was killed."

Monsieur? Did he mean Bastien? "A tall gentleman? Fair of face and hair too?"

"That would be him, my lady. A relative, his lordship said."

Then her instinct had not led her astray. How fortunate Francis had apparently met with Bastien. If he knew the dead man, her task would prove a deal easier.

"Do you not intend to see the corpse yourself, Mr Overy?"

"Indeed, indeed, my lady. But I hoped to hear more precisely what you saw first so that I may look for it also."

Ottilia obliged with a detailed description of the findings which had led to her conclusion. Justice Overy nodded several times, although he began to look harassed. He tutted when she came to the end.

"A bad business, my lady. I do not know what we are coming to when persons unknown seek to take the law into their own hands."

Ottilia sought to steer him in a better direction. "I must stress that the notion of an execution is only one supposition, and it is by no means certain. Also, if it was one, there is no saying the action would have been undertaken had it come under the law. I imagine there is a private matter underlying the killing."

The justice looked even more anxious. "How so? What sort of matter might that be? I cannot myself think of anything to make a man kill in such a manner."

Because he was not in fact thinking, but still in shock. But Ottilia did not say so. She offered options. "Revenge perhaps. Betrayal is a powerful goad."

"Good heavens! Revenge? Betrayal?"

"Or it may be a justification of jealousy."

"Jealousy?" Tobias Overy's cheeks suffused with colour and his tone changed. "You speak as if we are living within the pages of one of these absurd Gothic novels, my lady. I beg your pardon if I am speaking out of turn, but these notions are preposterous."

Ottilia eyed him. Was he going to prove difficult? She tried a gentle tack. "Does it not seem to you that the manner of the killing is itself preposterous?"

He looked struck, staring at her with those bulbous eyes positively popping. He expelled a frustrated breath. "I dare say it is. Yes, you are right. I dislike the notion, but I must say that you are right. The whole is preposterous in the extreme."

"Then perhaps we may look at equally preposterous reasons, do you not think?"

"I could wish the perpetrator had done the deed in a more conventional way. Execution!"

Using her most soothing voice, Ottilia oozed sympathy. "It is excessively frustrating for you, sir, but let me remind you that solution is merely a suggestion."

"Why, what else could it be from what you have described?"

Ottilia was loath to expound her own theories, as yet vague and unformed. "It is always best to be cautious, do you not think?"

"Yes, yes, indeed, my lady. I am with you there. But I cannot for a moment imagine how else one may interpret it. I do not know how I am to proceed."

Ottilia produced a fluttering sigh. "It is difficult indeed, sir. I hope I may be permitted to try to ease your path a little. I would not for the world tread upon your toes, but if you feel my assistance could be of use to you?"

Overy became emphatic, nodding the while. "Indeed, indeed, my lady. I will be only too gratified. This business is well beyond my ken, I admit it freely. If your ladyship is good enough to proffer assistance, it would be vain of me to refuse."

"In that case, Justice Overy, I am quite at your service."

He bowed several times. "The obligation is all upon my side, my lady. I hope you may advise me what I must do."

"Are you certain, Bastien?"

The young man's green gaze met hers in a sombre fashion. "It cannot be otherwise, *ma tante*. Any one of his friends must at once recognise it is Carlton Green who lies there. He does not look as he used to, as my uncle warned me it would be, but I cannot mistake."

Ottilia eyed him with some anxiety. "Are you troubled by his death? Was he a good friend to you?" Could the pair have become so close in these relatively short few weeks?

Bastien pursed his lips. "I am not troubled for myself, *ma tante*, but for Miss Green."

"Ah, yes, his sister, is she not?"

"His sister, yes. It is useless to say so, but it was my hope that I would not bring her such tidings."

There was something in his tone that aroused suspicion in Ottilia's mind. "Forgive me, but is she important to you?"

He looked surprised and a hint of colour rose in his cheeks. "Why do you ask? Ah, no. I speak as any man must. She has lost her brother, no? Grégoire cherishes such feelings, not I."

Ottilia was not convinced. She let it pass. "Is Miss Green a resident? Does she have other family here?"

"Not family, no. A lady resides with her. *En chaperon*, you understand. She is one of those who play whist with *Grand-mère*."

"Heavens, is it so indeed? It cannot be Mrs Peckledon. I hear from Henrietta that she is a widow with a collection of children to her credit, although all have flown the nest now. It must be Miss Ospringe then."

Bastien looked dubious. "I do not recall exactly. Mademoiselle Green speaks of 'Ivy' and says she is happy for this lady to enjoy whist."

"But not today. I have it from Henrietta that she is nursing a cold or some such. Which presupposes you will find your *mademoiselle* at home, if she is a girl of conscience, taking care of her chaperon."

Bastien's fair brows drew together, marring the smooth alabaster of his forehead. "May I request, *Tante*, that you go with me? My uncle said that if the dead man is Carlton Green, then it is better for you to tell his sister the terrible news."

Ottilia let out a sigh. "Did he indeed?"

"He tells me that a lady, more especially one with your skill, may say these things better than I."

"But I don't even know the girl." She tutted. "I shall have words with Fan when he finally reappears." Must he shuffle off that duty upon her shoulders? "Where has he gone now? Why did he not return with you?"

"He went again to the body. The justice made this request." A twitch at his lip suggested amusement. "I do not think it pleased my uncle, but the justice looked to be most fearful and so he complied."

Her heart sank. If her husband had been obliged to visit the wretched corpse yet another time, his temper was like to be sorely tried. The prospect of avoidance in breaking the dread news of Carlton Green's death to his sister began to look attractive.

"Is it still cold out? Let me but fetch my cloak and we will go together." Ottilia made for the door, but paused. "If your grandmother comes down in the meantime, for heaven's sake don't mention your liking for this Green woman."

Bastien looked startled, his colour once more flying. "But I have said —□

"Yes, yes, I heard you, my dear boy, but I am not blind. I do not say you have a *tendre*, but you will never make me believe you do not find her alluring."

She hid a smile at the chagrin that overspread his features and left the room.

Miss Cecily Green, discovered as anticipated in attendance upon her unwell chaperon, did not at first glance strike Ottilia as the sort of girl to attract Bastien. She was petite, in contrast to his tall and powerful masculinity, and her countenance was pretty enough under dusky curls, but nowhere near the perfection of her would-be cavalier. Which went to show, Ottilia reflected in passing, that one should not judge by appearances.

Miss Green received her visitors in a parlour one could only describe as poky. A glance as they entered, led thereto by a maid, was enough to assure Ottilia that the Greens were not well-to-do. The furnishings were sparse, consisting of a sofa to seat two against one wall, and one easy chair near the fireplace, upon the mantel of which reposed a clock and a couple of figurine ornaments. Two straight-backed chairs were set either side of a small bureau, and a central rug of oriental design provided the only colour in a dull environment. The house itself, one of a row in a narrow lane a couple of streets off from Aldborough's High Street, had not been promising. One could fit two of them into the Fanshawes' lodging. Ottilia had an instant vision of her brother-in-law the marquis's face should he hear that his son had taken a fancy to a young woman of this ilk. His French wife would no doubt be horrified.

When Miss Green joined them, Ottilia's first assessment was tempered at once by the manner of the girl's greeting, spoken in a soft voice and accompanied by a sweet smile.

"How do you do? I do beg your pardon. I was upstairs with Ivy." The smile came and she held out a hand to Ottilia. "Forgive me, but I did not catch your name. Mary was flustered and I was distracted."

Her frankness at once appealed, and Ottilia returned her smile and took her hand. "I am Lady Francis Fanshawe, Bastien's aunt, you know."

For the first time, Cecily Green's gaze turned on the Frenchman. Her eyes, though friendly, did not light. "Oh, of course, it is Monsieur Guizot. I should have realised."

"Miss Green." Bastien's bow concealed his features, but not before Ottilia had seen the curious mixture of appreciation and trouble in his eyes. Consciousness of the dread nature of his mission?

Miss Green turned immediately back to Ottilia. "I did not quite recognise you, my lady. I have seen you, of course, but we have not previously been introduced." The oddity of her guest's presence seemed to occur to her, a tiny frown catching between her brows. "But why are you here? I mean — I am honoured and happy, but…"

Did she speak the words as a matter of form? She was looking now from Ottilia to Bastien and back again. Sparing a glance for her nephew, Ottilia found him gazing at her in anguish. Clearly, he had no notion how to approach the matter that brought them.

Drawing a breath, Ottilia moved a step closer and reached for the girl's hand again. "Pray don't look so confused, my dear child. Sit with me a little, if you please."

Without waiting for an answer, she drew the young woman to the sofa and obliged her to be seated. Miss Green looked bewildered and, not surprisingly, showed the beginnings of apprehension. Bastien was hovering, looking anxious.

Ottilia retained her hold on the girl's hand, indicating with a look to her nephew that he should remain at a distance. He stepped back and she returned her attention to the young woman at her side.

"I fear there is no easy way to say this, my poor child. We are the bearers of sad tidings which will distress you. Your brother—□

Miss Green started, her gaze flying to Ottilia's. "Carlton? What has happened to him? Is he ill? I have been so fearful. Oh, what is it? Tell me at once!"

Ottilia said it as gently as she could. "I am so very sorry, my child. Carlton has died."

The shock hit hard. The young woman's eyes dilated, seeming to become huge as they stared into Ottilia's. She did not speak for a full minute.

Ottilia waited, neither flinching from that tragic gaze, nor releasing her hold on the suddenly stiffened fingers. There was no saying how Miss Green would react once the initial shock passed. Ottilia was ready for her to swoon or burst into sobs.

Cecily Green did neither. The light slowly drifted out of her eyes, leaving them dull. Her fingers relaxed and she drew them out of Ottilia's grasp, setting them in her lap and clasping both hands together. Her gaze also left Ottilia's and settled upon her hands. Her voice came, soft but with an edge to it. "I see. Thank you."

At a loss for a moment, Ottilia glanced towards Bastien and found him frowning. Was he puzzled by this calm acceptance? Did he think it would last? Ottilia's heart ached for the girl. This was but the beginning, if she only knew. How to burden her with the worst of the business? Yet it must be done.

"I understand you have been anxious for a day or two?"

Her head came up, but her response was mechanical. "Yes. Carlton went off on one of his expeditions. Fossils."

"He collects them?"

"He draws them. They have long fascinated him. I think that is why he wanted to live here."

There was absence in her face, but at least she was able to talk. Ottilia suspected she did so without thinking, unable to move beyond the fact of her brother's death.

"Bastien said you did not expect Carlton to be away for so long."

"He usually does not stay away beyond two days, for he knows I worry." Still the dull tone, but now she turned back to Ottilia. "It has happened before."

"He has overstayed his time in the past?"

Her senses were showing signs of a return. "A few weeks ago. He was injured. Wounded, I thought. When he came back at last, I mean."

Ottilia's instincts were prickling, but she kept her tone neutral to avoid startling the young woman. "How wounded?"

"His arm was badly cut. We had to send for the surgeon. Carlton insisted he had gashed it on a sharp rock."

Ottilia threw a questioning glance at Bastien, but he grimaced back in the negative. Then he had not known about this wound. "When was this, Cecily? I hope you won't mind the informality."

Cecily shook her head. "Five or six weeks ago."

"Ah, before we arrived here then. That is why you were concerned when he put in no appearance this time, I take it."

Cecily did not reply directly, her mind evidently still on that past event. "I thought it had been a wound from a blade. That is what the surgeon said. But when I taxed Carlton with it, he laughed. He said I read too many Gothic novels, that I should curb my imagination."

Ottilia drew a breath. "My poor child, I fear you may be found to have been correct."

She was treated to a fresh stare, a quiver beginning at the girl's lips. "Why?"

Straight to the point. There was a deal more to this girl than first appeared. Ottilia took the plunge. "You have been very brave, Cecily, and I need you to be braver still."

Her eyes dilated all over again, growing enormous as her face steadily whitened. No word was forthcoming, however. Ottilia kept her gaze on the girl's, but beckoned low towards Bastien, who moved silently to the side of the sofa.

"Carlton's death was no accident, Cecily. He was killed."

"Killed?" A thread of a voice, the girl's figure deathly still. "How?"

"He was shot in the head." She refrained from speaking of the possible notion of an execution. "The only consolation I can offer you is that Carlton did not suffer. He must have died upon the instant."

The girl's stoicism was at an end. Her eyes rolled and she would have slipped off the sofa as she fainted if Bastien had not been there to catch her.

CHAPTER FOUR

The bedchamber afforded little else beyond the four-poster itself, a chest at its foot and a press to one side. Ottilia negotiated the narrow passage that allowed her to reach the prone figure on the coverlet, where Bastien had laid Cecily down. She sat on the edge of the bed and felt the young woman's forehead.

"She is not running a fever." She checked the beat at her wrist. "Her pulse is tumultuous, however." She straightened Cecily's clothing and glanced up at Bastien, hovering at one corner. "Fetch water, if you will. Brandy would be better, but I should doubt of there being a decanter in this establishment."

"I will check." He crossed the room and slipped out of the door, his progress down the narrow stair echoing through the house.

Ottilia returned her gaze to the sufferer. Cecily's pallid features were a worry. She ought by now to have regained consciousness. Setting a hand on the young woman's arm, she called her softly.

"Cecily! Cecily, wake up now, my dear."

There was no response, but a sound from without caught Ottilia's attention. The swish of clothing against wooden floorboards? She looked towards the door and called out louder.

"Is anyone there?"

A figure in a bedgown slid into the room, one hand on the wall for support. An elderly face peered at Ottilia from under a lawn cap tied under the chin. Her voice quavered a little as she spoke. "Such a commotion! Is that Cecily? What has happened? Is she ill too?"

Recognising the dame, Ottilia stood and pushed through, catching her by one elbow. "Good day to you, Miss Ospringe. Ought you to be up? You look none too steady."

The chaperon ignored the entirety of this speech, her gaze fixed on Cecily. "Why is she lying down? Has she succumbed to this horrid malaise too?"

"I am afraid she is in shock."

"In shock? Why? What has happened?"

Ottilia gently steered her back to the door. "Pray allow me to guide you back to your bed, ma'am, and I will explain everything. I do not wish to speak of it before Cecily."

Miss Ospringe allowed herself to be ushered out, still protesting. "But what has shocked her? She was all right a moment ago."

"Which is your chamber, ma'am?"

The dame pointed to a far door. "That one, in the front. But why are you are here, Lady Francis?"

"I will tell you it all presently. Let me first tuck you up again."

"But Cecily…"

"Cecily will recover soon, I promise you. I have sent Bastien to fetch a glass of water. Unless you have brandy in the house?"

"Brandy? Oh, Carlton keeps it somewhere. Mary will know. If Cecily is unwell, he ought to be sent for. Not that anyone knows where he has gone this time."

She continued in this strain as Ottilia inexorably led her into a room better than that occupied by Cecily, which boasted a wide front window and a standing full-length mirror beside the bed, a press and a washing stand. Once she had been persuaded to get between sheets and rest against banked pillows, Ottilia sat on the edge of the bed, ready with a spurious explanation of Cecily's current state. She did not feel the exposure of the whole to Miss Ospringe at this juncture could serve any useful purpose.

"I am afraid I was obliged to disclose some distressing news to Cecily. I fear it will also be upsetting to you, Miss Ospringe."

"Oh dear, poor Cecily." Eyes a little rheumed, presumably from her present ailment, widened a little. "It is not Carlton, is it? Has he sustained another injury?"

Ottilia hesitated. Of what use was it to prevaricate? She abandoned her notion of concealing the worst. "It is worse than that, ma'am. Carlton is dead."

Horror leapt in the elder lady's eyes and she waved agitated hands. "Oh, no! Oh, poor boy. Poor Cecily."

"Indeed." Ottilia caught her hands and held them. "You must be strong for Cecily's sake, Miss Ospringe."

"Yes, yes. I will do all in my power, poor love. But Carlton dead? Upon what occasion?"

"I hesitate to burden you with this, ma'am, but it is what has shocked Cecily so badly. Her brother has been murdered."

Miss Ospringe stared in an uncomprehending way. "How could that be?"

Ottilia squeezed the hands she still held. "I do not yet know, but I assure you I mean to find out."

She was not sure whether the dame had taken in her words. Was her shock equal to Cecily's? For a long moment, she simply continued to stare. Then she gave a little nod. "Yes. That is what you do. Lady Fan, they call you. Lady Polbrook spoke of your prowess."

Did she indeed? A faint ripple of amusement rose up in Ottilia but she quelled it. This was scarcely a moment for levity, albeit her mother-in-law's contrariness was typical.

"I will do my best, Miss Ospringe. More I cannot say." A heavy tread on the stairs signalled Bastien's return. "I hear my nephew, I think." She released the other's hands. "I expect you could do with a tot yourself, ma'am."

Miss Ospringe did not speak, but she nodded again and Ottilia saw tears were gathering in her eyes, one already spilling down her cheek. On impulse, she leaned forward and clasped the frail lady in her arms, giving her a warm hug.

"Have a good cry, dear Miss Ospringe. You will be the better for it and more able to help Cecily."

She pulled back and the elderly dame sniffed and groped under her pillows, bringing forth a handkerchief. She used it, her voice now throaty as she spoke again. "You are very kind, Lady Francis. I am grateful."

"Oh, do not be. Pray call me Lady Fan. Everyone does, and it is so much easier."

"So kind, Lady Francis," repeated the other, not availing herself of this permission. She sighed gustily. "That poor boy."

"Do not hold back your tears, my dear." Satisfied Miss Ospringe would not succumb to shock as Cecily had done, Ottilia patted the lady's shoulder and rose. "I will return directly. Let me check on Cecily first."

Bastien was waiting in the corridor outside Cecily's chamber. "Brandy I have, *Tante*. The maid found it for me."

"Excellent." Ottilia took the tray from him, upon which reposed two glasses, one containing a measure of golden liquid, the other filled with water. "Pray go down again, Bastien, and fetch up another tray. Miss Ospringe needs brandy too, and water as well, I shouldn't wonder."

She did not wait for his compliance, but re-entered Cecily's bedchamber and found her awake but still lying where she had left her.

"There now, we are just in time, my child."

Cecily turned her head and looked up, but she did not speak. Ottilia set the tray down on the bedside table.

"Come, sit up. Let me bank the pillows for you." Cecily did as she was bid, still silent. "There, that is better. Lean back, my dear child." She picked up one of the glasses. "I hope you will take a sip or two of this, Cecily." The girl's gaze went to the liquid in the glass and she frowned. Ottilia let out a little laugh. "It is simply brandy, my dear. Purely medicinal. You will find it remarkably efficacious." She put the glass to Cecily's lips. "Come, just a little."

Cecily brought up a wavering hand and set it to the glass, tipping it up. Ottilia did not let go, but she allowed her patient to control it as she sipped. She was obliged to take it back as Cecily coughed, setting a hand to her chest.

"It feels hot."

"It will do. Only for a moment, mind. Try a little more. There, that is very well done."

The next few sips clearly went down more easily and Ottilia was gratified to see a little colour returning to Cecily's face. She did not finish all the liquid, but presently pressed the glass upon Ottilia, who took it and set it down.

"You look a degree better, Cecily."

"Thank you, but I feel as if my head may explode."

"That will pass in a little while. I dare say you will find that talking eases you."

A little sigh escaped and Cecily rested her head back against the pillows. "I cannot remain here for long. Ivy will be needing me."

"You need entertain no fears on that score. She came in here, but I put her back to bed."

"I cannot imagine how she will take this news."

Ottilia hesitated, but perhaps it would save Cecily a modicum of worry. "I have already told her. She took it well and is determined to be a support to you."

"She is always so." Cecily took in a sobbing breath and let it out again. "Ivy has been as a mother to me. She was my governess and then, when Mama died, she remained to chaperon me. But she is more than that. Ivy is family."

Ottilia smiled. "I am happy to know it. You will need her at such a time more than ever."

Cecily looked up at her. "I do not know what is to become of us without Carlton."

"That is a problem for a later time, my dear. At this present, we must find out why he became a target and who did this terrible deed." She had chosen her words with care, hoping not to resurrect Cecily's shock.

"I do wish to know it, ma'am, but I cannot think about that today."

"I understand perfectly, Cecily, and once you are feeling well enough, I will leave you." She did not add that there were questions to which she badly needed answers. They would do for another day. "Pray don't hesitate to ask for help if you need it. These occasions entail a great many formalities. You may find these will steady you."

Cecily agreed to it, but it was plain she was not yet ready to grapple with the exigencies of the death. Ottilia could but hope Miss Ospringe would prove more resilient than she appeared.

A thought occurred. "Should you object to it if I called in my nephew?"

"Monsieur Guizot? Is he here?"

"He fetched the brandy for you. I sent him for a glass for Miss Ospringe and I dare say he is waiting outside. May I bring him in?"

"I have no objection."

Ottilia called to Bastien, who popped his head round the door. "Come in a moment."

He came in and stood just inside the door, his gaze going directly to Cecily. He was burdened with another tray and Ottilia rose from the bedside.

"You have Miss Ospringe's measure there, thank you. I will take it to her." She possessed herself of the tray and jerked her head towards Cecily. "See if there is any way in which you may serve Cecily, Bastien. You and Carlton's other friends may be able to assist with certain formalities. I will not be long."

Bastien left the house in the wake of his aunt with reluctance. It felt churlish, even cruel, to leave Cecily to digest this horror alone. But the dismissal had been unmistakeable.

"I thank you, Monsieur Guizot. Pray do not incommode yourself any longer."

He had tried. "I have said, ma'am, that I am at your service. It grieves me to leave you in distress."

"You and your aunt have been more than kind. I could not impose further upon you."

A slight emphasis on that last *you* could not but prick. Yet it was plain she wanted him gone.

"As you wish. Tell me if there is anything I may do for you."

She had made only one request and Bastien had retired discomforted. His aunt, to his surprise, declared herself as quite ready to leave and he had therefore nothing to do but to follow her out. In the roadway, he paused.

"Where do you go, ma'am? I must find the friends of Carlton Green. His sister desired me to inform them myself."

His aunt was looking up at the front window, but she met his eyes at this. "An excellent notion. I dare say she will not feel ready to speak with anyone for a day or two."

Impatience gripped Bastien. "That is clear, ma'am."

He received an odd look from under raised brows. "But what have I said?"

He schooled his features and voice. "Nothing, *ma tante*. Do not heed me. This affair becomes a little troubling."

Lady Francis gave one of those laughs that came seemingly out of the blue. "An understatement, Bastien. Though I suspect you are referring to Cecily's condition. You cannot hope to relieve her, my dear boy."

"That is not —□

She rode over him. "Cecily's grief must take its course. The best you can hope for is to be at hand at a crucial moment."

Must she speak in riddles? His uncle had complained of this tendency, but it had not before come into Bastien's orbit. "What is it you mean, *Tante*?"

He was irritated to receive an enigmatic smile. "Where do you think to find these young companions of yours?"

Bastien suppressed his frustration. "I shall first try at Woulmer's."

Lady Francis gave vent to an unintelligible expletive. "That is a nuisance. I thought to accompany you. It might profit us if I could be present when you break the news."

This proved a distraction from his thoughts of Cecily. "How so?"

"People are never more apt to give themselves away than upon the receipt of bad news."

"How give themselves away?"

His aunt eyed him. "You are persistent, my dear boy. Are you intrigued or merely sceptical?"

He was betrayed into a grin. "I find your mind of interest. *Grand-mère* told me you do not think as others do. She says we all are — what is the word she used? — ah, yes, we all are plodding, but Lady Fan has a mind most convoluted." He had to smile. "You laugh, but my uncle spoke of you in this way also when we rode to the cave together."

The laughter vanished. "Do you tell me my wretched husband says I have a convoluted mind?"

"No, no. It is lightning is how he said it."

"Oh. Then I forgive him. As for my mother-in-law..." The smile that seemed to grace one appeared. "Pay them no heed. My knack is in noticing what others do not. It is a matter of observation. Perhaps also, to keep one's mind open to possibilities. Never dismiss anything, however unlikely, unless it proves to be incorrect."

Impressed by this reasoning, Bastien readjusted his intention. "It may be better if I do not say anything when I find them until I can bring them into your presence."

"An excellent notion, but you will alert them by this means too. I think I must defy convention and enter Woulmer's with you."

"Ah, yes. It is not proper for you to enter a coffee house, no?"

"Your grandmother would certainly say so, unless perhaps I was accompanied by my husband. But since I am quite in the habit of *not* doing what is proper, let us disregard that."

"But *Grand-mère* will accept me in the way of a substitute for Lord Francis, perhaps?"

He received one of his aunt's warm smiles. "How right you are, my dear boy. She would consider you more than adequate. I wonder I did not think of that myself."

Bastien offered his arm to Ottilia as they began along the little row of houses in the side lane and entered Crabbe Street, which ended at its crossing into the High Street, Woulmer's being fortuitously situated almost opposite. He was conscious of a smidgeon of relief to have his aunt's company in his task. He had not been looking forward to telling his friends of Carlton's demise, especially Grégoire, whom he knew to be close with Cecily's brother. A niggle of what he felt to be inappropriate jealousy arose at the thought that Grégoire's condolences might well be more acceptable to Cecily.

Woulmer's was reached within a few moments, an unprepossessing building with a long ground-floor window, panelled and paned. Bastien opened the deal front door for Ottilia to enter before him. Within, there was the usual bustle of tray-bearing waiters weaving between the little service booth with Mrs Woulmer presiding and the tables whereat relaxed gentlemen either read the papers or engaged in desultory talk.

One glance served to locate two of Bastien's friends, although Grégoire was missing. A pity, but it could not be helped. He led his aunt towards the far table, notwithstanding the odd glances cast at her. Both Mundell and Rampton had seen their approach and were showing surprise at Ottilia's presence. Both men rose and executed a bow, Mundell throwing a questioning look at Bastien. He did the honours.

"Lady Francis, allow me to present my friends, Messieurs Ince Mundell and Bryan Rampton."

Ottilia had not failed to take in the young men's reaction to her arrival. She inclined her head as they both bowed a second time.

"I caught sight of you both in The Rooms once or twice. I am glad of this chance to have a formal introduction."

First to respond was the one pointed out by Bastien as Ince Mundell, a slim fellow whose dress touched on dandyism with brass buttons to an elegant coat and high points to his collar, his neck-cloth an elaborate tie. His superior tone was at variance with his words. "You do us too much honour, Lady Francis. Who could not be happy to scrape acquaintance with your good self?"

Suppressing an instant feeling of dislike, Ottilia produced a smile as spurious as his own. "How kind. I have a sufficient reason to be seeking you out, you must know, albeit in this unconventional fashion."

This prompted a smirk from his companion, the one named Bryan Rampton. He was no dandy but a stocky man, countrified in a frock coat over buckskins and a complexion verging on ruddy. "Not for the sheer pleasure of our company then?"

Ottilia turned upon him her smile, falsely bright. "Alas, no. I trust you will not be too disappointed." She did not wait for a response, but wafted a hand in Bastien's direction. "My nephew has something of import to disclose to you both."

Mundell flashed Bastien a look but pulled out a chair. "Will you not be seated, ma'am?"

She inclined her head in her most gracious manner and sat down, nodding at Bastien to begin as the other gentlemen reseated themselves. He did not comply and remained standing, his eyes on the other two.

"Where is Grégoire, do you know?"

"No idea, old fellow," drawled Mundell.

"You have not seen him this morning? Nor you, Rampton?"

The other man raised his brows. "Why do you ask?"

"Because it will be easier to speak of this matter while you are all together."

"Grief, you sound portentous, Guizot! What's to do?"

Ottilia caught her nephew's eye and gave him a brief nod. The less these two were prepared, the better. So far neither had shown any sign of being forewarned about Carlton's death. Bastien took the hint and went directly to the meat.

"There is grave news. Carlton Green has been killed."

"What?" This from Rampton, who blinked several times.

The other man did not speak at first, his gaze fixed upon Bastien. When he did, his reply was terse and to the point. "Killed, you said?"

"Murdered."

The word brought both men to their feet, exclamations coming thick and fast from both tongues.

"You can't mean it!"

"Carlton murdered?"

"How in the world…?"

"Why? For the Lord's sake, why?"

"This must be nonsense!"

Bastien quashed this without hesitation. "It is true. I have seen his body. It is I who was able to identify him." He hesitated as his friends stared at him. "There is more. His hands were tied and he had a blindfold. The shot was to the forehead. Lady Francis here says this may point to an execution."

For a moment longer the stares held. Then Mundell dropped into his chair, seemingly stunned. Rampton remained standing, his gaze turning on Ottilia.

"You saw this, ma'am?"

She met the obvious disbelief in his eyes. "I did, sir. My small son discovered the corpse while he was exploring a cave."

"But … this is scarcely a sight for feminine eyes."

Ottilia smiled. "No, and it is not generally acceptable for women of my ilk to frequent coffee houses and sit with a collection of gentlemen."

Her nephew cut in. "You have not heard, Rampton, how my aunt is also Lady Fan. She has expertise in matters of murder."

Bryan Rampton looked incredulous, but Ince Mundell, evidently recovering from his stupor, reached out and tugged at his coat. "Sit down, man. You ought to pay more attention. Miss Ospringe and Mrs Peckledon have been chattering about it forever."

The other took his seat again, but blinked uncomprehendingly. "I've not heard them."

"Because you don't listen. They play whist with Guizot's grandmother. They are bound to know everything about the Fanshawes."

Ottilia intervened. "Hardly everything. Lady Polbrook is no chatterbox. But that is beside the bridge. Will you object to it if I ask you a question or two?"

Rampton instantly balked. "Ask us? Why?"

Bastien took this, at last pulling out a chair for himself and joining them at the table. "It is how Lady Fan works. She will find out the murderer with questions."

The other man exhibited agitation, repeating, "Why ask us? We didn't kill the fellow." He let out a snorting laugh. "At least, I know I didn't. Can't speak for Mundell."

"I should hope you wouldn't try, man. I can speak for myself, I thank you." Ince Mundell threw Ottilia a twisted smile. "Not that a mere denial is likely to serve, am I right, ma'am?"

Ottilia batted it straight back. "You are perfectly correct." Pleased she had taken him aback, she pursued it. "I am not here to make accusations, however. I merely desire to gather information. You are Carlton's friends. It is of importance to first discover his habits. For instance, I understand from his sister that he was absent too long upon an earlier occasion and came home with a wound upon his arm."

"Gad, yes," said Mundell. "Gashed it on a rock, he said."

The other threw up his eyes. "That's what comes of poking about in crevices and such, I told him. Dashed foolish way to waste his time." Rampton's brows drew together and his tone changed. "Ought not to say so now the poor fellow is dead."

Ottilia let this pass. "Whereabouts did he conduct this poking about, do you know?"

"All over. Combed the beaches round here. Known him to wander as far south as Orford. I went with him once or twice, just to see what he would be at. Dull work, if you ask me."

"Miss Green says he drew these fossils. Did he in general carry a sketchbook on these expeditions?"

The two men looked at each other and Mundell raised his brows. "I never saw him with one. Did you?"

"Can't say I recall it. But that don't mean he didn't have one. Likely he carried a pocket book like the rest of us." Rampton turned back to Ottilia. "You'd best ask du Guet, ma'am. He went along more times than I ever did."

Bastien cut in, his look a trifle disgruntled to Ottilia's eye. "He is talking of Grégoire, *Tante*."

Who was more her nephew's friend, or so she had supposed. Or was that only since their arrival in the town? She essayed the point. "I know Bastien has been much in Grégoire's company of late, but is it the case that he and Carlton are friends of long standing perhaps?"

Mundell made a moue. "Not to my knowledge. No more than Rampton here or myself. We all three met the Greens when they arrived, of course, but du Guet took to Carlton. Stuck to him, frankly."

"Indeed?"

Rampton threw a glance at Bastien. "No surprise there. Carlton spoke French and du Guet is what they call an émigré, like our friend here."

"Ah, but my father has brought us out of France at the beginning. We do not figure as émigrés."

"No daring escape like the one du Guet claims to have made, eh?" Mundell gave a sneering smile Ottilia deemed sarcastic. "Says he disguised himself as a sailor and was shipped under a pile of ropes." His laugh was mocking.

Ottilia took it up regardless. "Claims, you say? You doubt his veracity?"

"Smacks of the sort of adventure you read in novels," said Rampton.

Here Bastien grew stiff, and Ottilia read danger in his eyes, although his voice remained neutral. "You say so, but I have heard even more fantastic stories while in the capital. Among my friends are many so-called émigrés who indeed escaped the Terror using ingenious methods. My mother befriended such people, who come with nothing, and thus I have heard such tales for many years."

Mundell's smile broadened. "Then I bow to your superior knowledge, my dear Guizot."

Ottilia backtracked. "Leaving that aside, just when did Grégoire come to Aldborough?"

Mundell looked to the ceiling as if he sought the answer there, but Rampton was before him. "Five years ago, perhaps? Matter of some three years since the Greens turned up and du Guet was a fixture by then. Wasn't destitute the way Guizot describes it, though."

Bastien jumped in. "You will not pretend Grégoire is — how do you say? — plump in the pocket? That is the expression, no?"

"Yes, it is, but no need to take a pet, old fellow. All I meant is du Guet has money enough to live reasonably well. He's not purse-pinched, that I can vouch for. He carries a gold fob watch and wears a ring with a diamond in a gold setting. He didn't get those for a song."

"You speak of what you do not know. These are heirlooms, which Grégoire brought with him from France."

Ottilia broke in before her nephew's defence of his friend could become heated. "Does he have employment of some kind, perhaps?"

"He makes translations now and then, *Tante*. It is not so lucrative."

"His English must be good."

Bastien laughed. "Better than mine. If not for his accent, you would not think he is French. My father made me study long hours." A sheepish grin emerged. "I did so when I could not manage to escape my tutor. English grammar was not so interesting to me as the stables and my horse."

Ottilia smiled but did not trouble to ask how Grégoire had become fluent in the language of his adopted country. With luck, she might find out from the man himself in due course. She returned to the victim. "How often did Carlton make these forays to search for fossils?"

Mundell and Rampton looked at each other, as if for guidance. The latter turned back to Ottilia. "Liable to go off at any time. Not for long, mind. He'd be away for a day or two, perhaps once or twice a month."

"You're forgetting the local treks he made. The beach at Thorpe is pretty rock-strewn, Carlton was used to say. He'd trot down there any time he didn't wish to dance attendance on his sister."

Before Ottilia could respond, Bastien jumped on this, his tone curt. "You would imply Miss Green was a hindrance to him?"

"I didn't mean —□

Bastien did not suffer the interruption. "On the contrary, I have observed him to be most protective of his sister. I also have a sister, and it is out of both duty and affection that I look to her welfare."

Mundell's mouth curved in the cynical way that seemed habitual to him. "Very right and proper, my dear fellow. Yet I'll wager you Frenchmen cherish your females more strongly than we do. I should not stigmatise Green as neglectful precisely, but let us ask Lady Francis here if she considers it appropriate for a brother worthy of the name to leave his sister without escort or protection for days at a time."

Bastien allowed Ottilia no opportunity to take up this challenge. "You forget the chaperon. Cecily is not alone."

"Ha! Can't argue that, Guizot." Thus Rampton, entering the lists in support of his friend. "Do you see the Ospringe woman tacking about the place after Miss Green? Balderdash! Plays whist six days out of the seven. Any blaggard could spirit the girl away and none would be the wiser. Wouldn't surprise me if du Guet don't take advantage of Green's demise to do exactly that."

Bastien was on his feet. "You impugn my countryman, sir! Unsay those words!"

Both the other men rose and Ottilia decided it was time to call a halt. "Dear me, gentlemen. Do you mean to start a brawl in my presence? Next you will be asking each other to name your friends. Come, sit down again, all of you."

The English pair glanced from her nephew to Ottilia and slowly sank back down.

Rampton growled an apology. "Beg pardon, ma'am."

His companion looked across with a cynical gleam. "If you don't object to my saying so, ma'am, it would be more to the point to call your nephew to order."

Ottilia took this in her stride. "Indeed and I mean to do so. Bastien, my remarks were not intended for your friends alone. Sit down, if you please."

He threw her a fulminating glance, but retook his seat. Ottilia picked up on the goad.

"You raise an interesting point, Mr Rampton."

He looked both surprised and puzzled. "How so?"

"Do you know if Carlton approved of Grégoire as a potential suitor to his sister?"

"Didn't seem to object to the fellow."

Mundell let out a laugh. "Object? The two of them were as thick as thieves. If you ask me, Green would have welcomed a match."

An explosive sound came from Bastien, drawing the gazes of the other two.

"What's to do now?"

"You are dreaming, Mundell. No man considers an émigré a suitable parti for his women. It is more usual for refugees to wed among themselves. Our aristocrats do not deign to mix blood with the English."

The bitter note was not lost on Ottilia. Did Bastien's illegitimacy trouble him? Did he deem it a bar to a good marriage, perhaps? From what she knew of his parents, they would ensure the Polbrook rank and title served him in this regard.

Rampton snorted. "Du Guet is no aristo. Says his family is quite ordinary."

"As bourgeois as they come," said Mundell. "His exact words."

Ottilia bypassed this irrelevancy. "Be that as it may, let us turn to a more mundane matter." All three eyed her, wariness in the English faces. "As far as we can tell, this murder occurred perhaps two or three days ago. Will you tell me what engagements kept you occupied during that time?"

The question remained unanswered. A flurry at the door to the coffee house hailed the hurried entrance of a fourth young man. He paused to glance round, spotted the coterie at the table and plunged in their direction, hat in hand and looking distraught. Seeming not to notice Ottilia, he addressed the men, a wild note in his voice, which possessed a slight accent.

"We are bereft! Our friend Carlton is dead! It is hardly to be believed, but he has been shot. Do not look at me in that fashion, for it is true. I saw him myself as they brought him into the custom house. He is dead, I tell you!"

CHAPTER FIVE

Bastien leapt to his feet. "We know it already, Grégoire. I too have seen him. I accompanied my uncle to the cave."

"Cave? What do you mean?"

Ottilia watched the new arrival with interest, noting how puzzlement entered his face. It was a personable countenance, if not in the league of that of her nephew, who began upon another recital of the finding of the body. Grégoire du Guet had dark curling locks, cut short in the current prevailing style. His eyes were expressive but one would be hard put to it to notice the rest of his facial features. There was nothing prominent to mark him out from his fellows unless one met his gaze, Ottilia suspected. He would readily blend into a crowd. What then had attracted Cecily Green?

He listened to Bastien's account without comment beyond the odd muttered expletive. At the end, Grégoire looked from one to the other of his friends as if seeking enlightenment before his gaze fell upon Ottilia.

She met it without expression, waiting for her nephew to do the honours.

"Grégoire, here is my aunt, Lady Francis Fanshawe. Grégoire du Guet, *Tante*."

The newcomer made a mechanical bow, a question entering his features. Ottilia answered it. "You are wondering why I am here, I dare say."

A flicker of a smile came and went. "I dare say you will tell me, ma'am."

Before Ottilia could answer, Ince Mundell cut in. "She's a sort of Bow Street Runner, old fellow."

"Means to find out who saw fit to see off poor old Carlton." Thus Bryan Rampton, adding his mite.

Ottilia intervened. "I thank you, Mr Mundell, but I am not employed by Bow Street or anyone else." She returned her gaze to Grégoire. "You are distressed, sir. I have questions, but perhaps you would prefer to answer them when you have had time to assimilate your friend's unfortunate demise?"

Grégoire gave a little shiver. "He was my good friend. I cannot believe he has left us, even though I saw it for myself. It seems a very dream to me." His face changed and he turned to flash a glance across the faces of the others, his speech rapid and urgent. "What of Miss Green? Has she been informed? I dread to think of how she will take this terrible news."

"She knows." Was there a hint of triumph in Bastien's tone? "My aunt and I told her together. It was my first duty after I found the body was indeed Carlton."

Grégoire became eager. "Then you have saved me an unpleasant task, my good friend. How is she? Indeed, how could she be after receiving such shocking tidings? She must be in despair."

Ottilia took this. "In fact, sir, Cecily took the news with a calm one must admire." She gave the Frenchman a measuring look, choosing her words with deliberation. "She is deeply distressed, but I believe this outcome was not entirely unexpected."

An instant crease appeared between his brows. "Outcome? I do not understand you, ma'am."

"Surely you must be aware how troubled she has been? Her brother's absence for too many days? The previous wound he sustained?"

"Ah, indeed, it is true. But that was nothing. Carlton himself dismissed it as of no importance."

"One could scarcely dismiss what looks to be an execution, however."

Bastien had omitted these telling details from his story. The shock was evident in Grégoire's eyes.

"What can you mean? He was shot, yes, but…"

Ottilia kept her eyes on him as Bastien filled in the missing items of the tied hands and blindfold. The Frenchman stared in an uncomprehending way.

"But this must be a fantasy. What, did he face a firing squad? What cause could anyone have to subject him to such a punishment?" Ottilia took due note of the turns of phrase he chose to use. His protest continued. "Carlton, of all people. It does not make sense."

"To you and all of us," said Rampton.

Mundell put his oar in. "Who would suspect the world of fossil hunting to be taken thus seriously? Rivalry, is it?"

Grégoire gave vent to an explosive sound of contempt. "Do not be ridiculous, my friend." He gaze swept back to Ottilia. "How could Cecily expect such a thing? How, moreover, could you speak of it to an innocent girl?"

"Cecily did not strike me as quite so innocent, Monsieur du Guet. I have no doubt she was already suspecting that her brother was involved in some sort of nefarious activity."

"That cannot be right."

"You seem to think little of her intelligence, sir. She did not believe her brother's story of gashing his arm on a rock. Even the doctor thought the wound had been made by a blade of some sort."

Grégoire looked sceptical. "Do you suggest he was injured in a brawl?"

"I have no notion." Ottilia glanced across at the other young gentlemen. "Was Carlton quarrelsome, do you know?"

The answers came without hesitation from all sides.

"Not to my knowledge."

"Quite a mild character, Green."

"A fight, *Tante*, is not at all like the Carlton I knew."

"Enough!" Grégoire, coming in on top of them all. "He did not engage in any fight. This is nonsense. Cecily is mistaken. There could be no reason for anyone to wish to kill Carlton."

"Yet someone did." Ottilia brought her gaze to bear on the Frenchman again. "Someone bore a grudge, or deemed himself to have been betrayed, or perhaps there was some other motive we have not yet fathomed. Whatever it was, it had sufficient force to cause that person to eliminate Mr Green."

Grégoire flinched at the word, and even Mundell looked sick. None spoke and Ottilia felt the point had been sufficiently driven home.

She rose. "I will leave you now, gentlemen. You may be interested to hear that Justice Overy has asked me to find out everything I can. I trust, therefore, that you will all be prepared to hold yourselves in readiness for further questions." She inclined her head and looked to her nephew. "Bastien, will you escort me home, if you please?"

Francis fairly stormed into the parlour. He swept the room for his wife and fixed upon her, ignoring the rest of the party. "I've had enough of this already, Tillie. Not content with dragging me back to that confounded cave, Overy must needs involve me in hunting for a smuggling den."

Ottilia was seated in her preferred position at the end of the sofa nearest to the fire, from where she cast him a sympathetic look. "My poor darling. What smuggling den is this?"

"Lord knows!" He walked across to his favoured spot by the mantel. "To my mind it's nothing more than rumour, but

Overy thinks some farmer fellow has goods stashed in a hidden barn. He's convinced the whole lot of them are in on the trade, burghers and all."

His mother gave out one of her familiar snorts. "I should not be at all surprised. Even Reverend Stewkley confessed to finding a keg in his church porch."

Francis threw his gaze heavenwards. "In that case, ma'am, he likely turns a blind eye to night owl comings and goings in his churchyard. Radway told me the smugglers leave such *douceurs* to those who help them."

"And show no mercy to those who don't," his mother's companion piped up.

"But they do not murder," said Ottilia. "I have it from Mr Overy that he has never had to deal with a killing before."

"Ah, but Mr Yelford — that riding officer, you know — believes otherwise. He was telling me tales to make your hair stand on end."

"Poppycock, Henrietta! He was teasing you. Flirting, I dare say. I've seen the look in his eye when you are present."

"Oh, nonsense, ma'am. He regards me in a friendly light merely."

But the companion's heightened colour did not escape Francis. Not much to his surprise, Ottilia ignored both that and his mother's interpolation. "Does Mr Yelford believe a smuggler would go so far as a killing, Henrietta?"

Francis cocked an ear for the answer. He'd been certain he was wasting his time when Overy had inveigled him into searching Farmer Munderfield's barn. Properly speaking, the task should have fallen to that idiot in the custom house, but Beith could not be persuaded to act without his senior's instruction and Radway had put in no appearance.

The companion, a tall woman with a generous figure, put her head on one side as she thought through her reply. "Well, I can't recall him speaking of any actual murders, but he definitely said there were no lengths to which these smugglers would not go if events went against them. Captain Turves of the militia here has had several of his men set upon and badly mauled."

Francis looked at his wife. "Yes, I know Turves and I've heard that from him too, Tillie. Once, when his men found and secured a landed cargo, the rogues sneaked in at night to where it was under guard and took it all back after putting Turves's fellows out of action."

"Mr Yelford says it is pure thuggery. He has a troublesome time of it in his position."

"I don't doubt it, Henrietta." Ottilia drummed her fingers on the wooden arm of the sofa. "This becomes interesting. I had concentrated my attention on Carlton Green's friends, but it seems we must look further afield."

Francis gave a heartfelt sigh. "Well, don't expect me to go anywhere without some sustenance under my belt. I'm famished."

He was treated to one of his darling wife's twinkling looks. "Have no fear, my dearest. I gave orders for an early dinner to be served. It will be ready in a trice. Hepsie has already fed the children."

His mother cut in again. "Where is my grandson, by the by? You said he escorted you, Ottilia."

"He did, Sybilla, but he went straight back. He is anxious for this Grégoire."

"That French fellow? I wish he would choose his friends more wisely."

Ottilia's smile was wry. "Did you not only this morning champion Bastien's need to keep up his mother tongue?"

"None of your impertinence, my girl."

"I am merely pointing out an inconsistency, ma'am. Besides, there seems little choice for poor Bastien to be exercising wisdom."

His mother sniffed and wafted an impatient hand. "That is beside the point. I don't trust that young man."

"Grégoire? Merely because he is French?"

"Certainly not. Do you think I am so prejudiced, Ottilia? I have watched him closely and he has a shifty eye."

When his mother could have spent any considerable time setting du Guet under scrutiny was a mystery to Francis. But he said nothing, not wishing to draw her fire. Ottilia was not so reticent.

"Sybilla, you are merely trying to be contrary. How can you know anything of this Grégoire? Even I have seen him before today only at a distance. Your eyes are, besides, constantly on your cards."

His mother, in the grandiloquent way she had, chose to ignore this. "Mark my words. He will be found to be quite other than he seems, and then you may thank me."

Francis frowned down his darling wife, who was obviously struggling to contain her laughter. Fortunately, Tyler entered at that moment to rescue the situation.

"Dinner is served, my lady."

Francis had no further interest in the murder while he satisfied his ever-ready stomach. The day had begun to seem interminable, but a good supply of his favourite beef mellowed his mood.

He signed to the footman to remove his plate and took up his glass of wine, looking around the table at the women. "What, did you all content yourself with fish?"

His wife glanced across the table. "We are living by the sea, Fan. It is good when it's fresh."

"Then why have you left quite half on your plate? You eat like a bird, Tillie."

"You always say that. I am perfectly satisfied, I promise you."

His mother had been pecking in a desultory fashion at her portion, but she laid her fork aside. "It was not well cooked. That woman is no hand at fish."

"You should have had the beef, Mama."

"You know I never eat beef."

Francis looked towards the companion. "Ah, at least one good trencherwoman is about this table."

Henrietta glanced up from the concentrated effort with which she was consuming a goodly portion of sliced beef. She laughed. "I have a large frame to keep up, Lord Francis."

"Her appetite is almost as ravenous as yours, my dear boy. She will likely eat me out of house and home before I shake off this mortal coil."

Too used to his mother's acerbic comments, Francis could only suppose the companion had become inured likewise, for she merely smiled and resumed eating. She had been with the dowager for some seven years and seemed to take the brickbats with aplomb. Was there anything serious in a flirtation with the riding officer? Selfish of him to hope not, since it would inevitably exacerbate his mother's uncertain temper.

After dinner, there remained too little of the day to make further enquiries. The children, bored with having been obliged to remain indoors due to the intermittent drizzle, demanded games and stories.

"Pray read to the girls, Papa," said Pretty. "They are driving us demented. Luke and I won't be able to finish battleships before bedtime because Di keeps moving the pieces and Nell won't stop asking why, why, why to everything."

Luke added his mite. "If you please, Papa. Neither of those two listen to Hepsie, but they always quiet down when you're there."

Ottilia hid a smile, for this was true of both Luke and Pretty too. Their papa's strictures and affections were equally acceptable. Unlike her own.

"You're too soft with them, Tillie, that's the trouble."

But Ottilia could not bring herself to scold with any degree of severity. How could she, when both her brother and her own doctor had stated positively that she would conceive no more babies? Francis had tried to comfort her.

"It doesn't matter, my dear one. Four are quite enough."

"But if we lose one, Fan?"

"Don't raise spectres. They are all as healthy as bedamned."

Yet Ottilia could never forget her first disastrous pregnancy and the loss of her firstborn at birth. A corner of her heart ached still, and the fear of some unnamed disaster affecting one of her offspring was never far away.

"You've attended too many murders, my loved one. It's inevitable that you have come to fear unnatural deaths. Only look at them. I defy you to find a livelier set of infants than our brood."

With her returning health, and as she became used to the vagaries of an early onset end to her monthlies, such fears gradually receded. But her tendency to be lenient remained.

With Francis engaged in reading one of Perrault's fairy tales, one twin perched on each knee, Ottilia abandoned all hope of pursuing the hunt. As well since Sybilla, having missed her whist that day, held her daughter-in-law captive with a history of her better games and complaints of the few occasions when she'd held bad cards.

It was therefore upon the following morning that Ottilia was able to look into the individuals as cited to her spouse by Justice Overy. Fortunately, the skies proved clear, enabling the nurses to take the children out to play on the shingle.

"Stay within sight of the house, Hepsie. I don't want them venturing far until the villain is apprehended."

Accompanied by both Henrietta and the dowager, and escorted by Francis, Ottilia strolled along Crag Lane and turned into the lane that crossed Crabbe Street and led on to meet the High Street. The elder lady and her companion were dropped off at The Rooms and Francis gave Ottilia his arm. She was clad today in a fresh muslin gown with a spencer atop and a bonnet over the strands of soft hair, and together they continued along the main thoroughfare to look first into the general goods merchant, Parbold. An easy target, since Ottilia might pretend an interest in making a purchase and tackle the proprietor in the course of doing so.

The bell jangled as Francis opened the door for her and Ottilia entered the large mart where several counters were backed by shelves along the walls, upon which stood all manner of goods, from rows of bottles and jars to bolts of cloth, stacks of tins, tobacco pipes, soap and other accoutrements of everyday living. Barrels containing a variety of dried goods were stacked to one side, and several baskets of odds and ends sat on a couple of the counters.

As it chanced, Ottilia had no need to find an excuse to bring up the murder. News had evidently spread, and no one wanted to talk of anything else. She ran directly into Mrs Peckledon, one of Sybilla's whist cronies, a known gossip. A small, bird-like dame, she pounced the moment she sighted Ottilia.

"Oh, Lady Francis, is it you indeed? Or should I perhaps say *Lady Fan?*" She tittered in a way that never failed to irritate. "That is your sobriquet, is it not?"

Ottilia produced a smile. "It is, ma'am, and you are welcome to make use of it."

Mrs Peckledon tittered again, peeking in an arch fashion from under a straw bonnet decorated with ribbon. "Especially as Mr Overy has requested you to wear it. Or so I understand?"

"How did you come by that, I wonder?"

"Oh, he told me so himself. He said how pleased he was that you happened to be in the town just when this dreadful event occurred." She spared a glance for Francis. "And you, my lord, of course. Mr Overy said he is so grateful for your help. He does not know how he would have managed without the Fanshawes."

Seeing her husband's tightened jawline, Ottilia quickly turned the discussion. "Were you acquainted with the unfortunate young man?"

"Carlton Green? Can you even ask?" The widow looked almost affronted. "When Ivy Ospringe is my close friend? I should say I am well acquainted with the poor boy indeed. A tragic loss to that child. I cannot think how she will fare without her brother."

Ottilia wasted no time. "It seems Cecily has been obliged to manage without him upon several occasions lately. For days at a time."

Mrs Peckledon gave vent to a series of disapproving tuts. "Oh, those wretched fossils! Ivy believes it is but a hobby, but mark my words, I told her, the boy is up to no good."

Even Francis leapt on this. "What makes you think so, ma'am?"

The widow simpered. "Well, you are a man too, Lord Francis. I cannot think you will find it difficult to imagine what a personable young fellow would be up to, absent from his sister."

Ottilia almost laughed, but her spouse looked incredulous. "A dalliance? What, do you suppose a rival for some girl's affections put a bullet through him?"

Too harsh, Fan. For Mrs Peckledon was losing colour from her withered cheeks. Ottilia intervened, speaking with gentleness. "Pray don't be distressed, ma'am. It is true that Mr Green was shot, but your supposition is not as far-fetched as it might seem." She threw an admonitory glance at Francis as she spoke. "There is a factor, however, that you are probably unaware of. This was not a duel. Nor, as it appears, was Mr Green attacked without notice."

Mrs Peckledon was beginning to regain her usual attitude of avid interest. "What can you mean, Lady Francis?"

Not wishing to induce further shock, Ottilia chose her words with care. "It was a deliberate act. We must assume Mr Green knew his killer all too well. The way the murder was conducted makes one think more of punishment than jealousy." If the scenario was to be believed, but this thought she kept to herself.

"Punishment? Goodness gracious, whatever for? I am sure Carlton never did anything to warrant such a terrible retribution. Besides, it is for the authorities to mete out justice, if a need for it exists, which I do not at all believe. Not in Carlton's case. I cannot credit that he has ever in his life committed any act against the law."

Ottilia did not gainsay it, although one might well suppose otherwise, according to the information she had so far gleaned. "I dare say you are right, ma'am. But —□

"Should you not be off to The Rooms, Mrs Peckledon?" said Francis, cutting her off. "We left my mother there on our way."

The effect upon the widow was almost comical. A gloved hand flew to her mouth and her eyes popped. "Lady Polbrook is already there? Goodness, I shall be receiving a scold if I am late!"

Ottilia detained her as she made for the door. "Mrs Peckledon!"

The little woman looked back. "Hm?"

"Have you visited Miss Ospringe? How is Cecily, do you know?"

Mrs Peckledon's features wrinkled in concern. "The poor dear! Yes, I went the moment I heard. I caught them at breakfast, and Cecily could only peck at her food. She looked wan, poor thing."

"Is Miss Ospringe up, then? Is she recovered?"

"You mean from her ailment? Well, she was up and about, but none too good from the looks of her. But who would be, after such tidings?"

"Indeed. If you go again, pray give them both my best wishes and say that I will come again as soon as I may."

The widow looked doubtful. "Yes, but I shan't go until I have given Lady Polbrook a game."

"Can you play without Miss Ospringe?"

"Oh, indeed. Dear Reverend Stewkley has prevailed upon Mr Hargrave to make a fourth. His curate, you must know."

With which, she flitted away, reiterating her desire not to keep Sybilla waiting.

Ottilia watched her leave the shop. "She places great trust in Carlton Green's integrity."

"And you don't?"

Ottilia turned back to her spouse, who was idly flicking through a volume he had picked up from a pile of magazines on one counter. "Those young men made me more suspicious than otherwise. Besides the fact someone clearly thought he deserved his fate."

"We don't know that."

"I am saying the murderer thought so. Yet Carlton must have been involved in some sort of nefarious activity."

"Which is what we are here to investigate," murmured her husband, setting down the volume and jerking his head towards the proprietor, who had not approached them while they were talking with Mrs Peckledon, but who was now heading their way from behind the main counter.

Parbold bowed upon reaching them. "My lady, my lord, how may I serve you?"

Ottilia eyed his round countenance with new interest. She had visited his establishment several times, but in these circumstances she must consider him in the light of a potential suspect. If one judged by appearances, he was the epitome of innocence. Guileless, smiling eyes and plump cheeks under a brown wig, neatly dressed in garments of sober hue, his manner welcoming but not servile. Ottilia remembered he was one of the burghers of the town and thus in some sort represented authority. Not that it precluded his involvement in the smuggling, the area being renowned for the trade. She opted for frankness.

"To tell you the truth, Mr Parbold, I am not here to buy anything."

He did not appear remotely disconcerted. His smile widened. "Indeed, my lady, I must confess to having overheard part of your discussion with Mrs Peckledon. A bad business is this." He schooled his features to sobriety and shook his head sadly. "It is not what we are used to hereabouts."

"Do you say so?" Thus Francis, his tone sceptical. "From what Overy told me, there is a good deal of criminality in these parts."

"Ah, but not murder, my lord. Such doings form no part of our dealings."

Ottilia jumped in fast. "*Our* dealings, sir? What dealings would they be, pray?"

He was not in the least disconcerted. "I meant, I need scarcely say, my lady, the day-to-day dealings of our little community here."

"Ah, did you? Would such dealings involve contraband goods, perhaps? Or should I not ask?"

The smile reappeared. A trifle oily, was it? "It is true there are those who turn a blind eye, my lady, but we burghers take our duties most seriously."

Francis cut in. "Duty is precisely where the problem lies. Or the lack of it, should I say?" He cast a glance about and waved his arm in an arc. "I wonder, for instance, how much duty was paid upon goods you have here for sale?"

The smile remained in place. "We import very little, my lord. I like to think we are supporting local industry."

"You have a local winery, perhaps? You grow tea hereabouts, do you?"

Parbold gave a little laugh and wagged a finger. "Ah, you are attempting to catch me out, my lord. Both tea and wine I leave to my friend Washbrook. We are too small a town to be competing with each other." He pointed to one set of shelves. "Those earthenware jars you see there contain not liquor, but Italian oil."

"I thought you said you imported very little."

"Indeed, indeed. Oil is one of those few items from abroad. Duty as paid, I assure you. Anyone may inspect my books."

His confidence engendered suspicion, but Ottilia hoped her spouse would refrain from pointing out that written records could be fudged. She intervened by way of prevention.

"No one is accusing you, Mr Parbold. As you must know, I am asked by Mr Overy to make enquiries regarding this event."

"Of me, my lady?" Both tone and aspect indicated his incredulity.

"Of everyone."

"But what has it to do with the matter of excise duty?"

Ottilia considered him. Was this genuine, or was he pretending not to know the circumstances? "Did it not come to your ears just how Mr Green met his end?"

Parbold let out a long sigh of realisation. "So that is what you were getting at when you spoke of punishment to Mrs Peckledon."

"Just so. You will allow, I hope, that this gives me a valid reason to be looking into the business of smuggling."

"I see your reasoning indeed, my lady. I should take a similar view in your place. Yet I would question whether Mr Green had any hand in those activities."

"Would you know if he had?"

At last she had taken him aback. He made no answer for a moment or two, looking from her to Francis's now impassive countenance. Silently thanking her spouse for not interrupting at a crucial juncture, Ottilia waited.

At length, the answer came. "All I can say, my lady, is that rumour is apt to reach me. We burghers have a nose to the ground, you must know." He wafted a vague hand. "My establishment too lays me open to hearing things."

Ottilia came directly to the point. "What have you heard, Mr Parbold?"

"Oh, a great deal."

"Anything that may bear upon this matter would be useful."

He considered for a moment, or appeared to do so, fingering his chin in a thoughtful manner while his eyes studied her. Wondering just how much to disclose? Ottilia's suspicions increased.

At length he spoke again. "If Mr Green was involved in the trade —□ He broke off, harrumphed a little and began again. "I say *if* advisedly, for I place no great belief in that option. If he was so involved, you might with profit look to the fishermen."

Ottilia took due note of his use of the term *trade*. A loose translation of smuggling as preferred by the so-called 'free traders', so Francis had learned from Lieutenant Radway. She was pleased he chose to pursue it on her behalf.

"Which fishermen precisely?" Francis asked. "I feel sure you know who they are."

A definite smirk appeared upon Parbold's lips. "It is common knowledge, my lord. You might with profit talk to both Wark and Deanraw. They are usually to be found along the shore, pulling in their boats of a morning."

"They fish at night?"

"Customarily, I believe. You would have to venture out early to catch them."

Catch them, or catch them out? Ottilia caught a flash of warning in her husband's eye and kept silent, waiting upon how he might pursue the matter.

Wearing his enigmatic face, he returned his gaze to the burgher. "Anyone else? Overy has already had me attend a search of Munderfield's barn."

The merchant's brows rose. "Munderfield? Why, he is one of us."

"A burgher. Yes, so I gather."

Parbold pursed his lips. "Our worthy farmer is above reproach, but I have sometimes wondered about one of his hands. Reapham is a surly brute. I would not put it past him to bludgeon a man if he held a grudge."

Ottilia cut in. "Mr Green was not bludgeoned, sir. He was shot in the head."

The burgher pursed his lips. "Indeed. I had forgotten it for the moment."

"That is why we are hunting for a man with a musket."

This elicited an incredulous laugh. "Then you are looking at half the town, my lady. Not to mention Captain Turves's militiamen."

A scoffing sound came from Francis. "Do you tell me it is common to possess a musket? For a farmer, yes, but why in the world would you, or any plain businessman, own such a gun?"

"Do you not own one, my lord?"

"I have my pistol."

"Hunting guns also, perhaps?" He did not wait for a reply. "I don't say every gun owner prefers a musket, but —□

Ottilia cut in before the discussion could become both acrimonious and pointless. "May we leave off guns for a moment, if you please? I accept your assertion, sir. Pray is there any other person who might be involved in smuggling — pardon me, in the trade, as you put it?"

He looked a trifle put out at this pointed remark, but rallied quickly. "Well, there is always Sugnall."

"Who is he?"

"Our blacksmith. I have no real reason to suspect him in that regard, but there is no denying his calling makes him a particularly useful fellow."

"How so?" Thus Francis, frowning now, to Ottilia's dismay.

"He's strong enough to haul and lift for one thing. For another, I'd swear there's a hidden cellar in the smithy. But principally, for your purposes, my lady, he's the nearest thing to a gunsmith in this town. Fixed the sight on my musket and did it well."

Ottilia jumped on this. "So you do own a musket, Mr Parbold."

"I never said I didn't. But I'd no call to use it on young Mr Green, that I'd swear to."

CHAPTER SIX

"What did you make of him?" Francis asked his wife. They were heading for the lane leading to Crabbe Street with the intention of reaching their next port of call, the Cross Keys.

Ottilia glanced up. "Parbold? An expert in obfuscation. I have no doubt he is up to his eyebrows in it."

"The murder or smuggling?"

"Smuggling, to be sure. I cannot be as certain about the murder, but I am inclining towards the negative."

"Why, Tillie? He struck me as a man quite capable of such ruthlessness."

"Granted, but I think the manner of the death was a surprise to him."

Francis made no immediate answer as they walked on. But when they were within sight of the ancient structure which housed the Cross Keys, he checked, bringing Ottilia to a halt beside him.

"Wait a bit, Tillie." He turned to face her, his brows drawn together. "If Parbold is indeed of the smuggling fraternity, he would surely know if young Green had been party to it also."

"A fair inference, Fan. What are you implying?"

"That either he is lying — which is only too likely to my mind — or Green's murder has another cause altogether."

"Very possibly, my dearest, but what that might be has me in a puzzle."

"You gleaned no clue from those friends of his?"

"None whatsoever. Except to make me suspect this fossil business was nothing but a cover."

"Then you really believe he was engaged in some illicit activity?"

"Don't you? Why in the world otherwise was he killed and tied up in such a fashion? In a cave too."

Francis looked dissatisfied. "There is that."

Ottilia tucked her hand back in his elbow. "Let us tackle the innkeeper here and see what we can dig up."

Coxheath, the present landlord of the public house claiming a history dating back to the early sixteen hundreds, was of rougher origin than Parbold. So Francis had warned, he having taken the odd pint of ale here in company with Lieutenant Radway. Ottilia had not previously met him, and at first sight he looked the epitome of a man likely to be involved in an illicit trade.

Thickset and stocky, he had a trick of looking at one from under a pair of heavy eyebrows, head lowered like a bull deciding whether to charge. Scorning a wig, he wore his own rusty hair cut close to his head in unruly curls.

"If only it were better arranged," Francis murmured into her ear, "it might pass for this Brutus cut the young fashionables favour."

Ottilia glanced at her spouse's lush hair, well suited now to the shorter style he affected, its waves under far better control than Coxheath's. Francis had learned the trick of keeping back the lock that swept his forehead and gave him a rakish air Ottilia found curiously attractive.

Suppressing the rise of warmth in her bosom, she returned her attention to the landlord and his establishment. There were few customers as yet, those present seated at one or other of the dark wooden tables under a low ceiling, smoke-stained between aged wooden beams. The walls and windows were likewise yellowed, the whole interior giving off a musty feel relieved only by a couple of lanterns hanging from beams at the sides. The place felt stuffy and could well have done with an airing. Coxheath was dressed for his working day, matching the dowdiness of his surroundings, in shirtsleeves with an open waistcoat atop, dun-coloured thickset cotton breeches and a serviceable apron tied around the waist.

Francis thankfully chose to open negotiations. "You will have heard of the unfortunate death of young Green?"

The lowering look persisted. "Aye. What of it?"

Ottilia was not surprised to see her spouse stiffen at the challenging tone, his gaze growing grim. Nor had the man added a courtesy address. Francis was not high in the instep, but he was apt to become haughty if his rank was not acknowledged. He made nothing of it, however.

"My wife here, Lady Francis Fanshawe —□ said with emphasis — "is desirous of asking you a few questions."

Coxheath spared Ottilia a glance but immediately returned his glare to Francis. "Said all I got to say to Justice Overy already."

"My wife is assisting Overy, so you may say it all over again to her." Her spouse's tone indicated that there would be trouble if he did not.

Ottilia felt it politic to intervene. "I dare say it is tedious to be obliged to repeat yourself, Mr Coxheath, but it would help me a great deal if you would."

This was said with the smile that served, in most instances, to gain a positive response. It failed today.

"That may be, ma'am. Said all I'm going to say."

To Ottilia's consternation, Francis lunged forward, seizing fistfuls of the man's shirt and pulling him in so that they were almost nose to nose.

"You will answer anything she asks you, and with courtesy. Unless you want your teeth knocked down your throat."

Ottilia held her breath, her gaze on the landlord's hands, clenching and unclenching by his sides. His face had grown ruddy and a sudden hush among the few clients rendered the atmosphere chilly and tense.

The pose held for what seemed to Ottilia an age. Then Coxheath took hold of Francis's wrists and wrenched them off, stepping back as he did so. He threw up both hands.

"I'll not brawl with you, m'lord. Not in my own house." He cast a glance of dislike at Ottilia. "Let her ask if she must."

Francis, clearly too irate to speak, gestured to Ottilia to begin, but kept his dark gaze on the landlord.

"Thank you, Fan," she murmured, moving a little closer. It was an ill beginning and she was a trifle uncertain how to open in a way that might elicit a worthwhile response. She opted for a light approach. "It is nothing arduous, I assure you. I am merely seeking information."

"Aye? About what?" The tone was scarcely polite, but the belligerence was absent, Coxheath keeping one eye upon Francis.

Ottilia maintained a neutral stance. "I am trying to find out if anyone had heard of Mr Green being in any way involved in illegal activity."

"How'd I know such?"

"You might not. But you must meet many people in your line of business. It is possible you might have heard something."

He sniffed and pursed his lips. "Not as I remember."

Ottilia sharpened her voice. "You might, if you chose to think about it."

"Folks talk. I don't listen."

She ignored this. "Smuggling, perhaps?"

That made him blink. He tilted his chin. "Folks hereabouts don't pay mind to the trade."

Trade again? Was the expression common to the area, or might she take significance from his use of it?

"They ignore it, do they? Unless they are involved in it, perhaps?"

The brows lowered again. "Because a keg or two is found by the back door don't mean them living there has to do with the trade."

"But they might facilitate it, or turn a blind eye?" She made it a question, but an odd flash in the landlord's eye was promising. "Have I hit it, Mr Coxheath?"

He took a shuffling step back, checking on Francis briefly before giving answer. "Look here, missus —□

"I think you mean *my lady*." Thus Francis, on a decidedly dangerous note.

The landlord pressed his lips together. Suppressing a retort? The smoulder at his eyes dissipated after a moment. "What I'm saying, my lady, is no one don't pay no mind, see. No talk, no consequence is how it goes hereabout. If that Green had to do with free trading, them in the custom house will know it better than me or anyone."

Ottilia was almost ready to abandon this line of enquiry. It appeared well-nigh impossible to get anything out of the man. Reluctant to admit defeat, she tried another tack.

"Was Mr Green a regular here?"

"Who ain't? Only one other public house in the town and the quality wouldn't go there. Nor would they be welcome."

Ottilia looked to Francis in question.

"He means the Mill Inn. It's behind the old town hall." The latter was still in use by the burghers and for town meetings, including in its facilities a makeshift prison. The Tudor building was visible from some of the windows in their lodging in Crag Lane. Francis leaned in, dropping his voice. "The inn is a haunt of labouring men and fisherfolk, but not, as far as Radway knows, in use by thieves and vagabonds."

Ottilia's burgeoning hope died again. There was no future in combing the Mill for smugglers, then. She tried again. "Well, did Mr Green come often?"

"Most evenings. Ain't seen him regular for a bit, though."

"A few days?"

"Aye."

A pity the wretched man was not given to gossip. She could not be said to have profited from this interview, except to feel the more suspicious. What was Coxheath withholding? If he had nothing to hide, why not respond without all this recalcitrance?

She changed course again. "What can you tell me about the fishermen? Wark and Deanraw, if I recall correctly."

The russet brows lifted a fraction. "They fish. What of it?"

Ottilia pressed on. "Perhaps they bring in other items than fish on occasion?"

"Crabbing? Lobster pots? How'd I know?"

Her spouse lost patience. "Don't be a fool, man! She's talking of smuggled goods. Are they in the trade or aren't they?"

"Mebbe you'd best ask Green." A low chuckle accompanied this quip and Coxheath showed his teeth in a travesty of a grin.

Ottilia felt her husband's rising wrath and quickly intervened, ignoring the facetious comment. "What about Sugnall?"

"He's well enough if your horse needs shoeing."

"Is he well enough if you need a musket mending?"

That hit home at last. The landlord's chin came up and his eyelids fluttered. He gave no immediate answer and Ottilia waited, praying Francis would not allow his ire to overspill. Thankfully he remained silent, his inimical gaze fixed upon Coxheath.

At length the latter spoke. "How'd you know I keep one?"

"According to another informant, most inhabitants of this town keep a musket. Or some other weapon."

"Well, and if we do?"

Ottilia brought it out flat. "Carlton Green was shot with a musket."

Silence. Coxheath's lips tightened. Preventing the wrong words from escaping? Did he know already? Word of the type of weapon used had not been released — or had it? She could not ask Francis at this juncture. He was eyeing the landlord with deep suspicion. His patience had evidently run out.

"Well? What have you to say to that?"

Coxheath shrugged. "Naught. Unless her ladyship thinks to imply I did for Green. Then I'd have a deal to say."

Ottilia seized on this. "Well, let us suppose I did imply it. Say on."

A crack of laughter gave notice of his surprise at this tactic. "Accusing me, are you?"

Ottilia did not back down. "If I am, then what?"

"I'd say as be damned to you, my lady. Prove it."

With which, paying not the slightest heed to the growl of rage that emanated from Francis, the landlord turned short about and marched away, disappearing through a door behind the counter.

Ottilia seized her husband's arm as he made to follow. "Wait, Fan! Pray don't. What is the use of getting into a scuffle with him?"

He paused, but the burning in his eyes gave notice of his continuing fury. "I'll not permit any man to address you in such a fashion. He needs a sharp lesson."

She detained him as he again made to move off, speaking rapidly. "Granted, my dearest, but what purpose will it serve otherwise? We are already failing with the man. If you assault him, it will make things worse. Besides possibly turning his associates against us. We will get nowhere if we cannot question people. If you please, Fan, let it be this once."

His breath was coming short, but the fury began to die out of his gaze. "The brute insulted you, Tillie."

"Yes, but let it pass, I beg of you."

The matter remained in the balance for a moment or two and Ottilia found she was holding her breath. At last he gave a curt nod, lips compressed.

"Thank you, Fan. Let us leave this place."

He consented to accompany her out of the Cross Keys. He did not speak again until they were at the entrance to the lane leading back to the High Street, where he halted, bringing Ottilia to a stop alongside.

"We'd best leave off questioning anyone else for now. If I have to endure any more insolence, I won't be answerable for the consequences."

Ottilia sighed with relief. "I was going to suggest as much. I would like to visit Cecily Green again. The house is in that little lane just off the end of the street. You might leave me there, Fan, and enjoy a soothing coffee at Woulmer's, which is conveniently close. I will be glad of your escort home, however."

He snorted. "Fear not. I'm not leaving you alone to be subject to that sort of treatment. There's no saying what anyone in this benighted smuggling haunt won't dare."

Cecily Green was a trifle wan in the face, her pallor accentuated by the sober gown she had donned, not black as yet but of a dark blue poplin, with long sleeves and the neck cut high to the throat. She was, however, surprisingly composed. Along with Ivy Ospringe she received Ottilia in the same small parlour, bidding her welcome and ushering her into the chair by the fire.

"It is not as cold today, but if you have been out, ma'am, you must be in need of warming."

Ottilia consented to take the chair but waved her hostess to the little sofa where her chaperon was already ensconced.

"Pray do not stand about, my child. You look peaky."

Miss Ospringe jumped in at that, taking the girl's hand and chafing it gently. "She is bravely coping, are you not, dearest? I have not managed to get enough food down her, which is why you see her looking so pale."

Ottilia waved this away. "It is understandable that Cecily's appetite is affected." She smiled at the young woman. "But I hope you will make the effort, my dear. You need to keep up your strength."

"Exactly what I told her. Not that I found it easy to swallow my portion either."

Cecily withdrew her hand and cast a frowning glance upon her companion, her soft voice sounding a little sharp. "Pray don't dwell on it, Ivy. I cannot think Lady Fan — as I understand you are known, ma'am — has come to listen to commonplaces."

Miss Ospringe did not seem to be abashed. "It is not a commonplace, dearest, to be talking of your bereaved state."

She was ignored, Cecily fixing her attention upon Ottilia. "Have you discovered anything of use? Do you have more questions for me?"

Detecting an undercurrent of anxiety, Ottilia opted for frankness. "All I can say as yet is that there are grounds to suppose your brother was engaged in an activity other than fossil hunting. But I think you knew that?"

Cecily took in a snatch of breath. "I feared so. Is it smuggling?"

"Oh, surely not." Thus Miss Ospringe. "If I have heard Carlton decry the practice once, I have heard him do so a dozen times."

Cecily spared her a glance. "True, ma'am, but he might speak in that way to throw dust in our eyes."

"How can you talk so of your brother?"

"How can I not when I know how he was killed?"

Ottilia intervened. "She is being admirably honest. Come, ma'am. Of what use to pretend? It is clear Carlton was involved in illicit dealings. As yet, however, I cannot positively state that he had anything to do with the free traders."

"But you suspect he did?"

"It is possible, Cecily." She eyed the girl. "Do you have something more to tell me?"

A sigh escaped Cecily and she put a hand up to shade her eyes. Ottilia glanced towards Miss Ospringe and gave a quick shake of the head. The dame's brows pulled together, but she took the hint and remained silent.

After a moment or two, Cecily's hand dropped and she straightened her spine, her gaze returning to Ottilia's face. "I was looking for something in his desk once — a letter from a friend who planned to visit and I could not recall the dates." The hand came up again and her fingers played against her upper chest. Acute discomfort? Another sigh. "I saw a document. It was in French. At the time I made nothing of it. I thought it might belong to Grégoire, or at least relate to him.

My French is not good, but Carlton speaks it well. I think that is why he and Grégoire became friends. He cannot converse as fluently as your nephew Bastien, but they were apt to go off into French together. Laughing, for the most part. I thought they merely enjoyed a private joke."

She paused, trouble visible in her countenance. Ottilia applied a prompt.

"But now you think otherwise?"

Anguish in her eyes. "I don't know. When it came to me in the night, I went to his bureau, but I had only my candle and I could not find it."

"Have you tried again this morning?"

Miss Ospringe jumped in. "So that is what all the banging was about?"

"I woke you, Ivy. I'm sorry for that."

Ottilia pulled her back to the point. "You hunted through the drawers in some haste, I take it?"

A mirthless laugh escaped the girl. "I became frantic."

"Then perhaps a systematic search might be in order?" Not that Ottilia supposed this document would come to light. If it was in any way compromising, Carlton must have disposed of it. "When you are calmer, Cecily."

She waved agitated hands. "I don't feel as though I will ever be calm again."

Then her initial composure had been a front. At this juncture, it was evident Cecily's distress sprang from the thought of the devilry in which her brother might have been engaged. The loss had not yet fully hit her. Ottilia went for the pertinent point.

"What was it about the document that caused you concern, Cecily?"

Miss Ospringe piped up. "Yes, I should like to know that too. It cannot be merely the fact it was written in French."

A grimace passed over Cecily's face. "No, not only that. It was quite old, I think, for the ink was faded, although I did not note the date. It had the traces of a seal under the signature, with a crest, I think. Of the words, I managed to make out *peur* and *salut public*."

Ottilia's mind was working. "Might it have to do with the Revolution? Does it mean a fear of the then French authorities?"

"Well, there was also mention of a château, so perhaps you are right."

"Was it those words you understood that troubled you — 'fear' and 'public safety'?"

"Yes, for what had they to do with Carlton?"

"Could you read the signature?"

Cecily shook her head. "It was not Grégoire's hand. I should have recognised that. It was written in a flowing script, but there were scratchings out and blotches, although what that may indicate I cannot imagine."

"That it was set down in haste, perhaps?"

Miss Ospringe was staring at her charge. "Why did you not mention this to me before, Cecily?"

"What was there to tell? I was surprised, but…"

"But it did not trouble you until your brother came home from one of these forays with an injury," Ottilia guessed.

"I did not remember it quite immediately. I was too taken up with ensuring Carlton was properly recovered. But later, I did begin to wonder."

Her companion took hold of her hand again. "You could have spoken to me. I would have taxed Carlton with it upon the instant."

Cecily gripped the other woman's fingers. "That is why I said nothing, Ivy. If there was anything … if he had been involved in something bad, he would have lied. I could not bear that."

Nor would it have stopped him. But Ottilia did not speak her thought aloud. "I dare say you were right not to interfere, my dear. You might have run into danger yourself."

A startled look leapt in the girl's eyes. "Carlton would never have hurt me."

"I don't mean Carlton."

A gasp emanated from Miss Ospringe. "You are saying the person who killed him might have harmed Cecily?"

"Just so. We are dealing with a ruthless mind." Could it be one which Bastien might better probe? It behoved Ottilia to find out more about Grégoire du Guet. In the meantime, in her current state of mind Cecily was ripe for further questioning. "Is there anything else you remember? Any little thing might be of use, however trivial."

Cecily's brow furrowed in thought and she was silent for a space. Miss Ospringe merely looked worried, but she had sense enough not to interrupt the girl's ruminations.

At length, Cecily looked up. "Nothing springs to mind. Except…" She hesitated.

"Except?"

It came out in a rush. "Carlton had been edgy lately, a trifle out of temper. Oh, not unduly, but he was apt to snap at me. I think he did not like it that Grégoire paid court to me."

"Well, one can hardly blame him there, dearest." Her duenna seemed ruffled. "I did not like it myself. A penniless émigré can hardly be regarded as a suitable parti."

"It was not that, Ivy."

"Oh, my dear child, I know you cherish a *tendre* for the man, but you are a sensible girl and you must feel yourself he is ineligible."

Cecily's pale cheeks warmed, a spark in her eye. "As if I should care for that if I loved a man! But you are wrong, Ivy. Carlton was less concerned for my future than for Grégoire's own."

Ottilia had let the brief argument run, but she could not let this pass. "In what respect, Cecily? What could be in Grégoire's future to give concern to your brother?"

"He did not say. To be precise, he did not specifically state as much. I gathered it from things he let fall in these last weeks."

"Can you remember an example?"

She set her fingers together, pulling one against another in a way that seemed unconscious. "Once he spoke of Grégoire *sailing close to the wind*. Upon another occasion he was muttering about boats."

Ottilia's senses prickled. "In what connection?"

"I have no notion. But he said — or I think I heard him say — that Grégoire ought to give over something and attend to the boats. I asked him if he was thinking of going further afield for fossils. He all but glared at me. 'What nonsense are you talking?' he said. I replied that he had mentioned boats, but he dismissed it. He left abruptly. When he came back later that day, I would have spoken of it, only his mood was amiable and I did not wish to make him angry again."

Miss Ospringe had uttered distressful sounds through this recital and now broke out in lamentation. "Oh, dear me, I wish you had spoken of all this. I had no notion Carlton behaved ill towards you, Cecily. I should have given him a piece of my mind had I heard of it."

"Do you suppose he was particularly careful in your presence, Miss Ospringe?" Ottilia probed.

The matron tutted. "Well, he was ever courteous with me, even as a youngster. Brothers and sisters will quarrel, that is natural, so I paid it no particular mind if the two of them exchanged words now and then." She laid a hand on Cecily's unquiet fingers. "You should have spoken, my child. I might have prevented…" She faded out, her free hand scrabbling in a pocket. A handkerchief made its appearance and the dame dabbed at her eyes.

"I doubt anything you could have done or said would have made a difference," Ottilia soothed. "Pray do not fall into the way of blaming yourself. Carlton's actions were his own choice, whatever they may prove to have been."

"He did not choose to be slain!" Thus Cecily, her voice turning husky.

"Of course he did not. That act we must attribute solely to his murderer." She regretted using the word as Cecily shuddered and Miss Ospringe gave a little cry of distress. "Forgive me, that was maladroit. Rest assured, I will make it my mission to find out the culprit."

Cecily recovered first. "I hope you may. I fear I have been of little use."

"On the contrary, you have confirmed what we all suspected. All that remains is to uncover just what activity had engaged your brother to put him in such fateful danger."

She did not add that Cecily had also inadvertently prompted a strong suspicion of Grégoire du Guet's involvement.

CHAPTER SEVEN

The first person Francis spied upon entering Woulmer's coffee house was his nephew. Bastien was seated alone at one of the tables and looked to be in a brown study as he nursed a cup between his hands.

Francis made for the spot and took a seat opposite, hailing Bastien as he did so. "Well met, my young friend."

The other looked up, his frown clearing as he saw Francis. "*Mon oncle*! What brings you here?"

Francis signalled to a hovering waiter. "The desire to mend my temper." He addressed himself to the man as he hurried to the table. "Coffee, if you would. Strong and black."

Bastien was eyeing him. "Who has made you out of temper, sir?"

"That cursed fellow in the Cross Keys. If ever I met such an ill-natured brute! He had the impertinence to insult Tillie, which is a thing I won't endure."

"Ah, he is indeed a brutish fellow, that one. It is said he aids in the smuggling."

Francis seized on this. "Exactly what we were trying to find out. Who says so?"

"Woulmer. Also the friends of Grégoire, Mundell and Rampton."

"Yes, you said they were not to your taste, if I recall."

Bastien made a face. "Very much not, but I must tolerate them for the sake of Grégoire. Indeed, it is this temporary time I needs must know them."

The waiter bearing Francis's coffee interrupted them. He set down a pewter pot and a cup and saucer, together with a bowl containing sugar lumps and a pair of tongs. Francis poured himself a cup and took a couple of sips, studying Bastien as he did so. Just how close had he become with his fellow Frenchman? Or was he also a convenient companion for the duration of this visit?

Before he could probe, Bastien spoke again. "Where is Lady Fan? Did she not go with you?"

"She's dropped in to see how Green's sister does." He noted the change that came over his nephew's face. "What's to do?"

A hint of colour stained Bastien's cheek. "It is nothing."

"I doubt that. You need not tell me if you don't wish to. Have you an interest there?"

The colour deepened and Bastien looked away. "It is of no use if I have. She is smitten with Grégoire."

Did Ottilia know of this? Little doubt she would have fathomed it out when Bastien escorted her to break the news. As well the other Frenchman had the girl's preference. Neither Violette nor Randal was likely to welcome the connection. Francis let the matter lie, sipping at his coffee as he reverted to the business of the day.

"Have you heard anything else likely to be of use? We have learned of a couple of fishermen possibly involved in the trade, as they speak of it around these parts. Also the blacksmith. Have you had dealings with that fellow? Didn't you have to get your stallion reshod after we arrived?"

Bastien appeared relieved at the change of subject, his colour receding. "Sugnall is the man. He is good at his work. Also a judge of horseflesh."

Francis cracked a smile, amusement at last chasing away his ruffled temper. "He had a word of praise for Tonnerre, did he?"

That drew a laugh from Bastien. "Several words, all to my taste. He spoke knowledgeably of Tonnerre's points, admiring in particular the beauty of his long mane."

Francis grinned. "A pleasing encomium. Sugnall must see many horses in his line of work."

"That is so, but now you say…" Bastien trailed off, his brows drawing together.

"What are you thinking?"

He gave a shrug. "I am not certain, but it seems to me Sugnall knows much more than one may expect in a blacksmith of this out-of-the-way place."

Interest sparked in Francis. "How so? What did he say to give you that impression?"

"He spoke of breeding and studs, of racing and the hunt. One would suppose he had experience in that field, but how could that be? Also, I remember that when I happened to speak of my first pony, he said men underestimated the value of ponies in favour of the blood horse."

"Well, is that significant?"

"Perhaps. I have heard it said that these smugglers use strings of ponies to transport the goods."

Struck, Francis stared at him. "Aha! I've heard that too."

Bastien grinned. "There is one smuggler at least, *mon oncle*."

Inclined to agree, Francis remembered his wife's dictum. "We cannot jump to that conclusion, but Sugnall will certainly bear investigation."

Before he could pursue any further enquiries, a voice hailed him.

"Aha, there you are, Lord Francis! The very man I seek."

Francis rose to greet the newcomer who had called out as he entered the coffee house. "Radway, well met."

He had become reasonably well acquainted with the lieutenant in these few weeks. Radway and he were much of an age and shared a common background in soldiering. Francis was thus able to enjoy discussions over coffee and the morning papers related to the progress or otherwise of the war, in which Radway also took an interest, learning in the process a little of the vicissitudes attendant upon the lieutenant's duties as chief of the custom house. He liked the man, a bonhomous type with an appealing ease of manner.

Radway held out a hand as he came up, a lurking twinkle in his open gaze. "I'm surprised to hear you say so, since I understand you've been obliged to deputise in my absence. I hardly dare approach you, sir."

Francis laughed as he shook hands. "Count yourself lucky I am already soothed with a good strong dose of coffee. Else I might have been tempted to engage in fisticuffs with you."

"By way of revenge? I am entirely at your service if you feel it to be needed."

Francis glanced down the lieutenant's hefty and well-muscled figure. "I thank you, but I must decline, since I should certainly get the worst of it." He grinned across at Bastien. "Unless I make my nephew my deputy. He might match up to your weight."

"This I doubt, *mon oncle*. Lieutenant Radway is, I think, much stronger than I."

Bastien had the advantage in height if not in muscle, although he far outshone Radway in looks. The lieutenant's face was weathered from a life spent largely out of doors and his nose was a trifle off-kilter — from a break during a scuffle, so he'd said. His bright eyes were smiling, however. "In that case, my luck serves me double."

Francis granted this sally a smile and pursued a thought in his mind. "Where were you, by the by? Beith said you and Yelford had a suspect barn to inspect."

Radway snorted. "A barn? If we combed through one, we combed through fifty. The place is a rabbit warren of barns. Not that I believe for one moment they are as innocent as their owner would have us believe."

Letting the obvious exaggeration pass, Francis probed for more. "What place is this? Far enough, I presume, to warrant staying over?"

"Yes, and in a demmed uncomfortable inn, so-called, with the wind whistling through the rafters and so many damp spots I'm astonished I came away with dry boots."

"Coastal, then?"

"No, inland. Yelford is set on finding the holding stations, but his luck was out."

"Unlike yours, sir."

"Ha! It didn't rub off on Yelford."

His nephew's quip proved unfortunately timed, taking Radway's attention before Francis could establish the location of these barns supposed to be the repositories of smuggled goods, for the lieutenant turned the subject.

"What's to do with this abysmally distressing shooting, Lord Francis? I was hoping to run into you, for I've had Justice Overy bending my ear for an hour or more, all to little purpose. I'd be glad of a round tale."

Abandoning his hope, unlikely as it was, of finding a possible lead via Radway's excursion, Francis once again relayed his doings over the last couple of days, together with what had been discovered, ending with the potential smugglers so far named. "My nephew here was just telling me what he knows of Sugnall."

Radway's brows flew up. "The blacksmith? Deeply involved in the trade, I'll stake my oath. I've never been able to catch him out, but he's too fly to be anything but a free trader."

At the back of his mind, Francis noted the lieutenant's use of the expression. He had heard Radway say it before, but Ottilia had taken it up as of interest. Was it merely common to the area?

"You believe Sugnall is involved then?"

"If I don't miss my bet. Mind you, that could be said of half the town, as I'm sure I've told you before. Experts at covering their tracks, these people."

Francis was about to steer the conversation back to the murder itself when Bastien did it for him.

"Does it seem to you that Carlton Green was perhaps also involved, sir?"

Radway pursed his lips. "Not that I knew."

Francis pushed for more. "Did you suspect him?"

The lieutenant blew out a scoffing breath. "I suspect everyone. So would you, in my position. You can't move in this town without bumping into a fellow involved in the trade." Radway picked up the coffee pot a waiter had produced for him and poured. "Does your lady wife have any theory as to the perpetrator?"

"Not as yet. It's too early to say beyond how the deed was carried out." He watched Radway add several lumps of sugar to his coffee and stir with vigour. "At present, she is simply gathering information. She will sift and shift a good deal before coming to any conclusion."

Radway swallowed a gulp of liquid and set down his cup with a bit of a bang. "Extraordinary ability. Overy was telling me Lady Francis has solved several puzzles of the kind."

Francis said nothing, too used to the scepticism, or even outright disbelief, that often greeted his wife's peculiar talent. Bastien was not so reticent.

"Lady Fan is a natural, sir. She began with an affair in the family and went from there. Is it not so, *mon oncle?*"

Francis could have cursed. The affair in question had caused him endless trouble, including his brother's absence from the scene. No doubt Bastien had been told that history, since it had culminated in his introduction to the family.

"We need not go into all that. Suffice it that my wife is willing to put her skills at Overy's disposal."

"At mine too," said Radway, "since it falls into my jurisdiction."

"Assuming it involves smuggling, of which there is as yet no actual evidence."

"True, true. Overy seems to think I ought to thrust my nose in regardless. Therefore, you behold me ready and waiting to add my mite, whatso'er it may be."

Francis took immediate advantage. "Then can you say if you know of anyone who might be skilled with a musket?"

"Ah, you're thinking of the weapon? Are you certain it was a musket ball you found lodged in the head?"

"I'm relying on you to check that once the doctor conducting the autopsy has removed it." Even as he spoke, it occurred to Francis that he ought to see it for himself. Ottilia would certainly prefer him to stand witness than any other. "Or no, perhaps you and I may go there together? Two pairs of eyes are better than one."

Radway made an odd sniffing sound. "Neither of us will be able to say whence the ball came, you do realise that?"

"I merely wish to establish that it definitely was a musket that was used."

"We'll have a devil of a job on our hands if so, since the town abounds with the demmed things."

Francis curbed a touch of impatience. "So I understand."

"You can count me among those who own one, not to mention Turves's men. What, will you inspect the lot individually?"

Bastien saved Francis from having to respond. "Such a search must be futile, no? The culprit will certainly conceal his weapon."

"There you are, then. Can't go hunting every dwelling in the place. It would take forever. Believe me, after barns galore, I know."

With difficulty Francis suppressed a pithy retort. "All we need is to know, first, was it a musket? And second, who of those possibly suspect might own one or have access to one? My wife will do the rest."

Radway's eye gleamed with a trace of what Francis read as contempt. "How? Can she read minds?"

"In a way, yes." He was conscious of satisfaction as Radway's expression changed. "You need not look incredulous. She is no witch, though I have been moved to call her so. She has an uncanny knack of understanding how others think and thus she sees beyond mere words. Ottilia will never take a witness statement at face value."

He watched the changing expressions on Radway's face and was pleased by his own ability to read them. Disbelief, then confusion. Was it also apprehension? Or merely dismay? His familiarity with Ottilia's skills was working in his favour. Doubtful the custom house chief had any notion how his face spoke for him.

Bastien filled the little silence. "I am very glad to hear this, *mon oncle*. It is most interesting how she does this, Lady Fan."

That brought Radway's head round. "Lady Fan?"

"It is the name my aunt goes by when she is solving such a death as this one."

Of a sudden, Radway grinned, turning back to Francis. "I confess myself intrigued. I look forward to furthering my acquaintance with your lady wife, sir."

Francis rose. "Speaking of whom, it is time I returned to her escort. Where do you go, Bastien?"

"I am awaiting Grégoire."

"Are you indeed? Then I suggest you bring him to the house. Your aunt wants to see him." He dipped his head to the other man. "Your servant, Radway. If it suits, I will call at the custom house later in the day."

Radway had also risen. "I shall be there."

"I hope you may by then have found out when the post-mortem results are likely to be available."

Bastien's French acquaintance surprised Ottilia. At that first meeting, she had barely had time to take in more than his general appearance. Now, as he rose from a bow and smiled, she noted tell-tale tiny lines running from the corners of his eyes and about his mouth. Nor had his skin the youthful freshness that characterised Bastien. She placed him at a few years her junior. Around thirty, perhaps?

"I am very glad to meet you again, Monsieur du Guet. Thank you for coming to see me."

He wafted a hand. "The pleasure is mine, ma'am. Bastien explained that you are looking to find out who killed our friend and for this I am truly grateful."

Would he continue to be once he took in that he was as much under suspicion as anyone else? Ottilia waved him to a chair. "I hope you may be able to help me, sir."

He took the indicated seat across from the sofa, where she resumed her own place. Francis was as usual occupying his favoured spot at the mantel while Bastien hovered. Ottilia eyed him.

"You had best sit down too, my dear boy. Unless you prefer to leave us?"

To her amusement, he sat in haste, choosing a chair conveniently situated at a slight angle from where he might readily observe both his friend and Ottilia. On guard then? Would he be dismayed if Grégoire du Guet proved to be other than he seemed?

"How may I assist, ma'am?"

Ottilia returned her attention to the Frenchman. "You accompanied Carlton Green upon his expeditions to find fossils, did you not?"

He shifted his shoulders. "Upon occasion. Not regularly. Carlton's interest was intense, mine less so." A faint look of distress came into his face. "If I had gone this time, perhaps I might have…"

"Unlikely, sir, since it appears Carlton's final journey had naught to do with fossils."

She had spoken in a neutral tone, but Grégoire took it hard. "Ah, that is the cruelty of it! Who could guess he might meet with such a fate? Who bore him such malice?"

Ottilia did not let up, notwithstanding this apparent distress. "It was more deliberate than malice, do you not think?"

Grégoire frowned. "I do not understand you. Was it not malicious to slay my poor friend in such a way?"

"Or at all, if it was merely an act of revenge or evil intent, but this was more than that."

Bastien broke in. "My aunt speaks of the possibility that Carlton was executed, do you not remember?"

"I remember, but I refuse to believe it. For what crime? What had he done to merit such a death?"

"This is what Lady Fan wishes to find out."

Grégoire's gaze turned on Ottilia. "But I do not know. How should I?"

A little irritated by the intervention, Ottilia opted to take the bull by the horns. "You may know more than you think."

"How so?"

"Well, let us essay. When you accompanied Carlton, did he perhaps meet anyone?"

"Naturally. There are always walkers on the beaches."

"Specifically, anyone he knew? Think back, if you please."

Grégoire was silent, frowning. Ruminating? Or looking for a way to deflect? Ottilia glanced at Bastien and gave a little shake of the head as he opened his mouth to speak. He closed his lips again and trained his gaze upon his friend as Francis was doing. Her spouse knew to observe the effect of her questions.

At length, Grégoire looked across. "I have no recollection of the kind."

Ottilia gave an inward sigh. This one was not going to be an easy target. She tried again. "Let us leave that, then. Can you tell me some of the places where Carlton went to find these fossils?"

"Everywhere. He travelled up and down the coast. It is rocky in these parts."

A scoffing sound came from her husband, who had not before added his mite. "You may say so with confidence. A more inhospitable spot I defy you to name."

"But it is therefore a good hunting ground if you have an interest in these ancient imprints in the rock. All kinds of old marine life abound. Carlton must have combed every beach from Orford to Dunwich."

Ottilia cut in. "Only beaches? Not caves?"

"Caves?"

"Such as the one in which his body was found."

The blunt remark clearly jolted Grégoire. His face changed and his gaze grew bitter. "You do not mince your words, Lady Francis."

"Not when I am trying to extract information from a recalcitrant source."

She ignored Bastien's gasp. Likewise the flash in Grégoire's eyes. She caught a puzzled glance from Francis and met it fleetingly. He must surely realise she needed to ruffle the Frenchman. That she had succeeded became evident as he rose to his feet.

"I came here with a good intention, ma'am."

"Which I fully appreciate. Pray sit down again, sir." She gave a spurious smile as he hesitated. "I do not bite, Monsieur du Guet."

"That is debatable." But he settled back into his seat. "Why did you speak to me so?"

"I will be frank." Which was a quality lacking in his responses. "Correct me if I am wrong, but you seem evasive. You don't recall Carlton meeting anyone he knew, nor will you name any locations where he went. Forgive me if I seem too harsh, but such vagueness leads to suspicion."

He reared a little. "You dare to say I had a hand in this terrible crime?"

Ottilia did not back down. "It is not impossible."

He appeared nonplussed for a moment. "But … he was my friend. One does not eliminate one's friends."

Ottilia pounced. "A good word to describe just what happened to Carlton Green. Why did you choose it?"

"I am only following your strange notion of an execution. I never dreamed of such a thing."

"Even though you were told Carlton's hands were tied and he was blindfolded before he was shot?"

Grégoire's voice shot into a higher register. "I did not know that. I was not told these facts."

"You were, Grégoire. I told you." Thus Bastien, on a note almost frantic.

"If you did, I did not take it in. The shock of seeing Carlton dead — the suddenness of it — the worry for Cecily ... is it any surprise I did not understand you? That implication escaped me utterly." He turned on Ottilia. "You want me to answer with detail, but to say truth, I cannot think beyond the fact my friend is gone forever."

Was this near-hysteria real or an act? Ottilia infused sympathy into her tone, changing tack. "I do understand, Grégoire. You do not mind the informality, I trust?" She pressed on without waiting for permission. "You have been friends for some time, I take it?"

"Ever since he and his sister came to these parts." His tone had returned to a more normal range. "Carlton spoke my language, which was a joy to me."

"Ah, no doubt. Have you been obliged to converse mainly in English? Is that how you have acquired your fluency?"

Grégoire made a deprecating face. "I took pains to learn after my departure from France. I had a rigorous tutor in a friend who picked at my every mistake. He took me under his wing, so to speak, as I have done here for Carlton."

Ottilia adhered to the gentle note. "It must have been a boon to have Carlton for your friend."

"In many ways. I had not myself been in Suffolk long."

"Indeed? Where were you before?"

"In the capital for the most part."

"What brought you to Suffolk?"

"Circumstance."

So she supposed. But what circumstance? She did not press the point. "You were able to guide Carlton, I dare say, a stranger to the place."

"It does not demand much guidance. Aldborough is a small town and the environs are not difficult to learn."

Ottilia's senses prickled. "You know the area well?"

"As well as one needs. I like the place." An odd light showed in his eye. "The scenery is magnificent and I enjoy the wildness of the weather. One is not bored."

A liking for excitement? "You surprise me. I would have supposed the life here to be a trifle mundane." She paused. "If one discounts the lives of those engaged with free trading."

Grégoire's brows drew together and Bastien cast her an anxious look.

Her husband emitted a scornful sound that drew all eyes. "By Radway's account, that includes the majority of Aldborough's citizens."

The Frenchman's gaze returned to Ottilia. "Is this what you imply? You suppose Carlton was also in this trade?"

She turned the question back on him. "Did it never occur to you to wonder?" He made no immediate answer and she pursued it. "There were frequent absences, as you know. I have it from Cecily that Carlton once came back wounded. Also that he was out of temper. Does that not suggest activity other than a wish to sketch fossils?"

Grégoire's brow cleared. "At last I understand you. No, no, you have jumped to a false conclusion, ma'am."

"Have I?"

"Carlton sustained an injury from a sharp rock. It troubled him from time to time. He told me it had not healed well. That is why he was occasionally impatient. Cecily's worry was needless. I told her so many times."

Ottilia exchanged a quick glance with Francis. Her spouse's reaction was obviously as sceptical as her own. A spurious explanation, if ever she heard one. She tried one more throw.

"Much as I would like to believe that's true, it does not account for the manner of Carlton's death."

Grégoire put up a hand to his mouth, his expression dimming again. "I see what you are saying." He looked across, a plea in his voice. "It is my fervent hope that you will succeed in discovering the reason for such a horrible end." He stood up. "Forgive me if I leave you now. You will understand that it is hard for me to endure such discussions."

Ottilia was barely able to express any suitable response before Grégoire hurried out of the room, after executing a flurried couple of bows in the direction of herself and then Francis.

Bastien chose to follow his friend, throwing a word of apology as he went. "I will see him out, *Tante*. I may need to accompany him."

Ottilia waited until the door closed behind them both and then turned to her spouse. "That was an exhibition, Fan, was it not? He might have been a play-actor."

Francis dropped into the Frenchman's vacated chair. "You believe him insincere?"

"Do not you? He told me nothing."

"Nothing to the purpose, I agree."

Ottilia clicked her tongue. "No, Fan, I mean precisely nothing. He asked more questions than he answered and he is skilled at avoidance."

She received a quizzical look from her spouse. "Top of the suspect list then, my dear one?"

Ottilia had to laugh. "If only it were that easy."

"But you do think he is hiding something?"

"Just so. He may be innocent of his friend's murder, but his close association with one who, we have reason to believe, was likely operating outside the law, might have implications, do you not think?"

CHAPTER EIGHT

The physician applied to for the post-mortem proved to be a youngish fellow whose excitable manner put Francis forcibly in mind of Ottilia's older nephew Ben, now in training at one of the London hospitals.

Doctor Grove, whom he visited in company with Radway upon the following day, seemed particularly taken with the manner of the killing. "Oh, it most certainly gives the appearance of an execution, without a doubt. I must concur with that view."

Lieutenant Radway, perhaps playing devil's advocate, chose to challenge. "An appearance of it? When the wrists were tied and he was blindfolded?"

"That is precisely the point which raises doubts." The doctor had a way of illustrating as he talked, holding up clenched hands. "The wrists are scarcely marked."

"Marked?"

"There are lines from the twine, as one would expect. But were these created by swellings after death? Had the victim struggled against his bonds thus —□ shifting his hands in demonstration — "as one might expect, the skin would be gouged to a greater or lesser extent."

Radway cut in. "Unless he chose to accept his fate. Some men go to their deaths in stoic fashion."

Francis could not let this pass. "He received only one bullet. We can dismiss the notion of a firing squad, I believe."

"Perhaps he thought he deserved it."

A spurious argument, but the doctor intervened before Francis could scoff. "You will wish to know about the ball."

Radway frowned. "What about the ball? Did you extract it?"

"I did, and there's a most interesting thing." Grove moved around the long table that formed the centrepiece of his surgery, flanked by sideboards banked to the rear with layers of little drawers. The arrangement was familiar to Francis from his brother-in-law's consulting room at Ash Lodge. Grove picked up a small bowl from the cluttered surface and returned, holding it out.

"It's bent out of shape, but as a military man, Lieutenant, I am sure you must recognise a musket ball."

A flitter of triumph lit in Francis. "I thought as much. May I?" He picked up the ball, now free of skin and the debris from the dead man's skull. "Yes, unmistakeable. You agree, Radway?"

The lieutenant sniffed as he took the ball. "With reluctance. I'd hoped it would prove to be a pistol. These demmed muskets abound in this town, which makes it all but impossible to find the one that shot out this ball." He dropped the offending object back into the bowl. "Anything else you can tell us?"

Grove became eager. "The cloth!"

Francis eyed him. "The blindfold, you mean?"

"If it was one."

"It may contribute to your doubts, Lieutenant. The cloth bore no signs of bleeding."

Francis jumped on this. "I thought that at the outset."

The doctor waggled his fingers. "It is not conclusive. But there was no different coloration across the area of the eyes where the cloth must have lain. Yet again, one would expect marks to have been left, even though Lord Francis says the blindfold had not been tightly tied."

Francis could have cursed. He had half hoped for confirmation one way or the other. What Ottilia would make of the doctor's remarks remained to be seen. For himself, it doubled the complexity and confusion.

Radway was evidently just as frustrated, his tone holding more than a hint of sarcasm. "You ought to abandon doctoring and apply for my role, Grove. You seem to have it all worked out. Could you not be even more inconclusive?"

The doctor's brows snapped together. "You asked for my opinion. If you don't like it, you need not take it."

The lieutenant slapped the other's back, laughing in a way that sounded false to Francis's ears. "No need to take a pet, old fellow. I don't like it, but I'll take it you know your business. Was that it now? Or is there more?"

"Well, I made no incisions into the inner organs, since the cause of death was clear. There can be no doubt the fellow was awake when he was shot, so I had no need to hunt for narcotics or anything of that nature. But if you insist upon it, I can —"

"No, no — no need, I agree with you there. We have sufficient for our purposes." Radway turned to Francis. "Ready to go, sir?"

He was already moving in the direction of the door and Francis was making to follow when Grove's voice arrested him.

"There is just one thing…"

Francis turned back. "Yes?"

"The man's arm. It looks to be an old wound, but —"

Eager now, Francis interrupted, hardly aware of Radway's grunt of impatience. "It was gashed on a sharp rock, so we've heard."

"A rock?" The doctor fluttered his hands. "Gracious me, I doubt that. He would have had to have taken a rattling fall to sustain such a wound, which must also have caused other injuries. Breakage, even. That cut was severe. For my money, he was slashed not with a rock, but with a blade."

"Blades and smugglers?" The dowager, who had returned in acidic mood from her game of whist, threw up her hands. "This becomes more absurd than any of your so-called adventures, Ottilia."

Her companion, seated beside her on the sofa, let out a laugh. "Certainly more exciting, ma'am. Next we shall hear that this Green person was a masked desperado who battled against poor Mr Yelford."

"Don't be idiotic, Henrietta."

Ottilia jumped in with haste. "It may sound far-fetched, Sybilla, but it is not beyond the bounds of probability."

"Aha! Lady Fan is open to any option, as usual. I must see what other ideas I can proffer."

"Henrietta!"

The companion laid a hand on her employer's knee and patted. "I am trying to divert you, Lady Polbrook." She looked across at Ottilia. "She lost badly and it has made her twitchy."

"So I perceive."

Sybilla's delicate brows rose. "Oh, you perceive it, do you? I suppose you also know why I lost, all-knowing as you are."

"No, I don't at all. Why, Sybilla? Unless it was because you had not Ivy Ospringe for your partner?"

Sybilla's response came close to a snort. "Pah! That idiot curate cannot tell one card from another. He made several stupid mistakes."

"Because you flustered the poor man, ma'am. Mr Hargrave was doing his best, but you would keep criticising his discards."

The dowager opened her mouth with the obvious intention of annihilating Henrietta. Francis, at his standard post at the mantel, intervened.

"Enough! If I'd known my information would elicit this much nonsense, I would have held my tongue until I had Tillie alone."

Grateful to her spouse she might be, but Ottilia's heart sank as the dowager turned snapping black eyes upon her son. She leapt in.

"What is most urgent is to discover with whom Carlton Green may have been fighting, if he was." She was glad to see her mother-in-law's gaze return to her and hurried on. "That is why I do not pooh-pooh Henrietta's offering, even though it was meant in jest."

"How so?" Thus Sybilla, showing interest at last.

"It may not have been a fight as such."

"What then?" Francis asked. "It seems certain he received a cut, either from a knife blade or a dagger."

"My notion hangs on whether he was smuggling. It occurs to me that if he was indeed involved in the trade, he would be armed against an encounter with the militia or the riding officer if Mr Yelford was patrolling the coast."

"You are saying the dead man himself had this so-called blade?"

Francis took this. "It is merely a supposition, Mama. If Green had been caught bringing in goods or some such, he could well use one to defend himself."

Henrietta was leaning forward in an attitude of avid interest. "But if he was smuggling, would he do so without his fellows? Could it have been a general melee? I know Mr Yelford has engaged with smugglers on a tip-off, but always in company with militiamen."

"That gives us three possibilities." Ottilia counted off on her fingers. "An encounter with an assailant, where one or other produced a blade. A scuffle with an officer of the law. Or a scrum involving a number of others." She found herself under scrutiny from all three pairs of eyes, a thing that always provoked her sense of humour. "I wish you will not all look at me in that expectant fashion. Do you suppose I have the answer?"

"You usually do, Lady Fan."

"Don't be stupid, Henrietta. How would she guess without further evidence?"

Her spouse directed that quizzical eyebrow at her. "You favour one over the others, though, don't you, my love?"

She had to laugh. "Fiendish husband you are. Very well. It seems to me that if it was a general skirmish, there would have been talk of it at the time. Perhaps other men wounded as well as Carlton."

"I grant you that. What of the others?"

"Well, I cannot rule out a scuffle with the law, but as Henrietta pointed out, either Yelford or some other officer would be more likely to produce a pistol. I am inclined to favour the notion of an assailant, known or unknown to Carlton. On the other hand, it could as easily have arisen from a quarrel between friends."

Sybilla tutted. "Which friends? I trust you do not accuse Bastien."

Francis laughed. "Hardly, ma'am. This event must have taken place before we arrived." Ottilia received one of his questioning looks. "But possibly a different Frenchman, am I right?"

She had to smile. "Well, Grégoire du Guet was known to have accompanied Carlton upon his expeditions now and then."

Before she could debate the question further, they suffered an interruption as the door was flung open and Pretty plunged into the room, flushed, her blue eyes sparkling with wrath.

"Papa!"

"What in the world is the matter?"

"It won't do, I tell you! She is impossible!"

Ottilia made to get up even as Francis took a step forward, but they were forestalled.

"Is that a way to enter a room, girl? How dare you come bursting in without so much as a by your leave?"

"Ma'am, pray hush!"

Henrietta's muttered protest went unnoticed.

"In my day, you'd be whipped for such a lack of manners, young lady."

Ottilia spared a brief glance at Francis's furious face, but had no chance to calm the waters. Pretty's temper flared.

"I'm not a young lady yet, and I don't care what you think of me!"

Henrietta gasped and Sybilla's face went white. "How dare you!"

At which point, Francis cut in, his ire turning on his daughter. "Rudeness I will not tolerate, Pertesia Fanshawe. Apologise to your grandmother at once!"

Pretty, to Ottilia's consternation, grew even redder in the face. "She's not my grandmother and I hate you!"

With which, she broke into sobs and fled the room before Francis could order her to do so. Uttering a violent expletive, he made for the door.

Ottilia leapt to her feet and hurried after him, catching at his sleeve. "Fan, wait! Something has badly upset her, my dearest. This is not like Pretty. Wait a bit, pray. Let me go after her. It will only make the situation worse if you punish her without finding out what occurred."

He sighed. "Very well. You may have ten minutes."

"Thank you."

Ottilia hurried out, carefully shutting the door behind her, and made her way along the corridor to the bedchamber Pretty shared with Henrietta, which was the likeliest place she would have run off to. It was still light out, but there had been no slamming door and she hoped the child had not escaped the house altogether.

Her mind replayed the words Pretty had used when she came in. *She is impossible.* One of the twins must have done something outrageous. Diana, in all likelihood. Her little daughter was a bundle of mischief — insatiably curious and not yet capable of understanding the limitations involved in sharing with her siblings. There had been incidents before when one or other of the older children complained of Di playing with their personal property.

Ottilia did not for a moment suppose Elinor could be the culprit. Even going on three years of age, the other twin was apt to be studious, calm and methodical. Francis invariably stated that Nell took after Ottilia, to which she would retort that Di was his daughter through and through, inheriting both his energetic constitution and his temperament. He was his mother's son in that respect, and Ottilia had no doubt that his fury with Pretty was worse because he was already rubbed by Sybilla's tetchy moods.

The sobbing was audible as she approached the bedchamber Pretty shared with Henrietta. She opened the door and saw the child prone upon the four-poster, her gown awry, shoulders heaving, face buried in her arms.

Ottilia went softly to the bed and perched beside the girl, putting out a hand to stroke back the tumbled blonde locks. "There now, my darling, have your cry out and then we will talk."

Pretty stilled, her body growing rigid as the sobs abruptly ceased. Ottilia let her hand drop to the taut back and began a rhythmic stroking, murmuring soothingly. Not words to be heard but enough sounds of love and reassurance, she hoped, to calm the child's frantic suffering. Pretty was no delicate plant, but it was plain from the words uttered in her fit of temper that there were deep-rooted scars from those far-off days when the toddler she then was had her natural protectors ripped from her life.

Had Francis missed that in his instant reaction to Pretty's apparent rudeness? Had the discovery of a dead body and the subsequent investigation that so intrigued Ottilia's mind proved a trigger to Pretty's buried memories?

To her relief, she saw the child's muscles begin to relax again and a bout of renewed weeping ensued, softer this time, without the edge of despair. It ceased within a short time and Pretty rolled onto her side, sniffing in a doleful way, drowned blue eyes looking up at Ottilia.

"I didn't mean to be rude."

Ottilia smiled and reached to help her. "Of course you did not. Come, sit up, my love, and dry your tears." She dove a hand into a pocket within her skirts and brought out a handkerchief, with which she proceeded to mop the damp cheeks and eyes. She handed it to Pretty. "Now, blow!"

"I'm not a baby." But the protest was muted and she made use of the handkerchief, balling it up in her fingers afterwards.

Ottilia waited a moment, but nothing was forthcoming. She applied a prompt. "What did Diana do this time?"

Pretty shot her a startled look. "How did you know?"

Ottilia laughed. "Well, you said she is impossible, and I am persuaded you did not mean Nell."

Pretty sighed. "I know she did not mean it, and it's my fault for taking my treasure box into the nursery."

This was the first Ottilia had heard of a treasure box, but she had no chance to make an enquiry as Pretty hurried on.

"I didn't see she had it because I was helping Luke with his letters. He's still struggling to read that story, even though it's the easiest in the world."

"Yes, my love, but let us leave that for now. What is this treasure box and what did Di do to it?"

"She broke it and I only found it this morning."

"Oh, dear, how unfortunate. Where and when did you find it?"

"On the beach, while we were hunting for shells. Luke got a pearly one but I won, because even though my box is old, you can still see the pattern and —☐

Conscious of the passing minutes, Ottilia interrupted the flow. "You said Di got hold of it?"

Pretty's eyes grew wet again. "She snapped off the lid and the secret place opened up and I nearly lost all the sparkles, only I managed to catch the little bag. It's quite frayed and worn, you see, so it might easily have torn."

Ottilia's head was reeling. A hidden compartment? Jewels, was it? What in the world had her adoptive daughter stumbled upon? But that must wait. There was a more urgent matter to probe. "What happened after Di broke the box?"

Pretty sighed, looking shame-faced. "I got wild with her and the nurses scolded me. Hepsie told me not to mind it. 'It's only a box,' she said, but it's not any old box, it's a special box, even if it is old and I did mind. Then both Olive and Jennet said it was my fault — as if I didn't know that — and I know I'm the eldest and I have to be responsible, but it's just not fair! Di is always breaking things and she doesn't care a jot if it doesn't belong to her, and I know she can't help it because she's little and I do try to be good with her and Nell, but — but —□

The tears were erupting again and Ottilia cut in fast. "Of course you do, and you do it very well in general, my darling. It was very wrong of Di, and Olive should have told her so. Don't fret. I dare say the box can be mended." Although Ottilia had every intention of inspecting the article before any such repair could be made. She was already revolving possibilities at the back of her mind. "It will pass, my love."

Pretty drew a shuddering breath. "No, it won't because Papa is angry with me, I know he is."

Ottilia knew not how to counter this, since she was aware that Francis would not let it pass, even if he accepted the provocation. She changed tack, for the most important point was yet to be tackled.

"Pretty, my darling, why did you say that Lady Polbrook is not your grandmother?"

A trifle of pink entered the child's cheeks. "It slipped out."

"Yes, but why, my love?"

Pretty looked her full in the face, a little of her customary boldness returning. "Well, she isn't my grandmother, is she? My grandmother is Lady Wem."

A frisson went through Ottilia. If this was not exactly what Francis had been dreading all along! She wasted no words on expostulation. "Who told you that, Pretty?"

The child looked away. "Hepsie. But just because I asked her."

"What made you ask her?"

A pause. Then, in a small voice, "I hear things sometimes. And I remember some things."

Ottilia hesitated. Of what use to ask what things the child remembered? They were bound to be vague shadows of unknown persons and environments. Inevitable that whispers would eventually reach her ears as she grew old enough to understand them. Ottilia opted for truth. "I am afraid your real grandmother died, Pretty, a long time ago."

Pretty's startled gaze met hers. "Then it's true!"

"Yes, it is true. You know already that you are not a child of my body, don't you?"

"Yes. Hepsie told me long ago that my mama died. But Papa…"

"Papa is as much your papa as your real papa, who also died when you were younger than the twins."

Pretty's chin wobbled and Ottilia hugged her. "My darling, you have been our child, and especially Papa's child, for many years. Papa thinks of you as his precious and beloved daughter, you know that."

The tears spilled over. "And now he's too angry to love me anymore."

Ottilia's sense of humour nearly betrayed her, but she held in the laughter. "My dearest, he doesn't love you any less for being angry, I promise you. He will forgive you presently."

As well she said so, since the door opened at this moment to admit her husband.

Francis had given his wife a good deal more than the allotted ten minutes. Not with intention. His mother's continuing animadversions had inevitably descended into her perennial complaint.

"You never should have taken that child in, Francis."

"You have told me so a dozen times, ma'am."

"And I will say it a dozen more times. She comes of vile stock and nothing will make me believe she has not inherited the worst of the Brockhurst traits."

With difficulty, Francis controlled the emotions roiling in his gut. "If you lived with Pretty, you would know that is manifestly false. As my wife said, this sort of conduct is wholly unlike her."

His mother snorted. "Merely because it is hidden from you? Mark my words. What is bred in the bone will come out in the flesh."

It was too much. He spoke in clipped tones. "You will have to excuse me, ma'am. I am needed elsewhere."

He had left the parlour on the words, his intense fury veering from his mother back to his daughter for placing him in an awkward situation. No matter what Ottilia said, she deserved to be chastised and he was determined not to yield.

He was making for the nursery, but before he reached the stairs, he had been waylaid by his small son standing in the way.

"Papa, I need to speak to you."

The portentous note caught at his senses even as he made to pass onward. "Not now, Luke."

His son moved into his path again. "Yes, now, sir. It's very 'portant."

Arrested, Francis looked down into the serious upturned face. "Well, what is it? Be quick."

Luke shook his head. "I can't be quick. Please come into the chamber." So saying, he ran back a few steps and opened the door to the room Francis was occupying with his wife and pushed in.

Beginning to be intrigued, Francis followed, closing the door behind him. Luke stood off a little to one side of the four-poster and stared up at him again.

"You're cross with Pretty, but it's not her fault."

It was an accusation. Francis eyed the boy, puzzlement driving down his ire. "What do you mean?"

Luke's features, as he stared up from his inferior height, were both bold and determined. Arms akimbo, he looked to Francis like a man in miniature, so grown-up was his attitude.

"Well? Out with it!"

"You have to listen to it all, sir."

"Very well. I am waiting."

"You ought to be able to guess it, for you know what Di is like. She got hold of Pretty's treasure box."

"Treasure box?" Momentarily thrown, Francis frowned down at the serious face. "What treasure box is this?"

Luke emitted an impatient sound. "It's one she found this morning when we had a discovering competition. I got a really good shell but I had to concede 'cos the box is first-rate." He flung up a hand. "But that ain't the point. Di got her little paws on it and 'course she broke it. The lid snapped off and she dropped that on the floor and that's when I saw what she was doing and yelled. Pretty leapt, but she was too late. The wooden bit came out and the little bag fell. Pretty caught that or the place would have been scattered with them things."

Francis was finding it difficult to keep up. What bit fell out, and what would have been scattered? But he had no chance to ask as his son kept on with his story.

"In any event, Pretty got cross and you can't blame her because she only had it half a day before Di went and broke it. Of course Di burst out crying, like she always does."

Francis gave an inward sigh. "Is the box irreparable?"

Luke blinked. "What, Papa?"

"Can it be mended?"

"I don't know. In any event, that don't matter now. See, what happened next is, Olive got into a fuss 'cos Di was crying and Hepsie told Pretty not to mind it. As if she could help it when her treasure was all spoiled! Then both the nurses got into a bigger fuss and moaned at Pretty like anything, and you know what Pretty's temper is — she got crosser and crosser and said she was going to tell you and … and that's what happened. So it's not her fault and she oughtn't be punished when it's Di who made her so cross."

Francis could not have interrupted this last rapid plea even had he wanted to. Despite all, his heart warmed to his young son for taking his sister's part and braving the storm to intercept him. But Luke likely did not realise the result of Pretty's tantrum. He temporised.

"I'm glad you told me, Luke."

"So you won't punish poor Pretty, will you?"

He knew not how to answer this. The anxious note touched him, but common sense dictated that he could not allow Pretty's lapse to go unpunished.

"We'll see."

"Yes, but —□

"That will do, Luke. You don't know what passed in the parlour."

Unexpectedly, his son set his hands behind his back, stiffening his spine. "Yes, I do. I was listening outside."

Francis was obliged to suppress a spurt of laughter. If the child didn't take after Ottilia! That was just the unscrupulous thing she was apt to do.

"Did you indeed?"

"Yes, and I don't care if you punish me for it, 'cos I came after Pretty in case Grandmama was there 'cos I knew she'd be mad as fire if Pretty said anything. She hates Pretty."

Shock ripped through Francis. "Who says so?"

"Oh, everyone knows that, sir. It's 'cos Grandmama hates Pretty's real grandmama."

This was undeniable, although in truth his mother's sworn enemy was Pretty's great-grandmother. But that his son knew this, let alone the rest of the household, was appalling. "Whom do you mean by *everyone*?"

"All of them." Luke made sweeping arcs with his arms. "Joanie and Tyler and Ryde and Williams. Mostly Hepsie, of course. But Hemp knew too, and so did Doro, but she warned me not to speak of it, so I never."

"Who told you, Luke?"

"Nobody. I'm not stupid, you know. I got ears and I hear. I did ask Doro if it was true and she said not to talk about it, but when Hemp had a talk to me before they went away — "

"Hemp had a talk with you?"

"'Course he did, Papa. He talked to me a lot, 'cos he liked to be with Doro and Doro was with me. Stands to reason."

His son's logic amused Francis, but he was dismayed to realise — as he ought to have done long before this — that domestic gossip was bound to leak the truth of Pretty's origins. All the servants mentioned, bar Dorote Gabon, had been with them in Tunbridge Wells when his now precious girl was the unwitting victim of a tragedy.

"Well, I hope you have the sense not to say anything about this outside of our own people, Luke."

His son rolled his eyes. "I just said I don't. Even Hemp explained why I oughtn't."

Francis was tempted to pursue the subject. However, he knew that Ottilia's former Barbadian steward, now married to Doro and running a boarding house in Brighthelmstone on the south coast, could be trusted to give sensible advice to the boy.

"Very well. Back to the nursery with you now." He opened the door and gestured.

Luke did not move. "Has Mama found the murderer yet?"

The abrupt change of subject threw Francis. He began to usher the child forth. "Not yet."

"She will, though, won't she? Tyler says she always does."

"Quite right." He was about to mount the stairs when Luke stayed him, holding up a hand.

"She's not upstairs. She went to her room."

"Thank you. Up with you now."

"I'm going to find murderers when I grow up."

Francis laughed. "Are you indeed? Shall you be a Bow Street Runner?"

"No, I'm going to be like Mama and find them wherever I go."

God help you then! But Francis did not say it aloud. He parted from his son and made his way to the bedchamber his daughter was sharing with his mother's companion. Upon his entrance, he spied Pretty sitting on the end of the four-poster with Ottilia, his wife's arm about the girl's shoulders. The instant apprehension in his daughter's face caused him a bump at the heart.

"No need to look so scared, Pretty. I've heard the whole story from Luke."

At his wife's questioning glance, he threw her a silent message of reassurance. He would give her the tale of their son's intervention in a private interview.

As he moved towards the bed, Pretty slowly rose, her lip trembling. Ottilia's arm fell away, but she remained seated, a plea in the gaze she kept upon him. Relief slid into his breast that Luke had succeeded in averting a painful interlude.

Pretty eyed him with those big eyes that never failed to melt him. Her voice shook. "I don't mind if you scold me. I mind that you don't love me anymore."

His heart contracted. "Sweetheart! Don't be silly. I'll always love you, however badly you behave."

A sigh came from Ottilia. "What did I tell you, my love? Of course Papa won't stop loving you."

Pretty continued to regard him with a measure of doubt in her eyes. "But if you're not my real papa, you don't have to love me."

He had dreaded the moment of discovery, but now it had come, it appeared to have lost all power to wound either of them. "I don't love you because I have to. You adopted me for your papa. That's why I love you."

Her gaze widened. "I adopted you?"

He lifted an eyebrow. "You claimed me, if I remember rightly, calling me Papa and clinging to my boot. I really didn't have a choice in the matter."

Pretty stared for a moment and then her bright smile appeared and she flung herself at Francis. He received her in a comprehensive hug, raising questioning brows at his wife over Pretty's blonde head. She put a finger to her lips and he nodded. Later would do for explanations.

When he released his daughter, he held her away from him and deliberately grew more sober. "But none of that excuses the way you spoke to Grandmama." Pretty opened her mouth to speak and he put up a warning finger. "It is true that she is not your real grandmother, but —

"She's your mama. I know that."

"And as such, she deserves your respect. I want you to apologise."

A mulish twist came to Pretty's lips. "I only said the truth."

"You spoke rudely and I won't have that. She's an old lady and you are a child. It was very bad manners and that is what you are going to apologise for. Is that understood?"

CHAPTER NINE

Ottilia did not accompany her husband and daughter downstairs, instead repairing to the nursery. The usual chaos reigned. Diana, always quick to put trouble behind her, was now engaged in creating a trail of wooden bricks about the carpet which was guaranteed to trip anyone who walked unwarily through. Olive's expostulations went unheeded and as fast as she and Jennet were removing the bricks, Di was replacing them. Concentrated upon her self-appointed task, the infant did not at first notice Ottilia's entrance. But Elinor, seated on a large cushion in a corner and quietly turning the pages of a picture book, looked up as her brother hailed their mother.

"Mama!" Luke, back at the table where Hepsie was supervising his reading again, leapt from his chair, scraping it back and nearly knocking it over in the process. "Did you see Pretty? Is she punished?"

"Master Luke, come back here this instant! You've not even finished one page."

Ottilia waved the chief nurse to silence. "Give him leave a moment, Hepsie."

The nurse had risen and she dropped a curtsy, moving to the other two, whose protests to the noisier twin became hushed as Ottilia concentrated her attention upon her son.

"Papa has taken Pretty down to Grandmama so that she may apologise."

"Ha!" Luke's look became mulish. "Grandmama won't care if she does say sorry. She'll just say something horrid to Pretty."

"That is untrue. Grandmama doesn't mean to be unkind. When a person is old, it becomes hard to do ordinary things and that makes people crotchety."

"Grandmama is always crotchety."

"Not always, Luke. I wish you won't say things like that in front of your sisters."

"Well, but —□

"I am not here to argue the matter. Where is this treasure box, if you please? Can you show it to me?"

Her son was instantly diverted, a fortunate effect of his mercurial temperament. In that he resembled Diana, and had been just as lively and rowdy as a toddler.

"We put it out of Di's reach." He moved as he spoke to the shelving against one wall, in which both toys and books were stashed without any visible order. As Luke reached up to one of the higher shelves, Ottilia's attention was drawn to a tugging at her petticoats.

"Mama!"

"Hello, my little dear." She lifted Elinor into her arms, not without effort. "Gracious, how big you are getting, Nell!"

"I want to draw, Mama. Don't want to read book no more."

Ottilia kissed her smooth cheek. "You may draw, my love. Jennet!"

The youngest of the nurses, a shy girl not much above fifteen years of age, came quickly up. "Shall I take her, my lady?"

"Here it is, Mama. It's quite broke, you know."

"Mama! Mama!"

Now Diana was tugging at her skirts, while Nell reiterated her desire to draw in Ottilia's ear. Her head felt as if it were spinning.

"Enough! Luke, wait a moment! Quiet, Nell! Di, for goodness' sake, stop that!"

She so rarely lost her equilibrium that her auditors were startled into silence, even Diana desisting in her efforts to demand attention. Ottilia blew out a breath.

"Thank you. Jennet, pray arrange for Nell to sit and draw. Hepsie will help you." She passed the child across and dropped to her haunches to be immediately confronted by Diana's beaming smile, dark curls rioting around the face of utter innocence. "Oh, Di, you little devil! No one would suppose you had caused such a commotion."

"I want to draw too!"

"Of course you do, just because Nell wants to. Well, you may. Olive will help you." She added, sotto voce, to the other nurse who had also come up, "Not that I expect she will do so for long. Humour her, my dear. She is a handful for you, I know, but she will learn to be better in a year or two, I promise you."

Olive, an older and far more experienced nurse than Jennet, gave an audible sigh. "Well, I hope so, my lady. I miss Doro. Miss Di used to mind her best, my lady."

Ottilia smiled but made no comment. The reminder of that particular loss was still painful. Her steward and friend had at last lost patience in the previous year, claiming Doro for his wife and insisting upon making the break from the Fanshawe household. While she appreciated Hemp's ambition to build an independent life, she could not but be hurt by his departure. In correspondence, she had vowed to visit Brighthelmstone where he and Doro now lived, but that had not been possible on this occasion. The building Hemp Roy had purchased was in the process of being renovated, with only a couple of rooms ready for letting. The Fanshawe entourage could not yet be accommodated.

"Here, Mama. See, the lid came off. I put the little bag back in but it won't hold, I don't think."

Luke was holding up two parts of what was clearly the broken treasure box. Ottilia thankfully turned her mind to the more immediate matter that could not but intrigue. She took the box in hand first. It was of a size suitable for knick-knacks but little else, made of dark wood marked with fading, no doubt from being washed by the sea. The surfaces were carved with a pattern of curlicues which might once have been inlaid with paint, faint lines of gold still showing here and there. Its interior was empty, the contents no doubt washed away by the ocean.

"It must have been a good box, don't you think, Mama?"

"I do indeed. It may be mahogany, which is expensive. Let me see the lid."

She exchanged with her son and was the more intrigued to note how the curving top, carved with an even more intricate pattern but significantly damaged in places, had a false interior that concealed a cavity.

"You have to be careful, Mama, for that flat bit is likely to come away."

A flitter of excitement ran through Ottilia, but she opted to keep her suspicions to herself for the moment. "Let me see how it fits together." She set the lid back on the box as Luke held it up.

Of the two hinges at the back, one had clearly come away at some earlier date while the other had snapped. A flap device at the front ought to have secured the lid, but the companion setting was missing from the box.

"It does seem to be very old. Or perhaps it has been damaged since it was lost."

"Who lost it?"

"Now, how should I know that?"

"You always know everything, Tyler says. 'Cos you're Lady Fan."

Ottilia had to laugh. "I certainly cannot know about a box that has just been found. Where exactly did Pretty find it, by the by?"

"It was wedged between two rocks. You couldn't see it if you didn't take off the seaweed. Leastways, I didn't see it, but Pretty catched up the seaweed 'cos she saw that gold bit through it, she said." He pointed to a gleaming streak that still adorned one section of the carved top.

Ottilia made up her mind. "I think I must take charge of it for the moment. Tell Pretty I am going to see if it can be easily mended."

She slipped out of the nursery while both twins were occupied with their drawing, bidding her son return to his reading. Luke shared Pretty's governess at Flitteris, but the need for a tutor was looming.

Dismissing these domestic problems to the back of her mind, Ottilia made her way to her bedchamber, determined to probe the secrets of the treasure box in solitude. Once alone, she was able to make a proper examination, taking a chair by the window to make the best of the remaining light.

She removed the top and set the box aside, concentrating on the compartment clearly intended to be hidden. If the mechanism had not been damaged, how was it opened? No catch was visible. Did one press the wood at one or other end? In the event, since it had already been shaken loose by Diana's mischievous fingers, it took merely a little prising before the flat sliver of wood dropped down at one side, allowing a dark little square to slide into Ottilia's hand. The bag of sparkles Pretty had mentioned.

The familiar riffle of anticipation was prompting Ottilia to inspect the contents at once. She held off, however, first submitting the bag itself to a minute inspection.

It had suffered from its immersion in seawater, becoming stiff with salt and subject to discoloration. She was nevertheless convinced it was made of silk, the stitching minute and neat, and although the cord that drew the opening tight was frayed, it looked to have been woven from golden thread. An expensive item altogether.

With care, Ottilia untied the cord and opened up the bag. An immediate impression of twinkling within gave notice of Pretty's *sparkles*. With a fast-beating heart, Ottilia tipped the contents into her cupped palm.

Diamonds, without a doubt. There were perhaps a dozen, of varying sizes. Removed from a necklace, perhaps? Her immediate thought was not of smuggling. She was haunted by the notion of someone's little hoard — a female, was it? — becoming lost in this fashion. Its owner must have been desperate to be concealing a collection of diamonds in a box with a cunning secret compartment.

She had set the lid on the windowsill and a stray glance caught a hint of yellow under the thin flap. She slipped the diamonds back into their bag and set it down, reaching for the lid again. The cause was visible as soon as she moved the flap. A folded parchment?

This proved to be more tightly wedged into the curve of the lid, perhaps due to its bulk and the length of time it had been in situ. Ottilia worked at it without haste, fearful of tearing the parchment. Once she had got it out, it crackled as she gently undid the several folds that had been used to make the single sheet fit into the narrow space available. Triumphant, she held it up to the light.

Patches of discoloration were visible here too, and the ink was so faded it was almost illegible. It was close-written in sloping characters, the lines tight, and it took but a few words for Ottilia to realise they were in French. The remains of a seal adorned the bottom, too broken to make out fully. Or was there a crest or crown?

Ottilia's mind flitted to the document mentioned by Cecily Green. Also in French. Also old and faded, with a crested seal. Or was that a jump too far?

Ottilia had returned to the parlour with the intention of enlisting the aid of Bastien, but he was still out. She hoped he meant to be back in time to partake of dinner. Meanwhile, she lost no time in showing the box, along with her finds, to her mother-in-law, successfully diverting that lady's mind from Pretty's lapse.

She did not ask how the apology had been received — her erring daughter had evidently come and gone, since Francis was alone — but focused attention on the possible origin of the box.

"Can these have been prised from their settings in a necklace?" Sybilla was poking at the diamonds which Ottilia had poured into a comfit dish for safety.

"Just what I thought, Sybilla. Which would indicate that the owner was female."

Henrietta, who was turning the box in her hands as she examined its markings, looked up at that. "I agree. Robina had a box of this style."

"Your former employer? Was it the same?"

"Not nearly as rich as this. But with just such an intricate design. She kept odds and ends in it, nothing of value. I recall she had a thimble in there, several pins and a brooch to which the catch had broken, but Robina liked it too much to dispose of it." Henrietta gave a laugh. "Not nearly as interesting as this one. There certainly was no hidden compartment."

Ottilia smiled but pursued the thought in her mind. "The owner might have had that specially made."

Sybilla left off poking at the diamonds. "For the purpose of concealing these?"

"Just so. And the document." Ottilia looked across to the window where her husband was submitting the parchment to a close inspection. "Can you make anything out, Fan?"

He lowered the sheet. "Not much. It looks to be a plea of some kind, presumably to whoever was intended as the recipient of the box." He traced a line on the page with his finger. "This is of interest. *Si on trouve ma fille* … but the rest is too faded to read."

Sybilla sat up. "If my daughter is found? She sent the diamonds to England in hopes of them reaching her daughter."

"How romantic!"

"It is more likely tragic, Henrietta. The writer probably died by guillotine."

"Gracious, ma'am, do you think the owner was an aristocrat?"

"If she was, one cannot but pity her." Sybilla gave a shudder. "So many slaughtered, and for what?"

Ottilia made haste to change the direction of the discussion. The so-called Reign of Terror had been bloody, but its end coincided with the fall of Robespierre several years ago. Her mother-in-law was apt to bemoan the decimation of the French upper classes, even though in reality the middling sort suffered quite as many losses while the regime change to the

French Republic was in effect. Better to keep the talk on the possibilities that were teeming in her mind.

"What is important is whether or not this bears upon our investigation here."

Henrietta became eager. "Do you think it may?"

"Cecily spoke of her brother possessing a document in French."

"That's a tenuous link, Tillie."

"True, Fan, but it may be worth following. The question is, how long had that box been wedged between the rocks and how did it get here?"

"According to Radway, there are enough crossings for any article to find its way to our shores."

"Yes, Mr Yelford has said the same, Lord Francis," said Henrietta. "Several vessels have foundered, he says. Do you suppose this box can have floated here from a wreck?"

The mention of both names gave Ottilia fodder to ponder. She had not thought of questioning Lieutenant Radway or the riding officer, but this find might make that procedure advisable. Although it equally might mean giving up Pretty's find to the authorities, assuming it had anything to do with smuggling.

"I do not think so," she said aloud.

Henrietta's voice penetrated her absorption. "If not from a wreck, then how did it get there?"

Ottilia looked at her, a trifle puzzled. "From a wreck?"

"We were speculating where the box came from, Tillie. Were you miles away again?" Her husband came away from the window and held out the document. "Thinking of this?"

Ottilia took it absently. "I was hoping we need not take this to the customs chief or the riding officer."

Francis subjected her to one of his searching looks. "Meaning?"

Sybilla chimed in. "I should like to know that too. You are being enigmatic as usual, Ottilia."

"I do not mean to be. For one thing, it would break Pretty's heart to be deprived of her treasure. For another, it does not seem to me that this box pertains to smuggling."

Her husband took up his usual stance, leaning his elbow on the mantel. "Does it pertain to our mystery, though? Is that what you imply?"

"Gracious!" Henrietta's eyes twinkled. "How in the world can you make that connection, Lady Fan?"

Ottilia laughed. "It would be premature to do so. But there is that document in French mentioned by Cecily Green to be explained, and here we have another."

Sybilla rapped on the arm of her chair. "You go too fast, Ottilia. How should they be connected?"

"That I cannot fathom at this present. They may not be indeed, but the possibility should not be ignored. Once Bastien has made a translation…"

"So that is why you asked for him. How fortunate it is that he came with us. Do you not agree, Lady Polbrook?"

Sybilla snorted. "His usefulness extends far beyond making translations from the French, Henrietta." Her gaze pierced Ottilia. "I hope you don't mean to upset the boy. He is distressed enough by his friend's demise. That is why he has gone off riding today. I know his moods."

Francis cut in before Ottilia could respond. "You are too severe, ma'am. How should it upset him to be asked to translate? Besides, I intend to use him to better purpose."

"In what way? You had better not run the boy into danger, Francis, or you will have me to reckon with."

"For pity's sake, Mama! He is a grown man and able to hold his own in a fight. Not that I anticipate any such, but — ☐

Ottilia took a hand. "Pray do not fall into a quarrel. Fan, is it to visit those fishermen?"

He turned to her with obvious relief. "Precisely. I am aiming to set out at dawn on Monday to accost them as they come in with the night's catch. We may also visit the blacksmith, if time permits."

Sybilla continued disgruntled. "I do not see why you must needs involve my grandson in these antics. Next you will be accusing him of doing away with his friend."

Ottilia had to laugh. "Sybilla, if you must provoke an argument, I will oblige you. Don't drive poor Fan into a frenzy, I beg." She cast her fulminating spouse an apologetic smile. "It is quite deliberate, my dearest. I wish you will not rise to the bait."

A choked laugh escaped the dowager, but she immediately put a hand up to her mouth to hide her amusement. Francis thankfully refrained from expressing his annoyance, and Ottilia seized upon a distraction.

"Have your whist companions chattered upon the subject of the murder, Sybilla?"

"Chattered? If I did not prevent them, the wretches would talk of nothing else."

"I spoke with Mrs Peckledon myself, but has the Reverend Stewkley said anything to the purpose, perhaps?"

Sybilla wafted a hand. "He at least talks like a sensible man."

"In what way?"

"Oh, he accepts there is no stopping the smuggling trade in toto. Stewkley believes such incidents as this, though shocking, are inevitable when men will engage in dangerous enterprises."

Ottilia eyed her. "He thinks the incident is related to the trade?"

"He did not say so directly, but it is a fair inference, is it not?"

"Has Reverend Stewkley any reason to suspect Carlton Green's involvement?"

Sybilla let out a sound of scorn. "How in the world should I know?"

"Well, do you know if he was well acquainted with Carlton?"

The dowager's brows rose. "Well acquainted? He was the man's spiritual advisor."

Ottilia's interest rose. "Was he indeed?"

"Heavens, Ottilia, will you make something of it? All that means is that Green attended his church of a Sunday, as we must do tomorrow. How well does one know one's local pastor? I could swear ours has little knowledge of me."

Here Francis evidently could not contain himself. "I doubt that, ma'am. Everyone around Polbrook, parsons included, must know you very well indeed. You are hardly a nobody. Nor are you slow to inform all and sundry of your opinions."

Ottilia was swift to deflect the issue before her mother-in-law could take umbrage again. "It might be worth probing, do you not think, Sybilla? If it is not a trouble to you, could you, do you think, discover the extent of Reverend Stewkley's acquaintance with Carlton? Just in a casual fashion when next you play together. After all, I can scarcely ask myself when he is conducting the service."

Sybilla's black eyes regarded her severely, but with a lurking twinkle. "You seek to drag me in too, do you? Why do you not co-opt Henrietta while you are about it?"

Ottilia was betrayed into merriment. "How did you guess?" And turning to the companion, she added, "I fully intend to use your friendship with Mr Yelford."

Henrietta gave a crow of delight and clapped her hands. "Excellent. I was hoping I might become of use. What do you wish me to ask him?"

Bastien intercepted his grandmother's companion as she was about to enter the chamber she shared with Pretty. "A moment, I pray you, Etta."

Henrietta halted with her hand still on the doorhandle. "Ah, you're here. Lady Polbrook was wondering if you would be home to dine."

He ignored both the observation and the smile that went with it. Having long got upon terms with Henrietta Skelmersdale, whom he found possessed both of common sense and a dry wit that amused him, Bastien never stood upon ceremony with her, nor she with him. Indeed, in an expansive moment, the companion had invited him to address her by her pet name. "No one else does so and it will make me feel quite at home." He well understood the feeling of isolation from the early years of his sojourn in England and could sympathise with Henrietta's loss of the circle of friends she had known when she lived in the same district as the Fanshawes.

"I hope you may consider me your friend, Etta," he'd told her. "Then you may complain of *Grand-mère* to me and I will complain of my impossible sister to you."

That made her laugh and so began an unlikely bond. He therefore had no hesitation now in pumping her for information.

"What has happened here, Etta? I hear whispers and the house is too quiet."

The companion's face lit with mischief. "Oh, we've had quite the dramatics, my dear, and your grandmother surpassed herself."

When he had heard the tale of Pretty's lapse and the subsequent shame-faced apology — "though grudgingly given, I suspect" — Bastien was more relieved than otherwise.

"I am glad it was only thus. I feared a mishap between my uncle and aunt."

"Nothing of the kind, thank heavens. Mind you, I gather it was Luke who averted a crisis. But I have not told you the most exciting part. Pretty had found a box and Di broke it, which is what set her temper off, but the box subsequently became of even more interest and Lady Fan really needs you now."

Confused, Bastien blinked. "You speak in riddles."

Henrietta laughed. "Do I? Well, that is appropriate for we are presented with one."

He was intrigued to hear what the box contained and expressed himself as willing to do the necessary translation. "But why does my aunt deem this document important?"

"Because she says Cecily Green mentioned a document in French too, so there may be a connection."

It sounded tenuous to Bastien, but he did not say so, for he caught Henrietta eyeing him in an odd fashion, as if in question. "Why do you look at me so?"

"You cannot have been riding all day. Have you been visiting Cecily Green?"

He felt warmth rise to his face. "I prefer not to, since Grégoire may go there."

To his surprise, Henrietta took hold of his arm, leaning close and dropping her voice. "You do realise that Lady Fan suspects him, don't you?"

Bastien hesitated. The albeit brief discussion the previous day between his aunt and his friend had caused him a good deal of anxiety. Grégoire had taken snuff at the trend of Lady Fan's questions and it had required tact to soothe him. Yet a niggle of doubt could not but trouble him. So much so, he had absented himself for most of the day, riding Tonnerre cross-country to shake off his fidgets as well as those of his horse.

"I am aware."

Henrietta sought his gaze. "Do you think she has reason?"

A mirthless laugh escaped him. "You are too acute, Etta." He threw up a hand. "I do not know of any reason, but my heart misgives me."

"Why?"

"Because Grégoire became defensive. As if he had something to hide. If not, why not speak with calm and tell what he knew?"

She patted his arm, smiling. "You have not known him long, Bastien. He cannot be what we call a bosom bow to you. I dare say there is a great deal you don't know about him."

Bastien sighed. "You speak truth. I do not wish to find myself so bad a judge of character."

"We are all apt to misjudge people. But make yourself easy. As yet you have no real reason to think that you did."

He agreed to this, not wishing to burden her with his troubled mind. If truth be told, a part of him hoped that Grégoire would be found wanting, since that must eliminate him as a contender for Cecily's affections.

"I had best make haste, especially if my Aunt Ottilia requires my aid."

He left her on the words, repairing to his own chamber to make the necessary change in his dress before the family dined. Not that he made much adjustment beyond tidying his person and clothes and arranging a fresh neck-cloth about his throat since a measure of informality was maintained, his aunt declaring that it was ridiculous to parade in evening clothes when they dined *en famille*.

"We are on holiday and one cannot be forever rearranging one's hair and changing clothes when we are so blown about by the winds with salt air and sand getting into everything."

Predictably, his grandmother had made instant objection. "You need not expect me to make an appearance at The Rooms looking like a ragamuffin."

"I defy you ever to look other than elegant, Sybilla. Naturally, we will dress appropriately should we attend any gatherings."

With which dictum Lady Polbrook had thankfully agreed and his aunt had been allowed to have her way, much to the relief of the rest of the party. Bastien entered the parlour ready for the call to dine to find only his uncle waiting. Lord Francis hailed him with an unexpected grin.

"The very man I wish to see. I have a mission for you."

Wary, Bastien eyed him. "I do not trust this look of yours, *mon oncle*. What sort of mission?"

That drew a laugh. "Don't fret, you won't be alone."

"Worse and worse. Who comes with me?"

"I do, my boy. I want to catch these fishermen smugglers we've heard about."

"Catch them? Why do you not have the militia do so?"

"I don't plan on capturing them. Apparently they fish at night and I want to beard them when they come in."

Bastien let his breath go. "Ah, that is different. In this case, I will be happy to accompany you."

His uncle grinned. "Who knows? If the wretches have contraband aboard, we may become heroes."

Bastien laughed. "We are more like to become dead like my poor friend."

It did not take Lord Francis's raised brows to make him realise what he had said. Uncomfortable warmth rose up his neck and he backtracked at speed.

"This was maladroit. I beg your pardon."

A snort came in response. "For pity's sake, man! One cannot be forever avoiding the mention of death merely because it reflects back on the present circumstance. Take a leaf out of my wife's book. She calls it her besetting sin, but she is apt to find humour at the most macabre moments. It can be intensely irritating, but at times it has proven the best medicine."

There was no need for his uncle to elaborate, since the direction of his recollection was obvious. Bastien was all too familiar with the tale of the horrific murder of his father's first wife. His own memories were hazy, having arrived in England as a youth just when the affair had reached crisis point. He had later been given accounts from several sources of just what had happened, and his Aunt Ottilia's part in the business as Lady Fan. He knew his father's absence at the time had placed a heavy burden on Lord Francis's shoulders.

He was not obliged to respond since his aunt entered the room at this moment.

"Ah, you have come home, Bastien! I am much in need of your assistance."

He gave a brief bow. "So I have heard from Etta. I am naturally at your service, *Tante*. Have you the document with you?"

"Can you doubt it?" She was already fishing within the recesses of her gown. She brought out a folded piece of parchment and gave it to him. "Take care! It is fragile and may easily tear." He opened it with due attention as she continued.

"The writing is faded, so I do not know how much you will be able to read. Francis managed a little."

"Scarcely enough to be of use."

"It did give us a clue, Fan, but I should like Bastien to see what he makes of it without our prior judgements."

Bastien had moved to the candelabra that stood upon the side-table by the inner wall, his eyes on the faintly written words, but he glanced back. "You have the box also?"

"Yes, but I won't show you that until you have done. It might prejudice your thinking."

"But Etta told me what it contains."

"I trust she did not relate the points of our discussion?"

She sounded a trifle put out and Bastien made haste to reassure her. "We had little time since I was late already. Mostly she explained to me the fracas that occurred."

He saw the Fanshawe couple exchange a glance and regretted mentioning it. Focusing his attention on the paper, he moved it to take best advantage of the candlelight and began to study the text, ignoring a murmured conversation behind him.

Engrossed, he did not stir until he heard Tyler announcing that dinner was served. Turning, he was surprised to find that both his grandmother and Henrietta had joined the party.

"Has she lumbered you already, my dear boy?"

Bastien laughed. "It is no chore to me, *Grand-mère*. On the contrary, I find it to be very *interessant*."

"I hoped it might be." His Aunt Ottilia was ushering everyone out. "Bring it with you, Bastien. You can relate what you have found while we eat, if you will."

There was no opportunity to do so until all were seated and dishes of various shellfish or roasted pork with sides of pickled French beans and artichokes had been served to the diners.

But once the plates were larded to each one's satisfaction, Ottilia proved eager.

"Did you manage to make out much of the document, Bastien?"

He swallowed a mouthful of buttered lobster. "Enough, I think, to make a tale of what is there."

Henrietta leaned in. "I can scarcely wait. Do tell!"

"He will if you give the boy an opportunity, Henrietta. Don't be so impatient."

"I fear I am far too impatient to be patient, Lady Polbrook. Such an exciting moment!"

Bastien met her gaze across the table. "It is perhaps more tragic than exciting, I fear."

He became at once the cynosure of all eyes and a hush descended upon the assembled listeners. Only Ottilia appeared unaffected.

"I suspected as much. What does she say?"

Bastien was betrayed into a short laugh. "How did you know it is a woman?"

"It does not take much deduction. Pray do not credit me with more wit than I deserve."

His uncle chimed in. "She thought so from the first. Both box and gemstones point to a female."

"The diamonds came from a necklace, we surmised," said his grandmother.

"And my previous employer had a box like this one," added Henrietta.

His Aunt Ottilia clicked her tongue. "May we allow Bastien to tell his findings, if you please?"

There was a flurry of protest, during which he took the opportunity to partake of the food on his plate. But when quiet descended again, he looked around the expectant faces and gave a wry smile.

"You are ready? Then I begin." He gestured to the paper which he had laid to one side on the white cloth. "When this was written, it was, I think, at the height of the troubles in Paris. The signature is not clear, but I believe she was a comtesse."

"Was?" asked Francis.

"Indeed, sir, for it appears she is expecting at any moment the *canaille* will invade. Her son is already taken, but she has, if I made it out correctly, managed to send her daughter away. She hopes these jewels will find their way to her daughter."

"Jewels? In the plural?" Ottilia had paused in eating, her fork in the air. "Does she mean the diamonds?"

Bastien looked again at the paper. "I make out *bijoux*."

"She hid them with that document."

"But perhaps there were more, *Tante*."

"How so?"

"It seems she had the intention to give the box of jewels to a messenger, but here —□ he pointed to a line on the discarded sheet — "she says she does not know who she can trust."

"Box of jewels?" Henrietta likewise paused in her enthusiastic consumption of both buttered crab and lobster. "Did she fill it then?"

Sybilla snorted. "More fool she. If she did, the temptation to this messenger might well have proved irresistible."

"Or, since it was found presumably washed up, the contents were lost at sea," came from Lord Francis.

Ottilia's voice cut across these suggestions. "Was there more, Bastien?"

"Much is illegible, but I think it is perhaps just the name of the daughter and messages to be relayed to her. There seems to be another name I cannot make out. Perhaps the one who helped the daughter or that of a relative already in England."

"She meant the box to be sent to England?"

"*Angleterre* is clearly written, so I think yes."

For a few moments, no one spoke as the meal was resumed. Bastien supposed everyone was digesting the detail he had given as well as the food. Once the servants were removing the debris and the customary platters of cheese, nuts and fruit had been passed around, Lord Francis looked down from his place at the head of the table to his wife, seated at the other end.

"What do you make of it, Tillie?"

Lady Fan was evidently in play, to Bastien's amusement, as his aunt looked up from her plate onto which she had been carefully placing slices of a hard yellow cheese.

"I have been mulling it, Fan."

"To what result?"

She smiled. "You always expect me to produce a neat solution, my dearest, but I fear it is mere guesswork."

"Let's have it then."

The request was echoed from both his grandmother and Henrietta. Not that Bastien was averse to hearing her conclusions, however they were arrived at.

Ottilia set down the knife. "Then let us suppose our comtesse made a last desperate attempt to provide for her escaped daughter. She was canny enough to realise the jewels might not reach their destination intact — as we see, for they must have been either stolen or lost at sea — which is why, I suggest, she hid the most valuable of them in the silken pouch, along with the document. From the fact that Bastien says there is another name, it seems the box was despatched to a particular individual. That is what interests me. It did not reach that person. How was it lost? Was it intercepted?"

Henrietta raised an objection. "But Pretty found it wedged between rocks. Surely that means it floated here on the waves and became caught, does it not?"

Ottilia met the companion's gaze. "Or was it deliberately wedged there by an individual? And did that individual intend that another should find it there? If not, why not dispose of it altogether? Has Pretty inadvertently unearthed a plot?"

CHAPTER TEN

Despite rising from his bed at the ungodly hour of four on the Monday morning, Francis was chagrined to discover they had missed the dawn. Not that the grey mist that overlay the coastline and a choppy sea would have been any different had his small party been early enough to see the sun rise.

He had half expected, scrambling into his clothes, that his nephew would be still asleep. In his army days, the younger soldiers tended to need kicking awake by the hardier sergeants of long-standing. Bastien, however, was awaiting him on the stairwell, drawing his instant approval.

"Good man! Have you been there long?"

"Long enough." A wry look was cast up at him. "You are tardy, *mon oncle*."

"I am aware."

In fact, he had been ready in good time, but Ottilia had woken despite his careful efforts not to disturb her slumber.

"Pray take care, my dearest dear!"

He had moved to her side of the bed and dropped down, planting a kiss on her forehead. "Go back to sleep, my loved one."

She had detained him as he made to rise, grasping his hand. "Those men may well be dangerous, Fan."

"I have my pistol and Bastien will be with me."

The anxious note did not abate. "Did you send to Ryde?"

"I did. Don't fret, sweetheart. Nothing will happen to me."

Ottilia sighed, releasing him. "Well, if you come home with a musket ball in you, do not say I did not warn you."

He sat on the edge of the bed, drawing her hand to his lips. "I won't. Moreover, if I do, I know well my darling wife will devote herself to nursing me back to health, even if I am obliged to endure a scold."

That drew a smile from her and she squeezed his fingers. "I shall be a very tyrant, I promise you."

He laughed and released her fingers, preparing to rise. But his wife reared up and threw herself into his arms, clutching him tight. Her voice came muffled and husky.

"You are my life, my darling lord. Never forget that."

Francis hugged her to him. "I will return safely to you, my dearest love."

A moment longer he remained thus. But there was no time to soothe the stifled tears he knew she was shedding.

"I must go, sweetheart."

He murmured the words into her ear and she at once drew away and nodded. Her attempt at a smile twisted his heart.

"Yes, go."

Francis had to will himself to leave her. He did not dare look back. When Ottilia reversed anxiety on him, it was ever a wrench to be away from her, even for a brief time. In general so engaged, she was the one who made him fearful for her safety. Yet it troubled him more to know she fretted for his. The thought of how his darling wife would cope without him was anathema. He was her shield and he knew it too well.

It was something of a relief to discover his nephew in buoyant mood, ready with a quip and a smile.

"I am armed, sir, with both dagger and pistol. These desperadoes will not get the better of me."

Francis grinned and clapped him on the back as he reached him. "I am relieved to hear it. Ryde will be armed too, and Williams is handy with his fists."

His groom and coachman were found outside the front door. Ryde touched a hand to his hat. "Looks like rain again, m'lord."

Francis snorted. "When doesn't it in this infernal place?"

"Aye, but I'm thinking these fishermen may have come in already. Word is they don't stay out if a storm is in the offing."

Francis regarded the sea as he led the way along the shingle in the northerly direction that led in due course to Thorpe, the fishermen in general landing their catch some way beyond the old town hall. The fishing community tended to live in the cottages out that way. The waves rolling into the beach were smooth enough, but further out there looked to be a trifle of motion. The greying skies held no hint of lowering clouds, however, and the wind, though chill, was not yet strong enough to suggest a coming storm.

"It might blow up later. My hope is that the boats are just coming in."

Once they had traversed some half a mile of beach, this was seen to be the case as Bastien, striding a little ahead, halted and turned, pointing out to sea.

"There, *mon oncle*! See them? Two boats, I think, heading this way."

Francis joined him, shading his eyes against the vista of greyish blue. "You've better sight than mine. I see nothing." Even as he spoke, he picked out two black specks rising and falling on the waves. "Ah, yes, I see them now. Capital. We are in time."

The boats took form as they approached, making no attempt to divert from their apparent intended course. A grunt from his groom brought Francis's head round.

"What's to do, Ryde?"

"I'm thinking they've no contraband aboard, m'lord. Unless they've not seen us yet."

Francis looked back at the boats, each with an outline of an oarsman now visible. "If we can see them, they can surely see us. We must stand out in this empty landscape."

"But it seems we are not alone, *mon oncle*."

Francis glanced to where Bastien was indicating. A figure was approaching along the shore from the north. He was at first a silhouette, but within a few moments Francis recognised the figure's form and stance.

"Radway? What the deuce is he doing here this early in the day?"

"You think it is the lieutenant from the custom house?"

"There is no mistaking the man."

Bastien's gaze searched his. "You do not want him, sir?"

"Not at this moment, no. He'll be very much in the way." He glanced again at the lieutenant and then trained his eyes on the approaching row-boats. Was Radway here in hopes of intercepting smuggled goods? Why then was he not accompanied? Assuming he found something, outnumbered thus he could not hope to make an arrest.

"It is not as if he was expecting us to be here," he said aloud.

"What do you mean?"

Francis cursed. "I'm not sure if we are interfering with his purpose or he with ours."

"He is also here to meet these fishermen?"

"Looks like it."

His muttered response was immediately succeeded by a hail from Radway, who threw up a hand. "Well met, Lord Francis! I thought it was you."

With reluctance, Francis returned the salute. The boats were still coming in. Safe to assume their cargo was just fish. Not that he had expected to find anything else.

The lieutenant gave voice again when he was within a few feet of the party. "Quite a reception committee you have gathered, sir. Do I take it you mean to quiz Wark and Deanraw?"

Francis concealed an inward sigh. "I had that intention. You know them both?"

"Those two rogues? Been trying to catch them at it for many a year. Slippery as the fish they carry. I've had them empty the baskets of their catch several times. To no avail, I fear."

He sounded quite cheerful about these failures, causing Francis a measure of disquiet. "Are you certain they are in the trade?"

"Without doubt. Haven't yet been able to discover where they land the stuff, but it keeps them on their toes if I pounce now and then."

Was this spurious? Francis could think of better methods to hunt down smugglers. He did not pursue it, turning his attention to the ongoing activity at the water's edge.

The two boats were scraping shingle now and both Ryde and Williams had gone down to help with beaching them. It had been part of the plan, in hopes of ensuring neither man had an opportunity to decamp before Francis could question them. The groom and coachman could pave the way with assurances that he merely sought information concerning the murder victim. No suspicion of their possible involvement was to be implied.

Radway's presence rendered the scheme abortive. Unless he could be got rid of? He spoke again before Francis could think how to achieve his departure.

161

"Had you in mind that these fellows might know something of this murder? I know for a fact they don't possess muskets, if that helps."

"I doubt they were directly involved. But if Green was engaged in the smuggling trade, these fishermen may have known him."

Radway made a deprecating face. "The more I think of it, the less I believe the matter is in any way connected with the trade."

Francis eyed him. "Why so?"

The lieutenant seemed to be squinting out to sea. Or was he watching the beaching manoeuvres? "Don't you think I'd have known it?" His gaze veered back to Francis, an odd light in his eyes. "Think I've acquainted myself with pretty much all these fellows over my time in Aldborough. Green was never involved in my book."

Francis refrained from the obvious query as to why, if he knew them all, Radway had not yet apprehended these members of the smuggling fraternity. "You think my wife is wide of the mark?"

Radway threw up a hand. "Far be it from me to tamper with the notions of an expert."

To his satisfaction, as Francis struggled to keep his rising bristles under control, Bastien took up the cudgels.

"You scoff, sir, but Lady Fan has indeed uniform success in these affairs. She does not fail."

This time, Radway threw up both hands in a gesture of surrender. "Did I suggest otherwise? My dear fellow, I merely bow to a superior mind —☐ suiting the action to the word in what Francis deemed an ironic manner — "and hope I may yet have the privilege of observing her methods." He wafted a hand towards the knot of men approaching from the shore. "I will leave you to your catechism, my lord."

Francis, suffering a diminution in his previous liking for the man, watched the lieutenant stride away towards the town. "Insufferable!"

"Take no heed, *mon oncle*. He speaks like these proud Englishmen who think too little of women." Bastien gave a wicked grin. "We should perhaps ask *Grand-mère* to shake his ears."

Francis had to laugh. "She would undoubtedly give him short shrift."

"M'lord?"

He turned to find his groom at his elbow. "Ah, Ryde. Any luck?"

"Seems the wives and Wark's sons will be here anon to sell the catch off the boat. Wark and Deanraw will repair to that hostelry up behind the old town hall to break their fast before they sleep."

"Then we'd best accompany them. Nothing in the boats?"

"Not visible, m'lord. But Deanraw took note of the customs chief being abroad and didn't bat an eyelid. Seems as there's no illegal goods this day."

"Did you tell them I want to question them?"

"Aye, m'lord. Both heard of the murder, they say, but neither appears to know the dead man."

Was it futile to proceed with questioning? Would it profit him more to head for the blacksmith's forge?

"Will you speak with them, *mon oncle*?"

Francis made up his mind. "We'll accompany them to this breakfast. A man talks better on a full stomach."

163

Not averse to partaking of the mounds of sizzling bacon piled onto platters and set upon the rough wooden table along with jugs of ale and fresh loaves ripped into by eager fingers, Bastien watched with interest as his uncle dropped into what looked like easy camaraderie with the fishermen.

His father the marquis, for all his bonhomie, was never thus casual with his subordinates. Was it the past soldiering life that gave Lord Francis this manner? Feigned or real, Bastien could not judge. Or had he learned from his wife who, by all accounts, was readily able to converse with any and all persons regardless of their status?

The whole party had invaded the Mill Inn, a timber-framed establishment with leaded windows overlooking the sea on one side, huge ceiling beams and a massive hearth to one end of the main chamber. Lord Francis had requested the astonished landlord to serve its members at his expense. Then he had sat down in the middle of the bench to one side of the long deal table, bidding the fishermen to join him. He signalled Bastien to sit opposite and both groom and coachmen to take their places a little apart but within earshot, one on each side of the table. The two targets were thus cunningly separated, Wark flanking Bastien and Deanraw beside Francis, with reinforcements close enough to foil any attempt at escape.

Bastien could not but admire these masterly tactics. If the fishermen were wary at first, their host's generosity and genial manner soon engendered relaxation. Not until the two men had downed pints of ale and wolfed a fair portion of the food on offer did Lord Francis bring up the subject of his investigation. The first foray astonished Bastien.

"I hope you won't object if I ask a few questions concerning the recent killing?"

Both fishermen paused in eating, exchanging a glance. Then Deanraw turned to Francis. "Nowt to do with us is that, yer honour."

"Sadly, however, it has to do with my nephew here. Carlton Green was his friend. I have promised him I will do all I can to discover just what happened."

Recognising his cue, Bastien dropped his gaze to his empty plate. "I am grateful, sir. The event has saddened me greatly. How could it happen to my friend?"

Francis took back the ball. "How, indeed?" His gaze fixed on Wark. "Do you know anything of the caves round about?"

The change appeared to flummox Wark, a wiry man of middle years with a sharp-featured countenance. "Caves, yer honour?"

"Green was found in a cave."

Deanraw, of heftier build than his colleague with broad shoulders and a wide jaw, cleared his throat. "There ain't no shortage of caves round these parts. Might've chose any to park a corpse."

Bastien jumped on this. "Do you know the one in which my friend was found?"

Wark took this. "Don't we all know it? Can't take a boat out in these parts without getting to know all the ins and outs."

"When the weather's bad, see?" Deanraw added his mite — with too much eagerness, perhaps? "You have to know where to put in. A small boat can be washed away nigh anywhere along this coast. If it's bad, nowt for it but to shelter."

"In a cave?" Thus Lord Francis.

"Quickest and easiest on a stormy day."

Wark cut in. "'Specially as you've a boat to save. Dragging it up shingle's better than having it dashed to pieces on the rocks."

"What about your catch?" asked Lord Francis, with what Bastien suspected was deceptive interest. "Can you save that too?"

"Have to," said Deanraw. "Ain't nobody going to compensate you if you fail to deliver the goods."

With difficulty, Bastien held back a startled response. Goods, not fish? Or was it a mere figure of speech? His uncle gave no sign of similar surprise.

"No, indeed. Your livelihood depends on your proving reliable, I would guess."

"Mouths to feed, yer honour."

"If we ain't doing our part, likely we'd end as yon friend of his did." Wark jerked his head at Bastien as he spoke.

For a brief moment, Bastien met his uncle's eye and read there a warning. He gave an infinitesimal nod. He was not fool enough to inject a word at this juncture, despite the thump in his chest at the realisation that these two were undoubtedly involved in the smuggling trade. To whom did they report? Someone who could serve them as Carlton had been served, according to Wark. How to proceed? He was thankful it was not his decision to make as Lord Francis picked it up.

"This is just what I was wondering. Could it be that Green was punished for not doing his part?"

At once the wariness returned. Deanraw eyed Francis. "What part would that be, yer honour?"

"Precisely what I would like to know. He must have had employment of some kind."

Wark gave a snort. "What, a gennelman born?"

Lord Francis's lip quirked. "Even gentlemen have duties to perform. Estates do not run themselves."

Deanraw gave a few nods. "Never thought of it like that, yer honour. S'pose every man has his duty."

"Not him." Wark slapped the table. "Not Green. He weren't nowise in it, far as I heard."

In what? The trade? Excitement mounting, Bastien was hard put to it not to glance at his uncle again. Wark had slurred his words slightly. Was he a trifle above par with too much ale? Or tiring from his night's fishing?

Deanraw was staring at his colleague, his gaze hard, though he said nothing. Was he hoping to frown him down?

Unhurried, Lord Francis was sipping from his tankard. He set the vessel down. "I must thank you for your company, my good sirs. If you hear of anything concerning this affair, pray seek out my fellow Ryde there. He's to be found at the coach yard." He gestured to the groom, who touched a hand to his forehead in agreement.

He rose and Bastien followed suit, conscious of disappointment. Why did his uncle not pursue it? At the first opportunity, once the party was clear of the Mill, he did not hesitate to put the question.

"It would be useless. Wark's tongue was loosened, but Deanraw had grown circumspect again. I think we have all we are going to get from them."

"You believe they know nothing more?"

Lord Francis set a hand to his shoulder as they walked the short distance back towards the lodging house on Crag Lane, which was fortuitously close. "If your friend Green was not engaged in the smuggling trade, as it would appear from what Wark let fall —□

"Also Lieutenant Radway said so, no?"

"He did, but I'm more inclined to take Wark's indiscretion at face value."

"Then, if it is so?"

"I think we can take it that neither Deanraw nor Wark was involved in the killing."

"But do you not think they know something? Wark said they might share such a fate if they did not carry out their part."

"Yes, that was telling. But only to confirm both fishermen are occasional smugglers."

"Radway was correct in this."

Lord Francis halted and Bastien received an enigmatic look. "Yes, I am becoming a trifle dissatisfied with Lieutenant Radway. I wonder if he is quite the man I thought him?"

Cecily Green appeared to have regained what Ottilia guessed to be her customary composure. Having bidden Ottilia to the chair by the fire, she had sat down on the little sofa next to her preceptress, folding her hands in her lap. Subdued she might be, but she proved better able to converse without falling into melancholy.

"Carlton's funeral is arranged for tomorrow afternoon. Reverend Stewkley has been most kind in hurrying the procedures since the doctor released my brother's remains. I could not bear to leave my dearest Carlton any longer before he is laid to rest. I hope you will attend the service, my lady?"

Ottilia reassured the young woman on this point. "I do not imagine you intend to hold a wake?"

Miss Ospringe took this, her tone deprecating. "It would be too much to expect of poor Cecily with matters in such question still." She glanced at Bastien, whose services Ottilia had commandeered for this further expedition once she had ascertained that the earlier one had been undertaken with no harm, in particular greeting her beloved spouse with heartfelt relief.

"I dare say you, Monsieur Guizot," Miss Ospringe continued, "may join his other friends. Monsieur du Guet spoke of raising a glass in Carlton's memory."

Bastien, looking altogether too large for the small parlour, gave a small bow of acquiescence. "It will be my honour, ma'am."

Ottilia returned to the purpose of her visit. "I brought my nephew in case we may come across a document in French. Will you allow us to make a thorough search through your brother's papers?"

Cecily's brows drew together. "I have spent a little time here and there, when I could seize a moment, to search on my own account."

"Did you find anything?"

A little sigh came. "Nothing that appeared to me to be of value. Do you seek a clue of some kind? What could there possibly be?"

Ottilia was loath at this juncture to mention the existence of Pretty's treasure box and its interesting contents. She prevaricated. "You did find a document in French before."

Cecily's dissatisfaction was plain. "A while back. Moreover, I suspect Carlton disposed of it."

"You have not, I gather, found any other in that language?"

"None."

She did not appear to care for the notion of a search being made. Did she fear the discovery of an incriminating piece of evidence? A wary tread was indicated.

"Forgive me, Cecily, if I cannot at this moment reassure you as to Carlton's activities." She took due note of the little shiver Cecily gave and leaned forward a little. "To discover the truth will relieve you of anxiety, do you not think?"

The young woman released another heartfelt sigh and Miss Ospringe reached to take her hand, holding it in a comforting clasp.

"Cecily, my love, you know Lady Francis is right. You have said as much yourself."

Cecily did not respond immediately, but a quick glance thrown at Bastien drew him into the fray. "Miss Green, if my presence is a trouble to you, I will go. My aunt may show me later anything she needs me to translate."

This would not do for Ottilia. "By no means, Bastien. I desire you will remain." She received a flash from Cecily's eyes and smiled at the girl. "My dear child, pray do not look daggers at me."

"Indeed, Cecily, it is not becoming." Thus Miss Ospringe in a voice typical of a sometime governess. "Lady Francis is trying to help you."

"I know that, Ivy." And to Ottilia, her tone begrudging, "I beg your pardon, ma'am."

"There is no need. Come, child. I cannot undertake to sift through everything on my own. Bastien's assistance will halve the time."

"But I can —

"No, my dear. Let us do the thing on your behalf. You will find it trying to have memories revived. I promise you we will handle Carlton's effects with the greatest respect and care."

She hoped she had left Cecily with not a word to say, but she reckoned without her host.

"I am not as poor a creature as you suppose, ma'am. I can quite well —

Ottilia cut in without ceremony. "Now, what can I have possibly said to make you believe I think so little of you? It is natural to wish to partake of anything concerning your beloved brother, and you have shown great courage throughout."

"Then, if you believe so — □

"I am on a hunt, Cecily. I mean to find out who is responsible in this dreadful affair and bring them to justice. That is my mission and it is urgent. I beg you will grant me the opportunity to do what I need to do here without let or hindrance."

That silenced the girl at last. Ivy Ospringe offered herself as escort to Carlton's chamber. As she led the way upstairs, she spoke confidingly to Ottilia.

"She has indeed shown great courage, poor Cecily. I trust you will make allowances, Lady Francis. The manner of Carlton's death has severely overset her, little though she shows her hurt."

Aware of Bastien at her back, Ottilia chose her words with care. "None could be surprised, ma'am. It has upset all his friends too. One can only imagine how difficult it has been for Cecily."

She was relieved when the companion, having shown them the room at the back of the house, withdrew. Ottilia gave her nephew a conspiratorial smile.

"Now we may make some headway. Do you take that chest first and I will attack the bureau."

Bastien moved to the end of the bed where a long chest was set. "What is it I must watch for, *Tante*? Apart from some document in French."

Ottilia, who was already seating herself at the small desk set before the window, looked round. "For one, anything that may prove this apparent interest in fossils."

Her nephew spoke as he lifted the lid of the chest. "You think it was a blind?"

"That we may discover when we see just how much engagement Carlton had in this so-called hobby. Other than that, keep in mind the contents of that letter we have. You are familiar with émigré stories, but keep an open mind."

"Smuggling then?"

"Unlikely, but possible. A methodical approach will serve us best."

So saying, she opened the first drawer of the bureau and eyed the contents. Disarranged papers and a jumble of pencils, wafers, sealing wax, candle stubs and tangled tape. "Ah. Cecily has been in here, I imagine."

"Not here, I think. It seems to be just clothing. Coats, a hat, gloves, a whip. It is all I can see."

Ottilia glanced across. "Take everything out, Bastien, and don't neglect to search every pocket and look inside the gloves. Oh, and try within the fold inside the hatbands too."

Returning to her task, she began a systematic search, sorting writing implements aside and setting the papers down on the leather blotter before her.

For some little while, she worked through the documents in silent concentration, half aware of motion and a growing pile on the floor as Bastien followed her instructions.

Sifting through paper after paper, for the most part she found tradesmen's accounts interspersed with a few letters. A cursory look over the bills gave her to understand that Carlton Green appeared to have had modest needs, although one or two were odd. Tea, candles and calico, yes. Even ball and powder if he owned a gun. But book binding? Oilcloth? The latter was particularly puzzling. What might oilcloth be used for? No mention of a sketchbook, unless the binding was for that. She supposed also a gentleman might get through more leather gloves than usual if he was pottering about on rocks.

She paused in her work, looking around at Bastien where he knelt beside the chest.

"Have you found any gloves?"

"Several pairs, *Tante*." The young man glanced over his shoulder. "They are worn, even split in places, like this one."

Ottilia swivelled in her chair, staring at the glove Bastien had picked up from a pile. "What is it like on the inside?"

Bastien pushed half a hand inside the glove. "Rough. The leather is hard. Also it is badly stained."

"Salt stains, perhaps?"

Bastien put the glove to his nose and sniffed. Then he touched the tip of his tongue to an edge and grimaced. "Yes, I think so. Do you suppose it has been in seawater?"

Ottilia's mind was working and she spoke in an absent fashion. "Submerged? Did he seek fossils below the waves?" She became aware of her nephew's gaze fixed on her. "What is it, Bastien? Have you a notion in your head?"

He let out a wry laugh. "I am sifting the notions of Lady Fan. One does not look for fossils under water, yes? Then whence the salt?"

"The very question I wish I might answer. Keep it to one side, Bastien."

Shifting back to face the bureau, she resumed her hunt through the stack of papers. A couple of letters in English from Carlton's bankers proved of no interest, except to suggest that he was possessed of a more substantial income than might have been supposed. She might discover from Cecily later just how matters stood.

Setting the contents back into the top drawer, Ottilia began upon the second, removing first a stack of unmarked paper. Beneath it, she spied a pocket book. Lifting it out, she opened it and flipped through the pages, scanning contents that proved disappointing. She had been ready to swear the fossil-hunting was a cover for a more sinister activity. However, the notations appeared to indicate otherwise. Under listed dates were details of fossils found and in which place, together with small, sketchy drawings. Were these coils and squiggles meant to show the shape of a fossil? Were there other, more elaborate drawings somewhere? One thing was plain. Carlton had indeed spread his search wide, taking in many points along a lengthy stretch of the east coast either side of Aldborough.

She had just turned her attention to the third drawer and found it locked when a stifled exclamation emanated from her nephew. Ottilia shifted about to look and discovered Bastien more or less transfixed, holding in one hand a small but serviceable pistol.

"Gracious me, where was that hiding?"

He glanced across. "It was caught underneath this greatcoat." He dropped the coat he had been holding, gingerly turning the pistol in his fingers.

"It is not loaded, I hope?"

"I think it cannot be." Bastien peered down the short barrel. "Powder residue may be in there, but it is safe enough."

Ottilia got up and came across, avoiding the pile of garments Bastien had unearthed from the chest. She did not take the pistol, instead examining it as her nephew turned it this way and that, with a recollection of the bill for ball and powder.

"Now why did Carlton neglect to arm himself when he met his murderer in that cave?"

"You think he went there on purpose?"

"Well, he was certainly killed there. Considering the manner of his death, it is idle to suppose he went in to look for fossils and was surprised. He certainly knew his killer. Therefore, he must have arranged a rendezvous."

Bastien hefted the pistol. "Even had he taken this, it would not serve against a musket."

"True. I think we must assume he trusted the man, even if he went there to settle a dispute of some kind."

"Dispute?"

Ottilia dropped to her haunches, setting a hand to Bastien's pile and moving items to check what was there. "You have thoroughly checked all these?"

"Indeed, but what did you mean about a dispute?"

Ottilia was feeling along the length of the coat Bastien had left half fallen into the chest. "Some matter of import took Carlton there. Had he suspected he might be attacked, he would not have gone. Or at least, he would have taken his pistol."

Bastien was watching the systematic movement of her hands across the coat. "What are you doing, *Tante*?"

"On a coat like this, it has just occurred to me that a good hiding place could be found behind the lining. Check the others, if you please. Feel for a lump or listen for a crackle."

Surprising her, Bastien broke into laughter. "I begin to understand why my uncle calls you a witch. How is it you think of such things?"

Ottilia smiled at him. "Logic, my dear boy, that is all." She left off feeling the coat and rose. "I will leave that for you to finish. I must find a key for that drawer."

Bastien looked round at the bureau as she moved towards it. "It is locked?"

"The last one, yes. I hope I may find a key in these compartments."

She had ignored the set of little drawers that surrounded the writing space, supposing that Cecily must have checked them and found nothing of interest. The need to locate a key, however, sent her fingers tugging at the little handles and peering within.

The first searches yielded the sort of odds and ends that must accumulate over prolonged use: Carlton's seal, wax ends, wafers, bits of loose string, a broken shirt stud, a couple of buttons and, as might be expected, a flask for gunpowder. In a corner drawer, Ottilia was intrigued to discover a little silver box. Had Carlton been a snuff taker? She took it out and flicked it open. A faint odour of tobacco wafted to her nostrils and there was indeed a brown residue within, silver gleaming beneath it. About to close the box again, Ottilia hesitated.

The silver of the box, was it? It could not have been a key, could it? She held it closer and poked a finger into the cavity, wiping at the stains. The gleam intensified, and Ottilia wet a fingertip with her tongue and touched it. Something adhered. Absently, eyes on her find, she set the box down on the blotter. With care, she eased the tiny item into her palm, caressing it to clean off the remains of snuff.

"Now, why in the world would Carlton keep diamonds in a snuffbox?"

CHAPTER ELEVEN

Ottilia found her nephew at her elbow, peering down into her palm. He looked astonished, as well he might.

"It is just like one of Pretty's sparkles, do you not think?"

Bastien let out an audible breath. "I cannot think, *Tante*. What does it mean?"

"A good question." She bent to the still open box and brushed the diamond into it. "Key! I must find the key to that drawer."

"But you do not explain. Do you think it has to do with that treasure box of Pretty's?"

Ottilia shut the snuffbox and replaced it in the little drawer. "Oh, there is undoubtedly a connection. I suspect the gloves may also play a part. But that locked drawer must be opened."

Bastien stepped away. "Which?"

"The bottom one."

"Shall I break it?"

Ottilia paused. "Can you?"

Bastien had dropped to his haunches and was pulling in a futile fashion at the locked drawer. "I will need a tool."

"Well, let me first establish that there is no key." He rose and Ottilia glanced at the chest with the pile of clothing beside it. "Have you gone through everything?"

"Even the boots."

"You checked the linings of the coats?"

"All. I did not feel anything there. Shall I put it all back?"

Ottilia looked at the pile. "No, leave it for the moment. Carlton appears to have been more circumspect than I thought."

Her nephew's frowning gaze met hers. "What is it you are thinking? Do you believe he did some wrong?"

Ottilia smiled and patted his arm. "I don't yet know, my dear boy. Pray don't jump to conclusions."

"It is just that I worry for Miss Green. If her brother…"

"We will allow Cecily to cross that bridge when and if it becomes necessary. Carlton is the victim, remember? Whatever he may have done, he has paid a heavy price."

She saw that Bastien was less than satisfied. Better to keep him occupied. A glance about the room provided an answer. "The press, Bastien. It will no doubt be mainly his clothes, but do the same as you did with the chest. Take care not to disarrange everything too much."

He glanced at the small press set against the inner wall but made no immediate move, eyeing her with a gleam Ottilia read as ironic.

"Is it that you mean to make me too busy to think, *Tante*?"

Ottilia laughed. "Caught! But do think as you work. Remember what we are looking for."

He gave her a wry smile as he moved across to the press. "I wish I knew what it is we look for."

"Anything odd or out of the ordinary. Like the gloves." She turned back to the desk and once again took up her task of hunting for the key. "Just do not expect to come upon another hoard of diamonds."

She found the key at last, but not from a fruitless search through the drawers. It was tucked under them in a recess in the back of the bureau which she had entirely missed.

Ottilia clicked her tongue. "I might have looked there at the outset." She sat down at the desk and leaned to see if the key would fit into the lock.

"But then you would not have found the diamond."

"Just so." The key slid into place and a click rewarded her. "Eureka!"

"It works?" Bastien was working his way with care through the press and had just started on the second drawer within. "*Bien.* I am spared from breaking it."

Ottilia did not reply, engaged in pulling open the drawer. "Aha. We have papers in abundance here. Drawings too. It seems fossils were indeed his hobby."

She took out a stash of worn parchments, nearly all decorated with pencil drawings, quite well done, of fossils. Ottilia wasted little time on them, returning her hand to the drawer to extract the rest of the pile. As she lifted it out, she found the parchments had been concealing a leather binder, tied in four places with thick red tape. A flurry attacked her pulses. Was this more promising?

She set aside the parchments and lifted out the binder. It was of that type to contain blank pages, used in general for the purpose of making notes or writing a journal.

"This may be something at last." She took hold of one of the knots in the tape, intending to untie it.

"What have you found?" Bastien was back, looking over her shoulder.

Ottilia paused, looking up at him with a lift of mischief in her bosom. "If I do not miss my guess, we may find Carlton's secrets in here."

"How can you tell?"

"For one, it was locked up." She resumed her task of untying the tape. "For another, this is just the receptable for personal thoughts, or necessary notes, that you do not wish anyone else to see." Her fingers ceased moving. "It appears your friend was particularly anxious for the contents to remain hidden. These knots are recalcitrant."

Bastien leaned over the desk. "Let me try."

Ottilia shifted in her chair to make room for him, watching as he wrestled with the tie. His fingers were too large to be deft, but superior strength won and the first knot came undone.

"Excellent, my dear boy."

"You may say so when I have managed all." Battling the next, he spoke in a near growl. "I do not believe he was so much my friend, this miscreant."

"We don't yet know he was a miscreant, remember."

Bastien paused, throwing her a scowl. "You do know, *Tante*. You are only trying to find proof."

Ottilia tried to stifle a giggle and failed. "Dear me. Have I underestimated your intellectual powers?"

"I hope it indeed." He was back at his task of unravelling the last knot. "My father tells me that his brother — my uncle — thinks he is a fool. Also *Grand-mère*. But to me it seems it is Lady Fan who thinks this."

A wave of consciousness swept through Ottilia. It could not be gainsaid that the understanding of her brother-in-law the marquis had been productive of both ridicule and distress in those quarters. She knew not what to say and was thankful to be spared from answering when Bastien abruptly rapped his knuckles to the binder and straightened.

"I cannot undo that last one. We should cut it."

"Let us not do that unless we have to. It may be evidence at a later date." She drew the binder closer and worked gently at the knot with her nails. "Ah, it is coming adrift." One point of the tape had yielded to her efforts. Within a few moments, she was able to pull the tape free. "Now, let us see."

With a rise of anticipation in her breast, she opened the binder and flipped through the filled pages.

Bastien was once more peering over her shoulder. "There is much writing. Is it a journal?"

Ottilia was glancing through random pages, reading a sentence here and there. "It looks to be more like information. *Crossing within two weeks.* And here: *Shipment expected next month.* There are several entries of the like."

"Smuggling then, as you thought?"

"It may be quite innocent."

"But you do not believe this."

She glanced up with a smile. "Just so. The question is, what was expected in these crossings and shipments?"

"Cognac? Lace? Tea?" Bastien sounded eager now. "We know such things are brought from France."

Ottilia was still turning pages, catching sequences of words here and there. "But we have the gloves to consider. Also the diamond."

She heard a sharp intake of breath. "I had forgotten it. But the gloves I do not understand."

A word in French caught Ottilia's eye and she flattened the page she had been about to turn. "*Madame la Duchesse d'Autin… Three cousins… Thorpe.* Was he smuggling people? Émigrés?"

"Of what are you talking, *Tante?*"

She pointed. "Look here. See the name, plus the cousins and a place on the coast here." She sat back as he leaned to read, her mind juggling ideas. One thing stood out and she gave it voice. "This is clever. He has sandwiched the information in between other writing. Innocuous writings for the most part."

Bastien read aloud. "*Fine weather for sailing.* Here is a date! This is for last year. Is there perhaps something more recent?"

Ottilia dragged her jumping thoughts back and saw that Bastien was riffling through the pages. He stopped, flipped them open and struck a finger to a half-empty page. "Here it ends. This must be the last he wrote."

At once, Ottilia's mind snapped in and she bent to the open binder again, checking the final lines: *Gone too far. Danger too great. Must put a stop to it. Will tell him I can no longer condone or participate.*

Bastien had evidently also read the words. "Then he was involved in some kind of smuggling."

"I think that is evident now."

"But tell who?"

Ottilia did not hesitate. "His murderer."

His mind reeling with questions, Bastien went in search of his friend, Grégoire du Guet. His aunt's words, as he escorted her along Crag Lane and back to the lodging house, had set him in turmoil.

"Where was Carlton getting this information? How did he know when and where a party of French escapees would be arriving?"

Bastien had entered a protest. "We do not know they were escapees, *Tante*."

"What else, pray? A legitimate visitor would arrive through the normal channels with relevant papers. Not that any but diplomats are likely to be admitted in a time of war."

He was obliged to admit she had a point. The obvious answer was staring him in the face. He could not doubt that his aunt, as Lady Fan, had already thought of it. He gave it voice, not without a stirring of resentment.

"Do you tell me this so that I may tackle Grégoire?"

He received a mischievous look as she glanced up at him. "Did I not remark upon how quick-witted you are, my dear boy?"

He produced a smile, but his heart was heavy. "You think Carlton and Grégoire were working together?"

"It seems likely."

"Was this a matter to the good, perhaps?"

The hand tucked into the crook of his elbow for support tightened briefly. "I understand why you wish it to be so, but consider, Bastien. If that was the case, why the need for such excessive secrecy? This book —□ indicating with a nod the binder she was carrying — "conceals a form of code, besides being locked away."

She had wrested the book from Cecily's grasp after showing it to her, but without demonstrating what she had found. "This may well help us determine Carlton's movements, my dear Cecily. I trust you will allow me to take it away for a space?"

Bastien had seen in Cecily's features her reluctance to part with anything belonging to the brother she had lost. Lady Fan must have seen it too.

"I promise I will take the greatest care of it. I know how much you must value such a record in Carlton's own hand. A day or two will suffice."

Cecily had hesitated, only to be urged thereto by her companion.

"Do not put a bar in the way of Lady Francis finding out the truth, my love. I am persuaded Carlton would himself desire you to do all in your power to assist."

Bastien was by no means certain of this, but it had the desired effect and his aunt was permitted to remove the binder with all its potentially incriminating details.

"What more do you hope to find, *Tante*?"

"In this? Oh, I think there may be quite a history to be garnered here. Whether we can narrow down the precise nature of Carlton's dealings is another matter. Unless there is coding I have not yet fathomed."

Bastien left her at the door in a distinctly disturbed frame of mind. Feeling in need of fortifying, he trekked back along the lane, taking a shortcut into Crabbe Street and thence around the corner to finish up at Woulmer's coffee house, where he at once ran into the two English members of the coterie of friends.

Ince Mundell greeted him with an acclaim Bastien felt to be false. "Guizot! Speak of the devil, we were just wondering where you'd got to. I hear the funeral is set for tomorrow. In a bit of a hurry, aren't they?"

"Miss Green does not wish to wait. There is to be no wake, but Grégoire has said we may all raise a glass afterwards."

"Yes, yes, all very well, but has this bloodhound of an aunt of yours yet found out the murderer?" Bryan Rampton waved him to a chair. "Sit down, man, and tell us what's to do."

Bastien signed to a waiter and ordered coffee before seating himself in a chair across from the pair. "Where is Grégoire? Have you seen him lately?"

Mundell's customary sneer appeared. "Now don't seek to change the subject, old fellow. But since you ask, I haven't seen him for a day or so. Dare say he's off on one of his forays."

"Not he," said Rampton, on a scoffing note. "Bowed down with woe the last time we spoke. Probably keeping to his room in company with a bottle." He rapped the table. "Never mind du Guet. Can't you see we're agog?"

"You're in the thick of it, seemingly," said the other. "Has this famous Lady Fan done the trick?"

Bastien concealed an inward sigh. "Not yet. She has been gathering information."

"Such as?"

"How can I know, Mundell? If I did, would I betray Lady Fan's confidence?"

His coffee having arrived, Bastien made a business of sipping at the steaming brew, in hopes his companions' interest might cool. The hope proved misplaced.

"Look, old fellow," said Mundell, adopting a persuasive tone, "the whole town is blabbing with this business. Rampton here and myself have been bombarded, because we are known to have been Green's companions. It's natural we'd want to hear where things stand. Is there nothing you can tell us?"

Absolutely nothing, he might have said. He was certainly not going to reveal Pretty's fortuitous find of the so-called treasure box and what had been discovered in Carlton's chamber. He compromised.

"It is difficult. It was hoped the matter of the musket ball would lead somewhere, but too many own muskets in this town. Therefore, one cannot discover the murderer by that route."

Rampton threw up his eyes. "If you ask me, he won't be discovered by any route. I mean to say, it could have been anyone."

Bastien eyed him. "But not just anyone can have a reason."

"Well, don't look at me. I'd no reason to be doing away with Green. Dash it, he was a friend!"

Mundell waved him down as he half rose from his seat. "Take a damper, will you? Not that friendship precludes a fellow from taking another's life. Am I right, Guizot?"

The sudden turn caught Bastien off guard. "It is possible, yes."

Triumph lit in Mundell's eyes. "Ha! So that's why you're hunting for du Guet. Lady Fan suspects him, does she?"

Bastien backtracked in haste. "She does not yet suspect anyone. She still seeks information. When she has sifted all, and everything fits together, she will point the finger. That is the way she works."

At this moment, Grégoire du Guet walked into the coffee house. It struck Bastien at once that he was looking haggard. There were shadows about his eyes and a gauntness to his cheeks, as if he had lost flesh. The trappings of grief? Or was there some other cause, one more ominous?

He spoke in a dull monotone as he came up. "You are all here, my friends. Good. I need not exert myself to appear normal."

The two English companions exchanged glances, Mundell raising his brows at the other. Bastien watched Grégoire as he put up a finger to hail the waiter and jerked out a chair. He plonked down in a pose that conveniently afforded a good three-quarter view of his features.

The waiter having taken his order, Grégoire threw a glance across the three. "You have nothing to say to me?"

Bryan Rampton let out a laugh. "Thought you preferred to be left alone, old fellow."

Grégoire emitted a sigh. "I have been alone too long. It makes me crazy."

"Ha!" Rampton turned in triumph to the others. "Didn't I say he was likely nursing a bottle?"

"Several, by the look of him," Mundell agreed, in that mocking way of his.

Bastien ignored them both, striving to keep the envy out of his voice. "I supposed you had been comforting Cecily Green."

Grégoire shrugged. "I went at first to express my condolences. The last time I saw her, I had it in mind to ask for my snuffbox that Carlton borrowed, but the moment was not propitious since she spoke of the funeral arrangements."

Snuffbox? Was it the one Lady Fan found in the bureau? Why would he be thinking of a snuffbox at such a time? He was loath to ask, and Grégoire spoke again.

"I am sorry I could not do more for her, but it was not fitting to burden Cecily with my own struggles."

With grief? Or did that mean he had difficulties elsewhere? "Have you remained all the time in your lodging?"

"What would you, *mon ami*? I have not been fit for company."

"Not much fitter now, if you ask me," said Rampton. "Want us to leave you to Guizot's commiserations?"

Mundell gave a laugh. "No need, old fellow. They can chatter away in their heathen tongue."

Bastien would dearly have loved to do exactly that, but it would not be politic to advertise his purpose. "We may be heathen, but we are not discourteous, my friend."

Grégoire flicked him a glance. "Why do you accept this insult? I protest I am more English than French after all these years. More, are you not half-English, Bastien?"

"My heart is French. Or in that heritage." He seized inspiration. "It is a pity I cannot visit there. Nor even assist my unfortunate countrymen who have been forced to leave their own land."

He received a sudden sharp glance from Grégoire, but it was swiftly veiled with a smile. "Yet your mother does much, you told me."

"By befriending them? She helps to integrate them perhaps, yes. Her rank is useful there." He chose his words with care. "Now and then, if she can persuade my father, she provides a little pecuniary assistance. So many come with nothing. Even now, it is hard to bring valuables out of France."

"Poor devils." Thus Rampton. "Always felt sorry for them."

Mundell's mouth twisted. "They were lucky to escape with their lives. Isn't that right, du Guet?"

An unnecessary dig at Grégoire's history. But that aside, he was shifting the talk away from where Bastien needed it. He steered it back.

"At first, this is true. But the means to live then becomes paramount. One wonders if perhaps valuables may be smuggled here by the hand of an acquaintance?"

Grégoire set down the cup of coffee with which he had been supplied and blew out his cheeks. "I do not call that smuggling. It seems to me a sensible course to pursue."

Rampton cut in. "It makes more sense to hide them on your own person if you are escaping."

"If one had the opportunity. Picture this." Mundell counted off on his fingers as he made his points. "They're coming for you. You've no time to get away. What do you do? Grab some valuables. Pack them up. Write a note. Hand it to a trusted messenger — a friend or servant. Tell them to get it to England. Give it to some relative or other." He beamed around in a triumphant sort of way. "There you are. I agree with du Guet. It's not smuggling, it's common sense."

Bastien's mind was reeling. How was Ince Mundell so well-informed? Was Lady Fan looking in the wrong direction altogether? Was it he who was in a string with Carlton Green? What of the alleged human cargo?

Grégoire spoke before he could think how to voice any of his thoughts without giving away his suspicions.

"That time of escapes is long past, so I believe. The authorities have no more aristocrats to execute. Now they persecute their own — anyone who voices disagreement. A pitiful and parlous state my country has descended into."

Bitter words but spoken in that same dull monotone. Did he truly care? Bastien knew as much from his acquaintance and his regret was genuine. The halcyon days of his childhood in the French countryside could never be recaptured. He had made England his home perforce, but he still hankered for the France of his memory.

All that was by the by. He was on a mission and it appeared his target must change. Truth to tell, he was not averse to switching his suspicions from Grégoire, whom he liked, to Mundell, to whom he had not taken in the first place. Yet therein lay a dilemma. From what he had learned of his Aunt Ottilia, she would urge him to caution. He ought not to trust either until innocence was proven.

The decision was taken out of his hands. Mundell rose. "I'm away. The mood is too maudlin for my money." He turned to Rampton. "I'm for The Rooms. Care to join me for a game of piquet? I believe I owe you a fleecing?"

His fellow Englishman pushed back his chair, laughing. "Never resist a challenge. But don't be too cocksure. Cards are nearly always with me." He hesitated, looking from Grégoire to Bastien and back again. "Shall we rendezvous at the Cross Keys after the funeral then?"

It was agreed and with a word of farewell, the pair were gone. Bastien eyed his remaining friend, who was staring into the cup now cradled between his hands. Opportunity beckoned, but how to begin?

In the event, Grégoire opened the way, speaking in French. "Does your aunt progress?"

Was his look too intent? Bastien chose caution. "She gathers information still."

"Do you think she will discover why Carlton was killed?"

"It is said she never fails. Thus, I believe she will."

Grégoire drew an audible breath. "It was foolish of me to take umbrage and choose to escape." His gaze grew narrow. "She is inclined to think I am involved, yes?"

Bastien felt compelled to prevaricate. "Lady Fan says one does not accuse until one is certain."

"But one may suspect, no?" A sour grin pulled at his mouth. "Do not disturb yourself, Bastien. I must expect always to be suspect. I am of the enemy in this time of war."

"One might say as much of me, Grégoire."

The other shifted a little, as if in discomfort. "You have an advantage, my friend. In this country, to be the son of a marquis is no liability."

"The illegitimate son of a marquis. Half-French to boot. I am received, yes, but the *ton* regard me with a wary eye."

Grégoire's tone became dry. "But as to this affair, situated as you are vis-à-vis Lady Fan…"

"This is a stupidity, *mon ami*. I am a mere visitor to Aldborough. How should I be involved?"

Grégoire set down his empty cup and wafted a hand. "Pay me no heed. This business has overset me more than I realised." Again, his gaze grew keen as it met Bastien's. "What is it Carlton was about? Do you know?"

Bastien hesitated. Dare he hint? Too dangerous to reveal anything pertinent. He took too long.

"I perceive that you do know, but you may not tell, is that it? No doubt I must contain my heart in patience."

Bastien took a chance. "Have you never thought Carlton could be doing other than this hobby of fossils?"

Grégoire glanced away, and back again. "I have had that thought."

"What alerted you?"

He grimaced. "It is not specific. It is just that, on occasion, he was altogether distrait." He paused. "At times with our friends, he seemed not to follow what was said. It made me wonder what preoccupied him that he could not participate as he used to do."

Was this all a blind? Did Grégoire seek to indicate what Lady Fan suspected? Had he too suspected? Or did he already know? Bastien could not say he had observed such a change. Carlton had ever been the quiet type, overshadowed by his two English friends.

"Did you ask him? On such occasions, did you question aloud this strange mood?"

Grégoire met his gaze again. "You may be sure I did, fearing perhaps some mishap or difficulty. Carlton shrugged it off, at once assuming an air of bonhomie."

This tallied with the secrecy surrounding his activities. Then Grégoire all but floored him.

"I have a confession."

"Yes?" Bastien's heart missed a beat.

"I denied this, but when I saw Carlton's wounded arm, I did not for one instant believe his story of how he gashed it on a rock."

Sugnall, the blacksmith, proved to be a genial soul, ready enough to answer the questions Francis put to him.

"Aye, I'd heard something of it, my lord. Your fellow there — □ indicating Ryde, who had accompanied his master and was waiting by the entrance to the forge — "spoke of it when he brought in one of your lordship's horses from the coach yard next door."

Francis did not take this in a literal spirit. His groom was no blabbermouth. He made no doubt the blacksmith had introduced the subject. Ryde would have given nothing pertinent away.

"I take it you knew Green?"

"I didn't know him as such. He owned no horse, but he came in once or twice with an article in need of repair."

"What sort of article?"

The blacksmith fingered his chin as he set his memory to work. He was a brawny fellow, who wore his hair short about a broad countenance. He was clad in stout brogues, breeches and shirtsleeves, no doubt against the heat from the furnace, with a worn leather apron over all. It struck Francis that his speech was a good deal more refined than one might expect in one of his calling. Might his background yield anything of interest? Had not Bastien hinted at such?

Francis refrained from asking at this juncture, intent on hearing what Green had brought to Sugnall for repair.

"Ah, I recall it now, my lord. One at least. He'd a pistol which was throwing off a trifle. I made a slight adjustment. Not sure what it was the other time."

The pistol was already enough. Not that it was unusual for a gentleman to possess a firearm. Francis had several himself and was never without his pistol. In light of the man's odd death, however, it spoke to the apparent peculiarity of his activities.

Francis took the bull by the horns. "We believe Green may have had dealings with the smuggling trade." He watched the blacksmith as he spoke, but the man gave no sign other than an interrogatory lift of the eyebrows. Innocent, cunning or merely cautious? "Have you perhaps heard of him in this connection, Sugnall?"

The man's features relaxed into amusement. "You can't live around these parts without hearing snippets of those engaged in the trade. I could give you some names, but I dare say you've heard them already. Mr Green wasn't among them, as far as I know."

Time to bite hard. "As it happens, your name was mentioned."

At that, the blacksmith laughed outright. "I'll warrant it was. There's a fond belief I've a hidden cellar beneath this floor." He stamped on the hard surface beneath his feet. "Solid, my lord. You're welcome to test the whole for hollows, if you wish."

"No need." A pointless exercise. If there was such a hidey-hole, it would be elsewhere.

The forge, as was common, adjoined a larger building with stalls for horses awaiting shoeing, so Ryde had told Francis. Adjacent, he had reported, there was a storage area containing odds of farm equipment in need of repair, a carriage wheel and other such articles one might expect at the sole establishment of the kind catering to the inhabitants of the town. The blacksmith's house stood a little way off, in its own yard behind the forge. A secret store, if such there were, might be anywhere.

He changed tack. "Where did you learn your trade?"

A keen look entered the man's gaze. "Is that relevant, my lord?"

Francis opted for the candour his wife so often exhibited. It usually paid off. "You don't sound as if you came up through the generations. It would surprise me to learn that you ran around this forge as an infant."

Sugnall's eyes crinkled at the corners. "You've a shrewd head on your shoulders, my lord."

"Well?"

A shrug came. "I've no secrets. I began in the stables of a fine estate. I'd no head for figures, though my father was a clerk for his lordship. Luck was with me when I found I'd an aptitude for this type of work. His lordship put me to train with his man and I took over at the last."

Plausible. But how had he come to build his own business? "What brought you to Aldborough then?"

Sugnall's lips pursed. "I didn't care for his lordship's heir. When he took the reins, I chose to sell on. I'd my wife and little ones to think of by then. Heard of this place by chance and the owner wanting to retire. I closed with him as soon as I saw it. Not a bad environment, Aldborough."

Francis could have argued with this opinion, but he reserved his criticisms. Chance appeared to have played a considerable role in Sugnall's history. No misfortunes of any kind?

"It seems you were in luck all round. Why didn't you care for the heir?" He threw it in casually, watchful for the man's reaction.

The blacksmith again displayed a moue of distaste. "He'd none of the old lord's good traits. Young, he was. Lived high and paid little mind to his duties. Preferred carousing with his cronies, filling the house with women of a particular sort and … other people."

Abruptly alert, Francis seized this last. "Other people?"

"Refugees. From France. Mr Green's friend is all right. Du Guet. He talks casually to me, which I like, and he pays his way. Most of them ain't like that. High in the instep, just as if they weren't battening on the English gentry. They won't even try to earn an honest crust. I don't hold with that."

Francis adopted a mild tone. "Even though you know these individuals have come to our shores with nothing, only to escape certain death?"

Sugnall snorted. "That might have been so several years since. I grant you the early arrivals were genuine enough. Now, you've got nothing but riff-raff coming across, and all to take advantage. It makes my blood boil, my lord."

Evidently. "Well, there can't be many around these parts."

"Not now so much, but it used to be that it wasn't just contraband coming over in those boats of a night."

"Is that how du Guet entered the country?"

"He's been resident in England for years. No, he's legitimate. He works for what he has."

"Works at what?"

The blacksmith's face closed. "There you have me. I don't know what he does for his living, but Mr Green said he'd got a proper occupation. Takes him out of Aldborough now and then, that's all I know."

Yet Sugnall had heard it from Green, whom he professed hardly to recall. Moreover, his expression of bonhomie had turned bland at the question. Francis began to wonder if he had been spun a tale. How much was true? How much deliberate embroidery?

He put this to his groom as they left the smith's premises, heading for home.

"I'd not trust him too readily, m'lord. Too glib by half. Nor did I think much of all that bluster against these refugees."

"Why not?"

"Suppose he slipped up when he mentioned this heir bringing the French the place? He had to find a way to cloud the issue, m'lord."

This mirrored Francis's own doubts. "Playing devil's advocate for a moment, Ryde, it's a plausible story and his anti-émigré stance sounded real enough."

"Yes, if he ain't an accomplished play-actor, m'lord. Could go two ways."

True enough. Francis could only wonder if his darling wife had acquired any information that might shed light on the business.

CHAPTER TWELVE

By the dinner hour, in between giving her customary daily attention to the children and hearing such further information as had been gleaned, Ottilia had found time to study much of Carlton's revealing journal. She did not hesitate to relate what she had found to the family as they dined, despite the presence of Tyler and Joanie, who were serving.

Both were trustworthy. Both had been in the Fanshawes' service throughout most of her so-called adventures. Her personal maid was necessarily an intimate confidante and Ottilia could not doubt her devotion. Tyler often served Francis as valet in place of Diplock and was always willing to take on whatever task was needed. Neither would dream of tattling outside the environs of the family.

Ottilia accepted a small portion of the artichoke pie the footman was proffering. "Carlton made references over several years, as far as I can make out. All appear to refer to arrivals and most specify French names."

Sybilla, who was picking at a fillet of fried sole, directed a keen gaze at Ottilia. "Most? What of those that did not so specify?"

"That is what I find intriguing. I am not yet certain I have identified what I suspect to be a code of some kind."

Her husband, seated at the head of the table and, disdaining the fish, making his usual hearty meal from a plateful of beefsteaks, threw her a challenging glance. "I hope you mean to give us an example or two?"

"It will be simpler to show you. I could do with more minds set to unravel the puzzle."

"That is all very well, Lady Fan," cut in Henrietta, "but you have whetted my appetite to no purpose. Can you not recall an example?"

This demand was echoed around the table.

"Quite right for once, Henrietta. Don't be provoking, Ottilia."

"You did not show me when we were looking in Carlton's room, *Tante*."

"Where did you leave this wretched journal? Shall I fetch it?" Thus Francis. Rescuing her? Or was he as impatient as the rest?

Ottilia swallowed her mouthful and set down her fork. "No need, Fan. I do recall the gist. Carlton wrote down a series of letters and sometimes numbers more or less concealed within the text, just as the names were. Something like: *N to 3 of D* or *Em* or *Sa*. Several were noted as R. Once I saw *T to 1 of D mixed*."

For a moment or two there was silence, all four faces, to Ottilia's secret amusement, showing puzzlement. The dowager recovered first.

"Say them again."

As she resumed eating, Ottilia obligingly repeated the words, adding, "Though I cannot be sure I have relayed them exactly."

Henrietta, always a good trencherwoman, had disposed of both beefsteak and a substantial slice of artichoke pie with obvious gusto. She laid down her utensils and set her fingers to the table with an air of one ready to bestir herself. "We need to work out what each letter might be. *Sa* and *Em* must be easier, don't you agree, Lady Fan?"

"I have no notion. All I have so far fathomed is that the first letter is a general term with the number denoting how many."

"Aha! Then the other letters are specific?"

"Just so, Henrietta."

"What in the world could they be? N? What were the others again?"

Sybilla took this. "R and T."

"Your memory is better than mine, ma'am."

"*Grand-mère* has always had excellent recall."

The dowager ignored these interpolations. "Were these three all, Ottilia?"

"All that I have noticed, but I have not yet had a chance to read through the whole. Much of the material is nonsense, I suspect, made to seem like a journal but meant to hide the gems within."

Sybilla slapped her hands together. "Gems!"

"What the deuce are you talking of, Mama?"

Ottilia's mind leapt. "Gemstones. That is what you mean, is it not?"

Sybilla became eloquent. "It came to me in a flash. Those diamonds in the box my granddaughter found, remember? Did not you say you found one in a snuffbox too? It must be jewels, Ottilia. N for necklace?"

A fleeting warmth had swept through Ottilia's heart when the dowager had referred to Pretty as her granddaughter, but the solution to the riddle superseded it, teeming in her brain.

"Genius, Sybilla! Then do we take D for diamond?"

"That is just what gave me the clue. One need not look far for the others."

"*Sa?*" Henrietta chimed in with an expression of delight. "Sapphires?"

"Yes, and *Em* must be emeralds. Do you see, Ottilia?"

Francis was laughing. "You are all very ready with this interpretation — I must congratulate you, ma'am — but I should like to know why Carlton Green was tracking gemstones, if he was, which is by no means proven."

"Oh, but it must be so, Lord Francis. Only consider. R must mean rings. Although I cannot immediately place that T you spoke of."

"Tiara, Henrietta. They were rare." Ottilia spoke absently, her gaze concentrated on her spouse, who lifted an eyebrow quizzically.

"Do you tell me you have the answer to my question, my wife of devious mind?"

She had to laugh. "I wish I had. You gave me to think, merely."

Bastien, who had not taken part in the revelatory discussion, here surprised Ottilia and drew all eyes. "I think I have it, *mon oncle.*"

"Well? Spit it out, man."

Did her nephew sigh a little? An inkling hovered at the back of Ottilia's mind. What else but anxiety about Grégoire's involvement would cause him upset?

"All along we have looked for smuggling, sir. It seems my friend was doing a trade in these jewels. If one takes also the names in French that he wrote, what else but that he trades with refugees?"

"What, you mean he brought them in safely in exchange for these jewels?"

"That is what I fear. A despicable trade, to take advantage of these émigrés."

Francis echoed Ottilia's own thought. "Yes, but that won't quite fadge. If he was accepting jewels for payment, where are they? Why, moreover, assuming he sold them all, was Green not living high on the proceeds?" He looked down the table. "Tillie?"

She had taken a meditative sip of wine. "It is a fair point, Fan. How and to whom would he have sold them? Why were there none to be found? He cannot have disposed of so many thus easily."

"An accomplice." Henrietta was in again. "He must have had a go-between who — □ She broke off, her gaze flying to Bastien as a look of consternation broke over her countenance. "Oh … I did not mean to suggest…"

Ottilia watched a bitter smile twist her nephew's lips. It did not reach his eyes.

"Grégoire? It is a possibility I must face, no?"

"Forgive me, Bastien. I spoke unthinkingly."

He flicked a hand. "Do not concern yourself, Etta. I have come also to this conclusion."

"Prematurely," said Ottilia. "As yet, this is all speculation. One cannot make wild assumptions based merely upon your friend's nationality."

"But you have yourself spoken of Grégoire in this connection, *Tante*."

"Yes, because I must examine all possibilities." She lifted a finger. "We have first to sift just what Carlton was about. It is tempting to accept the notion of taking payment, but that strikes me as too simple an explanation for a matter demanding such an elaborate system of secrecy."

Once again, Ottilia found herself the cynosure of all eyes. Even, to her amusement, those of the two servants, both in the act of removing platters from before each diner.

"What, then?" Thus her spouse, one eyebrow flying in the way he used to quiz her. "If Carlton was not smuggling, what else could it be?"

She glanced about the other faces, Henrietta's eager, Bastien's apprehensive and Sybilla's delicate brows drawn together. The thought floating at the back of her mind took on coherence.

"You are all forgetting Pretty's treasure box."

"You believe it is connected?"

"I think it must be, Sybilla. That letter haunts me. I was expecting to find another when I came across Carlton's binder."

"But what are you thinking, Lady Fan?"

Ottilia drew a breath. "What if, under the pretence of assisting refugees, and without payment, he was defrauding them?"

Her announcement was not productive of the reception she might have expected.

"But you said he helped them to enter the country."

"How, pray, Ottilia? How defraud them?"

"Does this still involve Grégoire?"

"Be still, all of you." Thus Francis, in his authoritative voice. "She obviously hadn't finished."

Ottilia smiled her relief. "Thank you, Fan. I had not." She paused a moment to gather her thoughts. "It is not fully formed in my mind, but I do not think the French names necessarily indicate arrivals. At least, not of persons."

"I don't understand at all."

"Have patience, Etta."

"Quite so, Bastien. Give me leave to explain first."

"Very well, I am dumb."

"So I should hope." Thus Sybilla.

The companion closed her lips in an ostentatious fashion, although her eyes twinkled. Ottilia accorded this mischief an amused look before resuming.

"Let us suppose for a moment that Carlton was indeed meeting incoming boats wherever he pretended to hunt for fossils. Further, let us suppose he was somehow given notice of the arrival in said boats of articles of jewellery belonging to French individuals."

Henrietta jumped, throwing up a hand. "Sent from France to relatives! I see it now. Like the diamonds Pretty found."

"Just so. We may assume — and Bastien can confirm this, perhaps — that émigrés here, as well as those unfortunate enough not to escape, might do all they could to arrange for secreted gems to be sent across."

"Like the diamonds which were meant for the comtesse's daughter," said Sybilla.

"Do you mean Carlton was employed as a go-between, Tillie?"

"Either that, or he was connected to the go-between, who relied upon him to collect the packages containing these gemstones."

Bastien's eyes were eager. "Then my friend was no villain?"

"If not, why was he killed?" Thus Sybilla.

"To be slain does not make him a villain, *Grand-mère.*"

Ottilia intervened. "Neither point is certain."

The dowager tutted. "You said a moment ago that he was guilty of fraud."

"Because of the excessive caution. He cannot have taken possession of all the jewels."

"He'd have been discovered long before this if he had."

"Just so, Fan. Most of them must have found their way to their proper destination. I do wonder if temptation proved too great and Carlton began to appropriate a ring here, a brooch there. Perhaps he might prize out a small diamond or two. After all, there was nothing to prove the jewels would arrive intact. Pretty's sparkles were sent already separated from their moorings."

Bastien's look had grown intent. "You are thinking of the diamond you found in the snuffbox?"

"Why hide it in such an awkward place unless it was illicit?"

"*Tante*, I did not mean to speak of it, but that snuffbox may belong to Grégoire."

"Indeed? How so?" She listened as Bastien related what his friend had said. "Hm. It seems sinister, but I wonder if Grégoire would let fall such a point if there was anything in it? He is a sharp young man, I believe."

"He might have made a slip."

"True, but inconclusive." Ottilia gave a little sigh. "All I have outlined is not the full sum of the business."

Francis gave her a sharp look. "Why not? What else have you in your head?"

"The killing. If these surmises are correct, that must have been carried out by someone either involved — the accomplice you spoke of, Henrietta — or someone who had found Carlton out and took that means to punish him."

Her auditors were silent for a space. Ottilia did not blame them. The whole notion was preposterous. But she had not participated in so many investigations without recognising that the ways of murderers could be both devious and peculiar. Their logic was not always to be fathomed by the working of normal minds.

Francis came out of his reverie first. "There has to be an accomplice. At least someone who passed the relevant information to Green." He refilled his wine glass. "I'd suggest we ought to look both at du Guet — saving your sensibilities, Bastien — and the blacksmith. Sugnall certainly had access to Frenchmen, and his ranting hostility towards them might well be meant to cause a false scent."

Ottilia accorded consideration to this notion, half aware of the discussion continuing as Sybilla enquired further into Francis's talk with the blacksmith. Was not Grégoire du Guet too obvious a suspect? If he was the accomplice, he must have known his name would come up at first. Admittedly, he was recalcitrant upon being questioned. It was yet possible, if he was involved, that his participation was entirely innocent. He might well be the source whence Carlton learned of the expected advent of a hoard of jewellery. That did not necessarily mean he was party to the theft of these articles. Which indicated that the hunt might have veered off course. Ought she to mentally revisit the interviews she'd conducted? What of those her spouse and Bastien had carried out? She had not yet heard from Henrietta of her dealings with the riding officer.

She began running over names in her head and presently became aware of silence about her. She blinked out of her reverie to find her husband's gaze upon her.

"You were far away again, my dear one."

Ottilia made a negative gesture. "I was merely weighing things up in my mind."

"Let's have it then. I know you too well, Tillie. You've fathomed something, haven't you?"

She laughed. "Just that it may not profit us to look only at those who have connections with émigrés."

"Why, Lady Fan?"

"I am not yet sure, Henrietta. It does seem to me that whoever profited from this enterprise, if we have it right, would not advertise his association with or knowledge of French refugees."

Bastien leaped on this. "Then Grégoire cannot be the murderer."

"You go too fast, I fear." Francis glanced at him and back to Ottilia. "You have not eliminated him altogether at this juncture, I take it?"

"Oh, no. He may indeed have provided information. I am mulling over the notion that this so-called accomplice, assuming they did the deed, may be someone quite other."

"Someone whom we have overlooked altogether, perhaps?"

Ottilia pondered. "Unlikely, Fan. We have questioned several persons. One of them must know something more than they have revealed. Moreover, it may well be one who has legitimate reason to obtain such information."

The ladies left the two gentlemen of the party to partake of their after-dinner port, a practice Francis had initiated for his nephew's benefit. Ottilia was glad of the opportunity to catch up with what her mother-in-law and Henrietta might have found out.

Sybilla, seating herself in a chair by the fire in her usual regal fashion, waved a dismissive hand. "You will get little out of me, Ottilia. You bid me discover how much Reverend Stewkley knew of this Green fellow."

"Or merely how well-acquainted they were," Ottilia amended.

"It is the same thing. The dratted fellow was not communicative on the subject."

"But did he say anything at all?"

"Nothing to the purpose."

Ottilia preferred to judge for herself. She knew the dowager to be shrewd, but she was apt to overlook minutiae. "Any little snippet may be relevant, Sybilla."

A near snort came in response. "What I am saying is Stewkley gave nothing away. All he would do was bemoan the man's demise and shudder at the manner of it."

She was beginning to wonder if she might be obliged to beard the reverend herself when Henrietta, who had settled on the sofa, intervened.

"My dear Lady Polbrook, you are forgetting the curate."

"Hargrave? That fool who can barely tell one card from another? What has he to say to anything?"

"Do you not recall, ma'am? He spoke of Carlton Green." Henrietta's gaze met Ottilia's. "Mr Hargrave echoed the reverend's words, but he added that Reverend Stewkley must feel it more than others since Mr Green had been a frequent visitor at the rectory."

Ottilia jumped on this. "Did you notice if Reverend Stewkley reacted in any way?"

"He did," said Sybilla, on a note of surprise. "It had not struck me before, but Henrietta is quite right for once. Stewkley immediately insisted we drop the subject and concentrate upon the game. Pah! Now I see it — he must have wished to silence Hargrave. I shall have to question the wretch all over again."

Ottilia put up a finger. "Let us be cautious, Sybilla. Such visits may have been innocent."

"Or they may implicate him in this farrago of gemstone thefts. We cannot leave it, Ottilia."

"I do not suggest that. As yet, this is all conjecture. It may be that I can glean more detail from Cecily Green as to why her brother visited the rectory. If he did so often, she is bound to know."

The dowager looked altogether dissatisfied. "What of Hargrave? He might know why Green went there. I may readily question him, for he is forever offering his escort when Henrietta has been late."

Here, her companion entered a protest. "Once only I was late, ma'am, and that merely because I had been pumping Mr Yelford on Lady Fan's behalf."

"So you claim." Sybilla waved this aside. "But let that pass. It remains that this Hargrave jumps up and proffers an arm every time I speak of stopping play. He has even suggested a turn around the card room for exercise. Faugh!"

Ottilia bubbled with mirth. "I had no notion you had acquired an admirer, Sybilla. Fan will be delighted."

"Don't dare mention the matter to my son. I had quite enough of his teasing about the general down in Weymouth. Besides, it is ridiculous to suggest such a thing. I might be the man's mother. I wish you will stop smirking, the pair of you!"

Ottilia hastily begged her pardon, frowning down Henrietta, who had given way to unseemly merriment. "Yet it is an excellent notion to find out what he may know of Carlton's relationship with the reverend, if you do not mind pandering to the curate's *tendre*."

"He does not have a *tendre* — don't be ridiculous. If anything, it is mere courtesy."

"If you wish to know what I think, Lady Polbrook —□
"I don't!"

"— it is that Mr Hargrave is impressed with your ability at whist and your wit, which you cannot deny you exercise at his expense."

"Only when I am unfortunate enough to draw him as a partner."

Ottilia called a halt. "Pray do not fall into a pointless dispute. Will you try him, Sybilla?"

"I have no desire to encourage him." The dowager threw a black look at her companion. "I will find an opportunity to ask Stewkley directly."

"Not tomorrow, since he is officiating at the funeral. Indeed, I doubt we can progress at all until Wednesday. But I have still not heard from you, my dear," Ottilia pursued, turning to the companion. "Did you glean anything useful from our riding officer?"

Henrietta wrinkled her nose. "I cannot say whether it is useful, since it does not bear upon the matters we have discussed tonight, but —□

"That is beside the bridge. Was he forthcoming about his movements?"

"In general terms only. Naturally, Mr Yelford could not disclose the specifics of the forays he has made. It seems he often has to go out at night if he wants to catch smugglers in the act. I gather he and Lieutenant Radway use informants."

"I don't dare hope you heard who these might be?"

Henrietta drew her brows together. "Not directly, but I would hazard a guess that one at least, who apparently reports to Lieutenant Radway, is a farmhand."

"How so?" Sybilla's voice was sharp.

"Mr Yelford let fall the odd phrase or word I am persuaded was accidental. 'Radway's fellow,' he said once. He spoke of 'livestock and cultivated fields'."

"In what connection?"

"Oh, in regard to where his duties took him, Lady Fan, other than beaches. I noticed it because he was not at that point talking of searches. Those he conducts either with Lieutenant Radway or the militia under Captain Turves."

Both names caught Ottilia's attention. "Have you formed any idea of his relationship with those two?"

Henrietta thought for a moment. "Well, I must suppose he is in better skin with the lieutenant. The captain and he are not precisely at loggerheads, as I understand it, but there is an edge to his voice when he mentions him or his men. I suspect Captain Turves does not relish being called out by a mere riding officer — so poor Mr Yelford has referred to himself once or twice."

"I have heard as much from my husband. He says army officers in general consider these newfangled riding officers to be jumped-up pretenders who know nothing of real soldiering."

Sybilla here chimed in. "How should they? It is a government appointment, after all. They are not servicemen."

"That is most unfair, Lady Polbrook. Mr Yelford says there are former officers among them, although he was never in the military."

"There you are then."

Ottilia intervened again. "That is not to the purpose. What interests me, Henrietta, is how much interaction Mr Yelford has with Lieutenant Radway?"

"Why?" Sybilla's black eyes probed hers. "What are you thinking?"

Ottilia held up a hand. "Nothing of note."

"But why does it interest you, Lady Fan?"

Ottilia sighed, capitulating. "Do not make too much of it, but it does seem to me that Lieutenant Radway has a tendency to be here, there and everywhere. I think it may be time I had a word with him myself."

CHAPTER THIRTEEN

"But you said you'd take me out on a boat as soon as the weather was right, Papa, you know you did."

Francis suppressed a flicker of impatience. His young son had bearded him while he was breakfasting in company with Bastien, his mother and her companion not having yet come down. Luke bounced into the room and gave forth his forecast of a fine day ahead.

"The sun is out and there's no clouds and it doesn't look like rain or wind or anything bad, sir. It's perfect for a boat, don't you agree?"

Not having given a thought to the matter, Francis was concentrated upon the task set him by his darling wife as she sipped hot chocolate while he was dressing. Ottilia had looked worn to his critical eye.

"I wish you will rest a little longer, my loved one. This wretched business is taking a toll on you."

"Well, I own I would've preferred not to have been obliged to attend Carlton's funeral service yesterday, but I had given my word to Cecily. It was something of a sombre affair, do you not think?"

"Sombre? The whole thing was macabre. I'd swear every man jack in the town thought it his business to be there. Be thankful you didn't have to attend the burial too. Radway described it as a raree-show, what with the crowding outside the cemetery, urchins shoving their heads through the railings to gawp. I've never seen anything to equal it."

His wife gave a tiny laugh. "It might have raised my mood. I found it depressing beyond bearing, if I am truthful, to see that poor girl trying to bear up and failing miserably. I would have done what I might to comfort her when the coffin had been taken out, but Ivy Ospringe hurried her away. For Cecily's sake, if nothing else, I must put forth my best efforts to solve this puzzle."

Francis entered a caveat. "But not today. Or at least, not immediately." He finished buttoning his waistcoat and moved to the bed, perching by her on the edge. "If you love me, dear heart, rest a little and spare my anxieties."

He received one of Ottilia's warm smiles. "If you put it like that, my darling lord, how can I gainsay you? I will remain abed for another hour or so, but in return…"

Francis eyed her with misgiving. "In return, what?"

"Nothing very arduous." She reached out and set a hand to his chest in the beguiling way she had. "It is only that I am hopeful you may have success with this farmhand."

"Oh, so you want me to pursue the hunt in your stead, is that it?"

"If you please, Fan. If he can be induced to talk, we may learn more of potential arrivals of contraband."

Francis had balked. "How can you be sure Reapham is involved?"

"He was named by Mr Parbold, do you not recall? Along with the fishermen you met."

"Was he? I've lost track, Tillie."

"Moreover, since we already know or suspect him of being in the trade, and Mr Yelford let slip the notion of a farm to Henrietta, he is the most likely to be the lieutenant's informant."

Francis picked up one of his boots, conveniently within reach, and proceeded to insert his stockinged foot. "Isn't he the fellow Parbold stigmatised as a surly brute? I should doubt of his proving amenable."

His darling wife had given him one of her mischievous smiles. "You are very persuasive, my dearest dear. I believe in you. I know you will prevail."

He had laughed and leaned across to kiss her. "I cannot match you for cajolery, witch wife of mine."

Now here was his young son demanding his services instead. Francis tried to deflect him.

"I fear I have a more urgent matter on this morning. Can it not wait for another day?"

Luke's jaw jutted in a pugnacious fashion. "You promised, Papa! 'Sides, I've had to wait ever so long already 'cos it rains all the time and if we don't go today, it most likely will start all over again and rain and rain and very likely storm too, and then the wind will be too strong and you won't take me out at all!"

Only too likely, the way things were going. Rueful, Francis eyed the boy. He did not want to disappoint him. Yet the sooner this murderous affair was settled...

Bastien's voice interrupted his thoughts. "Why do I not take you, Luke? I am strong and can row just as well, no?" He grinned, flexing an arm.

Luke's gaze veered and he frowned, as if considering the question. Then he executed a neat little bow. "I thank you, sir, but you didn't promise. Papa did." His reproachful eyes returned to Francis's face. "Mama says it's 'portant to keep your promises."

"True enough, but you see, I promised Mama I would do an errand for her this morning."

Luke stared him out. "Your promise to me came first, sir. If you like, I'll go and ask Mama."

Francis was obliged to suppress his burgeoning amusement. There was not a doubt that Ottilia would take Luke's part. "Tenacious little beast, aren't you, my boy? Very well, you win."

His child's instantly brightened features rewarded him. Eyes sparkling, Luke turned back to Bastien. "You can come too, if you like. I dare say Papa might like a rest. He's getting old now."

Bastien gave a shout of laughter and Francis shook a finger at his son. "That will do if you don't wish me to change my mind. Old indeed!"

Luke grinned engagingly. "I just thought you'd like a bit of help, sir."

Before Francis could again protest, Bastien clapped a hand to Luke's back. "I agree, my young *cousin*. I will row the boat and your papa may enjoy his leisure."

Francis gave it up. "Wrap up well, Luke. I'll go and square it with your mother. Meet me at the front door, the two of you."

Ryde having had the forethought to arrange the hire of a suitable boat whenever the weather might permit, a message despatched through Tyler ensured the vessel was at the rendezvous, already pushed down the shingle to the water's edge, both the groom and the fisherman owner in attendance.

"If you'll board, m'lord, we'll push you out. No need to get your boots wet."

In high excitement, Luke leaped nimbly into the little boat, taking his place on one of the benches. Francis followed, choosing a position in the stern from where he might guide the rower, while Bastien placed himself in the centre and took the oars from the fisherman, who was quick to proffer advice.

"I'd not take her out past the buoy, sir. Them winds are like to spring up without warnin', and you don't want to be swept out. Waves are strong round these parts."

Bastien thanked him. "This is wise, since you know these waters best."

Francis cut in. "We don't mean to do more than tack close to shore, never fear. My boy here just wants a taste of seafaring, eh, Luke?"

His son gave an emphatic nod. "Can we go as far as the buoy, though, sir?"

"That's up to Bastien. Ready? Let's be off then. Ryde?"

Groom and fishermen set to and shoved the boat off the shingle. It rocked alarmingly as it took to water, and Luke clutched the seat beneath him with both hands.

"Whoo, it's really wobbly!"

"It will settle in a moment."

Bastien was already pushing into the water with his oars and presently, as he got into rowing rhythm, the regular motion steadied the vessel. He headed out into deeper waters and then straightened the boat, setting a course parallel to the shore. Francis kept an eye out for the buoy. He spotted it at length, a red bell-shaped splodge bobbing on the waves some two hundred yards out from the shore.

"It's off to your east, Bastien. Best to turn here and tack back again."

His nephew looked over his shoulder. "I see it. We can go around it, perhaps."

"As long as you don't take too wide a circle. Tillie will slaughter me if anything happens to Luke."

"I'm perfectly fine, Papa. I can swim too, if I fall in."

"Don't fall in, for pity's sake! We'll never hear the end of it from Hepsie."

Luke was clearly enjoying the treat, looking this way and that and commenting as he watched on how the boat cleft a path through the water, how the oars dripped as they lifted out on each stroke.

"I can't see any fish."

"They tend to be much further out, in deeper waters."

His son subsided for a space, looking ahead as the buoy grew in size the nearer they approached. Francis took pleasure in watching his face. The child's delight was palpable, his interest captured by each new moment of experience. A lesson indeed. He ought not to sacrifice his family's entertainment to another of these infernal adventures merely because his darling wife rejoiced in them. He had neglected Pretty and the twins too — that little rascal Diana and her angelic counterpart. Nell was a sweetheart, as good as gold. For his money, she would grow up to be a bookworm. How in the world had he sired a girl who promised to become a bluestocking?

Luke's sudden cry cut across his roving mind. "I see a fish!"

Francis pulled his concentration together. This was Luke's outing and he needed to pay attention to the child. "Where?"

"There, by the buoy. Do you see it, Papa?"

They were almost within touching distance of the bobbing buoy. Francis caught sight of an alien object in the water. Just as he realised it was no fish, Luke cried out again.

"It's not a fish, it's a … well, I don't know what it is. Look, there's a string. It's tied to the buoy!"

Francis's senses came alert. "Bastien, try to move in closer. It looks to be a package of some kind."

A grim note sounded as Bastien spoke. "More importantly, *mon oncle*, another boat approaches."

The notion Ottilia had raised about Carlton Green's possible activities concerning gemstones and jewellery leaped into Francis's mind. Urgency grew in his breast.

"Get us closer, Bastien. If whoever is in that boat is after the package, we must get to it first."

The boat had shifted under Bastien's careful manoeuvring and the bobbing package was almost within reach. A very lump it looked, wrapped in some kind of shiny material. As Francis leaned out, stretching his arm towards the object, Bastien's voice came low, a note of heavy disappointment within it.

"It is Grégoire."

Francis glanced back at the approaching vessel, a rowboat like their own, and saw the lone occupant was indeed the young Frenchman. It was obvious he had recognised them, but he gave no sign, heading his vessel directly towards the buoy on its other side.

Did he hope to intercept the package before Francis could take it? Determination settled in his breast and he leaned further out, his hand stroking the water as the boat shifted on the waves. "Hold her as steady as you can, Bastien."

The oars whispered in the water as his nephew struggled to control the vessel, keeping it as near to the buoy as he could.

A murmur reached him. "Shall I try, sir?"

Francis glanced at his son, who had pushed along his bench to the edge of the boat and was half out of his seat. Too perilous.

"Stay back, Luke!" Next instant, his hand connected with the object and he closed his fingers on it. "I have it!"

He pulled back, bringing the package with him. It dragged taut as the string that held it reached its limit.

"I'd best cut it. Luke, reach into my left pocket."

Nothing loath, his son closed with him and scrabbled inside the pocket of his frock coat. He brought out a folded knife and held it up. "Got it! Shall I cut it?"

"Just unfold it for me. Take care you don't cut yourself."

Luke had just managed to open the knife when a voice called across from the other boat.

"Will you give that to me, if you please, Lord Francis?"

Bastien answered for him, anger throbbing in his voice as he called back. "What is it you want with this, Grégoire? I did not wish to believe you were involved, but now I see you have lied to me."

"It is not what you think, Bastien. Just let me have that package and I will explain."

"You do not get this package, *mon vieux*. It goes to Lady Fan. You too should go, if you have any honour."

Francis did not bother to become embroiled in the argument, which switched in any event to French. He was intent upon securing the package as he took the open knife from his son, passing him the soggy wrapped lump. "Hold this, Luke."

The boy took it with alacrity, hugging it to his person with both arms. "He won't get it from me, sir."

"My reliance is all upon you," said Francis, in a bid to grant his son the excitement of being in the thick of the situation. It took effort to cut the soaked string, but the package came loose in a moment. Francis shut the knife and slipped it back into his pocket. "Give me the package."

Luke handed it over with obvious reluctance, but Francis was not going to run the risk of it slipping from his grasp.

"Bastien!" His nephew looked round. "Bastien, we have it. Let's get back to shore."

"But this rascal must come also."

"Never mind him. We can catch up with him later."

But this apparently would not do for his nephew. He raised his voice again. "Grégoire du Guet, if you have any honour, you will follow and explain yourself *immediatement*!"

Then he took up the oars again and began to push into the water, turning the boat shoreward. The vessel was soon ploughing against the tide.

Francis, the package secure, looked back. The Frenchman, whether for honour or otherwise, had opted to follow.

Joanie having brought up a tray, Ottilia breakfasted in bed.

"It's only a bite of toast and your favourite cheese, my lady. I didn't think you'd want egg or bacon if you're feeling poorly."

Ottilia sat up against the banked pillows, allowing the maid to set the tray across her knees. "I am not poorly, Joanie, just a little fatigued."

"I don't wonder at it, my lady. These doings always do tire you out. I've not forgotten your coffee. Soon set you to rights, that will."

Ottilia thanked her. "You always know just what to do for me, Joanie. How in the world I should manage without you, I cannot imagine."

The maid was busying herself pouring coffee, larding it with sugar and cream just as Ottilia liked it. "Well, you don't need to do without me, my lady. I'm not going nowhere."

The slight emphasis was not lost on Ottilia. She knew Joanie missed the company of Doro, with whom she had struck up a friendship. She was tempted to reassure the maid that the pair would meet again once Hemp Roy and his now wife were ready to accommodate their entourage. Best not to prick the wound, perhaps.

"Will you fetch my hot water, if you please, Joanie? I must get up after this."

The maid became motherly, as she often did. "Take your time, my lady. Nothing so urgent as it won't wait for you."

She bustled out on the words, leaving Ottilia to reflect, as she placed a sliver of her preferred hard yellow cheese upon a portion of buttered toast, that the matter promised to become all too urgent if she could not unravel it soon. She ought to hand over to the proper authorities both Pretty's treasure box and Carlton's spurious journal with their possibly incriminating contents. She was reluctant to take this course. After all, her conclusions were not yet certain. Nor, if she was honest, could she be satisfied of the integrity of those to whom she might entrust these articles. As of this moment, Lieutenant Radway, and even the riding officer, were to her unknown quantities.

If anyone ought to take charge, it was the Justice of the Peace. But Overy had been flustered and relieved to have her assistance. On the whole, it behoved her to withhold what might well prove to be evidence until she was sure of her ground.

A pity Francis had been obliged to postpone tackling the farmhand Reapham, but Ottilia would not have her precious young son forego his pleasure on that account.

"Of course you must take Luke, my dearest dear. He has been remarkably patient. It would be too bad to miss this opportunity."

Her spouse had grimaced. "Luke was vocal on that point, let me tell you. He predicted incessant rain, storms and wind for the remainder of our stay."

Her amusement had served to set Francis off laughing too. A blessing, for the change of plan had clearly been an irritant.

She had just finished off the last of her coffee when Joanie returned, bearing a jug of hot water for her ablutions. "Seems as your restful morning can't last, my lady. Tyler has told the gentleman you aren't ready to receive visitors, but —☐

"What gentleman is this, pray?"

Joanie set the jug down. "It's the justice, my lady, Mr Overy."

"Justice Overy? Good heavens!" Pat upon her thoughts? Coincidence. Tempting to think of it as intuition, but could one trust such notions?

"He said as he'd wait," the maid went on, "and Tyler showed him into the parlour."

"Here, Joanie, take this. I had best make haste." The maid removed the tray and Ottilia threw aside the covers. "Stay! Is Lady Polbrook downstairs?"

Joanie was setting her burden down on a convenient whatnot in a corner. "Oh, no, my lady. Her ladyship and Miss Henrietta went off to The Rooms not half an hour ago."

Then Tobias Overy would be obliged to kick his heels until she was dressed. Nevertheless, Ottilia bid Joanie hurry as her maid tied her stays and helped her into the bodice of the muslin gown, wondering how much of what she had discovered she ought to disclose.

Mr Overy's anxiety had not abated one jot. "From all I have been hearing, my lady, this obnoxious criminal could be anyone hereabouts."

Ottilia took her place on the sofa, waving the visitor to a chair opposite. "Not quite anyone, sir. But do pray be seated. I cannot converse with you comfortably if you continue to stand."

The justice harrumphed, looked behind to establish the indicated chair and consented to perch thereon, still maintaining an upright mien. A hopeful look crept into his face as he regarded Ottilia.

"Have you an idea of his identity perhaps, my lady?"

"Alas, no." She hastened to continue as his face fell. "But certain options have presented themselves."

"Which? Or should I say who?"

How to deal with his eagerness and yet not commit herself? She did not wish to send authority after any particular individual without certainty. She opted for candour.

"Pardon me, Mr Overy, but I fear it is yet too early for me to be naming names." She smiled. "Pray do not be disappointed, sir. I have several persons in my sights, but it would be too bad to be accusing an innocent."

Tobias Overy pursed his lips. "I had hoped to be done with this appalling affair in a trice, yet here we are almost a week in and nothing settled."

Ottilia ignored this. "Have you discovered anything on your own account, sir?"

He harrumphed again. "You bid me talk to those fellows at the custom house, which I did. Also the doctor in the case. He confirmed your findings, my lady. To my dismay, I admit. But it is useless to be wishing this horror had been perpetrated in some other fashion."

Ottilia prepared to soothe. "Just so, sir. Let us not waste time and energy upon what cannot be helped."

"Have you not progressed at all then?"

She was betrayed into a laugh. "I did not say that. We are somewhat forward." She hesitated, eyeing the troubled features before her. "If I give you the gist of what I believe may have occurred, will you allow me to reserve the evidence for it?"

Mr Overy chewed his lip for a moment. "If it pertains to smuggling, my lady, I fear I cannot give such an assurance."

"It does not. At least, not in the sense you mean."

He looked mystified and Ottilia was obliged to suppress a devil of mischief that prompted her to confuse him further. "Bear with me, Mr Overy. I will explain myself."

"I hope you may, my lady. If it is not smuggling…"

"I believe it does involve contraband, but no one is defrauding His Majesty's revenue."

"I beg your pardon?"

Ottilia held up a finger. "The goods being brought in are not, I believe, subject to duty. They belong to French émigrés. If I have gauged the matter right, that is."

"Émigrés? French? How should such goods escape taxes here?"

"Personal property is not subject to tax, sir, unless I have mistaken the law."

The justice blew out his cheeks. "I hope you mean to tell me of what this property consists."

Ottilia had not intended to do so, but she had not bargained for the man's tenacity. Knowing it would likely complicate matters, she gave in. "It is jewellery, Mr Overy."

"Jewellery?"

"Gemstones."

She waited for what he might say next, amused by his obvious non-comprehension.

He opened his mouth once, twice, and closed it again. Then he fetched a heavy sigh. "I do not pretend to understand how this can possibly relate to this horrid murder."

"Yet I believe it does." She thought for a moment, and then smiled. "I see I will have to trust to your discretion, sir. I will tell you the whole, as far as I understand it at this present. In return, I must beg for your promise you will not discuss any of these details with anyone else."

He did not immediately provide his assurance. "Until when, my lady?"

"Until I am certain. Indeed, until I have identified the perpetrator you are anxious to apprehend."

Still he hesitated. "Why do you wish me to keep mum?"

No sense in beating about the bush. "Because I cannot be sure of those individuals you might most likely talk with on this subject."

His eyes popped and Ottilia knew her words had gone home. "You cannot mean those in authority?"

"Aside from yourself, sir, I do indeed mean exactly these."

"But…"

She hastened to reassure, as he seemed lost for words. "I have two persons in particular in mind. Once I have spoken to them myself, I hope I may be able to eliminate them from suspicion altogether."

He appeared reluctant. "Do I understand that you will not give me the particulars if I refuse to make the required promise?"

Ottilia gave him a limpid smile. "I am not holding a gun to your head, Mr Overy. If you prefer, I will hand over everything so far known which would, I dare say, allow you to solve the matter without my assistance."

She had to bite her lip on a bubble of mirth as chagrin spread across his face. A sliver of unholy satisfaction slid into her breast as he backtracked in haste.

"Not at all, not at all, my lady. I am only too relieved you are willing to put your time and trouble at my disposal. Naturally, if it is your wish, I shall say nothing of what you disclose to me. My word on it."

Ottilia relented. "Thank you for that, Mr Overy. I am indebted to you."

"No such thing, I assure you. If only this business may be resolved, it is I who must owe you a debt of gratitude."

Judging it time to be done with these formalities, Ottilia embarked upon a judiciously expurgated version of her discoveries, outlining those aspects that gave credence to her understanding of Carlton Green's activities. Justice Overy was inclined to wish for a sight of the binder in question, but Ottilia managed to deflect this into a recital of what she intended next.

"There are still several persons I need to question, or even revisit. The dead man's sister, Cecily Green, may be able to shed light on certain aspects of her brother's conduct. In due course, I hope all these threads may come together and reveal the culprit."

Mr Overy looked dubious, but he was careful not to say so. "I must trust your experience in these matters, my lady. Do the threads in general come together?"

"Invariably. The truth has a way of coming to light if one persists, without allowing prejudice to rule."

The justice nodded in a grave fashion and then rose. "I have taken up too much of your time, my lady. I will take my leave."

Before he could make an exit, however, sounds below betokening an arrival heralded the return of the rowing party. Hasty footsteps sounded, the door was flung wide and Ottilia's young son burst into the parlour.

"Mama! We found a package in the water. It was tied to a buoy and Papa grabbed it out and we cut it and —□ He broke off, having evidently caught sight of the stranger. "Oh! Beg pardon, sir, I didn't see…"

Ottilia had no chance to respond since her husband entered the room, closely followed by Bastien, ushering before him, to her astonishment, Grégoire du Guet.

All four were still clad in their outdoor garments, bringing with them a distinct aroma of brine. Francis, setting a hand on Luke's shoulder, spoke first.

"Well met, Overy. I take it you're here to find out what we've all been up to?"

Tobias Overy bowed. "You are correct, my lord. Her ladyship has been kind enough to bring me up to date."

"Not quite, I suspect. She doesn't yet know about this latest fetch."

His gaze veered to Ottilia's as he spoke and curiosity drove her to her feet. "What is this package Luke speaks of?"

"We don't yet know." He held up a wet, lumpy object and grinned. "I would by no means allow them to deprive you of the pleasure of finding out."

She laughed, moving to reach for the item. "Another set of gemstones, do you think?"

Her spouse held it away. "Take care. It's still wet and particularly slimy. You'd best wear an apron or some such thing. I've sent Tyler to have Joanie fetch something suitable."

Ottilia acknowledged this briefly and turned her attention to her nephew and his French friend. "Monsieur du Guet, welcome. I am glad to see you, if a trifle surprised."

The Frenchman bowed, but the sullen look upon his countenance did not abate. "It was not by my wish, my lady, but I was given little choice."

"None." This from Bastien in a harsh tone. "In such circumstances, you could not expect it, *mon vieux*."

Grégoire cast him a measured glance, but refrained from making any reply. Bastien's gaze veered to Ottilia's. She detected both spleen and distress therein. "He will not speak, *Tante*, beyond this demand that we give him the package. This I have refused, as has my uncle."

Francis quirked an eyebrow. "With reason, if it contains what we suspect." He gestured to Tobias Overy. "He remains, I take it?"

The justice drew himself up. "I have every intention of remaining, my lord. However, I must protest at the continued presence of this boy."

He indicated Luke, who piped up with indignation. "But I found it! It's my treasure, isn't it, Papa?"

Amused, Ottilia watched her spouse pluck the hat from their son's head. "You can't wear that in the parlour."

Luke grabbed the hat, but continued to stare up at his father. "You don't answer me, sir. It is my treasure, you know it is."

Francis flicked at the dark locks falling across the child's forehead. "It is your find, yes. Treasure, if you will. But you see, it's likely to be evidence. Like Pretty's treasure box. I'm afraid you can't keep it."

Luke's sudden smile warmed Ottilia's heart. "I don't care for that. Didn't I say I'm going to find murderers like Mama? See, I already started."

"You did indeed. However —□

If he was about to suggest their son left the parlour, he was forestalled as Joanie entered at that moment. She dropped a curtsy and approached Ottilia, holding out a folded cloth.

"I got this from Mrs Forncett downstairs, my lady. I hope it's what you need."

Ottilia took the cloth, opening it out and letting the folds fall to reveal a large kitchen towel of coarse linen. "This is just the thing. Please convey my thanks to our landlady, Joanie."

The maid withdrew and Ottilia glanced around. "I wish you will all sit down." She resumed her own seat in the general bustle as those present found chairs and laid the cloth over her lap. Her husband came across and set the package in her lap before taking his customary stance at the mantel.

She studied it with interest for a moment or two, turning it this way and that. It was more awkwardly shaped than large, bulging in places. The wrapping was of oilcloth, which explained the bill found in Carlton's bureau. String, much stained and stiff from its sojourn in salt water, was tightly packed around the object. Salt? Did this explain the worn gloves in his chest? But one thing was missing.

"No markings? Nothing to identify either from whom it came or to whom it is addressed?"

"That is precisely why it is suspicious. Moreover, it had been tied to the buoy. Du Guet here knew of it, however, since he was in the way of picking it up."

The Frenchman spoke up at that. "It was my intention, yes. But that proves nothing."

Ottilia opted to soothe. "You will no doubt explain your part in due course, sir. I think we must open it. Fan, have you your knife?"

Her husband sat down at her side as he brought out his pocket knife. "Give it to me. I suspect that string won't cut easily."

Ottilia handed it over, but a motion in the periphery of her vision drew her glance towards the door. She spied her young son hovering to one side of it. Luke had taken advantage of the convenient distraction provided by the maid and picked a spot where he might remain without attracting notice. His eyes widened as he caught her gaze. Worried he would be ejected? Ottilia gave him a conspiratorial smile and returned her attention to Francis, working his knife at the saturated string.

It gave at length. He stripped the remnants away and handed the package back to Ottilia. The onlookers were silent as she tugged at the folds of the oilcloth covering. They gave and exposed a further container, one of leather, with a drawstring opening, which had been knotted tight.

"Cut it, Fan, if you please."

"Are you sure? We can't close it again if the drawstring is broken."

"I suspect it is too much deteriorated to be of use."

He slid the knife under a fold and cut the leather thong holding the purse together. Ottilia found she was holding her breath as she pulled at the opening and spread it wide. The contents at once loosened, chinking within. She upended the purse and a cascade of gold slid from it into her lap.

"Coins?"

"Yes, Fan. Rings too."

"Treasure!" Luke, clearly unable to contain himself, dashed forward, dropping to his knees and plunging his fingers into the mass. "It really is treasure! And it's better than Pretty's, isn't it? Wait 'til she hears!"

Ottilia leaped on this cue. "You had best go straight up and tell her, my love."

Luke scrambled to his feet. "Yes, and she can come and see for herself that I win!"

"No, don't bring her down here. Not now. She may look at it later." Her son was already making for the door in haste and she called after him. "No squabbling, if you please."

"Little chance of his obeying that injunction, my dear one," said her spouse as their son hurtled through the door. "I don't envy Hepsie."

Ottilia sighed. "I suppose they are bound argue over which is of more worth."

Bastien, who had risen to close the door behind her careless son, came over to look down at the find. He picked up a coin and studied it. "These are *Louis D'Or*."

Francis was also studying one of the coins. "I doubt they are worth much now France has introduced their *franc*, unless one was to melt them down."

"What is the worth to the death of my friend?" Bastien said bitterly as he dropped the coin back into the collection in Ottilia's lap.

Brought back to the more important issue, Ottilia looked towards Grégoire du Guet. "Perhaps your other friend can tell us?"

Before the Frenchman could answer, Justice Overy was on his feet. "What does this mean, my lady? Is that fellow the scoundrel responsible for this terrible slaying? You cannot claim these items are not contraband either, found as they have been. No, no. They should be appropriated for the Crown."

Ottilia held up a staying hand. "Let us not put the cart before the horse, sir. May I request, if you mean to remain, that you allow me to proceed in my own fashion?"

Mr Overy harrumphed, plainly disgruntled. "Very well, my lady, very well. But that hoard must be looked to."

To her relief, he subsided, retaking his seat. Ottilia could well have dispensed with Tobias Overy's presence, especially if he meant to interrupt when she was bent upon eliciting information. It could not be helped, however. He was clearly not disposed to leave now.

She set her sights back on the Frenchman, seated near the door. His features had grown a trifle haggard, she thought.

"Monsieur du Guet?"

He eyed her for a moment. Then his gaze travelled to the justice, to Bastien and back to the sofa where Francis still remained at her side.

"I will speak only to Lady Fan."

"Will you, by God?" Thus Francis. "What makes you think you have a choice?"

Grégoire lifted his chin. "Do you arrest me?"

"Don't be a fool, man."

"Then I am free. Therefore I may choose to whom I am willing to speak."

Did this reticence spring from a wish to keep Bastien out of it, as well as Justice Overy? Ottilia made a decision.

"In that case, sir, let us remove to a more private location." She wrapped up the coins and rings, cloth and all, and handed them to her spouse. "Keep these safe, dearest." Then she rose. "We will appropriate the dining room, Fan."

CHAPTER FOURTEEN

"Why did you insist upon privacy, sir?"

Ottilia had opted to take her usual hostess's seat opposite the head of the table, bidding the Frenchman to the first chair to one side. She positioned hers at an angle, the better to observe him.

Grégoire du Guet set his elbows on the wooden surface and surveyed his joined hands. "I fear Bastien is too impatient to give me a fair hearing."

"Can you blame him?"

The Frenchman did not look at her. "I understand he feels betrayed. Yet he misjudges my involvement."

Ottilia watched his face. He no longer appeared as wretched as he had earlier seemed. Was it an act? Or was he the more relaxed to be subject only to her judgement? Did she represent a less threatening object?

"Do you mean to disclose your precise involvement?"

He did look at her then, a light of resignation in his gaze. "It seems now inevitable."

"Then let us not waste time, my dear sir." She softened her tone, allowing a slight smile to appear. "Would you object to it if I addressed you as Grégoire? I so much prefer informality."

Surprise flickered. "As you wish. I do not object."

"Excellent." She plunged in. "I take it you were aware that Carlton was collecting packages of valuables from France, mostly jewellery? We had not got so far as to count in gold coins."

Grégoire's lip curled. "I was aware, of course. He was employed for the purpose."

Ottilia was unsurprised. "By you?"

"By my masters, but through my agency."

She took a guess. "Your masters being émigrés?"

Grégoire gave a brief nod. "A certain marquis began it. He was acting on behalf of a compatriot. Word got about within the community. In due course, a network grew, using trusted individuals in both countries."

"Of which you were one?"

"An acquaintance drew me in."

He paused and Ottilia, her mind piecing together the possible needed grouping of such a network, waited in hopes he would reveal more. When he remained silent, she applied a prompt.

"You in turn recruited Carlton?"

A look of disgust entered his face. "For my sins. We needed a man permanently on the spot."

The reason sprang to Ottilia's mind. "Because this coast is already a smuggler's haven? Your people might sneak in without attracting particular notice since the customs officials were likely to be otherwise occupied."

For the first time in their dealings, Grégoire seemed disconcerted. "Well reasoned, ma'am. A shrewd guess."

"It was not a particularly difficult one. Come, Grégoire, be plain with me. Was Carlton possessing himself of items from the jewellery he collected?"

A gasp escaped him. "How did you know?"

Ottilia rapped the table. "Was he thieving?"

Grégoire sighed. "Alas, yes. I did not know it until after his death."

"How did you find out?"

"He gave Cecily a ring. She was wearing it — in fond remembrance, she told me. I recognised it. A ruby stone.

Unmistakeable as one of a set that had come through some months ago. The recipient showed me both necklace and brooch, saying she supposed the ring had been lost in transit."

Ottilia digested this, not quite convinced. After all, the letter from Carlton's bankers showed he might readily afford to buy such a ring. "When did you hear of the loss?"

"When I delivered the jewels. It is my task to courier the items from here to the capital, or, upon occasion, to other parts of the country."

Plausible, but Ottilia was not yet satisfied. "Why did you not collect the items yourself? Why use Carlton for the purpose?"

"I was obliged to collect today since Carlton is no longer with us, but in general I avoided that work. I am too conspicuous. As a Frenchman myself, I might attract the attention of the customs authority. Besides, Carlton had the perfect cover."

"Fossil-hunting."

Grégoire's lip curled again. "His interest was genuine. He knew this coastline well."

"You accompanied him on occasion, I gather?"

Grégoire let out a scornful sound. "I was obliged to do so. We were supposed to be friends."

Ottilia cast him a sharp glance. "Supposed to be? Was it then a false friendship?"

"Let us say a cultivated friendship. It helped to be seen to be a duo, especially in sight of his English friends. Also it allowed me to make my frequent trips away, thought to be in his company. If you will have the truth of it, I was not mourning in my lodgings for two days. I had to report his unfortunate demise to my superiors."

His candour served to induce a growing distaste in Ottilia. Granted, Grégoire had a duty to his fellow countrymen whom he was serving in this way. But the evidence of deliberate subterfuge could not but disgust. Was Grégoire necessarily ruthless, or was it innate in his character? She probed a little more.

"You or your superiors had no previous reason to suspect losses? Had none other mentioned missing items?"

"It was not possible to keep track of everything. Too many individuals had become involved. Often we failed to secure packages."

"Or they were appropriated here, perhaps?"

Grégoire let out a sigh. "Now, I may choose to suppose it. Before, I would not have called Carlton's honour into question."

Ottilia thought it time to turn the screw. "You realise you have given me sufficient motive to name you as a suspect for Carlton's murder?"

Grégoire met her gaze. "I have said I did not discover his perfidy until after his death."

"I heard you." Ottilia gave a spurious smile. "Yet you have condemned yourself for a charlatan friend out of your own mouth. How can I know you did not make this discovery before he died and took this means to punish him for it?"

She half expected a vehement denial, but it did not come. Instead, he drummed his fingers on the table, seemingly lost in a brown study for a moment. Then his fingers stilled and he looked up.

"You are right. You cannot know if I am speaking the truth. However…"

He paused and Ottilia waited. Was this a prelude to the production of a convenient alibi? At length, she was obliged to ask.

"However?"

His eyebrows drew together. "It has been in my mind that perhaps Carlton was forced to act thus."

"By whom?"

"I cannot tell that. He never struck me as a dishonest fellow. Also he had been out of temper lately. Anxious, I think. I did tax him with it once or twice. He complained of headaches and said he was thinking of consulting a physician."

Ottilia's mind was working. It was not inconceivable that Carlton had been a victim even prior to his murder. Of blackmail? Had someone discovered his occupation and threatened to report him to the authorities? All well and good to say the items brought in were personal belongings, but for all her bravado to Justice Overy, Ottilia knew well the customs personnel would take a contrary view to anything entering the country in a clandestine fashion.

Grégoire broke into her thoughts. "There was also the wound he sustained."

"Cecily said he claimed he cut his arm on a rock, but she did not believe it."

"No more did I, ma'am. That arm was cut by a blade, and Carlton was no fighter."

"Who uses a short blade, Fan? A dagger is not carried by the military, is it? Do individuals keep them upon their person these days, do you think?"

Francis had succeeded in ridding the house of extraneous persons in a bid to provide his darling wife with a respite. No sooner had the Justice of the Peace departed than their two eldest children came in, clamouring for attention.

"Pretty won't believe me," complained Luke.

"He says he found gold coins. How am I supposed to believe that?"

"You will when you see them. Where are they, Papa? You didn't give them all to that man who came, I hope."

Before he could quell the pair, Francis was obliged to re-open the package he had in charge and expose it for his daughter's inspection.

Pretty remained unimpressed. "Well, all right, I concede it's gold. But my diamonds were better and I still win."

Francis cut off his son's instant objection. "Enough! Take your bickering elsewhere. Far away, preferably."

"We only came down for —□

"Hepsie sent us because —□

Francis pointed to the door. "Out!"

Pretty tweaked her brother's sleeve and tugged him forth. "Come on. Hepsie said we can go out if the rain holds off."

"Yes, but you still won't —□

Their voices became muted as Bastien shut the door behind them, a grin appearing. "I do not think the question will be easily settled."

Francis cast his gaze heavenwards. "Not 'til Doomsday. Wretched imps."

Bastien shifted back, watching as Francis once more wrapped up the morning's find. "Do you think Grégoire makes a confession?"

"I highly doubt it." He set the package aside. "Let us hope he is at least able to shed some light on Green's actions."

When his wife returned to the parlour, it was evident by the Frenchman's demeanour that no confession had been forthcoming. But Francis read Ottilia's expression with ease. She had learned something of import and it had clearly provided her with much food for thought.

On impulse, he turned to his nephew. "Bastien, why don't you accompany your friend to wherever he is going? I'd like your aunt to rest awhile."

While farewells were said, he crossed to the bell-pull and tugged on it, intending to call for refreshments when Tyler appeared. These being duly supplied in the dining room, he plied his wife with coffee and a roll buttered and larded with her favourite honey, himself consuming a substantial sandwich of beef washed down with ale.

By the time the repast was finished, Francis had been put in possession of all that Ottilia had learned. Her query about the use of a dagger piqued his interest.

"You're thinking of this wound? Well, an officer must wear a sword, but some purchase a dirk for close combat. I had one myself. You are surely not thinking of Turves? I doubt a captain of militia would need one. What have you in your head, wife of mine?"

Ottilia set her cup in its saucer and gave him one of her conspiratorial smiles. "I am happy enough to eliminate Captain Turves, thank you. It allows me to concentrate on a couple of others."

"Which others?"

"One I trust you may be able to put me in the way of meeting in person, my dearest dear. Lieutenant Radway. Also the riding officer, but I may rely upon Henrietta for that."

"Henrietta already said Yelford carries a pistol." The other notion was not welcome, despite his own vague stirrings of doubt. "Do you seriously suspect the fellow in charge of the custom house? I suppose it's possible he uses a dirk, though I would have thought a pistol would be more useful. But if you are serious, that would imply corruption, as well as murder."

The clear gaze he loved so much met his. "It would not be the first time an officer in authority abused his position."

"I dare say not, but…" He trailed off, beset by a rise of dismay.

"What troubles you, Fan?"

He shifted his shoulders, feeling all the discomfort of an unpalatable solution. "I've made a sort of friend of the man."

"If it helps, I have not settled upon him for the culprit. I had meant to talk to him in any event, but this fresh light has made it imperative. Tell me, Fan, can I eliminate a person merely because they have authority?"

There was no use prevaricating. Better to open his mind and hope in this instance Ottilia was wrong.

"If you must have it, I have been a trifle wary of Radway ever since I met him on the beach that morning. It seemed too pat that he came upon us just as those fishermen — both known smugglers — came in to shore."

"Did you think he was in a string with them, Fan?"

"Or he could have been, as he said, hoping to catch them in the act."

Ottilia appeared to digest this as she absently picked up her cup. Apparently finding it empty, she set it down again. Francis lifted the coffee pot but merely a trickle came out as he went to pour.

"Shall I send for more?"

She waved the suggestion away, still deep in thought. Francis waited, conscious of a touch of impatience. Must she go off into one of her reveries at this juncture?

Just then, her gaze returned to his. "Had it occurred to you that our lieutenant may be legitimate in his duties, and yet not so in his dealings with Carlton?"

"For pity's sake! If he did make away with that fellow, he is a villain through and through."

"Is anyone so? Only consider, Fan. To be hand in glove with smugglers must lay him open to discovery."

Francis snorted. "By all accounts, that has not deterred half the inhabitants of the town."

"True, but Lieutenant Radway's duty is to protect the king's revenue. His defection would be a great deal more serious a matter than if it were, say, Coxheath or one of the other burghers."

"Granted. But there is no denying it gives him an advantage. He seems to know who is and is not engaged in the trade."

"It is his duty to know, I imagine."

Frustration seized Francis. "You've made me condemn the wretch now. I no longer know which way I'm arguing."

Ottilia's laughter did nothing to soothe. "My dearest dear, pray stop fretting. All I am trying to establish is the feasibility that a method of enriching himself by taking a cut from Carlton might be simpler than jeopardising his position and standing."

The notion proved no more acceptable to Francis. "How would Radway even know of Carlton's involvement with this émigré network?"

His wife put up a finger. "Ah, that is the interesting part. What say you to the possibility Radway caught Carlton in the act?"

"And then?"

"Let us suppose he takes Carlton for a smuggler and challenges him. We must account for the blade wound somehow. To save himself, Carlton is forced to explain, at which point Radway perhaps conceives a plan of blackmail."

"What, he injures the fellow and then enters negotiations when Green is bleeding half to death?"

He received a smile of great charm. "Just so."

Francis found his annoyance dissipating in spite of himself. "You are a witch. I've said it before. But I protest, it's nonsensical."

"Perhaps. The cut may have been made to persuade Carlton when he refused. A warning?"

"I don't accept any of it and so I tell you."

"But will you facilitate a meeting with Radway, my dearest dear?"

"Not if you mean to confront him with this preposterous notion."

"Do you think me a fool, Fan?"

"I won't tell you what I think at this moment, you wretch."

"But you will help me, won't you? I promise I will be circumspect. You may say that I am hoping he can corroborate some of the facts I have heard elsewhere. He need not suspect my motives."

"If there is the slightest truth to your fantastic notion, I guarantee Radway will suspect you the moment you open your mouth. He is not a man to be trifled with, that much I can vouch for."

Bastien did not know whether to be glad or sorry to be a recipient of Grégoire's new confidence, although his reasoning was just.

"Now that your aunt has dragged the story out of me, there is little to be gained by concealing it from you."

When he had heard the sum of Carlton's activities, his first thought was of Cecily. "How could he so deceive his sister?"

"More to the point, he deceived me." This said with some degree of asperity, though in a low tone so as not to be overheard by other persons in the coffee house, despite the conversation being conducted in French. "If Carlton was harassed by someone, he should have told me."

Bastien eyed him. "You think he was coerced?"

Grégoire's lip curled. "It is my hope. If not, I cannot forgive this perfidy. It makes him nothing less than a petty thief."

"Have a little compassion, *mon vieux*. It cost him his life."

Grégoire did not soften. "Had he been discovered, his life would have been forfeit in any event."

"I hope you mean by means of the law." Bastien spoke with a deliberate edge to his voice. It was galling enough to find how poor his judgement had been in making a friend of Carlton Green. Worse, to realise Grégoire was of a ruthless bent.

The other man met his gaze with a cool stare. "For what do you take me?"

"I do not know. That is why I ask."

Grégoire's lip twisted. "You are disturbed to learn of my calling. *Mon ami*, it necessarily demands secrecy, but you will admit the motive is pure."

"How do I know you are not the one who pressed Carlton to act dishonourably?"

"You accuse me of this murder?"

Bastien did not flinch. "I have learned enough from my aunt that I should not be making unfounded accusations. But if not you, then who?"

Grégoire's gaze dropped. "Ask your Lady Fan."

"Did she name any?"

"Not to me." Grégoire raised his eyes again, a speculative gleam now visible. "It would be interesting to hear whom she might suspect."

"Other than yourself?"

The other shrugged. "I think she believed me. I hope you may come to do so also."

Bastien was far from satisfied. "If I could think of an alternative. Would you prefer I suspect Mundell or Rampton?"

At that, Grégoire burst out in a laugh that seemed altogether genuine. "Those two? Neither has the head for such subterfuge. Mundell thinks only of exercising his wit, while Rampton is merely a fool. I knew them, of course, when Carlton arrived here, but do you think I would have befriended either so closely if he had not drawn them in?"

This point of view could not but appeal. Bastien had ever found the two to be of a type of Englishman he despised. But not Carlton Green, whom he had respected. To find out his weakness was a disappointment. Yet, if truth be told, he was more distressed to feel so distanced from Grégoire.

His fellow Frenchman seemed to feel it. "You need not consider me a friend if this deception troubles you. I doubt we will meet once you leave this place."

It was Bastien's turn to curl his lip. "How not? I too have friends among the émigrés in my mother's circle."

Grégoire gave a grimace. "In the capital, my friend, I do not move in the echelon of the English aristocracy."

This was unanswerable. Du Guet's family connections were not precisely bourgeois, but distant in terms of the upper level in France. Such had been decimated during the Terror, but Bastien knew that pride in their lineage still ruled those who had escaped. No doubt Grégoire was tolerated for his usefulness in the tasks he had undertaken, but he would not be welcome in the social whirl of the elite.

"If you prove innocent in this affair, *mon vieux*, I have no desire to break our friendship." A smile was the only response. Bastien dropped the subject, returning to the main issue. "Do you have any in mind who could blackmail Carlton?"

"In this town? Throw a stone and you will hit a suspect. If they are involved in the so-called trade, to add a mere matter of such a theft is to them a bagatelle. I would not put it past even such a fellow as the pastor who serves the church where Carlton worshipped."

Ottilia's senses prickled. "He mentioned Reverend Stewkley by name?"

"He did not name him," said her nephew. "But that must be the pastor he indicated."

A snort emanated from the dowager Lady Polbrook. "Preposterous! My dear boy, you are dreaming. Reverend Stewkley is an astute player, but to suggest he would coerce that young man into sin is utterly ridiculous."

"Not so, *Grand-mère*. It is said even the pastors turn a blind eye when a keg is found in the churchyard."

"Condoning smuggled brandy is one thing, but for that Frenchman of yours to be accusing the poor man of blackmail is the outside of enough."

Ottilia intervened in haste. "It certainly sounds unlikely, Sybilla. But let us not forget Carlton did make frequent visits to the reverend's house. I have still to ask Cecily about that."

"Ask away, Ottilia. I make no doubt you will find he did so for his soul's sake or some such thing."

"Only too likely. In the meantime —□ turning to the companion, who was consuming her usual hearty meal — "do you think, Henrietta, that you might contrive a meeting for me with your riding officer?"

Henrietta waved her fork. "By all means. Although he is not *my* riding officer. We are merely friends."

Sybilla looked round, bending a severe gaze upon her. "I hope you do not mean to marry the wretched fellow and leave me stranded."

A trill of laughter came from her companion. "Good heavens, ma'am, where came you by that notion? For one thing, I am past the age of marrying. For another, Mr Yelford is not at all the sort of man to inspire me with a romantic fancy. I merely find the tales of his dealings with smugglers fascinating. I dare say he is quite tired of my questions." She looked towards Ottilia. "I should think he would be glad to talk to you, Lady Fan."

Ottilia doubted that, but the connection was useful. "Tomorrow, do you think, if the rain holds off?"

"Oh, indeed. He was occupied today, but I'm sure he said he would be in Aldborough again tomorrow."

"Then if I accompany you both to The Rooms, we may accost the man once Sybilla is absorbed in the game."

This plan being approved, Ottilia set out after breakfast on Thursday morning with her mother-in-law and Henrietta, while her husband went off with Bastien to find the farmhand Reapham, the task delayed by his foray in the rowing boat with their son.

"If we repair to the Tea Room, we may watch for Mr Yelford through the window," Henrietta advised.

Ottilia followed her out of the Card Room, where Sybilla and her cronies were already deep in their game of whist, and across the hall. Rather than the strategically situated card tables, this apartment was equipped with chairs and sofas placed to facilitate comfort for chatterers. Two waiters hovered in readiness to supply tea or lemonade, accompanied by sweet almond biscuits or little cakes. Henrietta chose a snug coterie of chairs near the bay window and plonked down into a straight-backed cane chair that afforded a good view of passers-by.

Ottilia settled in the more comfortable armchair with a cushioned seat. "Will he come in here, or must we go out to catch him?"

"You need not move, Lady Fan. I will dash out and bring him to you."

Ottilia glanced about the room. There were few persons occupying the seats provided and none close enough to overhear. "That should work. If the place becomes crowded, we may have to think of taking a walk."

In the event, this proved unnecessary as the riding officer put in an appearance within a short time.

"There he is. I will fetch him to you."

As Henrietta sprang up and made for the hall door, Ottilia craned to catch sight of the individual heading towards the northern end of the High Street. Mr Yelford looked to be a lanky fellow, thin in both face and form. When Henrietta presently led him into Ottilia's presence, this impression was borne out. He was of a height with the tall companion, but in contrast to her robust form, he had a slight stoop accentuated by the loose fit of his green frock coat; his figure was all limbs and angular corners, his countenance narrow, the nose jutting out. He seemed older than Ottilia expected as he removed his three-cornered hat and bowed. He wore his dark hair, peppered with grey, cut short to the collar and lines of care or age were deeply carved from nose to mouth.

"Mr Yelford, I must thank you for taking the time to talk to me. Pray sit down."

He hesitated. "Miss Skelmersdale intimated that you had questions?"

"I do indeed."

"Concerning this killing?"

"Just so."

Ottilia waited, but Henrietta became impatient. "For goodness' sake, sit down, Mr Yelford! She won't bite."

He threw her a fulminating glance. "I am hardly likely to fear that." But he nevertheless took the chair opposite Ottilia.

Henrietta reseated herself. "Now then, you may begin, Lady Fan."

Ottilia was betrayed into a laugh. "I thank you for your permission, Henrietta."

"You are most welcome," said the other in her impish way, as she turned back to the riding officer. "You see. She is perfectly amiable."

Mr Yelford frowned. "No doubt. The subject, however, is scarcely one for amusement."

"Oh, don't be so stuffy, sir. Come, you are not as a rule this stiff." Henrietta turned to Ottilia. "Or he isn't with me."

"Miss Skelmersdale!"

Henrietta put a hand to her mouth in a mock self-deprecating gesture. "I am dumb."

Ottilia took a hand. "So I should hope. You are embarrassing the poor man. Mr Yelford, pay no heed. The matter is serious enough, I grant you."

He nodded agreement. "How may I assist, ma'am?"

Ottilia waded in. "How well did you know Carlton Green?"

She watched closely, but his shrug gave nothing away. "Hardly at all. He did not come much in my way. None of these younger men do. Besides, my duties do not permit of a great deal of social interaction. I am but one officer for this stretch of coast."

"That must be difficult for you." Ottilia infused interest into her tone. "I dare say you rely a great deal on the militia quartered here?"

His features became pinched. "Captain Turves assists at need, yes."

Henrietta chimed in. "Did you not tell me he is not amenable to his men being called out?"

"To my regret."

Ottilia took this up at once. "Why not? Is that not his duty?"

A little sigh escaped the man. "Too often these forays prove abortive. A cunning lot, these free traders. They will draw one in to raid at one place and carry out a haul at quite another."

Ottilia produced a smile of sympathy. "That must be excessively frustrating."

"You may well say so. Try as one might, it is hard to make a successful intervention."

Once more, Henrietta jumped in. "But you have had success, Mr Yelford, for you told me several —

"I did, ma'am, but I wish you will allow me to answer for myself."

Ottilia took a hand as Henrietta's gaze grew merry. "Do stop interrupting, Etta." And to the riding officer, "She is a dreadful tease, sir. I am sure you must have had a deal to bear from this quarter."

He reddened as Henrietta burst into her customary laugh. "He has, poor man. Never mind me, dear sir. I won't say another word."

The riding officer looked relieved. He turned back to Ottilia. "I did not intend to give the impression there have been no successes. We have indeed caught them several times."

"I would not have supposed otherwise, sir. You would hardly have remained in post without achieving your objectives."

"Yes, but I fear we lose more than we recover. Moreover, once the produce has been distributed, there is no chance of identification, even though one may subsequently see suspect items in the shops here."

Ottilia thought it time to introduce her own agenda. "You work with Lieutenant Radway upon occasion, I gather?"

Another shrug. "When there is word of a hoard of contraband. He has his own methods and I have mine."

"Then you are not colleagues in this work?"

"Our objectives are alike."

His reticence was telling. No love lost there, perhaps? Which did not augur well for her desire to hear more of Radway's dealings. She tried another tack.

"Why do you remain in this employment, Mr Yelford, if you do not have the support of these authorities?"

"Just what I asked him myself," said Henrietta, breaking her word all over again.

Mr Yelford gave a sour smile. "A riding officer necessarily works alone, ma'am. It is the nature of the job. Unlike the preventives, who patrol in pairs or groups in small boats."

Ottilia returned to her own requirements. "When you heard of this murder, were you much astonished?"

To her surprise, he neither balked nor prevaricated. "At first, no. They are a sorry bunch of criminals here. It was only a matter of time before some poor fellow lost his life."

"You said *at first*?"

He let out a breath. "When I learned of the precise circumstances, I will admit to being shocked."

"Which of the circumstances shocked you, if I may ask?"

"The manner of the killing. Also the man's identity. I'd had no word of that young man being involved in the trade."

"You would have heard if he had been then?"

"I have my ear to the ground, ma'am. I could name you half a dozen or more persons of apparent respectability who are up to their chins in it. If I had proof, I'd have them behind bars instanter."

Not that confirmation had been needed after Grégoire's testimony regarding his actual activities, but Ottilia was glad to have her supposition vindicated. Mr Yelford was suitably forthcoming. She could not imagine, however, that he would willingly confide the names of his informants. Thankfully, she need not tackle him on that score since Francis was in a way to discovering one out in Reapham at this very moment.

Yet Yelford clearly knew or had suspicions of individuals involved in the trade. She threw a glance at Henrietta in a bid to discourage her from bursting out again and received a mischievous smile in response. Satisfied, Ottilia tried a throw.

"What would you say to it, sir, if I were to suggest that a person or persons in authority might be responsible for Mr Green's death?"

The riding officer stared. Perplexed? Surprised? Ottilia held her nerve with patience and was rewarded.

His gaze dropped to his hands, dangling between his knees, the fingers joined. When he looked up again, there was sharpness in his gaze. "You won't name names, I take it?"

"Not at this juncture."

He drew a breath and sighed it out. "I would say, ma'am, that is it not beyond the bounds of probability. Unlikely, I think. But in my years in this post, I have learned not to place full trust in anyone."

Ottilia altered direction. "Is this a coast where refugees might seek asylum?"

Mr Yelford's gaze became intent. "From France?"

"Unless you are aware of them coming from elsewhere?"

"Holland, I believe, is one route by which those unfortunate enough to fall foul of the *Directoire* have escaped."

"You are still talking of the French?"

"There used to be such landings. They are rare these days. Although most contraband is smuggled in from that country."

Was it time to come into the open? Ottilia put a tentative question. "Have you ever come across coin or gemstones, perhaps?"

The man's gaze narrowed. "Why do you ask?"

Ottilia produced a smile. "Indulge me, if you please. It is pertinent."

"So I must suppose, ma'am. Yet I say again, why those items in particular?"

She hesitated. A dilemma. Could one raise the issue without involving Grégoire du Guet and his associates?

"My daughter came across a beached box. It contained concealed diamonds." She refrained from mentioning the letter at this point.

Yelford frowned. "Beached? From a wreck?"

"That is what we supposed to begin with."

"You have then gone beyond that supposition?"

The man was shrewd, she had to concede as much. "I have, sir."

She said no more, hoping he would take the bait. He turned his gaze to the window for a moment or two. Ottilia found

Henrietta's questioning eyes upon her and gave a quick shake of the head.

Presently, Mr Yelford's gaze returned to her face. "There was one such discovery."

"Yes?"

"I surprised a row-boat up near Thorpe. It was pulled on shore and manned by a lad. He ran away at sight of my pistol. When I conducted a search, I found an oilcloth package."

"Ah, did you? What was in it?"

"A collection of jewellery. Not, I think, of any great value. Some silver, with perhaps a few small stones. One may have been an emerald, I cannot be certain. In any event, it did not constitute a smuggler's hoard."

"What happened to it, sir?"

"I gave it into the charge of Lieutenant Radway."

CHAPTER FIFTEEN

The farmhand had been described as surly. Francis, accosting the fellow as he was sifting straw in the cowbarn, had no fault to find with the description.

Reapham, a small, wiry fellow dressed in a smock over shag breeches with a spotted bandana tied about his neck, paused in his work upon being hailed and turned his head, his hands still clutching the forked implement he was using to turn the straw. A sullen gaze took in the two visitors.

Francis sought confirmation. "You are Reapham?"

The fellow's chin came up. He hefted his fork and turned fully to face them, holding it in a defensive position. "What's it to you?"

Francis bristled. "I have a sufficient reason for asking. Are you or are you not the fellow I'm seeking?"

The sharpened tone elicited a grunt. "If I be, then what?"

Bastien stepped forward. "If it is you, then Lord Francis has questions. I advise that you answer well."

Francis set a hand on his nephew's arm, speaking in a murmur. "Easy, man." He raised his voice. "You will have heard of the recent killing." The man's face changed, shock entering in. Francis maintained an even tenor. "I am investigating the matter on behalf of the Justice of the Peace."

The fork was lowered a trifle and Reapham took a step back. "I know nowt about it. 'Cepting as what every man jack hereabouts has heard."

"That's as may be. You might, however, be able to help me with what you do know."

"I tell you I know nowt."

An impatient sound came from Bastien. "Do not be a fool. He does not ask if you have done this deed."

The farmhand eyed him for a moment before turning his gaze back on Francis. "I ain't done it."

"Have I accused you? What I am after has no direct bearing on the murder."

Reapham turned the fork, setting the prongs into the straw. "Ask then."

It was said with belligerence. Francis began to doubt he would get anything useful out of the man. Might a direct attack startle him into response?

"I have it on good authority that you are one of Lieutenant Radway's bloodhounds."

Consternation spread over the fellow's face, but his tone was as aggressive as ever. "Who says so?"

"Never mind that. Is it true?"

The fork swung up again. "He tell on me? Is that it?"

Francis lost patience. "For pity's sake, is that likely?"

Bastien cut in. "But he admits it with this question, no?"

"I never said so!"

"You speak like an idiot, *mon vieux*. Do you think you deal with fools?"

Francis waved him to silence, once more taking charge. "Let us waste no more time, Reapham. Tell me this: do your tip-offs include information about jewellery coming into the coast?"

The farmhand stared. "Jewellery?"

"Have you never heard of such hoards?"

Reapham shrugged. "Not as I know." He made a thrust with the fork. "I ain't saying as I heard more'n any other man. Can't dwell hereabouts without learning a thing or two."

Francis opted to accept the caveat. "Very well, but what have you heard?"

"Far as I did hear, them in the trade mostly run tea, brandy, lace and such."

His fluent recital gave the lie to his denial. He was clearly au fait with what went on in the smuggling fraternity. Francis pressed his point.

"But no gemstones or gold coin?"

A crack of amusement greeted this. "As if any'd have hold of such. Where'd they get it, I'd like to know?"

Francis weighed this. There was nothing in the fellow's demeanour to suggest cunning and concealment. Hostile to questioning he might be, but his utterances had a ring of truth. There was still a matter to explore, however.

"You said you hear things. Such as notice of a run? A concealed hoard?"

A wary look returned to the farmhand's face. "Anyone might hear of such."

"But not everyone would think to tip off Lieutenant Radway."

Reapham became sullen again. "I dunno nowt of that."

"Come, man. No doubt he paid you well for such information."

The farmhand evaded the issue. "Said you was looking into that killing. I ain't heard nowt of that. Nor have I told no one nothing to get my fee for it."

Francis seized on this. "So you are in Radway's pay!"

"I never said so."

"*Peste!*" Bastien, losing patience. "You speak of this fee. Do not lie!"

"Said I didn't get none, didn't I?"

Francis frowned his nephew down and changed tack. "You knew Carlton Green was not a free trader, am I right?"

"Didn't know him neither. Nor do I know who went to kill him."

"What if it was Radway?"

The fork clattered to the straw-covered floor. Reapham drew back, fearful now. "What do you mean? Why would he?"

Francis pressed on. "I believe he may have had reason."

"Why? He weren't in the trade, that dead man. Why would the lieutenant go after him? Sugnall, he might. Wark or Deanraw mebbe. He'd no call to go after a gennelman born. Not as some won't refuse a keg or packet as ain't paid no duty, but I'd swear as the lieutenant wouldn't harm no one unless he'd to take them to gaol. I know him. He'd not do nothing like that."

Was he altogether too vehement? Francis let it go. He had at least confirmed that Reapham was in Radway's employ as an informant. But as to the lieutenant's possible involvement with Carlton Green, they were no further forward.

An unexpected stroke of fortune befell Ottilia after she left The Rooms, intending to return to the lodging. Henrietta came with her to the door.

"Shall I accompany you, Lady Fan? I know Lord Francis dislikes you to go alone."

Ottilia demurred. "It is but a step. Besides, I mean to drop into Parbold's first. We have stayed here so long, I must replenish one or two cosmetic items."

An eager look came into Henrietta's face. "So must I. Let me go with you there, and then —☐

"Sybilla will fret if you are absent too long. I have already kept you beyond your time."

It was true enough, for Ottilia's mother-in-law was apt to snap if she felt neglected. But that was not her real reason. She wanted to mull over what she had learned from Mr Yelford and much as she liked Sybilla's companion, Henrietta was bound to ply her with questions she could not yet answer.

The latter emitted a little laugh. "I see what it is. You are afraid I will plague you about Mr Yelford's testimony and you prefer to keep your ideas to yourself."

Ottilia was obliged to smile. "Are you reading my mind, Etta?"

Delight lit Henrietta's features. "Have I hit it? Your abilities must be rubbing off on me." She touched Ottilia's arm. "Very well, I will return to my charge. Do not forget your umbrella. And take care, I pray you. I do not wish to earn a scold from your zealous husband for leaving you to go by yourself."

"Don't be foolish. What can possibly happen to me? A few minutes at the shop and I shall be home in a trice." Henrietta was inclined to argue the point, but Ottilia cut her short. "The sooner I am away, the sooner home."

She set off, armed with the indispensable umbrella, taking a route opposite to the way back to Crag Lane. There were, as ever, few people about. An elderly couple passed on the other side of the road, a maid hurried into one of the shops, a girl burdened with a basket of fish carried on her head trudged by, and a fellow muffled in a rough greatcoat slouched along, the hat low on his forehead.

Within a few moments Ottilia was entering by the general merchant's portal. Among the few customers waiting or browsing, she espied Cecily's companion, apparently examining cloth items laid out upon one of the counters.

"Miss Ospringe! How do you do?"

Ivy Ospringe turned, glancing across from under a beribboned straw bonnet. Recognition brought a smile and she moved at once to greet Ottilia.

"How good to see you, Lady Francis. We have missed you these last days." With a glance at a man nearby whose back was turned towards them, she lowered her voice to a murmur. "Cecily is anxious to know how your quest is faring."

Ottilia took the proffered hand, clasping it warmly. "We are a little further forward. Indeed, I had the intention of coming to see you both, but I have not yet had an opportunity. How is Cecily?"

Miss Ospringe's face clouded. "She is not doing well, I fear. She puts on a brave front, but her heart is sore. I have gone into her at night when I've heard her weeping, but she tries to discourage me. The dear girl wants me to believe she is coping."

"Which she clearly is not. I dare say she will not be at peace until she knows the truth."

Miss Ospringe sighed. "I fear you are right." Her gaze became both apprehensive and pleading. "Have you anything to tell her that may set her mind at rest?"

Ottilia hesitated. In truth, her information was more likely to trouble the young woman unduly. How to avoid saying as much? She was reluctant to worry Ivy, who was clearly anxious already. She temporised.

"I cannot speak of it in public, you understand. I will make a point of coming to you tomorrow, if I may?"

"Oh, please do. Cecily will be so relieved. What time would suit, so that we may be ready for you?"

"Pray do not go to any trouble."

"But you will take tea? Or no, you prefer coffee, do you not? I have heard Lady Polbrook say so."

Ottilia laughed. "She decries my taste. My husband calls me an addict."

"Coffee it shall be then. And perhaps a biscuit or cake? I have been at pains to bring home little delicacies to tempt Cecily's appetite."

"She is finding it hard to eat?"

"I am sure she has lost flesh. I do try to distract her. Indeed, I am hoping to persuade her to indulge in a little baking. She used to make treats for poor Carlton. I was just looking for a colourful remnant to fashion an apron." She gestured at the counter. "This necessity to be clad in black is most depressing."

"Just so. It is an unfortunate aspect of mourning, since one cannot forget it for a moment. A colourful apron will be just the thing to cheer Cecily."

Miss Ospringe sighed again. "I suspect you may prove to be the only bearer of cheer. If, that is, you have some ray of hope to impart."

Ottilia chose to avoid a direct answer. "I ought to be clear by late morning. Eleven or thereabouts? Would that suit?"

Miss Ospringe assented and Ottilia went with her to the counter, where she evaded attempts to secure her opinion on the various remnants, requesting the hovering assistant to produce soap and tooth powder. Mr Parbold was absent, but his minions were eager enough.

Ottilia had just extracted the small purse she carried from an inner pocket when Miss Ospringe, who had at last chosen her cloth and was waiting for it to be wrapped in brown paper, surprised her with an exclamation.

"Here is Lieutenant Radway. I had wanted to thank him for attending the funeral, so this is fortuitous."

Ottilia had already turned at the mention of the customs chief's name. Fortuitous for her too. Of typical soldierly bearing, he was impressive in muscle with a tanned countenance which looked well worn, as if he had seen much action.

Might she seize this opportunity? She caught Ivy's arm as that lady made to approach the officer. "Pray will you introduce me, Miss Ospringe? I have been wishing to meet this gentleman."

Nothing loath, Ivy performed the necessary presentation and Ottilia found herself the focus of a pair of keen eyes.

"Lady Francis? I am acquainted with your husband."

Ottilia took the bull by the horns. "I know, and I had requested him to engineer a meeting with you."

His brows rose. "You wish to speak to me? In connection with this death, I take it."

"Just so." Inspiration struck. "I am about to return to our lodging at the end of Crag Lane. Fisher Cottage, do you know it? Perhaps you would be kind enough to escort me there? We may talk on the way."

He did not answer immediately, looking her over in a way that raised Ottilia's hackles. She held them in check and waited.

Miss Ospringe, who had been hovering, intervened. "I wish you would, Lieutenant. It cannot be right for Lady Francis to be strolling about the town unattended."

A sudden grin altered the lieutenant's countenance and the faintly sinister air vanished. "How right you are, Miss Ospringe. I should not wish to incur Lord Francis's wrath. He is a very tartar where you are concerned, Lady Francis. Or so I have heard?"

"My husband takes excellent care of me, yes. My health is ever uncertain. He is wary of mishaps." *Let that be a warning.* But she did not say it aloud.

"Then if you are ready." He gestured towards the door.

Ottilia hung back. "I must complete my purchase first. Did you not wish to buy anything on your own account?"

The lieutenant gave a flourishing bow, one Ottilia felt to be tinged with mockery. "It is wholly unimportant. I am at your service, my lady."

Dislike burgeoning, Ottilia settled her account with the assistant, collected her umbrella and said her farewells to Miss Ospringe.

"Tomorrow then? We will expect you at about eleven."

"As we arranged, yes. Pray give Cecily my regards and say that there is no need to be apprehensive."

"I will do so, but I dare say such a wish is in vain."

Lieutenant Radway was holding open the door, so Ottilia merely smiled and went through. She was relieved when he failed to offer his arm as they set off along the High Street towards the first of the side lanes leading through to Crag Lane. How Francis could have found the man congenial was a puzzle. Her suspicion of Radway could not but deepen.

But she must not waste this opportunity. As it chanced, he brought up the subject first.

"Do you mean to give me the substance of your findings, ma'am? Or am I a target for your investigations?"

She glanced up at him. There was a smile upon his face, but it smacked more of disdain than true interest. Francis had been right. It was plain her suspicions of the man were returned twofold, and she had not even begun. Ottilia opted for an attack direct.

"Astute of you, sir. How did you guess?"

He gave a small laugh. "Since I understand you have spared no one, I could not deem myself a likely exception."

"I wonder you did not then present yourself before this."

"And give my head for washing? I am not such a fool, ma'am. What is it you wish to ask of me?"

Ottilia slowed her pace, throwing him a spurious smile. "Come, this is excellent, Lieutenant. I do hate wasting time."

"Then?"

She halted and turned to face him. "Was it you, sir, who used a blade of some kind on Mr Green and gave him a wound?"

He looked taken aback. "Me, ma'am?"

Ottilia eyed him. Was this genuine? She pressed the point. "Someone did so, as you must well know. I have it from my husband that Doctor Grove brought the matter up after the post-mortem when you were present."

His brows lowered and a look of faint amusement came into his eyes. "I gathered the victim claimed he gashed it on a rock. Might that not indeed have been the case? After all, why should Green lie?"

This was dangerous ground. Dare she reveal at this juncture what she knew of the jewellery thefts? Was it too soon? She temporised. "He might wish to conceal the truth in order to protect someone."

"Protect who?"

"The manner of his killing suggests Mr Green was involved in some nefarious activity. That being so, others must be involved. Or one other, at least."

"How so?"

If he was indeed that other, he had himself well in hand. Was it possible to break his nerve?

"He was shot, sir. Someone held that gun. It rather leaps to the eye that he was not acting alone."

Lieutenant Radway pursed his lips. Thinking it over? Then he indicated the way ahead. "Shall we?"

With reluctance, Ottilia began to walk again, maintaining a slow pace. She was getting nowhere. Would he proffer anything if she used her tactic of silence?

For a moment or two, it seemed not. Then he spoke. "Do you have some idea of the nature of this nefarious activity? I doubt it is smuggling."

Ottilia leaped on this. "Why do you doubt it?"

"Because I have never heard of his being so involved."

"Ah, yes. You have an informant, have you not?"

He glanced round. "You found that out?"

"By chance."

"Did you rule out smuggling?"

"Yes, I did."

"Well, then?"

Was he testing her? If he was Carlton's accomplice, he would wish to find out how much she knew. If he was innocent, the question could only be idle. She turned the tables.

"I was hoping you might have a notion yourself, sir. You are in the business of keeping His Majesty's revenue from being appropriated. You must have ears to the ground all over this area."

"True, true." He fell silent for a space. "I cannot say I have heard anything to Green's detriment. I had no reason to suspect him. He seemed an ordinary young fellow, after all. Apart from his association with that Frenchman, that is."

The rider rankled. Yet was there an edge to his voice as he said it? Ottilia picked it up. "You do not approve of Grégoire du Guet?"

She was treated to a riffle of mocking laughter. "What would you, ma'am? These émigrés are an infernal nuisance. Or they have been in earlier years. We do not find ourselves obliged to pick them out of the water quite so many times these days."

Ottilia probed a little. "Their fate is often pitiful, do you not think?"

"Faugh! That business has been over for some years. Don't we have enough to deal with, keeping these free traders at bay without having to succour foreigners landing on our shores?" He seemed to recognise the harshness of his words, for he bent an apologetic look upon her. "You think me unsympathetic, I dare say. Yet if you had my task, I believe you might feel as frustrated. I don't know how many times I have been called out to intercept a smuggling vessel, only to find the craft packed stem to stern with escaping Frenchmen, who become nothing more than a burden upon the good citizens of this country."

This was telling indeed. At last his words rang with sincerity, such as it was. If he despised émigrés this much, Ottilia could well believe him capable of defrauding them of their precious valuables. His ranting shone, moreover, a different light upon his character.

He seemed to sense it, for he again broke out into laughter. "You will be thinking me a very ogre, am I right? To be frank, my quarrel is far stronger with the free traders. The bane of my existence, I assure you, ma'am."

They had reached Crag Lane, the shingle edging one side of the narrow fairway, where he paused. "Was there any other point upon which you wished to consult me?"

Consult him? An avoidance tactic supposed to indicate he was no subject for questioning? Yet it was hard to know how to proceed without alerting him to her knowledge. Ottilia tried a different avenue as she began to stroll towards the lodging.

"What do you make of Mr Green having been tied up and blindfolded, sir?"

His face expressed surprise as he kept pace beside her. "What do I make of it?"

"Since you are experienced with the actions of criminals, I wonder if you might have come across something similar?"

The lieutenant put up a hand and scratched his chin in a meditative fashion. "I see what you would be at. No, no, ma'am. If a free trader seeks to punish one of his own, he takes a cruder path."

"Such as?"

"Forgive my bluntness, but one is more likely to find a fellow with his head shoved down a privy or covered head to foot in dung. Tying his hands would be a little too refined, and hiding his eyes for him would be far too merciful. Besides, if these fellows were to go as far as slaying a man, they'd be more likely to string him up than perform an elaborate ritual of the kind."

Ottilia's heart jumped. Though Radway of necessity knew how the killing had been carried out, this manner of describing it was telling. An elaborate ritual? It seemed as if he knew the truth of the matter. They were within sight of the house now and Ottilia halted. She cast off caution.

"A fascinating comparison, Lieutenant. Your candour urges me to be likewise frank."

He did not look in the least disconcerted, his brows raised in question. "Say on."

"You spoke just now of émigrés. Had you any inkling that packages of valuables are picked up here from time to time? Sent, I need scarcely add, from relatives or associates of those who have sought refuge in our land from the scourge of France's revolution."

Radway's brows drew together in a thick line above his eyes. "Valuables? Of what kind?"

"Jewels or gemstones mostly. Some gold coin too." Ottilia watched him closely as she spoke, but could not flatter herself she gained anything by it.

He pursed his lips for a moment as if he considered further, and then gave a slow shake of his head. "I vaguely recall something... Ah. Did not Yelford find something of the sort some time back? What was it now? A few gewgaws, not worth much as I remember." He gave a nonchalant shrug. "It did not appear to me to need further investigation. We have a collection of such odds and ends at the custom house. However, you may well be right about the French connection. Dropped possibly by one of those who came ashore here?"

Ottilia gave an inward curse. Impossible to tell whether this insouciance was genuine or if Radway was lying to her face. She dared not risk revealing her full knowledge. The man was too smooth an operator, regardless of whether or not he was involved.

"Have you then eliminated Radway?"

The question, posed by her husband, presented Ottilia with a dilemma. She was partaking of her customary beverage while resting in the parlour with Francis, who had returned from his expedition a little in advance of herself. She had heard his report of the farmhand in exchange for hers of both Yelford and the lieutenant.

"I find that difficult to answer, my dearest. He was not overtly evasive, but his responses could have been cleverly so."

Francis was propping up the mantelpiece as usual. He set down his glass, now empty of the Madeira he had consumed. "I've not found him enigmatic."

"He is ready enough to speak out on the surface."

"You think he is hiding his teeth?"

Ottilia sipped and then looked up with a faint smile. "He was forthright enough about his contempt for émigrés."

Her spouse's gaze became keen. "Was he so? Did he rant like Sugnall?"

"Not with the vehemence of the blacksmith as you spoke of it."

"But?"

"It did point to a man who would not hesitate to take from those he considers undeserving."

She was treated to one of Francis's snorts of derision. "You might say the same of Sugnall then."

The notion struck Ottilia as she saw the change in her husband's face. Her exclamation chimed with his.

"The blacksmith involved?"

"Sugnall an accomplice?"

She exchanged a look of surprise with Francis and broke into laughter. "We are of one mind, my dearest dear."

He did not join in with her amusement. "Yes, but does that let Radway out? Are we looking at two of them? Or do we go after Sugnall alone?"

Ottilia sobered at once. "A pertinent point." She recalled her interview with the lieutenant. "There is the manner of the killing to be taken into account. Radway would have it that the free traders would never approach the matter thus."

"Meaning?"

"How did he phrase it? I took note of it, since it was singularly telling. He said they would not perform *an elaborate ritual*. Their methods would be cruder, so we might judge the blacksmith by the same —□

"Not so." Francis rapped the mantelshelf with his knuckles. "Sugnall comes of the middling sort. His father was clerk to the owner of an estate. Sugnall chose the smithy in preference to working for his late master's heir."

Ottilia's ideas were churning. "Would you call him refined?"

"Hardly that. But he's an educated fellow who might well have rivalled Radway's status in other circumstances. Moreover, the bee in his bonnet concerning émigrés is a good deal harsher than Radway's. With the exception of du Guet, he can't abide them."

Ottilia stared at him, her mind readjusting and sifting the information gathered. "Have I been on the wrong track altogether?"

Her husband shifted from the fireplace and dropped down beside her on the sofa. "We don't know that, my loved one. After all, you had no reason to include Sugnall. We were checking for his being involved with smuggling."

"True."

Then Francis smote his own knee with his fist. "It's I who have been remiss. I ought to have thought of him the moment you began talking of émigrés. I confess it did not occur to me."

Ottilia took the offending fist and held it between both her hands. "Why would it? We had dismissed the man from our deliberations. You had spoken of his dislike of the French, but I did not pick up on that either."

Francis unclenched his fist and slipped his fingers between hers. "I wish you won't put this on yourself, you wretch. Don't make me feel worse."

Ottilia squeezed his fingers. "We are putting the cart before the horse again. It is pure conjecture based upon little foundation."

"How so?"

"Well, only consider. Carlton did not even own a horse, so why would he frequent the smithy? Moreover, how would

Sugnall have discovered he was collecting packages? We have also to account for the blade wound."

Her husband blew out a breath in frustration. "Then you will have it we are back to Radway, I dare say."

"I cannot rule him out, however convenient it would be to do so."

"What will you do then? I could return to Sugnall's and see if I can unravel those questions."

Ottilia mulled over the notion for a moment or two. "Let me think on it. My priority is to visit Cecily. I have still to find out about Carlton's dealings with the Reverend Stewkley."

"Will you tell her what has been found?"

Ottilia sighed. "I fear I must. It will undoubtedly cause her more upset."

"She may know more than she's told you. As I recall, most witnesses hold back something which usually proves to be of importance."

"You are quite right, my dearest dear. You remind me to be on the qui vive when I speak to her. It is all too easy to be swayed by sympathy for her distress."

Accordingly, when Ottilia set forth upon the following morning, she determined to hold sympathy to a minimum. Francis was pledged to take Pretty fossil-hunting, his daughter having claimed her turn for a treat.

"Luke got to go in a boat, Papa, and we have not searched for fossils for an age. And I've been good and done all my lessons, and helped Luke into the bargain. It's only fair."

No match for his adored daughter's cajolery, Francis had assented, confiding to his wife when they were alone that night, "We have neglected them for this blasted murder. Bastien may go with you in my stead. He'll likely jump at the chance to see Miss Green."

The rain held off, but Ottilia's escort had nevertheless armed himself with an umbrella. "It does not promise well, *Tante*. Better to be safe, I think."

Ottilia agreed, but as they walked, she took the chance to say what was on her mind. "Come in with me, by all means, Bastien, but I will be grateful if you don't remain long. I must tell Cecily about the gemstones, and I suspect your presence may embarrass her."

"Because I am myself an émigré? I will not come in, *Tante*."

"There is no need to avoid Cecily altogether. I did not mean—☐

He cut her off. "It is of no concern. I have come to think it is foolish to be putting myself forward."

"Because of Grégoire?"

"Not at all. I do not believe Grégoire is serious. My father once told me that one should not raise expectations if one does not intend to fulfil them."

Disappointment arose in Ottilia. "You are not serious either then? I thought you liked Cecily."

"To like is not enough. More, she does not favour me."

So that was it. "Ah, I see. If she did?"

Bastien drew a breath and let it out. "That would be another affair altogether. But you know, as do I, that Cecily is indifferent to me."

Ottilia accepted this. Was it wounded pride? Cecily clearly had a preference for Grégoire. Perhaps it was wise of Bastien to pull away. Neither the marquis nor his French wife would have been pleased to see him courting a woman of neither means nor status. Illegitimate he might be, but his father's rank put Bastien into the first circles regardless. One might despise the system, yet one must abide by its rules — to an extent.

Aware that she crossed its lines all too often, Ottilia could only be thankful for her beloved husband's tolerance.

Bastien left her at the door of the Greens' home, promising to return.

"Give me an hour, my dear boy. I will wait for you."

Ivy Ospringe jumped up when the maid announced Ottilia. "You have come in excellent time, Lady Francis." And to the maid, "Bring the refreshments, if you please, Mary. Do take a seat, ma'am. Cecily will be down directly."

Ottilia made herself comfortable on the indicated chair, dropping her voice. "How is she today?"

Miss Ospringe shook her head as she settled into the little sofa. "No better, I fear. She revived for a while when I gave her the cloth, but she has not yet attempted to do anything with it."

"Understandable. It is bound to take time. How are you both managing, by the by, if that is not an indelicate question?"

The older dame looked puzzled. "In what respect, ma'am?"

Ottilia smiled. "Financially, Miss Ospringe. I received the impression Cecily was concerned?"

"Oh. Oh, yes, I see." Miss Ospringe fluttered her hands. "Matters are left a little uncertain, but dear Cecily was not wholly dependent upon Carlton. She has a little income of her own. Her papa made sure of that. We will be able to manage. Once probate is granted on Carlton's will — it is in his lawyer's possession, and he has promised to do all that is necessary — that will ease Cecily's path. He has — had — an income from investment in the Funds."

"And your path, Miss Ospringe?"

A trifle of colour entered the lady's cheeks. "I will not abandon her, be sure, even if it means we must retrench a little."

There was time for no more as Cecily Green entered at that moment. She looked wan to Ottilia's eye, her black gown emphasising her pallor. It appeared to hang a trifle in the bodice, as if it had become loose on her slight figure. Ottilia put out a hand.

"My dear child! Miss Ospringe said you had lost flesh, and I see it is indeed the case."

Cecily came across and took the hand briefly, making a pathetic attempt at a smile. "I have been anxious, perhaps." A look compounded of eagerness and apprehension came into her face as she took her seat beside her duenna. "You have news for me, I hope?"

Ottilia fought down a craven desire to prevaricate. "I have, but I doubt it will sit well with you."

Cecily's eyes opened wide. "Do you know who…?"

Should she be frank? Better to feed it in moderation, perhaps. "Not quite yet."

She received a straight look. "What does that mean, if you please?"

Ottilia had forgotten how astute the girl was. "I have a suspicion which I cannot yet substantiate."

"Will you share it?"

"Excuse me on that score for the moment. There is other information I must impart first."

Cecily's gaze clouded. "You have discovered why my brother was killed."

"I think so. What I know for certain is that he was working with Grégoire du Guet on a mission to help émigrés."

She was treated to a blank look, immediately followed by puzzlement. "I beg your pardon?"

Ottilia concealed an inward sigh. This was going to be difficult. "Grégoire gave Carlton news of packages arriving here from France."

"Packages? Of what, pray?"

"Gemstones, for the most part. Some gold coin. Carlton's task was to collect these packets and hand over the contents so that Grégoire could pass them to their owners."

"Gracious heaven!" Thus Ivy Ospringe. "Do you mean he was not hunting fossils at all?"

Cecily said nothing, her eyes intent upon Ottilia. Had she known or guessed?

"He did hunt fossils, which is why Grégoire enlisted his aid. It made an excellent cover for this work." Ottilia eyed Cecily. "Had you any idea of this, my dear?"

She was clasping her hands together in her lap and Ottilia noted how they tightened. "This does not explain my brother's wound, nor his terrible death."

Ottilia drew a breath. "Not entirely. In telling you the rest, let me say that I believe Carlton was coerced into acting as he did."

"Coerced? By whom?"

"Blackmailed. By his murderer."

Miss Ospringe jumped in. "But why? What had the poor boy done to be blackmailed?"

Ottilia put up a finger. "Give me leave. What I mean to say is that he was blackmailed into doing what he did."

"Into doing what?" Cecily's tone was curt.

"He stole items from these various hoards." Ottilia glanced at the young woman's hands. She wore no adornment. "Carlton gave you a ring. Grégoire recognised it for part of a set."

Cecily half rose from her seat. "Then it was Grégoire who—"

"No, it was not Grégoire. He saw the ring only after your brother's death. He supposed you wore it as a reminder."

Cecily subsided, speaking low. "I did wear it. Not for many days, for it made me too sad." She looked up again. "You tell me now that my brother stole it?"

"Among other pieces. We cannot know how many."

"But if he was doing that, why…?"

Beside her, Miss Ospringe gave a shudder. "That is just what I cannot understand either, my love. Do you know, Lady Francis?"

"I can only tell you what I suspect, since I have no proof." She looked to Cecily again. "You told me at the outset how Carlton had become irritable so that you thought he was anxious about something."

"He was so ever since he received that horrid gash."

The pieces seemed to be falling into place. "That is just why I believe he was forced into this thieving. It did not sit well with him, and I dare say he suffered agonies of conscience."

Cecily's head came up. "Then why did he not refuse to do it?"

"I think he did at last. If my surmise is correct, it is possible he threatened to expose his blackmailer."

Miss Ospringe gave a shocked gasp and Cecily drew in a ragged breath. "And the villain put him to death!"

"Just so." Although Ottilia had hardly expected the girl to encapsulate the circumstance with such precision.

The duenna was visibly shaking and Cecily, after a rigid moment, threw her hands over her face and gave vent to a heartfelt groan.

To Ottilia's relief, the maid entered at this opportune moment, bearing a loaded tray. Disposing of its contents served the combined purposes of keeping her from noticing the atmosphere in the little parlour and allowing both the women time to recover themselves. Ottilia embarked upon a flow of gentle commentary meant to assist this goal, addressing herself to the maid.

"Ah, this is most welcome, Mary. Do I see macaroons? How delightful. I am sure we could all do with a cup of your delicious coffee. Cream for me, if you please, and two lumps of sugar. You will know how your mistress likes it. Thank you, set it down on this little table, if you please. I will take a biscuit, yes."

By the time the coffee and macaroons had been served, both Cecily and her companion looked to be sufficiently in command of themselves again for Ottilia to be able to desist. She sipped her beverage and waited for the maid to withdraw before changing her tone.

"There now, how fortunate your maid chose to enter just at that moment. I am sorry to have given you both such a horrid shock."

Miss Ospringe had begun upon her coffee and Cecily picked up a macaroon. "You had no choice, ma'am. I am glad to know at least that my brother's honour had not been compromised."

Ottilia agreed to this, despite her private conviction that Carlton would have done better to confide the whole to Grégoire at the outset. Together, they might have taken a stand against the blackmailer, if everything the Frenchman had told her was true. Time to move on, for she still had one last avenue to explore.

"I do need to ask you something further, Cecily."

The girl set down the little cake uneaten and picked up her coffee cup. She acted absently, Ottilia was persuaded, but she answered calmly enough.

"What is it, ma'am?"

"Have you any notion why Carlton made frequent visits to the rectory? I understand he went there to see the Reverend Stewkley on several evenings."

Surprising her, Ivy Ospringe took this. "Oh, I can vouch for that. Dear Carlton told me he liked to read with the reverend. The rector is a most erudite man, you must know. I think Carlton felt a lack in his education and went there to improve himself."

A mirthless laugh came from Cecily. "Oh, piffle, Ivy! Carlton did not give a fig for education. Papa was in two minds whether to send him to the university, do you not remember?"

"But my dear Cecily, why else should he visit the reverend, a man years and years his senior?"

"That I cannot say. But it is far more likely he went there for social reasons, to play at cards, I dare say. You of all people know how much Reverend Stewkley enjoys a game."

"That is certainly true. He has revelled in having so keen and shrewd a player as Lady Polbrook. He is a fine player himself, you must know."

"There you are then. As like as not Carlton went for that reason. He liked to gamble." Cecily's gaze came back to Ottilia. "Not in any serious spirit. But he did enjoy a risk. When we played together, he always took a chance instead of playing safe as I did."

Which explained the attraction of the secret game he was involved in with Grégoire du Guet. He must have revelled in creating his coded record. Until he was drawn into acting against his own integrity.

Did all this mean she could strike the Reverend Stewkley off her list? Ought she to verify it? Why not make a detour to The Rooms on the way home? If the whist players were still at it, she could seize the opportunity to check with the man himself.

The decision made, she returned her attention to her hostess. At Cecily's request, she related how she had come to her conclusions via Pretty's treasure box and Carlton's record, together with the confirmation that came from Grégoire. By the time she had finished, her coffee was drunk and the macaroons eaten. Yet she still had a little time before Bastien was due to collect her.

Chafing, she thought it could do no harm to nip across to The Rooms on her own. It was no great distance. A glance through the window told her the clouds were lowering, but rain not yet falling. She made up her mind.

"Pray tell Bastien when he arrives to look for me there."

A few words of farewell and she was stepping out of the front door. The maid shut it behind her and Ottilia began the short walk along the narrow lane that led to Crabbe Street and thence to the High Street.

She had not taken many steps when she heard a flurry of movement behind her. Next moment, something heavy fluttered over her head and fell about her face and shoulders, smothering the light. Ottilia gave a muffled cry. She felt a blow to the back of her head. Her senses spun and blackness descended.

CHAPTER SIXTEEN

Driven by the onset of rain to cut short his expedition with his daughter, Francis sent Pretty off to the nursery.

"Get yourself into dry clothes quickly, sweetheart. We don't want you catching a chill. Hepsie will help you."

Pretty hovered on the stair. "You're wet too, Papa. Aren't you going to change?"

"I'm right behind you. Up with you, child."

She sprinted ahead and Francis slipped into his bedchamber, where he stripped off his damp coat and rang for Tyler to help him remove his boots and find a spare pair. The exercise took longer than he anticipated, as he had also to take a towel to his hair and run a comb through while the footman found the necessary footwear.

"Your boots, my lord. I'll take these down to the kitchens to dry by the fire."

"Good man." He sat on the bed to pull them on. "Fetch me the blue frock, will you? And a fresh neck-cloth. This one is ruined."

At last refreshed to his satisfaction, he turned from the mirror. "Bring coffee to the parlour, Tyler. I dare say her ladyship will be back at any moment."

But when he entered the parlour, he found his mother in possession, having claimed her usual seat by the fire, at which she was warming her hands.

"Back already, ma'am? Where is your companion?"

The dowager straightened, looking up. "She's gone to see to our coats. It began to rain and we were obliged to give up our game. Drat this coast and its miserable weather!"

Francis went across, leaning to hold his palms to the welcome warmth. "Yes, it's foul. Though I gather from the journals it's much the same across the country."

His mother looked him up and down. "I am surprised you did not get caught in it yourself."

"We did. I've just changed. Pretty was drenched. I sent her to change."

"Very sensible. It is distinctly chilly. I had my coat and an umbrella and thus escaped the worst of it. At least Mrs Forncett had the forethought to have the fire made up in here. They ought to have one up in the nursery too."

"They do." Francis moved a little away from the heat, setting his elbow on the corner of the mantel. "Hepsie knows to keep the children warm. Tillie won't countenance negligence that might endanger the little ones. She is so afraid of losing one of them now she cannot produce another."

He received one of his mother's beady-eyed looks. "Is it certain?"

Francis sighed. "She has not resumed her monthly courses, and the twins are going on three now. Patrick believes she has ended her childbearing years. Prematurely, but even so."

"That doctor brother of Ottilia's is not infallible. She is young yet."

"She is not far off forty. Besides, I don't wish her to go through again what she endured with our girls. I've almost lost her too many times."

The words were barely out of his mouth when the door was thrust open and Bastien strode into the room.

"*Tante!*" He stopped short. "Where is she?" His glance swept the room. "*Grand-mère*, did Lady Fan return with you? Is she perhaps in her chamber? Or with the children?"

The import of his words sank home and Francis felt ice enter his veins. He started forward. "What the devil do you mean, Bastien? My wife was with you!"

"I left her at Cecily's home. When I went to fetch her, they told me she had gone to The Rooms. Do you say she is not in the house?"

"For pity's sake! If she was, I'd have seen her. Didn't you follow her?"

Bastien came up. "I went there, *bien sûr*. When I could not find *Grand-mère*, I was told she had gone home. I thought *Tante* must be with her." He cast a glance at the dowager which was redolent with the same anguish burgeoning in Francis's breast. "But is it not so?"

His mother spoke up, sharp and urgent. "I have not seen her since we left here this morning." Her eyes veered to Francis. "She must have chosen to go elsewhere. Likely she is sheltering from the rain."

Francis's mind was beginning to work, clicking into gear over the initial freeze that had engulfed him. There had been too many similar instances in the past. He gave himself a mental snap.

"Do you know why she didn't wait for you, Bastien? Did the Green woman say anything?"

He gave a typically gallic shrug. "Miss Ospringe thought she wished to speak to Reverend Stewkley."

"Then she wouldn't have gone elsewhere." He spied his footman standing just inside the door, a loaded tray in his hands. His attitude of shocked attention showed he must have heard what had just passed in the room. "Tyler, send to Ryde and Williams. Bid them come here immediately and bring the rest of the stable crew with them. We'll organise a search." Tyler set down the tray and hurried off. "Bastien, you're still in outdoor gear. Go the custom house and see if Radway is there."

His nephew slapped the hat he was holding back on his head. "If he is?"

"Bring him back with you."

He did not add what to do if the lieutenant was not at his place of work, the unpleasant thought roving in his mind that Radway's whereabouts might be of crucial importance. But he had not bargained for his nephew's common sense.

"If I do not find him at the custom house, shall I go to Captain Turves?"

Francis vetoed this in no uncertain terms. "As yet, we don't know if we need to call out the militia."

His mother intervened in some agitation. "But you won't hesitate if the need arises, I hope."

"I won't, never fear. What are you waiting for, Bastien?"

His nephew started. "I go, *mon oncle*, I go."

Next moment, he was out the door, his footsteps clattering on the stairs. The dowager was eyeing Francis, her delicate brows drawn together.

"What do you want with Lieutenant Radway? Is he not on Ottilia's list?"

"Nothing is certain."

"What do you mean to do, Francis?"

"Scour the town, if I have to. And more."

His mother got up from her chair and came to where he stood in the middle of the room. She set a hand to his shoulder. "What is it you fear, my son?"

He removed the hand and held it. "It's not like Tillie, Mama. She knows how much I fret if she is absent. She would not cause me unnecessary anxiety. If she meant to meet you, or

Stewkley, at The Rooms, that is where she would have been had she been able."

"You believe she is not able? For what reason? Do you suppose she has fallen ill, or…?"

Francis released her fingers. "Too many people in this town know what she has been about. She has likely questioned the culprit already. What if he has chosen to prevent her investigation coming to a conclusion?"

The dowager's black eyes darkened. "You fear the worst?"

Francis let out an exasperated sigh. "I always fear the worst."

His mother's features became stern. "Then desist! You are not thinking straight, boy. What, do you suppose this villain would dare lay hands upon a lady of notable rank?"

"What should stop him?"

"Don't be a fool, Francis! We are not nobodies. Whoever he is, this creature must know he would bring the might of the law down upon himself, not to mention the peerage."

For a moment, the argument had an effect, but it did not wholly ring true. "He might not go so far as to kill her, but if he has her in his clutches, he might use threats."

"To make her stop?" His mother settled back on her heels, her gaze intent. "You suspect Radway, is that it?"

"Or the blacksmith. We spoke of it only yesterday, Tillie and I. I mean to send Williams to the smithy, and the other lads can scour the town. I need Ryde with me. But I'll wait for Bastien's return before I set out."

A sensation of cold and motion penetrated the clouds in Ottilia's mind. Awareness came in brief pockets of semi-consciousness in between bouts wherein reality was a miasma of strange dreaming images. Someone carried her? Blood pounding in her head. Was she upside down? The crunch of booted feet and a vague rhythmic shushing she ought to recognise. How came she to this? She forced heavy eyelids apart and saw only dark. Nausea dizzied her mind and she sank back into oblivion for a while.

When she came to again, all motion had ceased. Bit by bit the cogs in her brain strove to make sense of her situation. The muffled feel was gone, although some restriction covered her mouth, which felt dry. Hardness at her back. Was she slumped against a wall? A dull throbbing manifested at the back of her head and her memory stirred.

She had felt a blow. Then consciousness had deserted her mind. A faint question arose but she suppressed it. Let her not yet fret over who. She must assess her situation first.

It was not happy. Discomfort manifested in several places, not least in the clamminess of damp clothes. Had she been carried in the rain? Upon what was she sitting that her posterior should feel numbed? Her eyelids were heavy and it exacerbated the headache when she attempted to open her eyes. The half-expected blackness was absent, giving way to glimmers of light. Not enough to judge her whereabouts, save for an impression of huge shadows, dimly seen. Yet also space. She blinked a few times in the hope of widening her vision.

The effort was rewarded. There was a slash of light coming from above which enabled her to see the immediate area. Beyond this, down a narrow tunnel, another source gave shape to shadowy outlines. People? No, too low, and unmoving besides.

Anxious for identification, Ottilia made a move to set down her hands in a bid to push herself up, and could not. Instinct made her yank, causing a sharp pain at her wrists. They were tied.

Thin string, was it? A chord flickered in her memory, but was overtaken by a different suspicion. Answering it, she tried to shift her legs and found them hindered. Had they tied her ankles too? Even at the thought, a twinge there confirmed it.

Her tongue, when she used it to bring saliva to alleviate dryness, came into contact with an obstruction. A gag? Yes, for she could feel its knot at the back of her head, pressing on the tenderness there. Was that where she had received the blow?

The gradual recognition gave hope that her brain was clicking into gear. So too was her vision beginning to adjust, her surroundings growing clearer.

Where was she? The atmosphere was dank with an icy feel. Ottilia became aware of a metallic and musty odour. Rain? She listened for the spattering and heard again the rhythmic swishing she vaguely recalled from earlier. It was louder here. Breaking waves?

Abruptly, the world about her made sense, the huge shapes clarifying into walls of rock, like the boulders between where she was and that tunnelling light. She had been left in a cave.

Her mind froze on the realisation of just where she was. And the possible why. Did the perpetrator seek to punish her as he had punished Carlton Green?

Or, no. Had that been her assailant's intent, she would have been lying, as had the victim, with a musket ball in her brain. The similarity was there, but not exact. No blindfold. She was meant to see, to experience her prison and know it for revenge. It was not merely prevention. A warning? Would he come to release her? When?

Too late, in all probability. Could she not effect an escape? Was she guarded?

Ottilia looked about to verify whether she was in fact alone. The cave's proportions had grown more recognisable. Was not that the very rock behind which Carlton had been murdered? She was situated further into the cave than where he had been found, a narrower part where the crevice above allowed a little light to penetrate.

Even so, there was no shape that might be human. Whoever had brought her here had dumped her, tied her up, and left.

Come, Ottilia, you are not yet dead. Best to rid herself of the restrictive gag first. She wiggled her jaw, trying to dislodge the band of cloth. It proved too tightly wedged between her lips. She tried to chew at it and succeeded only in wetting the folds.

Might she loosen her bonds? Her hands were tied in front and she managed to twist them enough to bend her elbows and bring them closer. Twine, not rope. Not too thick then. Had Carlton's been tied with similar twine? If her mouth were free, she could use her teeth, but she had failed in that attempt.

Surely she could reach her ankles? The action of drawing up her knees produced a series of twinges and was difficult to do besides. The position was hard to maintain and she could barely see what she was doing, but she worked at the twine, trying to locate the knot.

How long she struggled, Ottilia could not have said. She was obliged to take rests and begin again. In between, her body's ills manifested, compounded at length by pangs of hunger and thirst. Her head swam. That was the lack of water, said her brother's voice in her mind.

The injuries aside, she was already chilled with cold and damp. Even if she did not raise a fever, which was all too likely, without water or food, her already weak constitution would inevitably fail.

She had been in danger before, but this isolation was unprecedented. No doubt that her beloved Fan, once alerted to her absence, would move heaven and earth to find her. With no clue to her whereabouts, and no reason to guess at this particular cruel revenge, could he do so before her precarious health betrayed her?

Hunger and thirst she might weather, but Ottilia had no illusions. If she was not found before night, she would be lucky to outlast the dawn.

"I wish you will stop pacing, Francis. You will not bring Ottilia back any quicker and you are wasting energy."

He heard his mother's words at the periphery of his mind, which was teeming with various hideous scenarios wherein his darling wife was lying dead, or injured. Or, most dreaded of all, washed away in the unforgiving sea.

"Francis Fanshawe! Sit!"

It was the voice of his childhood. Without thinking, he dropped into the nearest chair. Realising, he caught the flash of those familiar black eyes. A mirthless laugh escaped him. "What, am I a boy again?"

The dowager flapped a hand. "Don't behave as one then. You have done all you can for the present."

He had, but it felt as nothing. Bastien was not yet returned, but Francis had despatched his coachman to discover what he might from Sugnall the blacksmith. "Discreetly, Williams. If he is absent, check his home. If he is not there either, report to me at once." Ryde was making a tour of the shops just in case, the rest of the crew splitting up to cover the streets of the town and beyond. His mother's companion, once in possession of the news, had offered to hunt down the riding officer.

"Mr Yelford may have heard or seen something. Moreover, he could be useful in a search, for he knows the area well."

Francis had agreed to it, thankful for any possible assistance in locating Ottilia.

"Of what use to fret," went on his mother, "when Ottilia may walk in at any moment?"

"I wish she might."

The dowager leaned forward. "I've had no chance to speak of it, but she would have found it out if she had met us at The Rooms."

"Of what are you talking, ma'am?"

"Stewkley."

"What about him?"

"Were you not paying attention? Bastien said Ottilia had the intention of speaking to him. But she need not, for I have forestalled her questions."

A faint stirring of interest focused his mind. "What do you mean?"

His mother looked triumphant. "Ottilia may cross him off her list. I said it was absurd to suppose he could be involved in this horrible affair, did I not?"

"Did you?"

"Most certainly. I dare say you don't recall, or perhaps we were speaking in your absence."

Impatience seized Francis. "Well, what of it?"

"I asked Stewkley direct. 'Why did that Green boy visit you so frequently?' I demanded. 'My daughter-in-law wishes to know,' I said."

Was she trying to distract him with this history? "What said he?"

The black eyes registered satisfaction. "He was teaching the boy to play chess. Stewkley was cast down about it being no longer possible to give himself a worthy partner. Not that he dwelled on that aspect. I believe it slipped out, for he immediately expressed his distress at the fellow's death."

"I imagine he might." It was something that there was one less suspect. If Ottilia had been certain of the villain's identity, he could have confronted them at once, assuming his fears had any foundation. He hoped they did not, but the conviction that something untoward had happened to his beloved wife was growing upon him.

The sound he had been half-consciously waiting for came at last. "I believe that is the front door."

He was up and hurrying out into the hall, moving to the top of the flight of stairs that led down to the ground floor. The door was just visible at the end of the square hallway and his nephew had just come through, followed by Lieutenant Radway.

Instinct sent him hurtling down the stairs. "He found you then? Have you seen my wife? Did you serve her a back-handed turn?"

The customs chief halted before him, throwing up a defensive hand. "Steady, friend! Of what do you accuse me?"

Bastien cut in before Francis could answer. "He has not seen her, *mon oncle*. He has been all morning in the custom house."

Relief, mingled with disappointment, washed through Francis. "Then you know no more than we do."

"Ah, but I did speak with her," he added as Francis suffered a reversal of feeling, "but not, alas, today. We conversed yesterday as I escorted her home at her request."

Francis brushed this aside. "She told me. I'm not interested in that. My sole focus is on where she is now."

"So your nephew says. I came to offer my services, not that I can guess where her ladyship may be. But I know the town, if that may help."

"Well, come up." Francis turned for the stairs.

"Leave your hat and coat here, sir." Bastien, removing his own outerwear, indicated a convenient stand situated to one side of the stairs.

Once the party had foregathered in the parlour, Francis presented the lieutenant to his mother, who eyed the man with hauteur and a touch of animosity. He frowned her down. He did not need the man, undeniably astute, recognising how he had been an object of suspicion under discussion there.

"Radway has offered to aid our search, ma'am."

The dowager's gaze went from the lieutenant to himself and back again. "What can he do, pray?"

Radway gave vent to a bonhomous laugh. "I should like to know as much, my lady. I am willing to do whatever Lord Francis may require of me, however."

Was his manner too insouciant? Hard to believe he could have had a hand in Ottilia's disappearance. The word in Francis's mind caused a ripple of anxiety. He had not wanted to confirm that this was what her absence indicated, yet he dared not suppose otherwise.

Radway was regarding him with a look of serious contemplation. "What have you set in train by way of enquiry?"

Francis refrained from mentioning the blacksmith. "We've a contingent in the stables which I've set to covering the town and its environs. My groom is at this moment checking the shops. I am about to despatch my nephew here to look for her at both the Cross Keys and Woulmer's." As Bastien started for the door, he called out, "If your other friends are there, ask them also."

"I will do so, *mon oncle*, and return immediately." He left the room.

"Surely your lady wife would not frequent those places without escort, would she?"

Francis turned back to Radway. "If she felt it necessary, yes, she would."

A snort came from his mother. "Indeed. Ottilia is nothing if not eccentric in her adherence to rule and custom."

A laugh came from the lieutenant. "So I apprehend. An admirable trait. Our women are hedged about with too many restrictions." He addressed himself to Francis again. "Might she have taken a stroll along the beach?"

"Not in the rain. Nor would she do so without escort. My wife is not strong. To be blown about by the winds that abound on this coast would not sit well with her."

The other raised his brows. "You would say she has a weak constitution?"

"Childbearing has debilitated her health." Francis cursed as he said it. He was too distracted to be circumspect.

But Radway appeared sympathetic. "That is unfortunate. The more urgent to find her then."

"Precisely."

"What can I do? Only say the word."

The words he wanted to say would not do. *Did you make her vanish? Is it to your account?* Instead, he chose the more subtle path.

"It is my fear the culprit in this murder has chosen to intercept her."

"Good grief, do you say so indeed?"

His mother chimed in before he could respond. "I don't agree. I cannot suppose he would dare to interfere with a woman of my daughter-in-law's rank."

Radway made a negative gesture. "Ordinarily I would agree with you, my lady. Unfortunately, on this occasion I suspect his lordship may be in the right of it. A bold fellow, this villain. Much of the temper of some of these smugglers. They care naught for rank or authority and will go to any lengths to achieve their objective."

If he had wanted to revive Francis's fears, the man was going the right way about it. But a thread of cynicism kept him from giving way to them again. Would it be possible to speak in such a way if Radway had been instrumental in this? Or could he be playing a double game?

"Can you suggest any individual who might act in such a way? Do you know anyone who might know something? One of your informants?"

Radway gave a shrug. "I could ask around. Put the word out." He gave Francis a straight look. "But do you want to advertise your wife's disappearance before ascertaining whether she has indeed been done a mischief?"

"By the time my groom and Bastien have asked around, the word will be out in any event."

"Or your wife may return of her own accord."

Francis drew a breath. "No. I know her habits. If she was delayed, she would send to me."

"Even if incapacitated?"

The word sent a shaft of agony through him, together with a leap of suspicion. He spoke with an edge to his voice. "If she is unable to send to me, my wife knows I will use every means in my power to find her."

A smile Francis could not read crept across the man's mouth. "Heroic, sir. Admirable. One trusts that if this is indeed the case, the villain has not served her as he served young Green."

Francis heard his mother's gasp and, with difficulty, withheld himself from planting a flush hit to the man's face.

Then Radway was heading for the door. "I will be off to do what I may for you, Lord Francis."

Then he was gone and the dowager exploded. "Insufferable! How dared he speak so? Don't heed him, Francis. I am persuaded it is all poppycock. Only consider what a stir such a proceeding must cause. Ottilia will be found safe and well, mark my words."

He did not share his mother's confidence but he refrained from comment. What more should he do? He chafed from inaction. Yet the urge to join the hunt must be resisted. He would likely exhaust himself without result. Better to wait for word from those despatched on various missions and hope for a tangible clue.

Of all, he most wished to know how Williams had fared. Yesterday, the blacksmith had emerged as a suspect, both himself and Ottilia jumping to the one conclusion. If Radway appeared to be uninvolved at this moment, the most likely must be Sugnall.

Within minutes, sounds of a second arrival gave him hope of acquiring some news on this point. It proved otherwise as Tyler entered upon a knock.

"Ryde is returned, my lord, and asks to speak to you."

"Has he news?" Thus the dowager. "Bring him in here at once."

Francis wasted no time. His groom would not consent to enter the parlour, especially as his boots were likely to be soiled and he was not appropriately dressed. "I'll go to him."

He left the room on the words, brushing past the footman who was holding the door and called after him. "In the hall, my lord."

Once more Francis ran down to the hall, where Ryde was awaiting him with his hat in his hand. "What news?"

"No sign of her ladyship, m'lord. The others have so far found no trace, but I've set them to try further afield. Myself, I tried every merchant along the main thoroughfare, and one or two in the side roads as well, though I doubt her ladyship would go to those."

"Better to be sure." It was no more than he expected, but the confirmation nevertheless stung. Where the devil was she? In one of these alleged secret holes, perhaps? Or was that clutching at straws? "I ought to have got Radway to hunt in them."

"Hunt in where, m'lord?"

"I don't know, that's the pity of it. It's said there are hidden hidey-holes where these so-called free traders stash their hoards. Cellars or the like, I imagine."

Ryde gave a grunt. "We'd need the militia for them, m'lord. Does that lieutenant know who has one of them holes?"

"I have no notion. He did not suggest as much. He said he will do what he can."

"Mayhap he means to try those fellows, then."

Yes, if it was not he who had effected Ottilia's vanishment. A thought occurred. "You remember those two fishermen we questioned?"

"Wark and Deanraw, m'lord?"

"Yes. See if you can run them to earth. They ought to be in the Mill Inn or home in bed at this hour."

The groom nodded. "Right you are, my lord. If any know of these holes, it'll be them two."

He departed the house and, with lagging steps, Francis returned to the parlour. Time was passing and he was beginning to feel despondent. If he had a lead, he would not hesitate to act. To do so without information was futile.

He relayed Ryde's report to his mother, who tutted with impatience. "We appear to be getting nowhere. Where is that wretch of a girl of mine?"

"If you mean Henrietta —☐

"Whom else should I mean, pray?"

"— it may take her some time to locate Yelford. Not that I have much hope of his proving useful. Tillie's opinion ruled him out."

The dowager was inclined to argue. "You don't know that she is delayed by villainy."

"The longer she does not appear, the more convinced I become."

His mother ignored his interjection. "Besides, according to Henrietta, the man does nothing but ride about the country chasing smugglers. He is bound to know where they are likely to hide a person."

Francis emitted an explosive sound. "You just averred there is no villainy involved."

"I did nothing of the kind. I merely stated that you do not know it for a fact. It is supposition, as Ottilia herself would tell you if she were here."

"She isn't here. That's precisely the problem, ma'am. Are you trying to provoke me? I'm frazzled enough as it is."

A snort greeted this. "I can see that for myself." She mellowed. "Do not drop into melancholy, my son. That will not help you."

He gave a wry smile. "Very well. I will contrive to remain optimistic."

Francis found it hard to adhere to this laudable aim, but before he could again work himself into a frenzy, his coachman returned. Francis met him in the hall.

"The quarry was in the smithy, my lord."

"Was he, by heaven? What did he have to say for himself?"

Williams blew out a breath. "Well, I couldn't rightly accuse him. And I didn't wish to say nothing of her ladyship going missing, seeing as you said to be discreet, my lord."

"But you questioned him?"

"Aye, I did. Said as you'd got it in your head as he might have heard summat of that murder, seeing as folks are bound to be going to him for shoeing and that."

A trifle of impatience seized Francis. "Didn't he protest that I'd already questioned him?"

A dour grin creased his coachman's broad features. "He did that. But I were ready for him. Said as time had moved on and all the world were talking of the murder, so's he might have heard since."

"Did he bite?"

Williams touched the side of his nose in a knowing gesture. "See, there's the thing, my lord. He ups and says as weren't it that Lady Fan as were questioning one and all? How'd he know that? I asked him. Weren't she your lordship's wife? he says. I said she was, but how'd he know she were called by that alias?"

Faint hope was stirring in Francis's bosom, while his mind flooded with suspicion. "How did he answer you?"

"He said as all the world knows it. But that ain't so, my lord. Lady Fan is what the gentry call her ladyship. To anyone else, she's just your lordship's lady wife. How'd he know it, my lord? Unless he numbers gentry in his associates."

It was hardly conclusive. "He might have heard it from one of those young friends of Monsieur Guizot."

Williams looked dubious. "Mebbe. But that ain't all."

"Well?"

"Sugnall ups and asks did she find out the murderer? What's your interest? I says. Did you know the young feller? He

295

answers as he knows all of them, for he's the only smith for miles around."

"That may well be true."

"Aye, but when I suggested that must mean as your lordship were right to ask if he'd heard anything, he turned sullen. Said he didn't know nothing about it, and didn't want to. So why'd he ask me just afore if her ladyship had found the murderer?"

"Did you ask him?"

"I should say I did, my lord. He told me to my face to shab off. Said he were shutting up shop. In the middle of the day, I asked? None of my business, he says, he can close up any time he fancies. So I left him to it." A finger slid to the side of his nose and he grinned. "But I were canny. Pretended to go off as he were closing up, but I found a stout tree and hid. Followed him along the High Street."

"To where, Williams?" Eager now, Francis grasped his arm.

But the coachman sagged a little, looking crestfallen. "That's what I can't tell you, my lord, more's the pity. I lost him. He nipped down a side street and by the time I got to it, there were no sign of the cove." He brightened. "But he knows summat, my lord. That I'd swear to."

Francis released his hold. "I believe you are right. A pity you did not see where he went." Would it have led to where Ottilia was?

His coachman appeared to have read his mind. "I doubt he'd have gone to where her ladyship is, my lord. Seemed to me as he took fright. Mebbe he'd to answer to someone and that's who he went to find. Warn him you're on the hunt, so to speak."

Francis thanked him for his trouble. "Stay within call, will you? I dare say Forncett will provide you with refreshment. Tyler will arrange it."

On his return to the parlour, he learned that his mother had sent for rolls, ale and coffee.

"I told Ottilia's maid to have the landlady make up a sandwich for you. I know your appetite, Francis."

While Ottilia's whereabouts remained unknown, he felt little inclination to eat. At his mother's urging, however, when the tray arrived, he began upon the beef sandwich and found hunger manifesting. He satisfied it without interest, his mind roving the recital given by Williams. To whom had the blacksmith gone, assuming that supposition was accurate? That Sugnall had knowledge of Ottilia now seemed certain. Yet it did not bring him any closer to finding her.

Henrietta returned in time to partake of the proffered fare. She had drawn a blank.

"I could not find Mr Yelford at any of the places where we have previously met." She glanced at Francis, a buttered roll she was eating poised in her fingers. "Nor, before you ask, did I see any sign of our precious Lady Fan. I even took a chance and went to Miss Green's and from there followed her intended footsteps to The Rooms, but to no avail. She seems to have vanished into thin air."

The leaden feeling in Francis's chest intensified. "She has not vanished. She was taken."

"By whom?"

"That," said his mother on a tart note, "is what we would all like to know."

Francis bypassed this obvious comment. "You didn't happen to run into Bastien?"

"I did, as it chances. He has had no luck either. Neither Mr Rampton nor Mr Mundell had seen Lady Fan today, and Grégoire du Guet is from home."

Francis fairly jumped. "He is what?"

"From home, Bastien said."

"Since when?"

"Yesterday, it seems. Bastien thinks he has been recalled to his associates to report that their scheme is found out."

The leaping hope died. Ottilia had more or less ruled out du Guet, but at this juncture, Francis was ready to believe any individual guilty.

Before Bastien could reappear in person, Tyler entered the parlour, bearing a note on a salver. "This was just delivered, my lord."

A sense of foreboding arose in Francis as he took the folded missive. "Who brought it?"

"A lad, my lord. Not in livery. He looked to be an urchin. He did not wait."

"Who is it from?" asked Henrietta.

"He cannot tell until he reads it!" Thus the dowager. "Open it, Francis!"

Francis unfolded the note. It was written in capitals, in an unknown hand. He read the missive out loud.

"*Be ready to leave this place, you and your people. You have until dawn on the morrow. When your coach reaches the cross road at Strafford, your wife will be returned to you.*"

CHAPTER SEVENTEEN

Bastien entered the parlour to find his uncle the centre of a scene of disorder and hubbub. For a moment, as he remained unnoticed by the door, he tried to make sense of the rapid fire of comment and argument.

His grandmother had hold of Lord Francis's arm. "Wait, boy! It is useless to act without a plan."

"Militia! We need the militia," Etta was repeating.

"What use in planning? While you keep me here, my wife is languishing in who knows what condition."

"Hold for a moment only. You —□

"Desist, ma'am! Let me go!"

"If only I had found Mr Yelford!"

"— are being rash, Francis!"

Bastien cut through the noise, raising his voice. "Enough! Quiet, everyone!"

An abrupt silence fell, all eyes turning upon him. Bastien strode into the fray. "What has happened, *mon oncle*? You have news, I surmise."

Lord Francis shook off his mother's hand, pushed between the two women and held out a crumpled sheet of parchment. "Read that!"

Bastien took it, cursing as he took in the matter of the note in a swift appraisal. He looked up. "Then we must search."

"That's what I'm saying." His uncle swept a hand through his dark locks. He looked agonised. "My only question is where to start."

"The militia must be called out," said Henrietta again.

Bastien threw up a hand to enjoin her silence. "Is this what you wish, sir? I can go swiftly, for I took time to bring Tonnerre. Your man Williams has him in charge."

A faint light of hope came into Lord Francis's eyes. "Well thought of. Go as speedily as you can to the encampment on the heights and ask for aid from Captain Turves. He must turn out his men and then come to me here. I'll send Williams to find Lieutenant Radway. We need to search any possible hiding places the smugglers use, and he will know them."

The dowager intervened. "Can you trust that fellow?"

"I agree, Lady Polbrook. Mr Yelford would be of more use, Lord Francis."

"But you didn't find him, Henrietta. What is the point of bringing him up?"

"I'll go again, ma'am. He may have got back to town."

Bastien cut in. "Also he may be the one who took Lady Fan."

Etta threw up her hands. "Oh, no, no, no, Bastien. Lady Fan entertained no suspicion of him at all."

Bastien's arm was seized by his uncle. "We are wasting time. Go!"

"Fear not, *mon oncle*. When I have alerted the militia, I will hunt on horseback."

"Where? We cannot be covering the same ground."

"I will take the open country in case she has been carried outside the town."

This plan being approved, he left swiftly, caught up his hat and coat and exited the house, only to find his young cousin waiting by his horse, along with the coachman.

Luke hurried across, intercepting him with a grab at his arm and staring up into his face. "Take me with you!"

Bastien shook him off. "Not today, Luke. I am in a hurry."

He made to move on, but the boy stood in his way. "Mama is kidnapped. I have to find her!"

Bastien cursed. "How do you know? Do you listen at doors?"

A brief grin lightened the serious look on Luke's face. "'Course I do."

"Luke, I cannot take you without your father's say so. Now, out of my way!"

Luke did not budge. "Papa won't let me. He'll say I'm too young. But she's my mother. I've a right to look for her. You'd want to if it was Aunt Violette, I'd wager. Take me up before you, Bastien! *If you please.*"

He did not please, but time was pressing. "What of your nurse?"

"Hepsie thinks I'm minding my book in my chamber. She won't look for me 'cos the twins are causing mayhem. At least Di is as usual, and Pretty is reading to Nell. I won't be missed. 'Sides, Mama is more 'portant than anything. She'd want me to find her, I know she would."

Not proof against the pleading note and the hint of distress behind it, Bastien gave in. "Up with you then."

Luke bounded over to Tonnerre, where he immediately fell afoul of the coachman.

"Was you meaning to take young master with you, sir?"

"I must, Williams. It will cause too much delay to argue with him."

"His lordship won't like it."

Luke, already reaching up to the saddle for a purchase, turned his head. "Then keep mum, Williams. Papa can punish me after, if he wants."

A scoffing sound came from the coachman, quite as aware as Bastien of how Lord Francis indulged his children. He lifted the youngster, who leapt nimbly into the saddle and settled his leg about the pommel. Bastien mounted behind him and took the reins.

"Let's go, *mon cousin*! Hold tight!"

He swung the horse about and put him to a canter, heading south via the shingle beach. A secondary thoroughfare led above the shore on a longer route to the town and from there a track led off along higher ground to where the militia were quartered in an encampment on the outskirts.

Captain Turves was absent, but his lieutenant took the message and promised to locate him and request him to attend Lord Francis.

"But you will turn out your men in the meantime, no?"

"Not without a direct order, sir. I can ensure they are ready to move out, however, the moment the captain gives the word."

Bastien cursed and remounted behind Luke, whom he had left in place to hold the reins. Tonnerre had tossed his head, but a blandishment from his master kept him obedient.

Luke handed the reins to Bastien. "Does he say they won't search?" he asked.

"They will, once the captain gives the order."

"That's no good. They should start now."

Bastien was in agreement, but it behoved him to appease his young cousin. "We will form the vanguard of hunters, never fear."

"Well, hadn't you best go faster?"

"Do you wish to be thrown off? Don't you see the track is not even?" He was keeping his mount to a walk as they retraced their route downhill, manoeuvring between the ruts.

Luke ignored this. "Where are we going to search first?"

Hard to answer. Bastien had blithely spoken of open country, but it now came home to him that to ride blindly about the environs of Aldborough would achieve nothing. "I have not yet decided."

He was still mulling over the question as the track rejoined the road they had taken from the beach. Bastien pulled up his horse and glanced along in the other direction, where the lane led back into the town. Would he do better to take that way and try inland? He recalled several isolated buildings on the route when he had gone with his uncle to the farm. Or should he head towards Hazlewood, where they had first gone to inform the Justice of the Peace of the murder?

The reminder that the killing was central to his aunt's capture proved timely. Unlikely she would be held in the town. Whoever took her must know that a thorough search through any and all of Aldborough's buildings would be made.

His thoughts were interrupted. "There's Ryde!"

Bastien looked to where Luke was pointing. Lord Francis's groom was coming on foot from a southerly direction and he looked to be in a hurry.

Luke was hailing the man and waving. "Ryde! Ryde! Over here!"

The groom checked a moment, looking across. Under the hat, his face changed and he broke into a run, covering the intervening space in seconds. He grasped the horse's bridle, looking up.

"Master Luke! What's to do? Why're you out with the monsieur?"

"We're going to hunt for Mama. She's been kidnapped!"

"D'you say so?" His glance went to Bastien. "Is it true, sir?"

He gave a wry grin. "If *mon cousin* will allow me to edge in a word… Lord Francis has received a threat."

"What, a letter?"

"A note only. There is no way to tell from whom it comes. He is warned to be ready to leave Aldborough, all of us, by dawn tomorrow. Then Lady Fan will be returned."

"Villainy!" Ryde snatched the hat from his head and dashed it to the ground.

Luke applauded. "That's just how I feel, Ryde. We've got to find her!"

The groom retrieved his headgear. "Beg your pardon, young master. Shouldn't have lost my temper."

Bastien intervened as a thought occurred. "But were you on an errand? Have you news?"

"I have. And this new turn gives me pause to think." The groom jammed his hat back on his head as if it aided the workings of his brain.

"What is it you think, Ryde?"

The groom's aspect became grim. "I went after those fishermen. Remember them, sir?"

"Wark and Deanraw? Whom we saw return in the boat?"

"That's it. Had to hunt them down, for they weren't in the Mill where his lordship regaled them with breakfast. The landlord said they'd gone to meet up with other fisherfolk this end. I caught them on their way back."

"Is it they, you think, who have taken my aunt?"

"I doubt that, for Deanraw said he passed a fellow carting a heavy load over his shoulder. He couldn't say what it was, for it was at a distance and it was raining besides."

Bastien felt his heartrate increase. "Who was the man?"

Ryde shook his head. "He didn't recognise him. Hat was low over his face and he was heavily coated. 'A big fellow' is all he could come up with."

Luke forestalled Bastien's next question. "Was the man carrying Mama then?"

"Can't be certain of that, young 'un, so don't get your hopes up. A heavy load is all, which could be anything."

Bastien cut back in. "More important, where did he see this? Also, at what time?"

"Well, that's why I'm in a rush to get back to the house and inform his lordship. The time tallies, for it was late morning, which is when her ladyship must have been abroad."

"Then there is hope."

Ryde shifted on his feet. "Trouble is, the where don't make sense."

"Why not?" Thus Luke, who had evidently been following the discussion closely.

"The fellow was trudging down the shingle."

Bastien seized on this. "From where? Which way? How far?"

Ryde gestured behind. "By Deanraw's account, he had come by one of the lanes back there. Seems he was going our way, but heading towards the sea."

"*Peste*, no! If that was Lady Fan — ☐ He broke off, recalling his cousin perched up before him. He must not put that terrible thought in the boy's head.

Ryde met his gaze. "You said the note promised to return her. It couldn't be what you're thinking, sir."

Luke's treble piped up. "If he had Mama, he must have put her in a boat."

"True, Master Luke. Or he just walked close to the water so's not to be seen. Tide would've been out at that time. Who'd have paid mind? But I don't think it could've been her ladyship. Seems too risky. Easier to take her somewhere close in the town."

Bastien made up his mind. "We must take a chance. This possibility we should not ignore. Tell his lordship I will ride along the shore. There are rocks and crevices in the cliff face where one might perhaps hide a person."

He gave Ryde a message regarding the militia and turned his mount towards the north. The groom was starting off in the same direction, but Luke called back to him.

"Don't tell Papa I'm with Bastien, Ryde! He'd worry about me then too."

"You are a smart one, *mon cousin*," said Bastien, "but I think I should drop you off when we pass the house."

"No! Don't set me down, Bastien! Pray don't, just when we might find Mama."

"It is not very likely, Luke."

"But we might."

The child did not cease to argue the point as they rode and by the time they came level with the lodging house, Bastien had not the heart to refuse his cousin's pleas. He had been hopeful himself when he learned of the sighting, but the notion of hiding Lady Fan somewhere along the shore was so bizarre, any expectation he had entertained had dropped.

Time had become unmeasurable. Ottilia knew she had faded once or twice, half-dreaming until a resurgence of discomfort jerked her back to consciousness. A steady dripping from somewhere deeper within the cavern impinged for a while, claiming her attention. She abandoned trying to work out its cause, focusing on the rhythmic swish of the waves, which steadily increased in volume.

How long had she been isolated here? If rescue did not come, would the seas encroach into the cave itself?

A horrid thought assailed her. Had she escaped death in the river years back only to drown here?

Before the notion could take hold, she recalled the corpse of Carlton Green and her fears subsided. He had been in here several days and his body was dry. Therefore, logic dictated that the waters could not have penetrated this far. She was safe from that fate at least.

Whether she could survive the perils of exposure in this dank prison was another matter. Her garments still felt moist and the cold seemed to seep into her bones. She tried now and then to shift her limbs where she sat, in a bid to lessen the various ills engendered by the hard rock pressing against her body.

If only she was not so bony, a result of her poor appetite during the long months of recovery. She could have done with spare flesh in this predicament.

Her mind drifted again, presenting her with a half-formed dream of lying in bed under Joanie's careful attendance, being plied with her favourite hard yellow cheese and sweetened coffee.

She came back to herself again to suffer acute disappointment to find it but a fancy of yearning. Her situation had not changed. Aches still plagued her, joined now by hunger and choking thirst. Even coughing was difficult, hindered by the gag.

When the attack subsided, her ears were assailed by a new sound. Voices. Muted, beyond her line of vision.

Hardly daring to breathe, Ottilia strained to listen for words. They came intermittently.

"…alive?"

"More dead than … breathing."

"…see for myself."

307

Footsteps sounded.

Ottilia let her head fall back and closed her eyes. Let whoever it was think her dead to the world, if not in fact deceased. Her mind remained on high alert.

The footsteps approached and she sensed a presence. Leaning over her? A musky scent assailed her nostrils, not the stale odour associated with a working man. A gentleman then?

The urge to flick her eyes open was strong, but Ottilia withheld it. She felt a touch at her wrist. Fingers on her pulse? In her own ears, her heartbeat began to race to a rhythm she was positive must be heard outside of herself. She forced herself to remain motionless while the fingers rested against her skin.

At last they were removed and she heard the shift of clothing that told her he must be straightening up. Sure enough, the footsteps retreated.

Not far enough to take him out of her earshot, as it proved to her gratification when he spoke again.

"She is alive."

A timbre to the voice struck a chord in Ottilia's mind, but the other one spoke before she could catch it.

"What if she doesn't last the night?"

"It will not come to that. If he is wise, Lord Francis will obey my demand long before then."

The voice, despite its low tone, was jarring at her memory, which fogged at the onset of the immediate questions besetting her. What demand had he made? Could Fan obey it? Would he?

"To my way of thinking, he's not as easily manipulated as you think." Who was this other? Ottilia could not think she had heard his voice before. "Like as not, he'll have the militia out. Then what do we do?"

Indeed, yes. That would be her dearest husband's first act. If, as she must suppose from this exchange, he had been given notice of her capture.

"Let him try. They will search every known smuggler's den before they think of this place. Why do you suppose I chose it?"

Ottilia's ear caught the trace of an accent. Identification came like a blow. Could it be? Had she wholly misjudged and given the villain free rein?

He spoke again. "Keep watch here, but out of sight. Don't re-enter the cave. I'll go by way of the clifftop and find out what's afoot."

Now she'd caught it, the reality of recollection was certain. She could not mistake him, and her mind was reeling even as she took in the now fading dialogue between the pair as both sets of footsteps withdrew.

"You'd best not be seen neither, or it'll all be for naught."

"I've concealed myself well enough this last couple of days. I won't be spotted at this stage of the game. Do your part and I will do mine."

The voices became inaudible and then disappeared altogether. In the ensuing silence, Ottilia struggled with the sudden reversal of all her previous conclusions.

Was she losing her touch? By her reckoning, the voice she'd heard ought to have been that of Lieutenant Radway. Not the voice of one who had allegedly left the town the day before. He had tricked her finely, had he not?

Then live she must. Justice for a wronged Carlton Green depended upon her survival. Determination settled in her breast. *You will not get the better of me, Grégoire du Guet.*

CHAPTER EIGHTEEN

Progress was of necessity slow, since the shingled shoreline was dotted with rocks and shallow pools where an unwary placing of a hoof might cause Tonnerre to stumble. Crossing rocky surfaces was even more risky, as his hooves were apt to slip.

"Keep your eye out for any hole or crevice, Luke. I must keep my attention on the ground."

"I am doing. I'll yell when I see one."

True to his word, the boy was craning his neck hither and yon, his gaze scouring the area.

Concentrating on keeping Tonnerre from stumbling, Bastien expected his cousin's shout at any moment. It did not come. In its stead, a report sounded in the distance and something whistled past him.

Instinct made him duck his head, his gaze hunting the source.

"What was that?" asked Luke, muted and fearful. Then he pointed. "Look! Up there!"

Bastien followed the direction of his finger. At the top of the cliff a man was standing, a long gun at his shoulder, its muzzle aiming down.

"God save me!" Bastien freed his foot from the stirrup and threw himself to the shingle. Reaching up, he dragged Luke off the horse.

"Run! Make for the shadow of the cliff!"

The boy took off and Bastien seized Tonnerre's rein and followed, hunching down to make himself less of a target. They must get into the lea of the cliff to be out of range.

Luke made it ahead of him, flattening himself against the cliff face. He beckoned, calling out. "Here, Bastien! I spied a holey bit just along there."

Bastien again followed his cousin's pointing finger, speaking low as he joined him. "I see it. Go, but stay close to the wall. He cannot see us from where he stands."

Luke was moving. "Who is it?"

"You ask me? How can I know?"

"Why did he shoot at us?"

"I do not know this either."

All at once, the edge of the wall sank inwards into a recess with a patch of overhang above. It looked deep enough for a temporary shelter at least.

"Move in there, Luke. Squeeze so that I may bring Tonnerre also."

Bastien drew his mount into the recess, hoping it was enough to conceal the party from the shooter above.

Luke's whisper came. "Are we safe now?"

"As long as that man does not think to come down from the cliff. It would take him time."

Luke squeezed past the bulk of the horse to his side and Bastien looked into his upturned face. "What troubles you? Are you afraid?"

Luke made a scoffing sound. "'Course not. Have you a pistol?"

"Not with me."

"Papa always keeps his in his pocket, Ryde told me. If you had yours, you could shoot the man when he comes."

"We do not need another dead body, *mon cousin*."

In truth, he was less exercised by the possibility of the shooter coming for them than the reason for him shooting at them at all. Was it a mistake? No, the fellow must have recognised him. He could not be firing at random strangers. Had he shot to kill? That made no sense if he was acquainted with his target. Moreover, he must have seen Luke was with him. Would he be so foolish as to risk hitting the child?

The answer came, as unexpected as the shot itself. A warning.

Even as Bastien formed the thought, he realised it must have been done in panic. Otherwise, why cause a stir and demonstrate that he was riding too close — to what?

He expressed his thought aloud. "They do not want us to search here."

"Who?"

"Never mind." Urgency struck. "We cannot remain here, Luke. We will move on, but stay in the lea of the cliff. I will lead Tonnerre."

While Radway made himself master of the kidnapper's demands, Francis watched him with close attention. Were the threatening words his own? If he'd penned them, could he feign the growing frown as he read?

When he came to the end, Radway looked up, a light in his gaze Francis had never seen before. "This goes beyond anything. I little thought the villain would go to such lengths." He thrust the paper at Mr Yelford, who had arrived almost on his heels. "We can't have this sort of havey-cavey nonsense on our patch, man. We'll get Turves to turn out his men."

As the riding officer took the note and scanned it, Francis cut in. "It's what I've been saying since we first discovered my wife is missing. You said you'd do what you may, Radway? Have you yet tried every avenue?"

"I made a few discreet enquiries of characters I know to be suspect, but with no result."

Impatience seized Francis. "The time for discretion is past. While we dally here, my wife may well be suffering. Lord knows what kind of condition she may be in, wherever she is incarcerated."

Here Yelford spoke up. "My lord, it looks as if the fellow intends no actual harm to her ladyship. We must hope her situation is not as dire as you suppose."

A curse hovered in Francis's throat and he held it back with difficulty. "I can't imagine why you think so, sir. You saw how he served young Green, did you not?"

"Yes, but this is — "

"He has no compunction, whoever he is."

"Indeed, but I submit there is no need to fear the worst."

Radway intervened. "We are wasting time, man. We must raid every hole we know of where a person might be concealed. Lord Francis, do remain in situ while we institute a thorough search."

Remain inactive? Not if his life depended on it. Yet as long as the authorities concentrated on the town, he would be free to hunt elsewhere. If Radway was the culprit, he would ensure that Ottilia's actual location would be overlooked. Given the notion revolving in his mind about where to concentrate his own efforts, Francis might circumvent the lieutenant's supposed scheme. He waved the two towards the door.

"Away with you both, then. I will rely on your local knowledge. If you turn up any clue at all, pray send me word at once."

As the pair left, Henrietta, who had been instrumental at last in finding the riding officer, came forward. While the discussion was in train, she had remained in the background.

"I'm glad I went again, Lord Francis. If you still harbour doubts about Lieutenant Radway, I am at least certain you may trust Mr Yelford."

If truth be told, he trusted no one but himself when it came to his darling wife. But he refrained from belittling the companion's efforts. "There is that."

"I thought you would have gone with them. Lady Polbrook made sure you would not remain idle. Indeed, she is quite as anxious. I had the greatest difficulty persuading her to rest a little."

"There's nothing she can do." Francis said it automatically, his mind focused upon his immediate intention.

"Will you wait for word?"

He answered with a harsh expletive. "My mother knows me too well. Do you suppose I can twiddle my thumbs while my wife is still lost to me?"

"Oh. What then are you going to do, Lord Francis? I confess I cannot think what more is to be tried. Bastien is still out, so we must suppose he is roving the outskirts as he intended."

Francis barely heard her. "Williams saw that fellow Sugnall leave the smithy. I am convinced he is involved in this, if he was not the thug who captured Tillie. He is burly enough. Where else should he take her but to his own ground?"

Henrietta struck her hands together. "You are going to look for her there. That is an excellent notion. But not alone?"

"I'll take Ryde and Williams. Please keep my mother from fretting. She has a great regard for Ottilia."

The words were hardly out of his mouth when the door opened to admit the dowager, who plunged in, both hands flailing. "As if things were not bad enough, here is your nursery woman in near hysterics. Come in, girl, and tell his lordship all!"

Before Francis could make any enquiry, Hepsie slipped into the room. If she was not in the condition his mother described, she was certainly agitated.

"My lord, I cannot find Master Luke!"

Francis froze, his heart dropping. "What the deuce do you mean? Was he not with the rest of you?"

Hepsie was just inside the door, but his mother thrust a hand between her shoulder blades, causing her to lurch forward. "Don't stand there, girl! Tell him what you told me." Her black gaze focused on Francis as she herself approached. "The wretched child was supposed to be minding his book, but when she went to check on him, he was nowhere to be seen."

Francis threw up a hand. "Let Hepsie speak, ma'am, for pity's sake!"

"I've been urging her to do so for these last several minutes. Very well, very well. Go on, girl."

Hepsie was twisting her fingers in her apron. "I'm sorry for it, my lord, because it meant I could not keep an eye on Luke, but it was chaos in the nursery — □

"Diana?"

"Yes, my lord. She is in one of her difficult moods today. Miss Pretty took charge of Nell and I told Master Luke to take his book to his chamber and work there. You know how he is, my lord. He would not concentrate if he could join in and set Di even more wild."

"You don't have to tell me." Francis knew his son would take any excuse to leave off studying.

"No, my lord. Well, by the time we had succeeded in bringing a measure of calm and I could go down to him, Luke was not there. We have searched the house, my lord, but he is nowhere to be found."

Francis cursed under his breath. "That pestilential boy! Must he choose today out of all others to play off his tricks?"

Once again, his mother's companion proved her worth. "Don't delay, Lord Francis. Let us deal with this fresh crisis. We will find him, never fear."

Instinct urged him to hunt for his son himself, but the more pressing matter of his beloved wife could not be set aside.

"I thank you, Miss Skelmersdale. Hepsie, let her aid you. She is very capable and will leave no stone unturned."

With that, he pushed through, followed by his mother's demand to know where he was going. "Henrietta will tell you. I must depart immediately."

He fairly raced down to the hall where Tyler was waiting with his outdoor gear, having previously been alerted to his intention to go off as soon as he had ensured the authorities were at last acting.

His footman opened the front door for him. "Can I do anything further, my lord? Joanie is also fretting."

Francis stepped out, waving at his groom and coachman, both on standby a few yards off. "The best thing she can do is prepare for her ladyship's return. I don't doubt she will need both rest and care. Joanie is best suited to provide both. As for you, Tyler, I wish you to hold the fort here."

"Of course, my lord. I am at your service."

"You're a good fellow." He nodded his thanks and turned to his henchmen, now awaiting his instruction. "We're for the smithy."

"Right you are, m'lord."

A thought occurred and Francis turned back to the footman. "If Monsieur Guizot should return before me, tell him I'll be obliged if he will join in the search for that wretched boy of mine, if he's not yet been found."

"Master Luke, my lord?"

"He's vanished as well, drat him. Hiding somewhere, I'll be bound."

He was interrupted by Williams, who coughed in the way of servants wishing to attract attention. "Begging your pardon, my lord?"

Francis turned, impatience gnawing at him. He wanted to be gone now he had a definite target at which to aim. "What is it, Williams?"

His coachman looked shamefaced. "I ought to have spoken before, only young master begged me to keep mum."

Hope leapt in Francis's breast. "You've seen Luke?"

A note of apology entered the coachman's voice. "See, he came out when I were holding the monsieur's horse. I can't rightly say as how it happened, but young master persuaded Monsieur Guizot to take him up."

"Dear lord! Bastien agreed?"

"Seemingly, he were in too much of a rush to argue, young master claiming as her ladyship is his mother so's he had a right to look for her himself."

"The deuce!" Images ran through his mind of potential dangers into which his son might have run. Could Bastien be trusted to keep the boy safe? "Tyler, go up and tell them inside. At least they will be spared a fruitless search."

He was turning again for the beach when Tyler stepped forward. "What more, man?"

"Setting aside this complication, my lord, I had understood that the monsieur was intending to ride outside the town."

"Correct. What of it?"

"Well, the landlady says she saw him riding along the shore. Seemingly, he'd been to alert the militia as you bade him, but he was riding in the other direction." The footman pointed.

Francis looked along the shore towards the north. For a moment, the significance did not register. "Likely Bastien had the intention to ride far enough down that way to pick up a route onto —" A thought struck. "The cave!" Where Luke had first discovered the body. How slow was he not to think of it before? Now he had, it fitted all too neatly.

Poetic justice, was it, for the villain to hide his nemesis in the very place where he had committed the deed?

Francis snapped into action, beckoning his two henchmen. "Change of plan, my good fellows. With me!"

Bastien would have preferred to keep his young cousin in the rear, but with the necessity to hold Tonnerre's rein he could not risk losing sight of Luke. At least the boy was obeying his command to keep close to the cliff wall. Although, with the eagerness of youth, he was apt to quicken the pace as he crept along.

"Don't get ahead, Luke. Stay by me."

The child glanced back. "Has that man come down yet?"

"I hope he will not do so."

Though in truth his hope was likely misplaced. Whether he had fired on purpose or on a foolish whim, he had given himself away. Had he been standing guard up there? Or had he been departing the scene and happened to spot them riding too close to the hideaway? Assuming there was one. A smuggler's hoard? Or had he and Luke inadvertently stumbled upon the place where Lady Fan was being held?

The latter seemed unlikely, except for the fact that an ultimatum had been sent to his uncle. It was too much to suppose the free traders were abroad on the same day his aunt happened to be kidnapped. That would be a coincidence altogether unbelievable.

Ought they to leave the shore and ride up into the country above? The shot had come from there. Was Lady Fan being held in a spot near to where the shooter had been standing?

If so, he could scarcely afford to descend, leaving his prisoner unguarded. Were they safe down here after all? If not for his cousin's presence, he would remount Tonnerre and investigate for himself. Luke must not be endangered.

Undecided, he watched the stealthy progress of his cousin's small figure, hugging the wall and half-ducking to make himself even smaller.

Abruptly, Luke halted, straightening up and craning his neck. Bastien set a hand on his horse's neck to stop him and took a step forward, dropping his voice.

"What is it?"

Luke glanced back. "There's a man sitting on a rock. See there?" He pointed.

Bastien moved close behind the boy, peering across the intervening shingle. The whole area was uneven and rock-strewn, some as hefty as boulders. Upon one of these, he caught sight of an odd shape.

"It is just a jumble of stone." Even as he spoke, his senses adjusted the outline, presenting a hunched back atop a boulder. "Ah, no, I see him now."

"Who is it?" Luke spoke in a whisper.

"I know no more than you," said Bastien in like manner, "but do not move or speak."

Luke obeyed, holding still at the wall of stone, his gaze fixed upon the figure. It was, Bastien judged, some fifty yards away. The rock was positioned a few feet from the cliff face.

Bastien looked along the wall, which curved into the shore. Was there a darker spot more or less adjacent to where the man sat? A half-formed thought was vanquished as Luke seized a fold of his coat and tugged.

"Hush, Luke!"

"But it's 'portant!"

"What is?"

"I recognise this place." His whisper was eager. He pointed again. "That's where Papa and Pretty were looking for fossils. The twins were down by the water building a castle." Luke's eyes were blazing as they came around and fixed upon Bastien's. "This is where I went into the cave and found the body!"

Bastien's pulse quickened. "You are certain?"

"'Course I am. The cave is just there, it must be."

A motion in the figure on the rock made Bastien clap a hand across the boy's mouth. *Peste*! Why had he not brought his pistol? If the man turned, he must surely see them. Tonnerre was too big to be missed. He would give them away.

He held his breath, his gaze trained on the figure. It seemed to be shifting position, but to his relief, the man remained in the same pose, looking out to sea.

Bastien removed his hand from Luke's mouth, but put a finger to his lips to ensure his silence. What to do? Any movement must immediately advertise their presence. He could not guess how significant it was that the man was situated outside the fatal cave. It could be a coincidence. But with the earlier shot, this seemed unlikely.

The most pressing need was to rid them of the apparent guardian. He could creep up on him and perhaps overpower him. One could not tell at this range how powerful his adversary was. Without a weapon, he was at a disadvantage. Did the man have one?

Then it came to him that he did have a weapon, of sorts. He leaned down, setting his mouth close to Luke's ear.

"I am going to mount Tonnerre. When I ride and the man is distracted, run quickly and hide yourself in the cave. Do you understand?"

Luke nodded, bracing himself.

Bastien felt a wave of admiration as he moved with a careful, silent tread to his horse's side. Though with two such parents, the boy's courage ought not to surprise.

Knowing he could not avoid making a noise now, Bastien set his foot in the stirrup and swung himself up into the saddle in one swift movement. Tonnerre's hooves shifted on the shingle, adding to the inevitable sounds.

As expected, the figure on the rock turned its head. It evidently saw them, for the man slid off the rock and began to come around to confront the intruders.

But Bastien's other foot had already found its place and he set Tonnerre at a canter with one terse command. "Go!"

He made directly for the man ahead, who froze. Evidently realising he was about to be ridden down, he uttered a loud yelp and took to his heels.

Bastien gave chase. From the periphery of his vision, he saw Luke rush for the cave. The entrance was clearly visible as the horse came abreast of it, but Bastien kept on.

With practised ease, he controlled Tonnerre's pace, holding him in enough to drive the man to keep running ahead and avoid the obstacles formed by rocks and pools. They had been going for several minutes before his quarry showed signs of tiring, glancing back at the oncoming horse.

Bastien saw a swathe of shingle ahead and made up his mind. As the man reached it, he urged Tonnerre to a faster pace. His quarry saw it and turned, heading for the sea.

Did he hope to save himself in the water? Bastien gave vent to a laugh and turned his mount to follow.

The moment he was close enough, he pulled Tonnerre up, kicked his feet out of the stirrups and threw himself off the horse. In a bound, he leapt upon the man, flattening him to the shingle.

"Your race is run, *mon vieux*!"

The figure below him made no attempt to throw off the burden. He was out of breath and panting.

Bastien lifted off enough to heave the fellow over onto his back. Then he sat astride him and delivered a heavy blow with his fist to the fellow's face, rendering him half-senseless.

As he did so, recognition hit.

"Sugnall? Villain! What have you done with Lady Fan?"

The new sound outside the cave impinged on Ottilia's consciousness, jerking her out of the semi-dazed state into which she had fallen. She had been trying to work things out in her mind to make sense of it all, but the ills of her body betrayed her and logical thought became confused with illusion. Or dreams? She no longer knew which.

At first, she failed to identify the rhythmic thumps. They came faster than the waves breaking on the shore, to which she had become adjusted. A different set of sounds overtook the thumps. Were they separate? Footsteps? They seemed to come closer and then, as she listened, they ceased.

Ottilia settled back, aware of disappointment. Had she hoped for rescue? If so, it had not come.

A surge of frustration overcame her and she released a moan from her throat. Without the gag, she might have screamed or called for help. Except that Grégoire had left a guard outside. She quietened again, afraid of alerting the man.

Something moved in the area beyond the rocks. Ottilia held her breath.

Yes, there were sounds. A soft padding. She peered into the gloom.

A shadow caught her eye. Something was creeping towards her, hugging the far cave wall. Was it an animal? A stray dog, perhaps?

In a bid to frighten it off, Ottilia emitted the only noise available to her with the restriction of the gag. She growled.

The shadow stopped dead.

"Mama? Is that you?"

CHAPTER NINETEEN

"Luke!" It came out more a gargle than his name.

Ottilia wriggled where she sat, lifting her tied hands and waving her arms, uttering words she knew were incomprehensible.

To her joy, the figure bounded across, landed beside her and dropped down. Her son flung his arms about her.

"I found you! I found you!"

Ottilia suffered the embrace, though it all but caused her to choke. Her eyes prickled as relief swept through her bosom.

Luke drew back, his gaze hunting. "Are you hurt, Mama? I can't see properly."

Ottilia brought up her hands and indicated the gag, trying to speak through it to urge him to remove it.

"Oh! You're all tied up! That's horrid." He grabbed her hands. "Don't fret, Mama. I'll soon have you free."

Ottilia leaned forward, dipping her head in the hope of urging him to untie the gag first. Thankfully, her son understood and she felt his small fingers in her hair, searching for the knot.

"They tied it pretty tight, Mama."

Questions were teeming in Ottilia's brain, but she remained still and quiet while her son worked at the knot. It felt an age that he struggled, but at last it gave way.

"Thank you!" She gasped it out, coughing a little.

Her son did not cease pelting her with questions she was in no condition to answer. "How long have you been in here? Why did he put you here? It's horrid and smelly and cold and damp. Shall I undo your hands?"

This last rang the most sensible with Ottilia. Her voice came out hoarse. "Try if you can, Luke."

As her son bent to the task, she put to him urgent questions of her own.

"How did you come here? Did you think I might be in the cave?"

Luke glanced up. "I came with Bastien." He returned to his efforts. "He was on Tonnerre and we meant to go looking for you outside the town, 'cos Papa is getting the militia."

A sliver of foreboding entered in. "Does Papa know you are out with Bastien, by any chance?"

A flash of teeth told Ottilia he was grinning. "He might now, but 'course I didn't tell him. He would've forbade me."

Undoubtedly. "Where then is Bastien?"

"He's catching that man who was on a rock out there. Bastien rode at him like a madman and he ran off. But Bastien got him, don't fret."

Was the guard then overpowered? Yet Grégoire was at large and none but she knew him to be the true culprit. Despite the untoward exigencies that plagued her physically, a sense of urgency crept in. "Where had Papa the intention to look for me with the militia, Luke?"

He did not look up from tugging at the twine about her wrists. "Not sure. Maybe in the town. I could only hear a bit and Bastien went first to call the captain, but he wasn't there, so I don't know if they came yet." He released his hold on her wrists and sat back. "I can't get it undone! We need a knife and I'll wager Bastien don't have one. He hasn't got his pistol either, or he could've shot that man who fired at us."

Ottilia's heart gave a lurch. "Someone fired at you? When, Luke? Where?"

"It was as we were riding near here. He was on the cliff. We had to jump off Tonnerre double quick and run to hide at the cliff wall."

That her precious son might have been hit sent a chill through Ottilia's veins. What in the world was Bastien about to be taking him up? She refrained from speaking her mind. Time enough for that. The probable identity of the man who had shot at them increased her rising anxiety. She must act, and soon.

Although how she was to do anything in her present condition was an unanswerable question. If she could at least use her legs…

"Luke, my ankles are tied. Try if you can to free them instead." She shifted her legs as she spoke, dropping her knees so that her son could more readily attack the ties.

Nothing loath, Luke took to the new task with a will. "I can't see very well, but if I can find the knot…"

Why had Bastien not yet come in? Had he no means of holding the guard? She recalled the way her son had addressed her at the first.

"Does Bastien know that I am in here?"

"How should he? I didn't either. He told me to hide in here when he went for the man on Tonnerre." He paused. "Ah, there. I've found the knot, Mama."

"Gently, Luke, or you will tighten it the more."

She had doubts her impatient child would do as she said, but at least he began thus, still talking as he worked. "I got a shock 'cos I heard you growl. I thought it was a bear or something."

"We do not have bears in England," Ottilia stated, then, "I am sorry I growled at you… I thought *you* were an animal."

Luke suddenly left off trying to undo the twine at her ankles and instead threw his arms about her and buried his face in her neck.

Unable to hug him back, Ottilia was obliged to content herself with leaning her head against his and murmuring soothing words. So insouciant he seemed, one was apt to forget Luke was still a little man, subject to the painful pangs of childhood.

Luke sat back, dashed a hand across his eyes and said, "Papa will have a knife. He'll cut you free in an instant. Ought I to run back to the lodging and fetch him?"

Moving at a steady pace, despite the inner voice that urged him to hurry, Francis covered the ground at speed. He took risks with the uneven terrain, uncaring when the leather of his boots scratched against rock. His mind painted for him the condition Ottilia must be in, assuming his hunch was correct, to be unable to escape the cave. By what trick she had been taken captive he dared not imagine for fear of being overtaken by rage. He needed his wits about him on this fetch.

Nevertheless, as he and his allies came to the spot he recalled from that now seemingly far-off day, his heart filled with fury. How dared this villain serve his darling wife in such a manner? If it proved to be Radway, he'd have the wretch behind bars before he departed the shores of Aldborough.

Ryde caught him up all of a sudden. "M'lord, hold hard!"

Francis slowed, but did not stop. "What's to do?"

"Look yonder!" Ryde pointed. "Isn't that Monsieur Guizot's horse?"

That did bring him to a halt. He lifted a hand and shaded his eyes to see better under the grey horizon. Sure enough, the outline of a horse was visible, standing out in silhouette.

"You're more familiar with the animal than I. Are you sure it's Tonnerre?"

"I know his shape, m'lord. Tossing his head, don't you see? Resty beast, he is."

"Then has Bastien found her already?" Francis set off once more, picking up his pace. Landmarks became familiar. "This is the place. The cave should be close."

As he neared, a figure came into view. A man, standing over someone lying on the shingle. He wore no hat and the blond head was instantly recognisable.

Francis cupped his hands around his mouth. "Bastien! Hoy, there!"

His nephew's tall figure turned, hesitated, and then waved. Francis headed in that direction, but he had crossed only half the distance when a treble voice called out from a different place.

"Papa! Papa, she's here!"

Francis halted and spun. "Luke?"

His son was standing in the entrance to the cave. "Mama is here! She's inside!"

A tumult of emotion cascaded through Francis's chest. Relief, elation, tempered with remembered frustration at the boy's antics.

As he started towards him, his son came running, calling out, "Have you your knife, Papa? They tied her up and I can't undo the string. I tried and tried."

Everything else went out of Francis's head. "Where is she? Show me!"

Luke skidded to a stop, turned and raced back the way he had come. Francis followed him into the cave, his vision at once impaired by the gloomy interior. Perforce, he slowed, picking his way on Luke's heels.

The sight of the huddled figure against the cave wall struck at his heart. "Oh, dear Lord, my sweetheart, what have they done to you?"

"Fan, thank heaven!"

He barely took in the hoarse note, overwhelmed with relief that she was alive and able to speak. In a moment, he was on his haunches at her side, gripping her shoulders and scanning her face.

"Are you injured? Did he hurt you a great deal?"

Her joined hands were at his chest. "I am merely bruised, my dearest." Her voice was faint, a little laboured, much to his distress. "But I feared the cold and damp would do for me."

"We'll get you home and into bed in a trice, my precious one." He found his son hovering. "Luke, go out and ask Ryde to think how best to bring Mama home. She cannot walk, tell him."

"Maybe she can ride Tonnerre. I'll ask Bastien."

He was off and Francis turned his attention back to his beleaguered wife. "I should doubt of your proving capable of sitting a horse, never mind riding."

Her teeth chattered as she spoke. "You know well I have never learned to ride. I think we may discount that option at the outset."

"We will find a way." He leaned in and planted a kiss on her forehead. "Luke said you are tied up?" He released her shoulders as he spoke and caught her hands, uttering a curse. "He bound your hands? Dastard!"

"My ankles too." She drew breath and sighed it out, and his heart ached for the effort in it. "I hope you have a knife. Poor Luke did his best, but he could not manage it. At least he was able to undo the gag."

His fingers were already diving for his pocket knife, but Francis froze. "He had the temerity to gag you too?"

Ottilia nodded. "I will not pretend it was easy to be so hampered."

"Easy? I should think not indeed. The wonder is you did not choke."

"Well, I am able to breathe easier now, my dearest. I imagine he did not wish me to call out." A tiny laugh emerged. "I could only grunt. Luke thought I was an animal."

Unable to bear hearing of her suffering, Francis brought out his folded knife and prised it open. "Hold still!" It took an effort to cut through the twine. "He made a meal of this, the blackguard."

"I likely made it worse trying to release myself. To no avail, I fear."

The twine came apart and Francis worked to untangle the strands. He cursed again as Ottilia winced. "I am hurting you, my loved one. I'm sorry for it, but I want to rid you fully of this vile string."

It came away at length and he heard Ottilia sigh. "That is such a relief. Can you do the same by my feet?"

She was nursing her wrists and Francis growled. "You must be sore."

"More aching than sore." She flexed her arms, her movements slow and clearly difficult. "I fear my muscles have seized." She reached out and touched his cheek. "My ankles, my dearest dear?"

"Dear Lord, what am I about?" He saw the twine that bound her ankles and let out another curse. "I'll kill that scoundrel when we catch him."

"I hope we may be able to do so … if he does not abscond the moment he learns of my escape."

"We'll send the militia after him if he does. Although I imagine Radway will persist in his charade."

Urgent now, Francis set to, sawing at the bonds with his pocket knife until the twine dropped away from one ankle. "There, that is done at last. Now for the other."

As he began upon her other leg, Ottilia spoke again, with an odd note of hesitance.

"It is not Lieutenant Radway, Fan."

"Not?" He paused in his task, turning his gaze upon her. "How do you know? Don't tell me your captor came here?"

"He did, but it was not he who pounced on me. That was some other — I don't know who, for I did not see him."

"Then who was it, if not Radway? Did you recognise him?"

"No, for I kept my eyes closed and feigned unconsciousness. But I heard him speak. I could not mistake, for that slight accent gave him away. It was Grégoire du Guet."

For a moment, Francis could only stare, disbelief his overriding emotion.

A small smile hovered at his darling wife's lips. "You are as shocked as I."

"Indeed. You wrote him off."

"Foolishly. I must revise all my ideas, but I … I found myself too debilitated to think straight."

Francis became brisk. "Don't try. Time enough for that when you are recovered. Let me finish this and we can get you home."

He returned to his efforts and at length succeeded in removing the remnants of twine from the remaining ankle. He took time to massage both. Ottilia's whimper made him desist.

"It is too painful?"

"Not as much as my wrists."

"Joanie will apply a salve. I only hope you are not cut, but I cannot see in this hellhole of a cave."

Ottilia made motions as if she would try to rise and he put out a hand to stop her. "Stay put, my loved one."

"I don't wish to remain in this place a moment longer than I must. A hellhole describes it exactly. Help me, Fan."

"If we can get you to your feet, I'll carry you. Come, hold onto me. I'll take your weight."

His heart hurt for the inadvertent groans she let out as, with as much care as was possible, he helped her to her feet. As expected, her muscles had seized and she slumped against him the instant he loosened his hold. Francis caught her before she could fall and lifted her into his arms. He had not been obliged to carry her for years and it immediately struck him that she was lighter than she had been.

"You've lost flesh."

"I've not eaten for hours."

"Yes, but I don't mean now. I hadn't noticed, but you weigh next to nothing."

A tiny gurgle greeted this. "I am scarcely a featherweight."

"It feels like it to me."

He began to pick his way towards the entrance to the cave, glad of the increasing light. It appeared to trouble his wife, for she turned her face into his chest.

"It's so bright."

"Because you've been stuck in the dark for so long. Hold on, sweetheart, we will be out of here in short order."

"Wait! Stop a moment, Fan."

Francis paused, looking down into her face. He took in how pale and worn she was and his heart ached for the ordeal she had endured.

Her voice, still hoarse and becoming fainter, dropped to a murmur. "Do not tell Bastien about his friend."

"He has to know, Tillie."

"Not yet … later, perhaps. If he knows the truth, his distress may well give the game away to Grégoire."

He perforce agreed to keep mum and started off again, his emotions mixed. Typical of her to be thinking still of what was to come when she ought to be concerned for her ills. As for his nephew, let him choose his friends with more circumspection in future. All that mattered to him at present was to get his darling wife back to warmth and safety.

Delivered into her maid's devoted hands, Ottilia was glad enough to be spared the necessity to think. She recalled little of the journey home, nestled in her beloved husband's arms atop Bastien's horse. Several hands had lifted her, but once secured, she sank into a semi-dreaming state and at last found herself alone with Joanie, an echo in the corridor beyond the chamber where Francis repelled all comers.

"Let her be. She needs rest. Save your questions for later." He came back into their bedchamber briefly, crossing to where she had sunk down onto the four-poster. "Let no one in here, Joanie. Warm her up, feed her and let her sleep if she needs to." And to Ottilia, "I'll be back soon, sweetheart. I must needs call off the militia and set in train a hunt for that villain."

That brought Ottilia alert and she caught his hand as he made to leave. "No, Fan. Not yet."

"We can't let him get away!"

"He will not try to run, now I think of it more clearly. Reflect that he does not know I recognised him."

"He'll guess it soon enough once he finds you absent."

"Only trust me, my dearest. We must fully trap him to secure a victory."

He had been dubious, but had thankfully agreed. Ottilia had added a further caution. "Pray do not relay the exact details of my capture lest he hears and becomes suspicious."

"I must give the truth to the authorities."

"Then warn them not to bruit it about. I need time to work things out, Fan."

The vague and partially thought-out notions she'd had while in the cave were in no way fully formed. Ottilia knew she was not yet up to making plans. In hopes of a swift recovery, she gave herself up to Joanie's ministrations, soothed by her gentle coaxing.

"That's the laces done. Are you able to lift your arms, my lady? There, that's far enough, I can slip the sleeves off easy. No, don't get up, I'll ease the petticoats down if you'll just lift a little where you sit. There, that's done it. Gracious, these are soaked through! Never mind. I'll soon have you dry and warmed up, my lady. Then we can see to fetching you something to eat. You'll be glad of your coffee too, I'll be bound."

Ottilia had gulped down proffered water upon first entering the room, relieving her dry throat and making speech easier, but this was music to her ears. "Coffee! Oh, Joanie, you are speaking to my depths."

Her maid gave a chuckle. "That and yellow cheese."

"With a roll and honey too."

It was bliss to be pampered and put to bed, and Ottilia sank gratefully into the pillows. Joanie tutted over the wounds on her wrists, which were severely bruised, the skin chafed and bleeding in spots.

"I fear I made it worse myself, Joanie, trying to free my hands."

"Well, I should think you might, my lady," returned the maid, busy applying an ointment she had dug from the recesses of Ottilia's dressing-case. "It's a mercy your ankles are not as bad. The salve will do for them, but I think we ought to bandage these wrists, my lady."

"No, leave them. They will heal the faster for exposure to the air."

But the maid refused to be convinced, saying she did not dare for her life leave them unbandaged, for his lordship would undoubtedly scold her for it. Ottilia allowed her to have her way and indeed felt the benefit when a thin layer of soft gauze was fastened about the sores. Once Joanie was satisfied she had done all she could to make Ottilia comfortable, she went off to fetch the promised coffee and viands.

Ottilia half wished for sleep, but her mind drifted, presenting her with pieces of the puzzle she must needs solve before confronting the Frenchman. She was certain he had killed Carlton Green, but why? Clearly, he had lied. Or told a half-truth. How far was his testimony accurate? How much of it was twisted to conceal the truth? Even on hearing it, she had been uncertain about the ring Carlton had given to his sister which had allegedly alerted Grégoire to his fraudulent actions. Again, *alleged* fraudulent actions. Which of them was cheating the émigrés of their hoards? There was also the wound Carlton had sustained, its explanation now in doubt.

The entire scenario she'd worked out in her mind had been overturned. Unless Radway was in cahoots with Grégoire? The rethink proved too murky for her present condition and she was relieved when her maid reappeared, carrying a laden tray.

"Ah, that smells so good, Joanie."

Her favourite beverage proved efficacious. By the time she had consumed as much of the repast as she could manage, with the discovery her mouth was a trifle bruised from the gag, Ottilia felt sufficiently restored to be able to think with more attention. Presently, however, the thoughts grew entangled as exhaustion claimed her.

She awoke to twilight and the rattle of the bed-curtains. Francis was pulling them across at the bottom of the bed.

Ottilia pushed up onto her elbow. "Heavens, what time is it? Is it growing dark?"

Her spouse left off his task and came to perch on the bed at her side. "It is past eight. Relax, my loved one."

"I must have slept for hours."

She sank back and he picked up her hand.

"You needed it, obviously." He brought the hand to his mouth and kissed her fingers. "How do you feel?"

Ottilia shifted her limbs. "Better, I think."

"Are you hungry? We dined ages ago, but I directed Tyler to ask for a tray to be made ready for when you awoke."

She set a hand to her stomach over the bedcovers. "I could eat a little."

Francis released her, rose and went to tug on the bell-pull. Ottilia watched him return to the bed and held out her hand. He took it and sat again, leaning to brush strands of hair away from her face.

"You look less worn, thank the Lord. You'll likely ache for a day or two."

She squeezed his fingers. "I can endure that, if my mind is clear enough to see this through. What has been happening?"

"That is readily told. The hunt is called off. That rogue Sugnall is in custody. He'll be charged, according to the Justice of the Peace, with kidnapping and causing bodily harm."

"You've seen Mr Overy yourself? What had he to say to it all?"

"He was shocked to hear of your ordeal." His hand tightened on hers and she returned the pressure in a bid to console. "Overy kept bewailing that he had dragged you into the business."

Ottilia wafted her free hand. "He did no such thing. I persuaded him to let me handle it."

"Not according to his account."

"Were they not disgruntled that the militia searched to no purpose?"

"As it chanced, Turves and Radway had not made much progress, as they encountered opposition from the owners of the places they wished to check."

"That is not much of a surprise."

"No, and Radway said both Parbold's and Washbrook's complaints that the militiamen were likely to cause damage were justified. Turves's men tend, he says, to be too rough and ready when they search premises."

"It is well you called them off in time then."

"Radway was all for coming here to get your statement, but I refused to allow it. He'll come over tomorrow, but you need not meet him if you are not up to it."

Ottilia's mind was already running over the problems she faced and she was glad to find her thinking a good deal clearer.

"I am already improving. A night's sleep will restore me, I am sure. Indeed it must. We cannot leave Grégoire at large too long."

"Well, I hope you come up with a plan or I'll be tempted to take the matter into my own hands."

"I will tackle him, Fan, come what may. Only keep mum about his involvement. Let us keep the truth between us until we have him cornered."

Francis agreed to this, if with reluctance, and Ottilia changed the subject, asking after the children. She received a comfortable account of the girls and was moved to ask about her son.

"I hope you did not scold Luke too severely, Fan."

He emitted a snort. "Don't talk to me of that wretched imp. He is quite incorrigible." That familiar quirk of his lip teased. "Like another I could name."

Ottilia smiled. "What did he do to deserve that comparison, my dearest dear?"

Her husband rolled his eyes. "When I taxed him with the crime of listening at doors, he retorted that he learned it from you." Her amusement elicited a wry look. "It's well for you to laugh, but how he learned of your using a tumbler to hear Mama and Randal that time, I cannot begin to imagine."

Ottilia sobered. "I don't recall telling him that story, but I might have done. Am I to suppose he was not in the least penitent?"

"Ha! He had the temerity to say I ought rather to scold Bastien. As if he hadn't wheedled his way into accompanying my nephew. Moreover, Luke thinks he deserves a medal for finding you! He reminded me of his intention to find murderers when he grew up and said his participation was good practice."

Ottilia's laughter drew a reluctant grin from her husband and she began to feel a semblance of normality returning. She made a good effort at consuming the light repast of tender chicken breast and buttered green peas that Joanie brought and was able to sustain a visit from her mother-in-law, anxious to see for herself that Ottilia was on the mend.

"I am a good deal recovered, Sybilla. I hope tomorrow will see the end of this adventure."

CHAPTER TWENTY

The Frenchman's audacity astonished Ottilia. Sought by Bastien at her request, he came with apparent willingness, expressing himself as appalled at the tale of her capture.

"Such villainy! What did he hope to gain, I wonder?"

Ottilia glanced at Bastien. "Did you not tell him of the note my husband received?"

Grégoire, who had taken a position a little away from the sofa where Ottilia was seated, looked from her to Bastien and back. "What note was this, ma'am?"

Bastien took this. "It was a threat, *mon vieux*, that my uncle should get ready to leave if he wished Lady Fan to be returned."

Her nephew was, to Ottilia's satisfaction, most fortunately situated between his erstwhile friend and the parlour door. Not that Grégoire would be permitted to escape. Both Ryde and Williams would by now be stationed in the hall, ready to detain him at need. Francis was absent, his part being to effect a search, accompanied by Radway, of the Frenchman's lodging. The lieutenant, who must know where Grégoire lived, was needed to lend the proceeding authority. Her spouse had agreed, though not without protest.

"You expect me to leave you alone with that unmitigated scoundrel?"

"Bastien will be here, not to mention both Ryde and Williams, ready to intervene at my call. I will have Tyler remain outside the parlour door."

The plan had come to Ottilia in the night hours. Contrary to her expectation, she slept little, despite the comfort of her husband's embrace that sent her into dreamland at first. While Francis slept on beside her, she drifted in and out of consciousness, ideas chasing one another through her mind until, at last, they coalesced into a coherent whole. By morning, she was confident she understood and the scheme came fully formed.

"It's very well, but I don't trust any other man to keep you safe. Radway can make the search and I will —□

"Can we fully trust Radway to make a thorough job of it? Besides, my dearest dear, your presence is bound to put Grégoire on alert. You will not be able to conceal your animosity, Fan."

He had been persuaded at last, contenting himself with swearing to brief his henchmen and Tyler. "They will answer to me if any harm comes to you."

Sybilla and her companion were likewise banished, although Henrietta entered a caveat. "It will be thought odd if we go to The Rooms. The news of your capture and rescue must have spread by this time."

"Well said, Henrietta. You know how these people gossip, Ottilia." Thus the dowager. "We will have to remain."

But this would not do. She would have difficulty catching Grégoire out if there was an audience. An alternative came to mind.

"How would it be if you accompany the children? I have asked Hepsie to take them all to the market square for ices, and then to choose a toy each from the booths. It will not be thought odd if you stroll around with them. If anyone you know should question it, you may say it is to allow me to have complete rest and that the children are too noisy."

This was not far from the truth. She was a good deal restored, but true to her spouse's prediction, her muscles protested and she was still fatigued, not to mention feeling tender where the blow had struck her head. The prospect of the coming confrontation, however, had the effect of giving her a lease of energy.

Her suggestion caused Henrietta to applaud. "Excellent, Lady Fan. Come, Lady Polbrook, I will fetch your cloak and hat."

"Don't forget my stick," the dowager called after her. "If I must dawdle about the market, I will need support."

Thus it was that when her unsuspecting nephew brought Grégoire as requested, Ottilia was alone and ready for him.

He responded to the contents of the threat with appropriate horror, feigned as Ottilia knew.

"But this is beyond everything. One sees that he must have wanted you to cease this investigation."

Marvelling at his smooth delivery, Ottilia agreed to this. "It seems so indeed."

Grégoire leaned back on his heels, giving a sigh. "Who would have supposed the blacksmith had carried out this villainy?"

Ottilia raised her brows. "You refer to taking me prisoner?"

"That also." He bent a puzzled frown upon her. "Does it not point to Sugnall having done away with my dear friend?"

Bastien stepped in. "He did not do this alone, *mon ami*. We believe there was another."

Grégoire turned to him, lifting one hand to his chin in question. "There was? How can you know that?"

"Because someone fired at me from the clifftop. It was not Sugnall. I found him moments later. But now I am convinced it was to warn me away from that place."

Grégoire moved to set a hand on his shoulder, sympathy entering his voice. "You said nothing of this before. Good God, man, you are lucky to be alive!"

"I do not believe he intended to hit me. Moreover, I had my small cousin up before me. Who would be so lost to humanity that he would shoot a child?"

Grégoire dropped back. "Or, one might say, take a woman captive." His gaze veered back to Ottilia as he spoke.

She gave a spurious smile. "Just so. Yet we may credit this person with a callous disregard for the lives of others, do you not think?"

"But you do not yet know there is such a person, ma'am. The shot Bastien describes might have been accidental. There are rabbits to be had on those hills."

Ottilia hit back. "Does a man take out a musket to shoot rabbits?"

"A musket?"

She turned to her nephew, her gaze deliberate and filled, she hoped, with meaning. "Did you not say you found the ball, Bastien?"

His brows drew together a little. "From the shot?"

"You said it was a musket ball." She willed him to take the bait without questioning her intention.

He hesitated a moment too long. "Ah, yes. It was so, *Tante*."

Too late. Grégoire's gaze met hers and she caught a flash of understanding there. He turned to address Bastien. "You were able to pick out a musket ball on the shingle, *mon ami*? You must have excellent eyesight."

Bastien reddened and Ottilia gave a little laugh. Time to shift the game.

"Do not look so conscious, my dear boy." She turned back to Grégoire. "Of course he could not have done so. Yet how easy it is to lie, do you not agree?"

His eyes narrowed briefly and then his lip curled in an apparent smile. "I have not the pleasure of understanding your ladyship."

Ottilia changed tack. "Do you care to sit down? I truly need your help to unmask the culprit."

For a moment he looked to be on the brink of refusing. Did he hope to make a run for it? An intelligent man, this one. She had likely given herself away. Would he brazen it through? If he had caught her drift, he must realise she had taken measures against his escape.

Bastien was looking troubled, his eyes shifting from one to the other. Was he beginning to suspect?

Then Grégoire glanced behind for a chair and moved to sit, throwing one leg over the other and leaning back in a pose of nonchalance. A bold villain this. One had to concede as much. Even his tone spelled confidence. It was misplaced, but he did not yet know the mettle of his adversary.

"How can I be of assistance, Lady Francis?"

Ottilia became tart. "You may begin by telling the truth, sir."

Grégoire spread his hands. "Which truth, ma'am? Do you accuse me now of lying?"

To Ottilia's chagrin, Bastien intervened, anxiety rife in his voice. "What is this, *Tante*? What do you imply?"

She held up a staying hand. "In good time. Try to be patient like your friend here."

Grégoire made a soft-spoken plea. "You should sit, *mon ami*. It seems your aunt is rendered a little confused by her ordeal. Humour her, I beg."

To Ottilia's admiration, her nephew proved to be made of sterner stuff. His handsome countenance grew stern.

"You shall not speak of her with such disrespect. I do not know Lady Fan's purpose here, but this I know: her wits are as clear as ever."

The other raised a hand palm-up in a gesture of peace. "Have it as you will."

Ottilia took back command. "I thank you for your confidence, my dear boy. However, you may as well make yourself comfortable. I suspect this may take some time."

As she spoke, she indicated the chair closest to the door which must place him in a convenient position to hinder Grégoire from leaving. Bastien threw an admonishing glance at his friend before taking the seat.

Ottilia returned her attention to her quarry. "Let us continue the bout with gloves off, Grégoire."

He merely raised his brows, a wary look coming into his eyes.

"If you wonder at my little demonstration, let me explain." Ottilia took a breath. "You told me Carlton was defrauding your émigré clients. Further, you said you found it out after his death."

Grégoire nodded. "Correct."

"I fear it is far from correct, sir. In fact, it was not Carlton but you — aided, I imagine, by Sugnall — who had devised a neat system of 'losing' items of value from these hoards."

An expletive from Bastien brought Grégoire's head round. "Did I not say, *mon ami*, that your aunt has become confused?"

Ottilia ignored the interruption. "Carlton, by means I cannot yet guess at, discovered these thefts. Since he was anxious for some weeks, I suspect he could hardly believe it and took time to ensure it was true."

Grégoire gave forth a sound redolent of cynicism. "He could hardly do so since this is a fabrication, a fairytale of your mind."

"Quiet!" This from Bastien, whose look of shock had given way to growing dismay. "Go on, *Tante*. I dread to hear it, but go on."

"What, you believe this foolishness? You are a fool, my friend."

Bastien accorded this a flashing look of warning, urging Ottilia to continue with a waft of his hand.

"In the end, Carlton must have become certain. I think he confronted you. Oh, I make no doubt you denied it. Clearly, at the last he was able to verify the truth or you would not have had reason to shoot him."

Grégoire set a hand to his chest, his face expressing the utmost astonishment. "I? You say I did this?"

What a play-actor! Ottilia pushed on. "Did Carlton threaten to bring the authorities down on you? Taking a line from your attitude today, I would guess he first questioned you. You must have taken umbrage, or pretended to, protesting your innocence. Was that when Carlton sustained his injury? Did you feign losing your temper and strike at him, gashing his arm? As for the finish, I must suppose Carlton spied upon you and at last was able to catch you and Sugnall in the act. Near or in the cave, was it? Did you keep your stash of stolen émigré wealth there? It seems likely, since you chose that spot to keep me captive."

Her nephew entered an objection. "But we found nothing there, *Tante*, for Williams and I made a search of the cavern after Lord Francis took you away."

"Oh, I am sure it had been removed once they were obliged to leave Carlton's body in the expectation it would eventually be discovered in the cave."

Grégoire emitted a scoffing sound. "Your discovery, ma'am, came as news to me. I knew nothing of the cave until my poor friend's body was found there."

Ottilia clicked her tongue. "Come, come, Grégoire, you put his body there. Carlton surprised you at the cave. No doubt you had your firearm to hand at that moment. You did not hesitate to use it."

Bastien burst out of his chair and loomed over Grégoire, fists clenched. "Scoundrel! You dare to call him a friend?"

The other did not flinch. "Peace! This is pure fantasy. Your aunt claimed at the outset that this was an execution. Now she will have it that I shot Carlton on sight."

Ottilia's pulse flickered. A telling description. But she saw Bastien hesitate, one fist still raised. He turned and caught her gaze. "*Tante?*"

"You heard him say it, Bastien. *He shot Carlton on sight.*" She returned her gaze to the Frenchman. "It is possible you acted from sheer panic. I don't doubt you came to regret it, once you began to envision the consequences."

"But this execution, *Tante?*"

"I am coming to it, my dear boy. Lieutenant Radway expressed it well. An elaborate ritual is an apt way to describe this exercise to make the death look like Carlton had indeed been executed."

"Then you think it was falsely created? But why?"

"Grégoire set the scene thus, I believe, to obfuscate any investigation. The killing occurred either in or just outside the cave. He and Sugnall must have carried the body to where we found it and created what was a most unlikely and confusing scenario."

Bastien fell back a little, his brows drawn together. "But did you not believe it was so, *Tante?*"

"I was never fully convinced, and the doctor's testimony made it certain that both the blindfold and the tied hands were applied when Carlton was already dead. The positioning of the legs was also puzzling. The trick almost worked, for it was well played. As was Monsieur du Guet's reaction to the death."

Grégoire slowly clapped, as if he humoured a child. "According to this account, I should perhaps try my hand at the stage. It had not before occurred to me that I had a talent for that profession."

Ottilia made no answer, her attention on Bastien's distressed condition. "You doubt it all, do you not?"

He threw up his hands. "I do not know. Do you have proof?"

Grégoire stabbed a finger at him. "The heart of the matter, *mon ami.*" He turned his eyes back on Ottilia. "Content yourself with Sugnall, ma'am."

"Ah, yes, you would have it so, would you not? While we sought information, you took pains to suggest other avenues, even to the Reverend Stewkley. You carefully pointed me in the direction of a possible accomplice, ready to sacrifice your associate to save yourself. Sugnall took me captive, did he not? I thought he had been tracking me, but I have had time to think and I recall making my arrangement to visit the Greens' home while I was in Parbold's and the blacksmith was not there. It occurs to me that you may well have been."

"How so? I have been away and have just returned to Aldborough."

"I doubt you have been anywhere but Aldborough these last days. However, I do *not* doubt that yours was the brain behind the jewellery thefts, as yours was the finger that pulled the trigger."

She received a mocking look. "I have heard that you are never wrong, but there must always be a first time. In this case, you will be obliged to admit you are mistaken."

Ottilia smiled. Time to deal her ace. "Will I, sir? If we are to talk of mistakes, what of yours?"

"Mine? Am I in error then?"

"Perhaps merely careless. You thought I was unconscious, did you not, when you came to the cave to check on Sugnall's work?"

For the first time, a look of doubt entered the man's face. He was too fly to comment, however. Ottilia pursued her theme.

"You were not so foolish as to speak when you checked my pulse. But I heard you talking with my guard, though you were speaking low. I did not know the blacksmith, but your voice I recognised, Grégoire. Your English is excellent, but you have not quite rid yourself of your accent."

Bastien's gaze, aghast now, was focused on his erstwhile friend. "It is true then."

Grégoire sprang to his feet. "This is no proof at all. The word of a woman tied up and gagged, whose senses were all but gone? Faugh! Who would believe you?"

Bastien swung on him, seizing his coat by its edges. "How did you know she was tied up and gagged? I did not tell you. None but the family know this."

"Release me!" Grégoire fought to free himself. "I tell you this is all lies! There is no proof to say I did these things."

A beloved voice, speaking from the doorway, smote Ottilia's ears.

"You ask for proof? What is this then?" Francis held up a long-muzzled gun. "This musket was found in your lodging. And that is not all." He moved into the room, throwing a word over his shoulder. "Come in, Radway."

The lieutenant followed him in, a sturdy wooden chest in his hands. "How do you explain this, du Guet?"

He set the chest down on the nearest chair and slipped the catch on the lid, flinging it back. A jumble of gemstones winked and sparkled within.

The task his aunt had set Bastien proved quite as distressing as he had anticipated. Cecily Green listened to his account with close attention. When he came to the end, she did not even refer to the events.

"How is Lady Fan? It must have been frightening, as well as causing danger to her health."

Bastien eyed her in some consternation. Had she taken in the substance of the tale? "My aunt is recovering well, but she is fatigued. That is why she asked me to visit you. She did not wish that you remained in ignorance until she was well enough to come herself."

Miss Ospringe, who had sat mumchance throughout, keeping a worried eye upon her charge, spoke up. "Gracious, no, indeed. She ought to rest. Such a terrible experience, poor Lady Francis." She glanced at the silent Cecily as if she hoped some remark might be forthcoming. "We are excessively grateful to you, Monsieur Guizot, for coming in her stead. It cannot have been easy for you either."

"Not at all, ma'am. I am glad to be of use."

"Oh, but to learn this dreadful truth of your so-called friend."

He saw Cecily wince and rushed into speech. "Yet it must be some consolation, to you and to Miss Green as well as myself, to know that Carlton was the more honourable man."

Miss Ospringe put a hand to her chest. "I could not speak when you said as much, sir. I felt quite overwhelmed with relief. The boy was a hero. We must think of him so, dearest Cecily."

Bastien's gaze went to the young woman who had drawn his interest. She looked up and met his eyes. "It is a blessing to hear that of Carlton. At least he did not betray us all."

The bitter inflection of this last was telling. "Forgive me, Miss Green, but is it not better that you found out Grégoire's true character before you wholly gave away your heart?"

The companion looked startled and Cecily's gaze flew to his. "You are very frank, sir."

Bastien smiled. "I have learned from my aunt. She is not afraid of plain speaking. Did you think your preference was concealed?"

Miss Ospringe made a frantic gesture. "Monsieur Guizot, this conversation is quite inappropriate."

Bastien made a bow with his head. "Then I beg your pardon."

"Don't," said Cecily unexpectedly. She lifted her chin. "It is true that I favoured Grégoire, though I am ashamed to confess it now. He was gracious and polite to me always. How could I know what he was?"

"Oh, that is so true. A most plausible gentleman. To think it was he who took the life of our precious Carlton!"

Miss Ospringe had recourse to her handkerchief, but Cecily remained stoic, much to Bastien's admiration. He could not doubt that her grief would find expression in private. He tried for a way to mitigate the worst.

"You must not blame yourself. My aunt has said Grégoire is an actor most accomplished. Even she was fooled by him. If he had not spoken within her hearing in the cave, it is possible she would not yet have uncovered his duplicity."

Cecily drew in a shuddering breath. "That does not bear thinking of! I wish it had not been in such a manner for her sake, but I am grateful beyond words that she found him out. Pray thank her on my behalf."

Feeling he had outstayed his welcome, Bastien rose. "I will do so, but you may say it yourself before we leave, we hope next week. My uncle waits only for Lady Fan to be fit to travel."

To his surprise, Cecily also got up, taking a step towards him. "You are leaving too?"

Was that a note of anxiety? Was she dismayed to see him go? "*Grand-mère* wishes to return home. I am her escort, you understand."

Miss Ospringe was now also on her feet. "What a shame! We will miss her at whist. Not that I have been able to participate these last days. Lady Polbrook is a fine player."

Bastien had to laugh. "She is indeed enthusiastic. In the family she cannot find a worthy opponent, so this has been to her a boon."

His attention was drawn back to Cecily, who asked, "Will you visit Aldborough again, sir?"

Bastien knew not how to answer. The likelihood was slim. "Time alone will tell."

He left a few moments later, his emotions mixed. If he made no special visit — what excuse did he have? — he might not see Cecily Green again before the cavalcade set off for home. On reflection, he did not think her sudden apparent dismay at his imminent departure betokened a change of heart. Was he perhaps a convenient, albeit temporary, substitute while her heart mended? He liked her, true. Enough to play second fiddle to a murderer?

Should he take counsel from Lady Fan? Even as the thought entered in, his wise aunt's probable answer settled in his mind. Cecily Green was a woman labouring under double griefs. Association with him could only serve as a reminder. If he gave his heart, let him choose a lady who could return his affection untainted by horror.

In the bustle of imminent departure, Ottilia had scant opportunity to mull over the events of the past weeks. So much to think about. All the little details to be arranged.

"Jennet, be sure to have with you a supply of those powders. You know how bad a traveller is Nell. Do you have the travelling set for that game she likes? Very well, be sure not to pack it. Di, my little darling, pray stop pulling at Mama's skirts. Hush now, my dear, I cannot hear myself think. Olive, for heaven's sake, take her and distract her. Pretty, have you collected all your bits and pieces? Pray do not leave it until the last minute as you did before we left Flitteris. Hepsie, make sure she packs them tonight. No, Luke! For the last time, Papa will not have you travel in our carriage. You'll stay with your sisters, if you please. Yes, I know they are noisy, but Papa cannot endure it when you will keep asking questions. Yes, you say now that you won't, but I know well you won't keep to it. Oh, dear heaven, what a cacophony! Hepsie! Hepsie, has he got his book? Don't pack it in the trunk, for goodness' sake. His lordship will be cross if Luke does not practise a little reading when we put up for the night."

When she was at last satisfied that all was in train for their departure on the morrow, Ottilia was exhausted as she sank onto the bed to begin her nightly routine of hair-brushing.

"I feel perfectly battered, Fan. Thank goodness for Henrietta. At least we are not obliged to organise your mother."

Francis began unwinding his neck-cloth. "You may thank your stars we are not obliged to travel with them. Mama is cock-a-hoop at having been proved right."

"About Grégoire? Well, she did say he had a shifty eye."

"I dare say she will be crowing all the way to Polbrook."

Ottilia ran the brush through her soft brown locks. "No more so than Luke, I imagine. He is in a fair way to believing he solved the whole thing because he found me. Heavens, Fan, those children of ours! How Hepsie is able to manage in the Bedlam they create I cannot fathom. I can only hope she does not take it into her head to abandon us."

"Have no fear. I can vouch for it that Hepsie would never leave Pretty. She dotes on that child."

Francis was stripping off his attire without help preparatory to donning his nightshirt. He had given Tyler leave to continue his own preparations, since the footman had to oversee all the domestic arrangements apart from the carriages, which were under the control of Ryde and Williams.

Ottilia set down her brush and moved to her side of the bed. "It has not been a satisfying holiday for our little ones." She sat on the edge, her mind shifting at last to the past days. "Do you think my affidavit will be enough, Fan? Mr Overy did not think I would be obliged to attend as a witness at Grégoire's trial, but I confess I am not sanguine."

"Don't fret, my loved one. If we are obliged to come for the Assizes, we will. The last thing we need is for that devil to escape justice."

"No, indeed." Ottilia let out a sigh. She lifted the covers and slipped underneath. "Draw the curtains, if you please. It is chilly tonight."

"Ha! When isn't it on this ghastly coast?"

Ottilia bethought her of her erstwhile steward. "I shall write to Hemp and beg him and Doro to prepare for our coming next summer. I am glad they have chosen the south coast. The weather is bound to be better."

Francis finished his task and climbed in beside her, pulling the last curtain to. "Well, warn him that if anyone gets killed there, we are coming straight home again."

Ottilia entered a laughing protest. "Is it my fault that wretched Frenchman chose to do his evil deed just when we came here?"

Her spouse turned and pulled her to him. "Of course it's your fault. You can't go anywhere without attracting murderers. We'd do better to remain at home forever."

Ottilia bubbled over. "You think we are safe at home? Have you forgotten, fiend of a husband, how people are apt to drop bodies on my doorstep? I refuse to be blamed."

"Once, just once, wretch of a wife, could we not enjoy a peaceful sojourn somewhere without you being obliged to solve a murder?"

"That is quite unfair. It has been three years since the last."

Francis turned his head and she received a gentle kiss. "I'm teasing you, sweetheart." He hugged her close. "I almost lost you again and it's the only way I can endure the anxiety."

Ottilia returned his embrace with fervour. "But I am still with you, my dearest dear, in spite of all. I bear a charmed life, do you not think?"

A NOTE TO THE READER

Dear Reader

Although Aldeburgh is now a sizeable town and famous for an arts and music festival held in June, at the time of Lady Fan's latest adventure, it was just emerging from its status as 'little more than a fishing village'. It grew as a sea-bathing resort through the nineteenth century, but when the Fanshawes were visiting in 1799, it had not yet become fashionable.

I set this story on the east coast because I wanted a haunt of smugglers and I happen to possess an old research book on that very subject, *Smugglers of the Suffolk Coast*, in which Aldeburgh featured, along with riding officers, militia and the fact that practically everyone in the town was involved!

Conveniently, at the end of the eighteenth century, Aldborough — as it was then named — was also sparsely populated, which suited my purposes. When I discovered that 1799 was a year noted in England for only eight days without rainfall throughout, the atmospheric scenario became perfect for the distraction of a local murder.

There is plenty of material available to show the shingle beaches and the rocky shores, along with cliffs further towards Thorpe. There are caves in the area, if not exactly where I put them along the shore!

An unusual feature of Aldeburgh is the location of the High Street, running parallel to the seafront. Crabbe Street existed at that time, named after George Crabbe the poet, who was born in the town, and we may assume Crag Lane was also extant.

The old town hall, the Mill Inn, the Cross Keys and the custom house are all old buildings that existed then and still do. All the other establishments, including The Rooms, are of my own invention.

The inhabitants are also imaginary, although the militia were in fact encamped on the heights, ostensibly to repel potential invaders and protect the town since the country was at war.

Thus, the background environment is a blend of the real with the fictional, the author's privilege of creation. To be honest, this is no different to the other stories in the Lady Fan series. One can only go so far with what was actual before adjusting things to suit the given structure of the tale. One reason why I tend to choose lesser-known spots is that it gives me a freer rein with the area.

As to the Fanshawe entourage, I do hope you have enjoyed the introduction of the twins, Diana and Elinor, for which I know expectation was high. How Francis will cope when all these girls grow up into young women I really can't imagine! Fortunately for Luke, he has plenty of male cousins to leaven the plethora of sisters. Speaking of whom, I've become rather fond of his French cousin, Bastien. I think we must not leave him heart-free for too long.

It's a joy to me to bring in members of the extended family and I am already looking at Bastien's sister Lucille, perhaps at some point revisiting the Hathaway boys, now nearly grown men, and the clutch of Fiske cousins may well be straining at the leash too. Let's hope I can stay fresh enough to write them all in!

I do hope you have enjoyed Lady Fan's latest foray into the world of puzzling mysteries, and if you would consider leaving a review on **Amazon** and **Goodreads**, it would be much appreciated and very helpful. Do feel free to contact me on

elizabeth@elizabethbailey.co.uk or find me on **Facebook**, **Twitter**, **Goodreads,** or my website **elizabethbailey.co.uk**. You might like to browse all things Lady Fan at **ladyfan.uk** too.

Elizabeth Bailey

Sapere Books is an exciting new publisher of brilliant fiction and popular history.

To find out more about our latest releases and our monthly bargain books visit our website: **saperebooks.com**

Printed in Great Britain
by Amazon

54462462R00201